CALEB

In his heart he was soft and loving. But the world had forced him to survive by the brute power of his bare hands. For trouble has a way of following a half-breed...

SARAH

Nothing could compare to making love with the man she treasured beyond all things, a man who had been her friend in childhood, her lover in their youth.

LYNDA

The daughter of the half-breed Caleb and his fiery-haired bride, she had a savage beauty that stirred needs in a man seldom satisfied in such a desolate land. Two men loved her, a Cherokee and a cowboy, but could either tame her wild spirit?

TOM

Every inch the son of the proud Caleb Sax, he went through hell to win the woman he loved, and to defend young Texas against the Mexicans... but could either desire quench the fires that raged within this child of the Cheyenne?

FRONTIER FIRES

Also by F. Rosanne Bittner

S A V A G E   H O R I Z O N S

Published by
POPULAR LIBRARY

F. Rosanne Bittner

FRONTIER FIRES

POPULAR LIBRARY

An Imprint of Warner Books, Inc.

A Warner Communications Company

POPULAR LIBRARY EDITION

Popular Library® and the fanciful P design are registered
trademarks of Warner Books, Inc.

Cover design by Barbara Buck
Cover illustration by Franco Acconero

Popular Library books are published by
Warner Books, Inc.
666 Fifth Avenue
New York, N.Y. 10103

 A Warner Communications Company

Printed in the United States of America

First Printing: June, 1987

10 9 8 7 6 5 4 3 2 1

With special gratitude to Claire Zion, my editor, for believing in my potential as a writer and guiding me down new pathways of creativity. Happiness to a writer is having an editor with whom it is easy to work, and who understands the writer's personal goals and abilities.

Hold not thy peace, oh God of my praise; for the mouth of the wicked and the mouth of the deceitful are opened against me; they have spoken against me with a lying tongue. They compassed me about also with words of hatred; and fought against me without a cause. For my love they are my adversaries; but I give myself unto prayer. And they have rewarded me evil for good, and hatred for my love.

Psalm 109: 1-5

This novel contains several references to historical characters, locations or events that actually existed or occurred during the time period of this story. All such reference is based on factual, printed material available to the public and has been researched to the best of the author's ability. Most dialogue attributed to actual historical characters is not taken from direct quotations but is the author's interpretation of what each character might have said, based on historical record regarding the nature and personality of those characters.

Primary characters in this novel, as well as the events in the lives of those characters, are fictitious and a product of the author's imagination. Any resemblance of the author's fictitious characters to actual persons, living or dead, or of the author's fictitious events to any occurrences of that time is purely coincidental.

This novel is based on major historical events in what is now the state of Texas during the years 1833 through 1842.

He was the hawk... all power and strength, sharp of eye and full of courage and daring, rising high and visiting far places. But she was the wind that carried him...

Introduction

Their name was Sax, and the land was called Texas. They fit each other, the Saxes and Texas, big men and strong women in a big and strong land. The year was 1833, a time of increasing turmoil in the Province of Texas, which still belonged to Mexico. Caleb Sax and his family were the owners of 49,000 acres of land northwest of San Felipe de Austin, the American settlement founded by Stephen Austin. It was an area of Texas growing rapidly with a heavy influx of new settlers, most of whom were from Southern states like Tennessee and Kentucky. The newcomers were seeking free land, offered by the Mexicans in return for a promise to settle and civilize Mexico's northernmost territories. But to do that they had to face the Comanches and Apaches, who considered the land their own and used any ruthless means necessary to prove it. The American settlers had only to promise to abide by Mexican laws, accept the Catholic faith and give up voting rights. It all seemed a small price to pay for vast amounts of free land, and so they came.

Mexico welcomed them—at first. Its own government was new, and the country hoped that the industrious Americans would help their land prosper. But they underestimated the American thirst for expansion; the American determination to live and do as they damn well pleased; and to worship as they wished.

By 1833, Texas was a land made up of many different

types of people, perhaps too many, with more arriving every day and many of them straining against ever-tightening Mexican rule. All-out war was not immediately considered, but the word was whispered. It was a worry to the common settler, already plagued by Indian raids, spring flooding, summer drought, grass fires, violent storms and marauding outlaws.

But the Saxes were accustomed to struggles and deprivation. And, for now, Caleb and Sarah Sax cared little for the outside world. They had found each other, after years of separation, and their love had not changed. Theirs was a passion as big and magnificent as the land in which they had chosen to settle.

Caleb had come to Texas first. He was the half-breed son of a Cheyenne woman who had been raped by a French trapper. His looks were all Indian but his eyes were a stunning blue, and his mixed blood left him a man torn between the white and Indian worlds. The first nine years of his life had been spent with the Cheyenne and Sioux, who called him Blue Hawk. But war among the Indians had left young Blue Hawk wounded and orphaned, and he had been adopted by a white man.

Ever since, he had lived in both worlds, once marrying a Cheyenne woman who was killed, then falling in love with his beautiful Sarah. That love had been violently stolen from him, and years later he had found solace in the arms of a gentle Cherokee woman, Marie, with whom he had settled in Texas. Marie died, but Caleb had lived to continue building his vast ranch, raising some of the finest horses in all of Texas and beyond, selling them at the Gulf to buyers from the States.

And then he found his Sarah again. He was united with his one great love, and finally had the home and family he had always wanted. More than that, he felt he had found a solid compromise for his two bloods—the wild land called Texas, which offered enough freedom to satisfy his Indian blood; yet was civilized enough to settle and build a future for the white woman who was his wife, and for whom he had chosen the white man's way of living.

Texas was home, where he and Sarah could forget their

tormented past and start over, in spite of the hardships of the land. Nothing and no one would ever again separate them. Even in death, they would be together, for such great love does not die with the human body. It goes on and on, living in the sons and daughters and grandchildren . . .

Chapter One

In June 1833, after a smothering heat wave, eastern Texas had been drowned by a violent storm that had brought a sudden and unusual chill to the air. Dawn broke through deep pink, wispy clouds that soon gave way to a brilliant blue sky that looked down on the vast acreage and beautiful horses that belonged to Caleb Sax. Low mountains sprawled around the borders of the Sax land, sheltering a broad, green valley broken occasionally by sloping hills and odd rock formations.

Normally all the Saxes would be busy doing the endless morning chores that came with caring for several hundred horses and more land than a man could ride in a day. But today only the hired help worked. The Saxes themselves were all gathered together in the modest adobe house belonging to Caleb and Sarah, where they anxiously awaited the birth of a new Sax child.

Sarah was thirty-five years old, and this was only her second child. Her first child, Lynda, was eighteen years old. Sarah was approaching the end of her childbearing years, and her health was not good. But this baby was her gift to Caleb, their celebration of being reunited, and their love gave her the strength to bear it with joy. She had left the civilization of St. Louis and made a home in the wilds of Texas to be with her Caleb. And to her new home she had brought the mixture of refinement and resilience that made up her own spirit.

1

Their "house of clay," as Sarah called the adobe house they lived in, was airy and bright, with high ceilings and ruffled curtains over the windows. The large main room had polished wood floors and was dominated by a fireplace built along one wall, which served for both heating and cooking. An oven was built into one side, and the smell of baking bread or pie often filled the Sax home.

Off the main room was Sarah and Caleb's bedroom, a spacious area closed off by a curtained doorway. Clothes were stored neatly in the closet, or in the drawers of two homemade pine dressers; the polished wood floors were decorated with cheerful hand-braided rugs. On a second floor reached by ladder from the main living area was a loft for sleeping. This Sarah kept as clean as the downstairs, its feather bed plumped up and covered with a hand-made quilt. Most every piece of bedding or clothing in the Sax household was made by Sarah, who once earned her living as a seamstress.

By the standard of their neighbors, the Sax house was very large but it had to be roomy, for Caleb Sax was a big, broad-shouldered man, standing six feet three inches tall. Tom Sax, Caleb's son by a Cheyenne woman, was just as big; his daughter Lynda's husband Lee was, like his Cherokee ancestors, not tall but a broad, burly young man who the family teasingly labeled a bull.

Normally, the Sax home was filled with laughter and warm conversation. But today groans from the pain of Sarah's labor filled the rooms. Caleb stoked up the fire in a small fireplace in their bedroom, where Sarah lay pale and exhausted in the big, four-poster bed she and Caleb shared. Both had known moments of ecstasy in that bed, for after finding one another again after years of separation, their passion had been fiery, their needs consuming, their love stronger and sweeter than it had ever been.

Caleb hoped keeping the room warm would somehow help ease Sarah's labor pains, but he knew deep inside that the only thing that would help was for the child to get born. He could do nothing but wait and pray. He didn't like this helpless feeling.

Their daughter Lynda stood near her mother, holding her

hand while a Cherokee woman named Ada Highwater acted as midwife. Sarah's red-gold hair was damp with perspiration, and she mumbled something about looking terrible. Caleb smiled sadly at the remark, for to him she was more beautiful at this moment than ever. She was his Sarah, still young to him, her green eyes and milky skin and lovely shape all as enticing as when he had fallen deeply in love with her so many years ago.

Their daughter was equally beautiful, but she had none of her mother's fair-skinned features. Lynda was dark like her father, and looked more like a full-blooded Indian than the mixed breed she was. Her form was exquisite, tall and slender and round in just the right places; and although her skin was dark, her eyes were as blue as her father's—and sometimes they showed the same fire and wildness for which her father was notorious.

"She'll be all right, Father," Lynda said, trying to reassure Caleb.

"Of course she will," Ada Highwater added, bustling around the room trying to gather her things. "I have to leave, just for a few minutes. My Jake, he goes far today for a roundup. I wish to pack his food and make sure he has what he needs." She glanced at Caleb. "Is it all right? I will not be long, Mister Sax. And I will be close by."

Caleb nodded. "This could go on for a while yet, and I don't want Jake riding off without the proper supplies. We know where to get you. Besides, you need a break, Ada."

The woman nodded, stroking Sarah's hair gently. "I will not be long."

She hurried out, and Sarah moaned just as the woman left. She arched with the pain, and her breath came in groaning gasps. She called Caleb's name and he strode to her bedside, clasping her hand in his own. He leaned over her lovingly, his eyes blazing as if he hoped to infuse her with his own strength. Those eyes were what made most people take a second look at Caleb Sax. Their startling blueness put the finishing touch to his stirring handsomeness. His thirty-eight years of hard living had made him a strong man, as if age only enhanced his rugged good looks. The sun caught his face as he bent over his wife, accenting the thin white scar that ran down his left cheek. Caleb had gotten the scar when he was only a teenager, and had killed the man who had given it to him.

"Don't let them . . . take this baby," Sarah muttered in her pain.

Caleb gently stroked the red-gold hair back from her beautiful face, realizing his wife, delirious in her pain, was lost in bitter memories.

"Nobody will take this one," he told her softly. "I'm right here, Sarah. I won't let anybody take this one."

Caleb looked away then, needing a moment to control the violent rage and pain he felt when he thought of the horror this woman he loved had suffered at the hands of a man named Byron Clawson. He would kill Clawson some day. Of that he had no doubt. The man had often beat and humiliated Sarah, then kept her so severely sedated that her health had been damaged. Clawson still lived in St. Louis, a wealthy banker, and it was only the daily demands of running a vast ranch in Texas, as well as Sarah's urgings, that kept Caleb from going to Missouri to murder the man. Sarah feared Caleb would get caught, and pleaded with him, knowing that to go to a civilized place like St. Louis would only bring Caleb a hanging.

Byron Clawson was a powerful man in St. Louis, but that mattered little to Caleb Sax. He knew that one day he would feel Clawson's soft flesh give way under his hunting knife, for besides his cruelty to Sarah, Clawson had once tried to kill Caleb. He was the worst kind of enemy—a back-shooter and a coward. Clawson had left Caleb for dead, but Caleb had managed to survive, although he had lain paralyzed for months. He still suffered pain and occasional numbness from the incident. Sarah, who had been told Caleb was killed, had been forced to marry Clawson, for she was pregnant with Caleb's child. Clawson had been brutally cruel to her, and had taken her baby daughter away from her at birth, put her in an orphanage, and told Sarah the baby had died. Clawson hated the child because she was Caleb's. For years Sarah, Caleb and their daughter had lived separate lives.

Although the horror of those years was behind them now, Caleb knew that in the pain of labor Sarah was reliving the nightmare of not being allowed to keep Lynda and raise her baby. That made this new baby so important. She would hold and love this one. She would put this one to her breast and feel it suckle its nourishment. She would love it, be the mother Byron Clawson had never allowed her to be. This baby had to be born healthy. Nothing must go wrong.

Sarah opened soft green eyes to meet Caleb's blue ones. Caleb stroked her hair as she rested from the pain of the last contraction. The love in their gaze was not just the emotion of husband and wife, or just lovers, but of friends in the deepest sense. Caleb and Sarah had known each other since childhood at Fort Dearborn, now a growing city called Chicago. Caleb had been just a small orphaned Indian boy called Blue Hawk. A trapper named Tom Sax had found and adopted the boy, giving him the Christian name Caleb and the last name Sax, and they became as much father and son as if they were blood related.

That was when Caleb had first met the little girl named Sarah, Tom's niece. They had become great friends, developing a brother/sister relationship. Sarah had taught Caleb most of what he learned about the English language and white man's customs. But the two of them had lost contact when Sarah was returned to St. Louis, to be raised in wealth and comfort.

After that Caleb left Fort Dearborn and returned to the Cheyenne. Only years later did he see Sarah again, and by then she was a young woman. The childhood friendship they had once known soon turned to deep love and unbridled passion, a love affair thwarted by the young man who was determined to have her—Byron Clawson.

It was all so long ago. But the passion lingered, as well as the great love they had shared since childhood. Sarah and Caleb—their love was as natural as breathing, as necessary as the sunrise.

"I'm going out for a while," Caleb told her softly. "I'll be right outside on the veranda. I won't go far."

Sarah forced a smile. He knew the toll this birth was

taking, knew her inner strength, not her physical strength, kept her going.

"It's a boy," she whispered. "I just know it's a boy."

He leaned down and kissed her forehead. "It doesn't matter, Sarah. Just so you and the baby are all right."

Her breathing quickened again. "I forgot how bad the pain is," she managed to get out before squeezing her eyes shut and arching against another ripping contraction that tore at her abdomen like a witch's fingers. He started to stroke her hair again.

"No," she panted. "Don't touch me." Caleb frowned and drew back. "It almost . . . hurts more," she groaned. "I have to do it . . . alone. I'm . . . sorry," Sarah breathed out then as the pain subsided.

"I understand," he told her. "I'll be close by."

He had been uncomfortable in the room anyway. His worry for Sarah had sent him to her side, but his Indian blood told him that he shouldn't be in the room at all. No Indian man was ever present in the tipi when his woman was having a baby. It was bad luck.

He walked out of the bedroom on the wide planks of the oak floors. This was his second house. His first had been a cabin, but it had been burned by marauding outlaws years ago—when his Cherokee wife, Marie, a son and his mother-in-law had been killed. Caleb still bore scars on his hands from trying desperately to save them from the fire. He had one son left from that marriage—twelve-year-old John, who was three-quarters Indian and looked it.

Years before that, even before falling in love with Sarah, Caleb had had a Cheyenne wife. They were both still very young when she was killed by Crow Indians, but she had left him his first son, Tom. At twenty, Tom was tall and broad and very Indian like his father, but with the bold, dark eyes of his mother. He was a strong, handsome young man, eager as a young colt, sometimes reckless in his ways as Caleb himself had been at the same age.

"How is she, Father?" Tom asked him now when Caleb joined him near the great stone fireplace in the main room. He understood his father's love for Sarah Sax, knew the story of how they had been torn apart. How many times had his father talked about the woman before they had been reunited, longed and mourned for her? It was Tom who had found her in St. Louis. He had gone with a delegation of men sent by Stephen Austin to give talks and try to get more people to come to Texas. Sarah had seen a newspaper article with Tom and Caleb's names, and through that had learned Caleb was alive and well in Texas. Tom had brought her home to his lonely father, along with his own half-sister, Lynda, who he had never even known existed before finding her in St. Louis.

The young man read the worry then in his father's eyes. What if Sarah died now, after only a year of being together again?

"It's hard to say," Caleb answered. "She's not that strong physically." Caleb turned. "I'm going out for a smoke." He took a cigar from a box that sat on the fireplace mantel. "Where are John and Lee?"

"Out cleaning stalls. They figured it didn't make much sense to stand around waiting any longer, and with a lot of the men getting ready for the roundup, somebody has to clean the barns. I'd be helping, too, but I was worried about you."

A soft smile was shared by father and son. No father liked to have favorites, but there was something very special about Tom. For years he was all Caleb Sax had to keep him going. Caleb had been a man forced to wander, a man of two bloods and two worlds and no roots. Tom had been the only stable element in his life.

"Don't worry about me," Caleb told him. "If you have chores to do, go ahead." He walked outside, standing on the veranda, his eyes scanning the several rosebushes that bloomed around the wooden porch. Sarah had planted the roses, and they seemed to mirror the gentleness and beauty Sarah Sax had brought to their lives in the wilderness. Caleb knew she would endure the worst deprivations to stay with him and that was part of what he loved about her.

He cringed when she cried out again. Closing his eyes, he whispered a prayer to *Maheo*, his Cheyenne god, the only god he'd ever recognized even though he had had to pretend to become a Catholic to stay in Texas. He saw no difference in the Catholic god and his own. They were simply called by different names.

He lit his cigar and stared out toward the barn that had taken them months to build. He could see young John carrying in some hay. Three children by three wives—Tom, by his Cheyenne wife; John by his Cherokee wife, Lynda born to Sarah, the white woman he had loved most of all. Now there would be another child by Sarah.

Lee came out of the barn then. He was the brother of Caleb's dead Cherokee wife, Marie. He and John were all that remained of the Cherokee family with whom Caleb had first settled in Texas. When Caleb had finally faced the loss of Sarah, he had married Marie. She had loved him fiercely and faithfully. Now she lay buried on the little knoll behind the house, along with the rest of her family and her second son by Caleb, David.

Lee had stayed on, helping with the ranch. He was a husky, strong young man with the round, friendly face of a Cherokee and a heart of gold that did not seem to match his powerful, bullish build. If any man was all good, it was Lee Whitestone. Once Lynda came to live with them, it had not taken long for the young man to fall crazy in love with Caleb's beautiful daughter. They were married now, as happy a couple as any two could be. Caleb was glad for both of them, for Lynda had had her own share of tragedy growing up in an orphanage. Lee loved and protected her with the fierceness of a lion.

Caleb's blue eyes moved to the distant hills, past thorny mesquite and the greens and yellows of chino and tabosa grasses. He could sit for hours and stare at this land and never tire of its barren beauty. But today he saw something that spoiled that beauty, something that made him throw down his cigar before taking another puff.

"Tom," he called out. "Get out here!"

The young man was out the door quickly, coming to his father. Caleb nodded toward the distant hills.

"What do you think?"

Tom squinted his eyes, seeing nothing at first, then focusing on several riders who were coming fast. In this vast land something could look far off and be close, or seem close and be very far away. After years of living in Texas, it was still hard to judge. "Comanche?" the young man asked.

"I'm not going to wait until they're close enough to find out. Run out and tell Lee and John to close up the barn. Keep whatever horses are in there inside and don't worry about the rest of them. Get your muskets and alert the hired help! I'll get the women into the hiding place."

Their eyes met. "Father, Sarah's in the middle of labor!"

"That can't be helped. Better to give birth in a dirt hole under the house than to have the baby carved out of her stomach by some Comanche warrior! Get moving!"

Caleb's Indian instincts went into action. In moments like this he became Blue Hawk again, the fierce warrior who had once waged a personal war against the Crow Indians after they had killed his young Cheyenne wife. To this day the name Blue Hawk struck terror in the hearts of those Crow who remembered the Cheyenne warrior's sudden raids and brutal attacks. The story of Blue Hawk had become a legend among them.

Caleb had a full family and a real home, land of his own to protect. No Comanche raid was going to spoil that for him. As Tom rushed to carry out his instructions, Caleb returned to the bedroom.

"I think Comanche are coming," he told Lynda. The girl's eyes widened. "You two have got to get down into the hiding place."

Sarah groaned, terrified at the thought of being moved. "Baby . . . my baby."

"Father, the baby is coming!"

"Then it will have to come down there, and it will have to come without Ada. There's no time, Lynda. I've seen pregnant women's bellies slashed open before. We've got to get both of you out of sight in case there are too many of them for us to handle." He bent down to scoop Sarah up into his arms.

Lynda knew better than to argue. Caleb Sax knew this land and he knew the Comanche. A part of him understood their own desperate struggle. If they had been willing to cooperate, Caleb would gladly let them camp on his land. But of all Indian tribes, the Comanche was perhaps the most difficult to reason with. The Mexican army was unable—or more likely unwilling—to help protect the American settlers in the north, so many had suffered the horrors of Comanche raids.

Sarah screamed as Caleb lifted her. "Move the rug away and open the door," Caleb ordered Lynda.

The girl grabbed towels and a couple of pillows before rushing to the main room. She pulled away a braided rug and lifted a heavy oak trapdoor that was so closely melded into the rest of the floor that it was difficult to see when it was closed. She moved around and descended a short ladder into the hole where they stored potatoes and other vegetables and which also served as a hiding place in time of raids. Caleb had learned his lesson the hard way when Marie died. Now his women had a place to go where they would not be found and where they would be safe even if the house were to burn.

Caleb waited a moment while Lynda lit an oil lamp. Then he moved around to the ladder, laying Sarah carefully on the floor near the door until he got his footing. His heart cried out at her groaning and weeping, and he prayed he was not harming the baby. He reached up, getting hold of her carefully and carrying her down the ladder. Her weight was nothing to him, but to hold her and keep his balance was hard. He gently laid her on the dirt floor.

"Caleb," she gasped, grabbing the front of his buckskin shirt. "Stay . . . here."

"You know I can't," he told her, bending down and kissing her forehead. "I'm so damned sorry, Sarah. I didn't want it to be like this for you." His eyes teared. "Try not to cry out." He took her hand and squeezed it. "It will be all right. I'll be back in no time, as soon as we chase off the Comanche."

She looked at him with terror-filled eyes. They all knew the horrors Comanche were capable of administering.

Caleb looked at Lynda. "Do the best you can. You'll have to put out that lamp when I close the door or it will smoke you out of here. There's a candle over where the canned peaches are stored. You can light that."

Their eyes held. "Be careful, Father. And watch out for Lee. I couldn't bear to lose either one of you."

He touched Lynda's cheek lightly. "After all we've been through to be together again, God's not going to let us lose that now."

He let go of Sarah's hand reluctantly, pain moving through his chest when she wept his name. He climbed up the ladder, hesitating at the top. "Don't come out of here unless Lee, Tom, or I come to personally open this door, understand? No matter what you hear above you, stay put and keep quiet."

Lynda nodded. Caleb quickly closed the door, pulling the rug back over it. Already he heard war whoops and a gunshot. He grabbed his pistol and musket, both of which he always kept at hand since he had learned the hard way that a man seldom had time to reload a musket. He would be lucky to get one shot out of each, so he would have to make them count, then rely on his knife for the rest.

He ran outside to see Indians circling the barn. Lee and Tom were shooting at them from doors that opened out from the loft. Young John was nowhere to be seen.

Caleb mounted a black mare he had tied at the house, leaping onto its bare back and riding off, calling out his own war whoops as he felt his blood running hot. These Comanche were shooting at his sons and his daughter's husband, and they were most likely after Caleb's prized horses. Caleb was determined they would not get those horses, nor harm any member of his family. At the same time, he wanted to keep the fight centered around the barn and away from the house and the women.

Most of his hired hands were still close by. There were fifteen men who worked for him full time. Most of them were Cherokee who had fled to Texas from persecution in Georgia. His best hand was Jake Highwater, Ada's husband. In addition to those who worked for Caleb, other Cherokee lived on his land, farming on their own and grateful for his generosity. He could even get more help from those Cherokee when necessary, but today he had no time to go and get them. He only hoped none of them had already been attacked. He looked over at the distant cabin where Jake and Ada lived with their three sons and was relieved to see no Comanche. He knew Ada was hiding inside. Jake was probably in the barn with Lee, Tom and the other men who were shooting it out with the Comanche.

Caleb spotted a Comanche trying to climb into the window of a closer cabin. He fired, and a red hole opened up in the warrior's back. The Indian screamed and fell out of the window.

Caleb charged up beside the cabin, dust swirling around him from the hard earth. He jumped off his horse and knelt at the corner of the building, taking aim with his pistol. Again he fired at one of the Indians who circled the barn and again he hit his mark. Several Comanche were already down, but so were several of Caleb's men. One lay nearby, his skull smashed by a tomahawk.

There was no time to think about Sarah and the hell she must be going through, giving a difficult birth in the dark hole under the house. The war whoops, thundering horses and gunshots had decimated the peace of the Sax ranch. An arrow whizzed past Caleb's ear. He turned to see a Comanche warrior nearly on top of him. He rolled away as a tomahawk came down and missed him. He leaped up again and grabbed the warrior off his horse. The man landed with a grunt, stunned by Caleb's strength and looking at him in wide-eyed surprise, for this settler was not white but Indian, as were most of the men the attacker had seen at this settlement. This surprised and confused the Comanche. These settlers didn't fight like frightened white men. They fought like proud Indians.

The Comanche warrior did not have long to ponder this curiosity. The big Indian who had thrown him from his horse was on him quickly, while the breath was still knocked from his lungs, and a huge knife was plunged into his chest. That was the last thing the warrior remembered before the life left his limbs.

Caleb jerked out the knife and quickly reloaded his rifle and pistol. He smelled smoke, and looked around the side of the cabin that sheltered him to see flames licking at the door to the barn.

"Sons of bitches," he growled. He looked up at the doors where Tom and Lee were perched. "Get out," he yelled. "Fire! They set the barn on fire!"

His shouting was to no avail amid all the yipping and whooping of the Comanche. Those left continued to circle, but they had lost several of their own, and Caleb could only hope they would give up. Just then the barn door was pushed open and young John came out and began beating at the flames with his shirt. Caleb's eyes widened in terror as he saw the boy exposing himself to the Comanche.

"John! Get back! Get back!"

A warrior reached for him, but John pulled away. Caleb started running. If the Comanche couldn't get the horses they wanted, they would settle for a child. They were notorious for stealing children and adopting them into their tribe. But if they were not pleased with their captives, a slow, torturous death awaited them.

Caleb stopped and fired his rifle at one of the circling Comanche, and the man sprawled from his horse. Caleb threw down his rifle and ran, but something hit him hard between the shoulders from behind. He stumbled forward and a horse thundered past him. He ignored the pain and managed to get to his feet, his eyes on John, who was wrestling with another warrior.

Everything seemed to whirl around Caleb as he ran toward them. He grabbed at John, at the same time stabbing with his knife at the leg of the boy's would-be abductor. The Comanche cried out, letting go of the boy. Caleb tried to carry John across the flames back into the barn, hoping to run through and somehow get out the other side, but the flames were leaping high. Horses whinnied frantically inside, and Caleb's head swam with the memory of the night outlaws had burned his cabin, killing Marie and their son David. He couldn't let anything happen to John.

Another warrior grabbed at John's hair. The boy screamed with pain and Caleb let go of him to reach up and jerk the Comanche off his horse. He pulled his pistol from his belt and shot the warrior in the head. But more Comanche descended on Caleb, intrigued by the man's great fighting skill and enjoying the challenge of getting the young boy away from him. They seemed to forget all about the horses. Getting the boy from his father's arms had become a game, and they all grinned as they took turns taunting and fighting with Caleb.

Caleb struggled violently while several of his men moved out from behind walls and doors and began yipping and running, shooting at those of the Comanche who had decided to give up the fight. Many of the warriors were riding off with the horses they had chased out of a corral while others had kept the ranch owners busy around the barn.

Tom and Lee scrambled down from the loft, opening the door at the other end of the barn and hurrying to yank at the Saxes' most prized mounts to get them out of the barn before it burned down around them. They could not even see through the flames at the other end to know Caleb was struggling with five warriors who were laughing and stabbing at him, trying to get John away. Caleb fought like a wild man, oblivious to several stab wounds, clinging to John desperately. Some of his hired hands came around the end of the barn to try to stop the fire, and they began shooting at the remaining Comanche. But they were too late to keep one of the warriors from finally wresting John from Caleb's arms as the big man went down under blows from several war clubs.

"Pa!" John screamed as one of the warriors held him tightly and rode off with him. Caleb tried to get up and run, but all he could do was crawl before collapsing completely.

Lee led a prized stallion out of the barn to see the remaining Comanche riding off. "Jesus, they've got John," he yelled to Tom.

Tom ran out, taking aim with his musket. But he lowered it without firing, his heart screaming with sorrow. He couldn't shoot at the man, not while he held John in front of him. His heart raced.

"Father! What happened to Father!" He ran around the other side of the burning barn. Some of the hired help ran back inside the barn with Lee to lead out more frightened, whinnying horses as timbers began falling.

Tom saw three Cherokee carrying Caleb away from the barn. He ran up to his father, who seemed to be bleeding everywhere, his face battered. "Father!"

The men laid Caleb on the ground. "John," Caleb groaned. "Got to . . . get him."

"We'll get him, Father! We'll get him back," Tom said in a determined voice. He looked at Jake Highwater, who seemed ready to cry. "Get him into the house."

Jake nodded, ordering the men who were carrying Caleb to the house. They laid him on a rug in front of the fireplace at Tom's instructions. Sarah would need the bed, and they couldn't carry Caleb's big frame up to the loft.

Tom quickly whipped the rug away from the trapdoor and opened it.

"Tom," he heard Lynda cry from below. "Where's Lee!"

"He's all right. But Father is hurt bad. The Comanche got John."

He heard a gasp. A baby started crying. Lynda climbed up the ladder to face her brother. She looked frantically over at her groaning father, then back at her brother. The baby below cried harder.

"It's a boy," Lynda told Tom quietly, her eyes tearing.

Tom nodded. It might be very important that this new child was a boy, for Caleb Sax might have just lost another son. "How is Sarah?"

"I can't tell. We've got to get her back into the bed." She looked at Caleb again. "Father will be all right, won't he? He won't die?"

She met her brother's determined gaze. "He won't die.

He'll live out of pure stubbornness. He'll go after John."
His jaw flexed in anger. "And Lee and I will go with him.
We'll get him back from those bastards!"

Caleb tried to move, but a blow in his back from a war
club had brought on a terrible weakness in his legs, awakening the awful paralysis that was always so close at hand
—an aftereffect of the bullet wound in the back he had
suffered from Byron Clawson all those years ago. How he
hated this horrible, helpless feeling!

"I'm here, Father," Tom was telling him.

"John—"

"We'll get him."

Caleb heard the baby crying, and his eyes opened wide.
"The . . . baby—"

"It is a son, Father," Tom answered. "A son for you and
Sarah."

A tear slipped out of Caleb's right eye, tracing its way
through the dirt and blood on his face. A son. He had been
blessed with another son. But what of John? How could he
lose a son and gain one all in the same day? But no. He
hadn't lost a son. He would find him. He would get well
and find John Sax!

Tom looked over at Jake. "Maybe Lee and I should leave
right away and go after them," he said. "Who knows how
long Father will be like this."

Jake shook his head. "No. Remember who your father
is—the great warrior, Blue Hawk. He will find those
Comanche, no matter how much time passes. You cannot
go out alone, Tom. You do not know those wilder Indians
as your father knows them. You must wait until Caleb is
well enough." He looked down at his employer and friend.
"It will not take him long. Caleb is a strong man, and his
son has been taken. He will go for him . . . soon."

Tom looked down at his wounded father. Jake was probably right. He and Lee couldn't go after the Comanche
alone, but when Caleb was ready, they would both go
along. Tom Sax wanted his share of vengeance, and Lee
would want the same.

Chapter
Two

"So, what is the report on the Americans?" Antonio López de Santa Anna asked, his dark gaze moving around the polished mahogany table at which he sat with his advisors. He did not care for the stories he was hearing about American resentment of his new dictatorship.

"Some say the *Americanos* speak of breaking away and forming their own republic," one of the men answered.

Santa Anna's eyes narrowed to slits of anger. "That could be quite unfortunate for them."

"They are angry, *Presidente*," another told him. "They approved of the federal constitution under our old government, and of being allowed to form their own constitution. But now they have been told none of these things are valid and that we will enforce Mexican laws even more strongly. These Americans—they do not like to be told what to do."

Santa Anna sneered. His black, wavy hair lay neatly around the collar of his white, ruffled shirt, and some of the men at the table could not help wondering how the man was able to always look so well-groomed. He put a foot up on the table, his black boots shining with a freshly polished look, covering his tight gray pants to the knee.

"They will learn that they must do as they are told, or suffer the consequences," Santa Anna said slowly. "These Americans will soon learn who rules this country and its provinces. They are no longer dealing with those sniveling

17

leaders who bow to every American within these borders. Those days are over. We were nice to the American settlers; we let them have all that land for nothing. It was their choice to deal with the Comanche, to struggle against the heat and the drought and whatever else they have had to put up with. That is not my problem. If it had been up to me, I would not have allowed them to come here in the first place."

"But, *Presidente*, if I may speak . . ." another aide said, sitting up straighter and looking nervous.

"Have your say," Santa Anna told him.

"The Americans . . . they do not truly want to break away from Mexico. They do not mean us any harm. They only ask for more say in the government, and for the ability to make their laws so that a man does not have to wait in jail for months until a Mexican court can hear his case. And they wish to have more protection against the Indians and outlaws who are always raiding and murdering, raping their women, taking slaves. If we send more soldiers—"

"Enough!" The word was roared and the man jumped, looking away and swallowing. Santa Anna took his foot from the table and shoved back his chair, standing up and walking to a window. "I will hear no more talk about helping the Americans. They no longer want our help, nor deserve it. They claim that their acts against Bradburn and Colonel Ugartechea at Velasco were not against Mexico but only against Bradburn for his unacceptable laws. I do not believe it! That was only the beginning."

"But, *Presidente*, fair treatment is all that they ask. It is so simple."

Santa Anna turned to the man who had spoken the words, and the man's blood chilled at the look he received. "Nothing is that simple," Santa Anna growled.

The man gripped the arm of his chair for courage. "But . . . they want only peace. They are proving it right now."

Santa Anna glared at him. "How?"

"A messenger came today to tell us Stephen Austin himself, the one who founded San Felipe and began bringing in all the settlers . . . he is on his way here . . . to Mexico City . . . to see you."

Santa Anna stiffened, moving quickly back to his chair but not sitting down. "And you have just now told me this?"

"I found out only moments ago myself, just before you called us here. He is bringing with him a petition, asking only for reforms in the judicial system and the right to have more local control over political affairs, better schools, a militia. They wish Texas to remain a province of Mexico, but that it be separated from Coahuila. Since they are so far away from Mexico City, trials can take months, and we do not have enough soldiers to—"

"Say no more!" Santa Anna smiled, sitting down in his chair again. "So the great Stephen Austin is coming here ... to beg before Santa Anna." He laughed. "It will be very interesting. I shall have to think about the best way to tell him none of his wishes will be granted." He flexed his fingers. "He is a brave man—coming here like a sheep to the wolves. It will be a good chance to show the Americans who they are dealing with—the kind of leader they have in Antonio López de Santa Anna." He rose again, puffing out his chest. "These Americans talk about freedom and cry like babies when they cannot have their way. I will watch Stephen Austin cry!"

Lee held Lynda close, while outside the crickets cried out their nightly song. Soon he, Caleb, and Tom would ride into Comanche country. The rescue attempt would be very dangerous, but it was a risk they had to take. Caleb Sax was determined to get his son away from the Comanche, and it was something they had to do as a family. It was a matter of pride.

Caleb had drawn on some deep spirit that gave him strength to ignore his pain and injuries and get him on his feet within three days of the awful blows of the Comanche warriors.

But even three days was too long when it came to finding John. The whole family knew Caleb was straining against agony as he walked about getting ready for their journey. The women would stay at the home of Wil Handel, a German immigrant and a good neighbor who lived closer to San Felipe. They would be safe there, and with Sarah not yet well, the companionship of Mrs. Handel would help her during the long wait for Caleb, Lee, and Tom to return.

Lynda moved closer, needing the comfort of her husband's strong arms. When she first met him she teasingly called him a bear, but his gentleness with his wife did not match the description. Lee was almost childlike in his open love for her. He worshipped his wife. He didn't care that after running away from an orphanage Lynda had lived with a gambler. She had been so young, alone, and frightened. The man had helped her, and loved her in his own way. But he had been killed after cheating in a card game, leaving her alone again. All her life Lynda had never known a real home, nor real love and security. She had finally found it in Lee.

"You'd better come back soon, Lee Whitestone," she said softly.

"Hey, for you I would walk over hot coals," he teased her, kissing her neck. "It will be all right, honey."

He studied Lynda's beautiful face and blue eyes in the dim light of the lantern. Those eyes were filled with love, and with tears.

"Lee, I'm pregnant," she blurted out.

At first his face did not change. Then he broke into a broad smile, showing even, white teeth. His dark eyes danced and he let out a howl, pulling her close and hugging her so tightly she could barely catch her breath.

"Pregnant!" He laughed. "We will have a baby! I will have a son!" He pulled back. "When?"

She smiled in return. "About six months, I think. Right around Christmas. But there's no guarantee it will be a boy."

He laughed again and kissed her hard. "What does it matter? Such good news!"

Their eyes held as they both thought about the Comanche. He was going to face them to help find John. "Don't you worry, Lynda. For our baby, for my Lynda, nobody can stop me from coming back."

He ran a hand over her slender, perfectly rounded body. He was still amazed that this beautiful creature loved him.

Lee never thought of himself as handsome. He was not tall, not compared to Caleb and Tom, and Lynda often teased that his stocky muscles were so tight he was incapable of even bending over. But to her he was so beautiful; a joyful, open, energetic young man who had been loyal to her father and had remained to help with the ranch even after his sister Marie had been killed.

Nor did Lee ever question that he and Lynda would stay forever on this land. Lee knew that Lynda would never leave the mother and father she had found after so many years. Caleb Sax's home would forever be Lee Whitestone's home, and that was all right with Lee. He had lived on this ranch many years himself, and as long as he could be with this beautiful woman, it didn't matter where they lived.

Lynda closed her eyes as his hand moved under her gown and over her bare hips. "We have to say good-bye the right way," he told her. He looked at her almost as though to ask if it was all right. He always approached her that way, as though he needed her permission. She knew he did so because he loved her so much he never wanted to offend her. She wondered if he would ever understand that her love for him was so great he always had the right to take his pleasure with her. But she loved him all the more for being so respectful of her wishes.

She moved a leg over him and kissed him hungrily, letting him know she needed this as much as he. Who could tell how long he would be gone?

He pushed up her gown with strong, callused hands, moving on top of her, neither of them caring about preliminaries. Their joy in each other was mixed with the sorrow of his imminent departure, bringing on an urgency that enhanced their passion so that in a moment he surged inside of her and she arched up to meet him in return.

The wonder of being one with this exquisite beauty had not lessened for Lee Whitestone. To him it was a dear privilege, and it brought ecstasy to his every limb and nerve, always making it difficult for him to hold on long enough to be sure she enjoyed herself in return. He knew by her gasps and whispered words of love that he was pleasing her. Surely she never failed to please him.

Lynda kissed his powerful chest, taking him deep inside herself, wanting to remember everything about him: every powerful muscle, his round, handsome, joyful face, his straight, dark hair, his rhythmic movement inside of her. *Precious Lee*. His life spilled inside of her, but it was not needed. His seed was already growing in her womb, and her joy should be boundless. It would be, if he were not leaving her to go after Comanche.

At the main house Caleb lay next to Sarah, staring into the darkness. Neither of them would sleep this night. Even if she were healed from the baby, he could not make love to her. John was out there with the Comanche. Would the boy have sense enough to cooperate with them, to be strong and not cry? If he fought them or showed too much weakness, they would kill him.

Again the horror of it surged through him. The agony of the situation was all the worse for Caleb because he was Indian himself, and understood the plight of the wild ones. Even now he could live among the Cheyenne with no trouble at all. He still remembered his own hatred of white men when he was small—remembered the white man who had cut him at Fort Dearborn, the one he'd killed. But since then, he had learned there was good and bad in all races. A white man had raised him, and Caleb had loved Tom Sax like a real father. He'd been a damned good man, and Caleb had named his own first son after him.

"It all boils down to survival," he said reflectively. "I'm going after my own kind, Sarah, because I want my son to live. When I lived among the Cheyenne, and the Crow killed Walking Grass, I rode against the Crow, killed a lot of them. I've called Indians as well as white men both enemy and friend. I'm mostly Indian, yet the Comanche came against me and took my son. I guess it never ends— the killing, the struggle."

"You could be living as a wild Indian yourself, if not for the paths fate has shown you," she answered.

He lay quiet for several long seconds. "In some ways

I've never stopped being Indian, not inside. That's the hell of it. But this time being Indian myself is to my advantage. That's how I'll beat them. I can think like them. No white man can do that." He turned to her. "That's why I can't take along any extra men, Sarah. Too many men and we would be too easily spotted. They won't be expecting just three."

She couldn't stop the quiet tears then. Their baby son was only three days old, and Caleb himself was not physically ready for this. She could not erase the memory of how he'd suffered, the realization of how quickly life can end. She could have lost him! Lost him, after all those years of separation. What hurt the most was realizing that part of his suffering was because of Byron Clawson, whose desire to possess her and her father's money had brought Caleb so much agony.

"Oh, Caleb, I'm sorry," she sniffed.

He frowned, resting a big hand on her still-soft stomach. "Sorry? For what?"

She swallowed, a painful lump in her throat. "For your pain," she managed. "For Byron."

She felt him stiffen. He pulled her closer and her head nestled against his shoulder. "None of that was your fault and you know it. All you did was love me. I wouldn't change any of it if it meant forfeiting those days we spent in that cave where I first made you Caleb Sax's woman. You were mine first and you've always been mine, even in the years we were apart."

"Oh, Caleb," she wept, pressing her face against him then. "I've had you back for such a little while. I lived without you once. I couldn't . . . do it again."

He stroked her lovely red-gold hair. To him she had not changed at all since he'd known her as a little girl, except to grow more beautiful. He knew she would regain her firm, round figure eventually, but he didn't care. He liked the soft fullness she had taken on because of the baby. He loved watching his new son feeding at her breast. To see what his seed had produced, to see what their love had created filled him with pride. Sarah had insisted on naming the baby James, after Marie and Lee's father, who had died during his family's journey to Texas.

"You won't have to be alone again," he assured her. "I just told you. It's my Indian instincts that will help me. I'll be back, Sarah. I have too much to live for—a daughter I never knew I had, a home and family, this ranch, now James. And you. Always you."

He winced with pain as he shifted his position, but he let out no sound. She had enough worries without his making her fully aware of how bad his pain still was. He had to learn to ignore it. There was no more time to be wasted lying about waiting to heal. He'd survived the ordeal of the Sun Dance ritual when only eighteen. He'd lived through the bullet wound Byron Clawson had opened in his back. He'd live through whatever the Comanche had in store for him.

He kissed her hair. Sarah. Surely God had not brought them together only to tear them apart again.

Charles Hafer settled into a leather chair near Byron Clawson's desk, worried over why the wealthy St. Louis banker might have called him to his office. Hafer had had problems paying off his loan from the bank, but he was at least making regular payments, and the manager with whom he had made the arrangements had assured him they had been approved by Mister Clawson.

Hafer glanced around the empty room while he waited for Clawson. He had been ushered into the plush office by a wiry, pompous young man in a dark suit, who had given him no idea of how long he would have to wait. The office was tidy, the hardwood floor was highly polished as was the great oak desk that loomed before Hafer. The large, black leather chair belonging to Byron Clawson sat menacingly on the other side of the desk, as though to threaten him, and Hafer shifted nervously, adjusting his tie and patting the sides of his hair. He reminded himself that Byron Clawson was just a man and no more important than anyone else.

An American flag hung in the corner of the office, and near it sat a large poster with a penciled drawing of Clawson—his face thin, his nose sharp and straight, his thick but receding hair combed into neat waves.

Hafer thought the drawing most certainly made Clawson look better than he did in person, adding a little hair and leaving out the odd shape of the man's nose. Clawson had a very crooked nose, as though it had once been not just broken but smashed. Perhaps the distorted look it gave him was part of the reason Clawson was not very popular. Hafer supposed the ugly nose was why Clawson dressed in such expensive, perfectly tailored clothes.

Hafer looked down and brushed at his own simple wool suit, angry at the way Clawson was keeping him waiting. Byron Clawson was pompous and arrogant. He was not well liked and had lost a run for mayor of the city, and Hafer wondered at the rumor that Clawson was considering a run for governor of Missouri in the '36 election. The man surely did not have a chance in the world, but perhaps the rumor was true. The poster drawing near the flag was a leftover from his bid for mayor. He could be planning to use it again.

The door opened with a loud creak that made Hafer jump. He turned to see Clawson coming inside and he smiled. "Good morning, Mister Clawson."

Clawson took long strides to his desk, not replying. Hafer gauged the man to be in his mid-forties. He stood close to six feet tall, but he had an almost feminine look to him. Hafer, himself six feet tall and built like a bull, knew he could pound a man like Clawson into the ground, but muscle power mattered little in this civilized world. Money was the real power, and that made Byron Clawson the strong man in this office.

Clawson threw some papers onto his desk and sat down in his chair, studying the papers a moment, as though deliberately wanting to put Hafer on edge. The man's dark blond but now graying hair was slicked back neatly with something greasy. Finally Clawson raised steely gray eyes to meet Hafer's brown ones.

"Good morning, Mister Hafer," he said slowly.

Hafer nodded. "What can I do for you, Mister Clawson?"

Clawson studied him closely, making Hafer uncomfortable. "The question is, what can I do for you?" he finally replied.

Hafer's eyebrows arched. "I don't understand. I really have to get back to my farm, so I wish you would tell me why I'm here."

Clawson leaned back in his chair, rubbing at his smoothly shaved chin. His gray suit seemed to match his eyes exactly, eyes that narrowed as he sighed deeply.

"Mister Hafer, you took a loan from this bank several months ago, quite a large one."

Hafer nodded, his heart tightening. "My farm wasn't doing so well—the drought—and my wife got very sick. It cost a lot of money to take care of her. She has since died. My son was killed in a fight with drunken Indians. He was my right arm. Times have been bad for me, Mister Clawson."

Clawson nodded. "And you seem to be having a lot of trouble paying back our loan. In fact, you recently asked for more. We, of course, had to turn you down."

"I'm paying as regularly as possible," Hafer added.

"I am aware of that. I am also aware that you have talked about leaving the St. Louis area for this wild new land called Texas, where you can get free land and start over." His eyes bore into Hafer. "You wouldn't consider leaving here and not paying back your loan, now, would you, Mister Hafer?"

The words were spoken with a definite threat, and Hafer swallowed. "I'm not that kind of man, Mister Clawson. Even if I left, I'd use the money from the sale of my farm toward the loan, and I'd send money whenever I could."

Clawson eyed him with smoldering gray eyes. "That would not be good enough, Hafer. If you left here under such circumstances, I would have little choice but to have you hunted down and arrested and thrown in prison for your debts. After all, that land isn't worth as much as it once was. Even if we took it over ourselves, we would never get enough to cover the loan." The gray eyes grew colder. "Hafer, I want *all* the money. Now."

Hafer straightened. "Mister Clawson, I have a daughter.

She's barely eighteen and has no mother now, no other relatives. Throwing me in jail and taking me away from her would be like throwing her to the dogs. You can't do that. I've been faithfully paying on that loan."

"A loan can be called in any time, especially one that is delinquent. You could try to fight it in court, but that would cost you more than you can afford."

Hafer gripped the arms of his chair in anger and near panic. "Why are you doing this?"

Clawson suddenly grinned, his teeth seeming too big for his mouth. "Relax, Mister Hafer. I was just testing you out—trying to decide just how desperate you really are. Be honest now. Have you seriously contemplated Texas?"

Hafer watched him carefully. "Yes," he answered boldly. "Why not? A lot of people are going there, in spite of the problems with the Comanche and the Mexican government. Maybe there I could get rich, pay off my loan, and start over." His eyes saddened. "Part of the reason I considered it is my wife and son. Everything is too familiar on the old farm. I need to get away from there."

"And your daughter?"

"She doesn't mind. She thinks it sounds exciting."

Clawson leaned forward, taking a pipe from a desk drawer. He took out a can of tobacco and began stuffing the pipe. "Tell me, Mister Hafer, how do you feel about Indians?"

"You mean the Comanche?"

Clawson shook his head. "No. I mean the civilized ones, if you can call them that. Ones like the Cherokee who are being booted out of Georgia and other places. The ones who claim to be peaceful and civilized now. How do you feel about Indians in general—the local ones?" His eyes narrowed. "Like the ones who killed your son?"

Hafer felt the rage he always felt at the memory. "They hung for it." He almost growled. "I'll be blunt, Mister Clawson. I have no use for Indians of any tribe. Those drunken Osage killed my son and burned my barn two years ago. That's what finally killed my wife, and ruined me. Far as I'm concerned, we're right to rid Missouri of *all* its Indians, and I'd gladly go murder them one by one if I could get away with it!"

Clawson slowly lit his pipe and puffed it for a few quiet minutes, while Hafer sat, actually shaking with anger. Clawson finally pulled the pipe from his mouth and eyed Hafer again. "I have a proposition for you, Mister Hafer. If you accept it, you will be a rich man, and your debt will be considered paid as well."

Hafer frowned, but his heart quickened at the thought of being completely out of debt. The only drawback was that Byron Clawson expected something of him, and Clawson could be ruthless. Hafer knew that in his bones. "I'm listening," he answered, in spite of his doubts.

Clawson kept his gray eyes fixed on Hafer, as though trying to detect any duplicity, any doubt, any thoughts of betrayal.

"I want you to go to Texas," he finally said. "I have already made arrangements with one of my investors, who has claimed a considerable amount of land there for me. But you will tell your neighbors there, as well as your daughter and friends here, that *you* have claimed the land yourself. You will settle the land, work it. Hire some good men to help you. You will be given the finances to build a home for yourself and your daughter, to buy some cattle, farm supplies, whatever you need. You will live there just as though you owned it, be paid by me, and your debt here with the bank will be erased. We will sell your old farm and send you the money."

"Send?"

"Yes. Part of the deal will be that you leave right away. You may tell others, if you wish, that you have acquired another loan from this bank pending the sale of your farm, to be handled by us. Tell them how generous this bank has been to you." Clawson grinned almost wickedly.

Hafer smiled nervously in response. "Pardon my bluntness, Mr. Clawson, but I can't believe you're doing this out of the goodness of your heart."

Clawson laughed. "Of course there is a catch, but it has no real effect on you. It's quite simple, Mister Hafer. The land is yours for as long as you want to live there. Even if I were to come there, you could stay. But I really have no desire to go to such an uncivilized, dangerous country at the moment. I simply want you to live there, settle the place . . . and do everything in your power to make trouble for one of your neighbors."

Hafer ran a hand through his hair. "Sir?"

"His name is Caleb Sax. He's a half-breed Indian, living with a white woman. My guess is they're married by now." Clawson rubbed at his nose self-consciously. "For personal reasons, I hate the man. For one thing, he's responsible for disfiguring me. The rest of the reasons for my hating him are none of your business. Your only concern is to give the man trouble: spy on him and let me know what he's up to, get him in trouble with your other neighbors if possible. I'm told if a man gets arrested down there he can languish in jail for months. And since he's part Indian, perhaps even longer, or perhaps even hang. I know there isn't much law down there yet, but see what you can do. Personally, I'd love to see him dead. I would sleep better at night."

Hafer shifted in his chair. "You afraid of him for some reason?"

Clawson began nervously shuffling through his papers. "He'd likely kill me if he had the chance. That's why I'm not going down there myself, and why it is important he doesn't know who sent you. He has to believe you own the land."

"You aren't suggesting I kill the man, are you?"

Clawson grinned. "When you meet him, you'll know how difficult that could prove to be. He doesn't go down easily. I learned that myself a long time ago. I just want you to make trouble for him and to keep an eye on him. Keep him busy down there so he doesn't have time to contemplate coming to St. Louis to pay me a visit. I never worried about it until the woman he lives with went down there a year or so ago. She'll stir up old hatreds and it's got me worried."

"Who's the woman, if I may ask?"

"You may not ask. The fewer who know, the better. I plan to run for governor of this state in a couple more years. She would love to ruin that. The whole Sax family would. That's why I want to be sure they're kept occupied and that you keep them so upset that they don't have time to think about me."

"From what I hear, trouble with the wilder Indians and with the Mexicans should take care of that for you."

"Well then, this will give me that much more protection, won't it? It's worth twenty thousand dollars to me—as well as freeing you of your debt. The land here and in Texas will, of course, belong to the bank. You won't actually own any land, but you'll live like a king."

Hafer sat up straighter. He let out a little gasp and rubbed at the back of his neck. "You must hate this man very much—or be awfully afraid of him."

Clawson's eyes flashed. "Don't think me a coward, Mister Hafer! It's simply that the man is half Indian, and being so, he is a sneaking, bloodthirsty savage at heart and cannot be trusted! You know how Indians are. And yes, I hate him very much. Will you do it?"

Hafer sighed and leaned back again. "Twenty thousand dollars is a hell of a lot of money. I've never had that much at once in my whole life and probably never would the way I'm going. But if this man is as dangerous as you say, I'll need protection."

"Hire all the men you want. There are plenty down there roaming around looking for work. Not all of them make it at farming or whatever, and plenty of volunteers are going there just for the adventure, thinking war will break out any time. Most of them are from the Southern states and are Indian haters anyway. You won't have any trouble finding men who will gladly help you."

"You have any suggestions as to just what I should do?"

Clawson shrugged. "Claim some of his land. Find a way to rob him of water. I hear that's pretty precious stuff down there. Kill off some of his stock. Steal some of his horses and sell them to the Indians. I don't care. Just think of things that can hurt a man in his position—and remember that he's Indian. The best thing you can do is keep sentiment stirred up against him. If Texas ever does become independent, they'll step up efforts to rid the place of all its Indians, not just the wild ones like the Comanche, but the settled ones, like Caleb Sax. You can use that, whatever it takes. I'd love to see him dead, but I'd love even more to simply see him fail. I want him bankrupt, Hafer. I want Caleb Sax to suffer—him and his wife both. I want him in a weakened position so that perhaps one day I can come down there myself and squash him under my foot!" The words were sneered bitterly.

Hafer ran a hand through his hair. "Well, sir, I guess I can accomplish that for you. I'm not in the best position to turn you down. And I've got no love for any Indian. But what if I don't succeed at what you're asking?"

Their eyes held, each man greedy in his own way. "You'll succeed. It's worth a lot of money to you. Twenty thousand now and ten thousand for each year you stay and keep Sax out of my hair and in trouble. If he ends up being chased completely out of Texas, there will be an additional ten thousand dollar bonus. I'll hire someone to go check out the situation now and then, to make sure you're doing your job. And I never, I repeat—never—want my name brought into the picture. If Caleb Sax finds out I'm behind it, my life won't be worth much—and neither will yours, Mister Hafer, if you get my meaning. If Sax doesn't kill you, I might find a way to do it myself. That should be inspiration enough for you to succeed."

Hafer silently clenched his fists. He didn't like being threatened. But if he did not agree to this, he would lose everything he had. The farm wasn't worth much, but it was his. And what about Bess? It was like choosing the lesser of two evils, for he was sure that taking Clawson up on his offer would be dangerous. Worse, he would be the man's puppet. But he would be free of debt, a rich man; better yet, he would be an important man. He had never been truly rich and important in his life.

And he could persecute Indians. Hafer liked the feeling of power that gave him. After all, they were an inferior race. The Osage men who had been accused of killing his son had said someone else had done it; that they were not there; and that his son was drunk that night and had started the fight and the barn fire. Bess foolishly believed that crazy story. But she had always hated her brother's drinking, and she was too naive to understand. Hafer did not believe the Indians were innocent, and neither did the neighbors, who tried and hung three young Osage men, who proclaimed their innocence until the ropes around their necks finally silenced them.

Hafer nodded then. "I'm tired of trying to make something out of that used-up land I'm farming, Mister Clawson; tired of always wondering where the next dollar will come from. I don't have a wife anymore, and my son is dead." He stood up and put out his hand, a big, rough hand, callused from years of hard labor. Clawson took it with his smooth, slender, cool hand. "I'll do it," Hafer told the man, afraid to squeeze too hard for fear of hurting him.

Clawson grinned, his eyes glittering with triumph. "Good. And surely you know that what has transpired between us here today must be told to no one, not even your daughter. Make up whatever story you want to give her. Come here at ten o'clock tomorrow morning and I will have a paper for you to sign. I will also give you a list of what you will need. I'm getting it from some men who have been to Texas. They'll help you find a good, sturdy wagon to take you there. They'll follow with supplies to build you a home right away. The extra men should be enough protection for your journey there, and you can quickly build a fine home for your lovely daughter."

Hafer studied the man carefully. Hafer was a man who liked to make his own decisions, but he would be far away in Texas. Clawson wouldn't be able to order him around. He would do what the man wanted, but in his own way and in his own time, and enjoy a good life while he was at it. Why should he be in any hurry to kill Caleb Sax? The longer the man lived, the longer Hafer could live like a king. Harassing the man, destroying him financially, that would be the slower method and the best one for Hafer himself.

"Well, you seem to think of everything," he said aloud to Clawson. "Wagons, supplies—"

"It's my business to stay ahead of the game, Mister Hafer. I should tell you, the men I have hired simply think

I am helping out an already-wealthy man who is going to Texas to do some investing for my bank." He opened a drawer and took out a small bottle of brandy. "A drink to close the deal, Hafer?"

Hafer grinned. "Don't mind if I do."

Clawson laughed lightly, pouring some of the alcohol into a small glass. He handed it to Hafer, then took his own drink straight from the bottle. Hafer sipped his shot, watching as Clawson drank with gusto. He had heard Byron Clawson was a heavy drinker and that was part of the reason he never got anywhere politically. From the way the man guzzled the brandy, he guessed the rumors must be true. But it mattered little to him, as long as Clawson stuck to his side of deal.

Clawson set the bottle down. "Have a good day, Mister Hafer. I'll see you in the morning."

Hafer nodded, downing the rest of his drink. "I'll do right by you, Mister Clawson."

"We're doing each other a good turn, eh, Hafer?" The man laughed wickedly, and a chill moved through Hafer. Clawson had an almost insane look in his gray eyes at times. He bid the man good-bye and left, quickly setting aside his concerns over Byron Clawson. He was going to be a rich man. And he had no moral qualms about destroying Caleb Sax. He didn't like Indians, civilized or wild.

Inside his office Clawson walked to a window, watching the busy street below. He took another swallow of brandy, thinking of Sarah Sax. He hated her for the power she had to expose him for what he really was, and how he'd treated her. Clawson had never received what he considered to be his proper due from that marriage. He had not seen one penny of Sarah's father's money when the man died; and that had been Byron's primary reason for marrying Sarah, who had first belonged to and, he found out later, would always belong to Caleb Sax.

"You won't win this one, Sax," he muttered, taking another swallow of whiskey. "You think you're so high and mighty now, married to Sarah, owning all that land. When I'm through with you, you won't even be able to step foot in Texas. Maybe you and your fine, prized sons will even die, and your precious Sarah will be alone again. She and that daughter you fathered would make lovely gifts for the Comanche or Mexicans!"

Chapter Three

The Comanche were good at hiding. The war party that had taken John had ridden deep into Indian country, heading for a red-rock canyon near the Colorado River, where their women and tipis waited.

The Comanche stopped in the canyon to celebrate the theft of the fine horses and a strong boy from the ranch they had attacked. John's captor was especially eager to have a victory dance, for the boy's father had been a warrior himself and had fought well to keep his son. Soon they would join a much larger village, but first they would rest and drink the firewater they had stolen from a supply wagon. The wagon had been left to burn, its driver tied to one of the wheels.

John's captor shoved him off his horse and laughed when the boy hit the ground hard. John refused to cry or show fear, remembering his father's warnings about the Comanche.

John shuddered with the memory of these men hitting and stabbing Caleb. Was his father still alive? The memory of the awful blows made the boy want to cry much more than the abuse he suffered from the Comanche now.

John had given up trying to get his hands loose from the leather ties that bound his wrists. They were too raw to pull at the bindings any longer. His captor pulled him up and shoved him into a tipi, barking something to him in the Comanche tongue that John was sure meant that he should stay put.

He looked around inside the conical dwelling. Paintings, mostly of horses and battles, decorated the walls. The tipi was bigger than he'd expected, and cooler. He was himself mostly Indian, yet such a dwelling was not familiar to him. He wondered at the fact that his father had lived this way once. Caleb Sax had been as wild and vicious as these Comanche.

The boy closed his eyes and prayed Caleb was still alive. If he was, he would come for him. Of that John had no doubt.

Outside, drums began beating and the boy's heart pounded. What would they do with him? So far he had been tossed around like a sack of potatoes, fed little, and given almost no water. He understood almost nothing of the Comanche language. Perhaps they intended to torture him slowly. Did they do that to twelve-year-old boys? He was already so numb from exhaustion that perhaps he would not feel the pain so much.

Again the lump rose in his throat. He missed home. Even if they didn't kill him, he would probably never see home again, unless his father came for him. But he felt selfish hoping for that. Surely to come for him would mean certain death. But that wouldn't stop Caleb Sax . . . unless the man was already dead.

Maybe he would die out here in the middle of nowhere, or at best be made a slave of his Comanche captor. He must draw on his Indian spirit now, perhaps learn to be Indian to survive. Caleb would expect that of him.

"Please come, Pa," he whispered. He sniffed, and unwanted tears spilled down his dirty cheeks. He bent up his knees and quickly wiped them away on his pants so no Comanche would see.

* * *

The drums pounded hauntingly, while men yipped and women chanted. The sounds were chilling to Lee and Tom, who had never really lived the life of wilder Indians, but the sounds were not unfamiliar to Caleb Sax. Caleb himself was not now the man Lee and Tom had always known. He was Blue Hawk again, and he would make war against the Comanche the same way he had ridden against the Crow in vengeance for his Cheyenne wife's death. Only now, he must rescue his son.

They had searched for over two weeks, and both the younger men knew only Caleb's Indian instincts kept them from being seen by the Comanche. They felt baked from the sun, and their skin was sore from constant battles with spiny ocotillo bushes, cactus, and the countless other thorny, mean plants that defied anyone to come to this land. Tom's left shirtsleeve was torn and the skin cut from catching on the long spike of a mesquite branch, and they had had more than one encounter with rattlesnakes.

Caleb's strength and determination astounded the two younger men, who ached from too many days of almost constant riding. They were weary to the bone from too little sleep and too little food, which was always cold when they got it, because Caleb refused to build any fires for fear of being spotted by the Comanche. Both young men knew Caleb had to be hurting, but he never showed it. The man had grown visibly thinner and his eyes looked bloodshot, but a hard strength could be felt in his very presence.

The Comanche they had been trailing had finally stopped to make camp in a red-rock canyon. Whether or not John was with this party, none of them could know. Only two days before, they had come across a burned-out supply wagon, its driver's blackened body lying slumped beside a wheel. Finding the man made Caleb ride even harder. They all worried that the next body they found might be John's.

The three of them sat in a hollow above the canyon where the Comanche were celebrating. They were out of sight of the village and its scouts. Their horses were tethered nearby behind thick yucca bushes, the poor animals' legs full of cuts and scratches.

Tom and Lee sat waiting for instructions. They watched Caleb quietly. He sat with his eyes closed, breathing deeply, remembering another time and place—another Caleb, the Sun Dance ritual and/its pain, the power and pride he had felt at surviving his test of manhood. He had not felt his Indian instincts so strongly for a long time, yet the way of life of his youth was coming back so easily.

"The Comanche feel this is their land," he told Lee and Tom after several minutes of meditation. He opened his amazingly blue eyes and studied them both. "Just as the Cherokee feel Georgia belongs to them. Everywhere such things are happening to the Indians. My white half battles with my red half. Always there is this war in my soul. I know the Indian is right in wanting to hold what is his, and it could work—Indian and white man side by side, if the white man would keep his promises. But all of us know he never does and never will. Your grandfather learned that, Lee, when he was forced to give up that government land and come to Texas."

He sighed deeply, from terrible weariness. The man was nearly spent, but Tom knew he would never give in to his aching bones, not until he had John back.

"All of us react differently when we're threatened," Caleb continued. "The Comanche react by attacking the settlers and trying to scare them out. They're angry, and they're dying. They steal young children, partly to bring heartache to the settlers, but also to add to their own numbers. They make Indians of them and intermarry with them. John is part Indian. He could adjust. But he's my son and I intend to get him back. Until he learns their ways, they'll be cruel to him. And if he offends them in some way, they'll kill him. We have to get him out."

He took a long, polished wooden pipe from his parfleche. "We will smoke, and pray. It's important to pray for strength. God is many things to many men. To me He is *Maheo*, the Great Spirit of the Cheyenne. To Lee, now a Christian, He is *Jehova*. To you, Tom, He is *Maheo*. I raised you on Cheyenne beliefs. But *Jehova, Maheo*, they are the same. We must be strong. And we must be swift, for John's sake."

He stuffed the stone bowl of the pipe and lit it, and a wonderfully sweet aroma from the smoke penetrated their nostrils. Caleb drew on the pipe, then handed it to Tom. "My first son, my beloved first son, who was all the reason I had to live for many years. Take the pipe and smoke it. Offer it high, first, to the God of the Sky, *Heammawihio*; then to the God of the Earth, *Ahktunowihio*; then to the Great Spirit, *Maheo*. Give the pipe then to Lee."

Tom did as he was told. It had been a long time since he had seen his father this way. He knew there was this side to him, this very spiritual, powerful being who drew on a certain strength few men possessed. How else could Caleb Sax have survived the many losses in his life . . . his Indian father; the white man, Tom Sax, who had become like a father to him; his Cheyenne wife; his Cherokee wife and son; and once thinking he had also lost Sarah. Now another son was in danger. Caleb Sax was determined not to lose this one.

They all sat quietly as the pipe was offered and smoked, then handed it back to Caleb, who held it out in front of him.

"We have followed these Comanche for over two weeks," Caleb said then. "We have found no trace of John. That means they don't know we're following. If they did, they would leave his dead and mutilated body for us to find, just to be cruel. It also means John is still alive. We have to be very careful. If they discover us before we get our hands on John, he's dead."

"So what do you want us to do, Father?" Tom asked.

Caleb took one more puff on the pipe, breathing deeply. "There are many of them—only three of us. They have not yet reached full camp. This is just a small camp on the way. If we don't strike soon, we won't have a chance once they reach the bigger village." He set the pipe aside. "When I was warring against the Crow, sometimes alone, I used the element of surprise. That's what we'll do now. They are not expecting us now like they were a few days earlier. They think we're too afraid to come into Comanche country to come after John. Our advantage is being Indian and knowing how they think—how to keep from being detected. We'll make our move after dark."

"But you don't know if John is even in any of those tipis," Lee said.

"I intend to find out—tonight. That drumming is a celebration. They'll all be drunk by tonight. I'm going down and see if I can find John in any of the tipis."

"You're going in there alone?" Tom asked. "They'll kill you!"

"They won't even know I'm there. When it's necessary I can be as invisible as the wind."

Tom looked him over with concern, wondering how his tall, broad father intended to make himself invisible. Caleb smiled reassuringly.

"Don't worry. I know what I'm doing. You two will wait for me. As soon as I've found John's tipi, I'll come back here and we'll all go down together. You will wait in the shadows while I cut the tipi skins loose from stakes in the back of the tipi, enough to allow me to crawl under. My guess is John is being watched by only one man—the one who captured him. He'll be celebrating tonight also. There might not be anyone at all inside the tipi, but if there is, I'll kill him quickly enough—and quietly. You two keep watch. If someone approaches, or if there's trouble, use your rifles and shout war cries. That will surprise and confuse them—I hope enough to give me time to get out with John. We'll ride hard and fast. They'll have trouble finding us at night. It will give us a head start. Besides that, the way they're situated, they have to come up the path to the top of the canyon no more than two at a time. That will slow them down even more. And if we're real lucky, they won't bother to come at all. They still have the horses. We'll leave them. There's no way we can get them out of there, and John is the only thing that's important. Between being satisfied with the horses, and their own hesitation to ride at night, we have a good chance."

"What if we're caught?" Tom asked Caleb.

Their eyes held. "A man's only hope then is to be brave. The Comanche have been known to release a prisoner who refused to cry out under torture—out of respect for his courage."

"That's not very reassuring," Lee put in.

"It's the best I can offer. Just remember that once we make our move, it's torture for all of us if we fail. So I have one order. Kill John if it looks like there's no way out. I don't want him to suffer, and by God, Comanche know how to make a man suffer. They have their own religious reasons, but I don't intend for my son to be a part of their ceremonies. Understood? You'll not be held to blame. Kill him and do it quickly."

A lump rose in Tom's throat. "We'll do it."

Caleb nodded. "First I will put on war paint for power, and the two of you will also wear the paint. Then I will go down there first. Be ready—and remember, surprise. It's our only hope. Surprise—and move fast. Use those Indian instincts you were born with. This one's for your sister, Lee—for Marie, God rest her soul. That's her son down there. We lost one. We're not going to lose this one."

Lee nodded. "For Marie. We can do it, Caleb."

Caleb held out his hand and the other two put theirs on top of it, feeling a certain power at touching Caleb Sax.

Sarah sat up and sipped the tea Mildred Handel brought her. The Handels were two of the many foreigners who had come to Texas to settle on vast amounts of free land, people from another world hoping to find a freedom they had never known before. None realized the dangers they were risking in coming to Texas until they were already there, and none wanted the war that now seemed imminent with Mexico.

The Handels had come to Texas four years before. Because their land adjoined Caleb's to the southeast, Caleb had soon befriended them. He was fascinated with their foreign ways, and the Handels were fascinated by the Indian next door. Sarah was grateful for their friendly helpfulness, and for the companionship of Mildred Handel, although the two women were always too busy to visit very often.

Now Sarah lay in bed in a spare room of the Handels'

small log house. She could only pray the help left at the ranch would be able to take care of things until Caleb returned—if he returned. It was the middle of the night, and twenty days since Caleb, Tom, and Lee had ridden off. Sarah wondered how much longer she could stand the suspense, and she worried about Lynda, who also had trouble sleeping and who sat in the outer room now knitting a sweater for her unborn baby, trying to keep busy.

"Drink it all," Mildred urged Sarah, her German accent so heavy she was sometimes difficult to understand. "You are still very weak, Mrs. Sax."

Sarah sighed, smiling sadly at the sturdy German woman. "I'd get well faster if I knew Caleb was all right."

"Ach! That Caleb! When he rode in here with you, I thought we were the ones being attacked—all that paint and wild look! Feel sorry for the Comanche, I say! Do not worry about Caleb Sax!"

Sarah had to smile, but it did little to alleviate the worry in her soul. "Still, there are only three of them, Mildred. And Caleb is . . ." Her eyes teared. "What would I do without my Caleb—now, after finding him again?"

The woman patted her hand. "You would survive. And we would help you."

Sarah set down her cup. "You're so kind to us, Mildred. Surely you know some of the others around here are speaking against Caleb—saying Indians shouldn't get to own any of this land. So far there's been no real trouble, but so many Southerners are coming into Texas, I feel it's going to get worse."

"It is terrible, what they say! Caleb Sax is a fine man— runs a good place—a hard worker like my Wil. We appreciate good workers, strong people. We will stick by you. Any time you need us, like now, you feel free to come to us. I am glad your husband took up my Wil's offer to help. There might be a time when you can help us. We cannot bicker over race in a place like this, Sarah. We all need to work together to survive."

Sarah nodded. "Yes, we do."

"Ah, and that baby of yours! Such a fine-looking boy he

is—so strong and healthy, too. I have never been able to give my Wil a child. It is a sad spot in my heart."

"It must be. I'm so sorry, Mildred."

The woman shrugged. She was forty now, but looked older, her hair starting to gray. She was a short, plump woman with a quick smile but a stern look to her face when not smiling. "There are worse things in life, I suppose, like what you are going through now—this terrible worry. It must be so terrible to love someone as you say you loved your Caleb, and then be separated from him for so long. All those years—thinking he was dead—and your daughter, too. And then finding them both. Every time I think about it, I want to cry," Mildred carried on in a singsong pitch. "Such a story of miracles. And now you have the little baby. Life will be good for you, Sarah."

Sarah sipped more tea, hoping it would help quell the tears. "I hope so," she answered. She sighed deeply and swallowed. "Sometimes it seems like only yesterday when Caleb and I were little children at Fort Dearborn—and other times it seems like a century ago. We've both been through so much since then."

"You never told me how it was you thought each other dead. Why don't you tell me, Sarah? You need to talk. You are lying around thinking too much."

Sarah smiled sadly, meeting the woman's steady brown eyes. Mildred Handel was a wise woman, a kind woman. "It's a long story, Mildred."

"I have all night. I, too, am having trouble sleeping."

Sarah looked down at the teacup, running her finger around its rim. "It would help me to talk, I suppose." She smiled softly. "I knew Caleb as a child. That was at Fort Dearborn, where I lived with my mother and stepfather. My stepfather was also my uncle, Tom Sax, brother to my real father, Terrence Sax, who lived in St. Louis. Terrence Sax was quite wealthy. It's a long and sad story—about my mother and the two brothers. But Tom Sax is the man she really loved, and I loved him, too. I thought of him as my father in those early years."

She sighed deeply. "At any rate, Tom adopted Caleb into our family, and we were like brother and sister. Then my mother died, and things were getting dangerous around Fort Dearborn, what with a war brewing between England and America. I was sent to St. Louis to be with my real father." She shook her head. "I hated it there. And I lost track of Caleb. He went west to find his Indian relatives, married a Cheyenne girl who bore his son, Tom. Then she was killed. My uncle died in an Indian raid while fleeing Fort Dearborn with the other settlers there. I had no one but my real father and stepmother in St. Louis. My father ... was a pompous, arrogant man. There was no warmth and love at home. I suppose he loved me in his own way, but I'll always hate him for what he did later to Caleb."

She sipped some more tea. "Then Caleb left young Tom with the Cheyenne and came to look for me in St. Louis. We were both older, and the moment I opened the door and saw him standing there—" She smiled. "He was so beautiful. We both felt it right away. We weren't children anymore. We were in love. In a way, I think we always were. We were just too young before to realize it. When he came to St. Louis I was seventeen and he was twenty."

She looked at Mrs. Handel, who appeared fascinated with the story. "To make a long story short, father did not approve of Caleb. He always felt my uncle, Tom, had 'stolen' my mother from him, and Caleb was a lot like Tom— rugged, a man of the mountains, someone my father claimed could never support me properly—all the things he hated about his brother Tom. Father wanted me to marry Byron Clawson, a young man I detested. But Byron had a future, or so my father thought. He was wealthy, and to my father that meant everything."

She set her teacup aside. "Caleb and I ran away together." She reddened slightly. "We were young, and so much in love. We decided not to wait until we could find a preacher to marry us." She glanced at Mrs. Handel shyly. "At any rate, in our hearts we were already married. But then I got sick, very sick. Caleb was afraid I was dying. So he took me back to St. Louis to find a doctor who could help me. The doctor told Caleb I was dead, but I had a strange sleeping sickness that only made me appear to be dead. Everything happened so fast. The doctor secretly sent a messenger for my father. He and some other men, including Byron Clawson, came after Caleb. Caleb thought I was dead, and he had no choice but to run. They would have hung him, and he had to get back to his son, who was still with the Cheyenne. Then his horse stumbled and fell on him. Caleb was unable to go on. The men caught up with him and Byron—" The name was still bitter in her mouth. "He shot Caleb in the back," she almost hissed. "I didn't know until years later that it was Byron who had done it. I didn't even know Caleb had been shot at all. They told me he was killed when the horse fell on him. My father was so apologetic, told me he would have let me stay with Caleb. But I didn't believe that and never forgave him, although I didn't imagine he had actually let Caleb be killed. Even worse, Father had Caleb dumped off on river pirates and paid them to get rid of the body." Sarah shifted in her bed, saddened anew by her memories.

"Oh, Sarah, what a terrible story. Such a past you have had."

Sarah smiled at the kindhearted woman and leaned back against her pillow. "I was a long time recovering, and by then I knew I was pregnant with Caleb's child. I needed a husband. I hated Byron Clawson, but my father forced me to marry him, telling me how disgraceful it was to be pregnant and without a husband, extolling how kind Byron was to be willing to make my baby 'legitimate.'" She shook her head. "Byron moved with me to Washington, D.C. He was cruel, Mildred. So cruel." The words were spoken in a near whisper. "He beat me, forced himself on me in the night. He was drunk more often than sober. Then when Lynda was born, he took her away from me—told me she had died..." Sarah broke down in tears. "He kept me so drugged after that, I never knew the truth and half the time wasn't even aware of where I was," she continued in a broken voice. "He put Lynda in an orphanage and later he divorced me, after discovering my father was going broke and there was no money for him to inherit. He left me a near cripple, sent me home to St. Louis. My father died shortly thereafter. I've never visited his grave."

"And Caleb? How did you find him again? And your daughter?"

Sarah fingered a tie on the quilt that covered her. "Caleb lived. A woman we had known as a young girl at Fort Dearborn, Emily Stoner, lived in New Orleans then. Caleb had seen her there a year or so earlier, when he fought at the Battle of New Orleans." She decided not to tell Mildred Handel that the woman was a prostitute. Emily had been good to Caleb, saved his life. That was all that was important.

"Caleb was nearly dead," she went on, "but he managed to tell the men who found him to take him to Emily. She nursed him back to health, and then he went back west to get Tom, thinking me dead. We went on that way for years, thinking each other dead. Caleb met a Cherokee family on their way to Texas. He got Tom and joined them there, wanting to start a new life for himself and Tom. That's when he met Marie, who he married several years later. They had two sons, and then Marie and one of the sons were killed in a fire after an outlaw raid. Of course you already know all about that."

"Yes. We had only just come here when that happened. It was so sad." Mrs. Handel patted Sarah's arm. "Do you want more tea?" she asked.

"Yes. I think I do."

The woman poured more from a pot, handing the cup to Sarah. "And you? What happened to you?"

"I stayed in St. Louis. My stepmother died and I stayed in the house and opened a sewing business. Then one night a young girl came looking for work. It was raining that night. She was dripping wet and looked so sad and lonely at the door. And she was so young. I had to let her in. She told me she was an orphan and later explained the man she'd been traveling with was killed in a fight over a card game on a riverboat. She got off in St. Louis, alone and afraid, knowing no one. She walked the streets looking for work. Since she had worked in a garment factory back East, I gave her a job helping me. Later she told me about a blue quill necklace that had been left with her when she was dropped off at the orphanage."

Sarah shivered at the memory. "I'll never forget that moment. Caleb had given me a blue quill necklace. Byron took it away from me the night Lynda was born. I asked her to show me the necklace, and we knew then—she was my daughter."

"Oh, such a gift from God!"

Sarah's eyes teared and she sipped more tea. "Yes," she said quietly. "It was a miracle. Byron, too, had returned to St. Louis by then. I confronted him, much as I didn't ever want to see him again. But I had to know for sure. He admitted Lynda did not die—that he had put her in an orphanage. We knew for sure then. Several months later, Lynda and I saw an article in the local paper about Texas, saw Caleb's name and read that his son Tom was in St. Louis. Lynda went to see Tom and found out it was indeed my Caleb Sax." She met Mildred's eyes then. "You know the rest. We came to Texas."

Mildred Handel clapped her hands. "Such a story! See what a lucky woman you have been after all? And that Caleb was lucky, too. All the time we knew him before you came here, always I saw such loneliness in those handsome blue eyes. Always we felt so sorry for that man, and angry at how some of our neighbors talk now—against the Indians who have settled here, too." She grasped Sarah's hand. "But no more bad things for you now, hm? God will be good to you—and He will bring back your Caleb from those Comanche."

She released Sarah's hand and Sarah took another swallow of tea. "You have a great deal of faith, Mildred."

"Ah, and you are stronger than you think. Now you try to sleep. Do it for Caleb. He'd not want you sitting up and fretting this way." She stood up and fluffed Sarah's pillow. "Tomorrow my Wil and I are going into San Felipe. You are walking around now some. Would you like to go with us—ride in the back of the wagon and perhaps visit one shop—buy yourself a new dress for Caleb's return, perhaps? You can show him how you are getting back your lovely shape."

Sarah handed her the cup and put a hand to her waist, which to her was still too thick but was at least improving.

"Yes. If the weather is good, maybe that would be a good idea. I need more exercise, and I'll do anything right now that will help keep my mind off Caleb."

James started to fuss, and Mildred lifted the baby from his cradle beside the bed, laying him next to Sarah. Sarah opened the blankets to study the tiny package. The boy was already putting fat on his knees and elbows. He drank as though the milk might run out any time and it would be his last meal. He was going to be a big, strong son. Her eyes teared again. What other kind of son would Caleb Sax father but a strong, healthy one?

"James. My beautiful James," she said softly. She snuggled down and opened her gown so the child could suckle his midnight meal. Outside the same yellow moon shone down on the Handel ranch that was shining down on Caleb Sax, as he moved on his belly like a snake toward the Comanche camp.

"Hey, you big bull, we'll kill us some Comanche tonight, huh?" Tom shook back his long, black hair, enjoying the feeling of being Indian.

Lee grinned and gave him a shove, the white war paint against his dark skin seeming to glow in the soft moonlight. "I will kill more than you. You think the Cheyenne are better than the Cherokee."

"Smarter and faster."

"You will find out, nephew."

"I will help you when those Comanche get you in a fix, uncle."

The two always teased each other about being uncle and nephew, even though they were nearly the same age and had grown up like brothers and were now also brother-in-laws. Both were trying to make light of what they knew was a dangerous situation, as they waited anxiously for Caleb to return.

"They won't get me in a fix. I've got a wife at home with a baby in her belly," Lee answered. "And it's about time you started looking for a woman, Tom Sax."

"Find me one as pretty as that sister of mine you married

and maybe I will get serious. You don't deserve her, you know."

Lee laughed lightly. "I didn't see you trying to stop me from marrying her."

"That's only because you both had such a lovesick look in your eyes I thought I would get sick myself."

They both laughed then, but kept everything on a low key, not wanting to be heard by Comanche scouts who might be about. Their smiles faded then and their eyes held in the moonlight. Both of them wore buckskins and moccasins, clothing that blended into the surroundings.

"You think he's all right, Tom?"

Young Tom fingered a small rock. How he loved his father—worshipped was more like it. "Sure. My father can do anything. He's all Indian, remember? At least right now he is. You've heard him talk about what he did to the Crow. And he painted our faces. We will have much power now."

"Yeah." Lee sighed, adjusting the weapons belt he wore crossed over his chest. "Hey, don't you sometimes wish you could have known your Cheyenne mother?"

"Sure I do."

"I bet she was pretty."

Tom nodded. "I think she must have been, the way father talked about her. It's funny about feelings. Your sister Marie was not my mother, but I loved her the same as if she was. Yet there is this real mother I never knew, buried somewhere in the mountains to the north. My father has had many experiences in his life—many losses." He swallowed. "I hope he doesn't lose John. It would be very bad for him."

They heard a call then, like a small night creature.

"It's Caleb," Lee said softly.

A moment later Caleb appeared, calling their names softly.

"Here," Tom answered.

Caleb moved closer. "I know which tipi he's in. They brought him out once, arguing over whether to sell or keep him. He looks tired and hungry, and his wrists look like they're bleeding from rawhide straps, but he's okay otherwise. The Comanche are drinking like crazy. We have to hope they don't decide in their drunken state to torture John for fun and games. If we wait just a little longer, a lot of them will be passed out. It should be easy to get into the tipi and get John out. If we ride off fast tonight, it will take them a while to get themselves together to come after us— probably not until later in the morning. We'll have a hell of a start on them by then."

"It is still risky. Are they all drinking?" Lee asked the question.

"As far as I can tell. I think if we're quiet and quick enough, the only ones we'll have to deal with are the two or three that might sleep in the tipi where John is kept. I can't stress enough to either of you the fact that we must be very fast—no hesitating, understand?"

"Sure, we understand," Tom told him. "We've gone against Indians and outlaws before, Father. We can do it."

Caleb pulled a huge knife from its sheath at his waist. "And we've always done it on our own land—never this deep in Comanche territory. Believe me, if they weren't drinking, they'd know we were here and we would be stretched out for a nice long death right now. *Maheo* is with us. He has helped us in the form of rotgut whiskey." He put a hand on Tom's shoulder. "You bring the horses. You're best at keeping the animals quiet. Stop about half-way down the path and wait. Lee and I will go in. If you hear a lot of shooting and yelling, get the hell out of here, do you hear me? Don't try to be heroic. There are too many of them and death would be better than what they would do to you. Promise me right now—both of you. If things look bad and you have a chance to get away, do it."

Tom sighed deeply. He knew it was important to his father that they agree. "All right. I'll get out if I have to, but I'll by God come back with half of San Felipe!"

"I wouldn't count on too many back there helping us. We're Indian, remember? That's why I didn't bother asking for help in the first place. Lee? I want to hear your promise."

"I promise. I'll get out. But I'll be carrying you and John both on my back!"

Caleb grinned. "Come on. We'll wait a little longer. Then I'll go in and slice open the back of John's tipi. Lee, you follow me inside and we'll take care of whoever is in there." He put a hand on Lee's arm. "Now is when you must be all Indian, Lee. This is our war now, and all our lives are at stake. It's important that no one survive inside that tipi so that everyone thinks they're just sleeping. That will give us a lot more time in the morning. The same goes for you, Tom. If anyone comes your way other than John, he's dead. Understood?"

Both men nodded.

Caleb put a hand on each of their shoulders. "*Maheo* be with both of you. Let's go."

The camp was quiet, the central fire burning low. Several Comanche lay sprawled in a drunken stupor near the fire, and more were snoring in tipis.

Caleb touched his blue quill necklace and ducked low, leaving his musket behind on his horse and moving toward the camp with only a side gun and his huge knife. He and Lee crept to the bottom of the canyon, then went onto their bellies. Yes, they were Indian this night; moving stealthily, slowly, being careful where they placed hands and knees so as not to crack a twig or make scraping noises on gravel.

It seemed to take hours for them to reach the tipi where John was being kept. Caleb snaked toward it, stopped at the back and lifted the edge just slightly to peek inside. Only a few feet away he could make out a Comanche warrior lying on his back, snoring. Caleb tapped Lee on the shoulder. Then he took out his knife and rose to his knees. He looked around carefully, quickly jabbed the knife into the tipi, and ripped downward.

Everything happened fast after that. Caleb ripped all the way through to the bottom of the tipi skin, throwing back the flap and ducking inside like a shadow. Lee followed. Inside, a small fire shed just enough light to see John and two men. John's eyes widened with joy and he started to open his mouth, but Caleb put his fingers to his lips. He moved to one of the men as Lee also moved inside, just in time to see Caleb grasp the Comanche's chin, pull it up, and slash the man's throat quickly and quietly.

Lee froze, surprised at the viciousness of Caleb Sax. Just then, a woman bolted up behind Lee and the second man inside the tipi stirred. Caleb knew the first danger was the second man. He noticed the woman had a lance in her hand and hoped Lee would make his move fast. But Lee just stared at her, his soft heart trying to drum up the courage to kill her.

The woman, however, was quick; she was defending her husband. She rammed the lance into Lee, just as Caleb slammed his knife with a soft thud into the second Comanche before the man could cry out. Lee stumbled backward and the woman stabbed him again. Caleb dove into her, knocking her to the ground. She started to cry out, but Caleb's knife slashed across her throat without hesitation before she could make a sound.

John was watching the scene in terror. Caleb rammed his knife into its sheath and knelt over Lee, who was shaking violently, blood pouring both from his chest and from a hideous wound between his legs.

Caleb's heart felt ripped in half, and his eyes filled with tears. "My God, Lee . . ." But looking at Lee's wounds, Caleb was too devastated to speak. Only by drawing on his deepest strength did he manage to say, "I'll help you out of here!"

Lee reached toward him as Caleb moved away to cut the ties on John's wrists. John quickly wrapped his arms around his father's neck.

"It's all right, John. There will be time for reunions later," Caleb whispered. "We have to get out of here fast! Tom is waiting a few yards up the canyon path. You know where it is. Get outside—and be quiet as a mouse. I'll bring Lee."

The boy let go, his dirty face stained with tears. "I can't leave you behind, Pa."

"Don't argue. Do what I tell you. Go, quickly." He shoved the boy toward the cut in the tipi and John ducked out, crawling into the darkness to wait. The boy shook with fear that his father would not get out in time. How could he possibly make it if he had to carry Lee? Lee was as heavy as a buffalo, and badly wounded. Surely he couldn't live.

Inside, Caleb bent over Lee to pick him up.

"No," Lee whispered hoarsely. "I . . . am dying."

"You'll not die! Think of Lynda." Caleb grabbed the man's shirt. "Goddamn it, Lee, why didn't you kill that woman? Don't do this to me! I can't go back without you!"

Lee's lips twisted in a grimace of pain. "You know . . . I am dying." He made a strange gasping sound and arched. "She got me . . . down there . . . Can't go back . . . to Lynda . . . like this . . . Not a man . . ."

Caleb's blood chilled with the horror of it. He moved his eyes over Lee's wounds. Blood had already soaked his chest, and it was pouring from between his legs. There was no way he would survive and even if he did, the hideous wound would leave him less than a man. For someone like Lee, that would be worse than death.

"Tell . . . Lynda . . . love her so much . . . take care of the baby . . ."

"Lee, I can't leave you here. You aren't dead. Maybe you're dying, but if you aren't dead yet the Comanche will only make it worse for you."

"Kill me."

Caleb froze. Lee lay panting and weeping while Caleb's mind raced. He had to get out if he was to have any chance of saving Tom and John. No man in his right mind would think Lee could possibly survive the vicious wounds from the Comanche woman's lance.

"Kill me," Lee repeated, a begging sound to his words. "Take care . . . of my Lynda . . . my baby."

Now it was Caleb who hesitated. If he tried to take Lee with them, they would never move fast enough to get out of Comanche country alive, and Lee would leave a trail of blood that would bring the Comanche right to them. He was dying, but if Caleb left him and he had the misfortune of not dying quickly enough . . .

He leaned over Lee. "God, I love you like a son, Lee. You know that."

"I know." Lee actually forced a smile. "If you really

love me . . . kill me now . . . quickly. Get away . . . Caleb
. . . do it . . . for me. Thanks for letting me . . . have your
daughter . . . for a little while. She made me . . . so happy."
He reached up with a hand that shook almost violently. He
grasped Caleb's arm. "Your God . . . would understand.
Hurry, Caleb."

Outside, Tom waited with the horses on a small, flat
stretch of ground several yards in the distance. His heart
pounded with anxiety. What had gone wrong? They should
be out and running for the horses by now. Minutes seemed
like hours, and his whole body felt numb with anxiety.
Should he go after Caleb? He was just as able a fighter as
his father and Lee. They had all fought together to protect
the ranch many times over. He had killed his share of men.
He could kill a few Comanche.

When a dark figure finally approached him, Tom ducked
into the shadows until he could clearly see that it was
Caleb carrying a quietly crying John. A chill moved down
Tom's spine. Caleb plunked John onto Lee's horse and
quickly mounted his own. "Let's go! There's no time to
waste."

"Where's Lee?" Tom asked.

"Dead," Caleb said flatly. "Let's get going. I'll explain
later."

He rode off, leading John on Lee's horse and leaving no
time for more questions.

A horrible sorrow swept through Tom. Lee dead! It
couldn't be. Not Lee. Not big, strong, strapping Lee. He
wanted to go back for the body—something, anything.
But he knew without asking that there was no time, and a
dead body would slow them down. He mounted his horse
and headed carefully up the rocky pathway. Riding away
was the hardest thing he had ever done in his life.

Lee! They were leaving Lee behind.

Chapter
Four

The Handels' wagon lumbered into San Felipe with Sarah and the baby riding in the soft hay in the back. It was a bright, sunny day, and Sarah was glad she had decided to come to town. She needed to get out, to do something that would help ease her worry over Caleb. In the light of day those worries lessened, but deep in the night her chest pained her with anxiety.

Would they ever come back? For the last two days, she had been especially anxious, sensing something had gone wrong. But there was only one way to find out and that was for Caleb to return. The waiting was excruciating for Sarah, as it was for Lynda. She wished she could have convinced her daughter to come to town with her, but Lynda had insisted on staying behind, always hoping Lee and her father and brother would show up any time.

Sarah noticed more people than usual milling about town as they approached. She had heard that San Felipe, the town Stephen Austin had built with dreams of a grand American settlement, had turned into headquarters for talk of Texas independence. Wil Handel halted his wagon near a crowd of men who stood listening to a speaker, a tall man with a full build and a commanding voice. He was warning those present that they must be calm and not act rashly if they wanted to save both their lives and Texas.

Despite the man's admonition, the crowd was rowdy and

angry. Sarah held James closer to her as shouting filled her ears.

"Kill Santa Anna and get somebody else in there," someone shouted. Others agreed, shaking their fists.

"What is going on?" stout old Wil Handel asked in his heavy accent. A man nearby frowned.

"What's that you say?"

"What is going on? Who are these people—and who is that man?"

"Mister, that's Sam Houston, a former U.S. Congressman and a great friend of Andrew Jackson. He's here to investigate our problems and help us."

"Sam Houston. I never hear of this man," Wil answered, waving his arm.

"That's because you're from over the water. Hell, everybody has heard of Sam Houston. He even lived with the Cherokee awhile. Him and Jackson went at it over kicking the Cherokee out of Georgia. But I guess we can forgive his Indian sentiment if he thinks he can help us Texans now."

The remark hurt, but Sarah took hope. She watched Sam Houston. He stood tall, spoke well. She felt relieved that he was a friend to the Indians. Perhaps her vague fears about many Southerners and Indian haters coming to Texas would be unfounded if men like Houston were going to be in charge.

"Where is Mister Austin?" she asked. "Why is this Mister Houston talking to these people, and why are they so angry?"

"You haven't heard?" The man screwed up his face in anger. "Austin went down to Santa Anna to talk peace and tell him our grievances, and Santa Anna arrested him! He's in prison in Mexico City. We want to go after him."

Sarah looked up at Mildred Handel, her heart pounding. No one could be more loyal to Texas and to the promises he'd made to the Mexicans than Austin. How could this Santa Anna do such a thing? Why was there never any peace? She didn't even know if her husband was dead or alive, and here these men were talking about rising up against Mexico.

Wil moved the wagon farther down the street, fuming in German mutterings. "We will lose all that we have built up, Millie," he said, shaking his head.

"It will not be all that bad. We have been through so much. We will get through this."

The man sighed and shook his head, pulling up in front of a general delivery store. Wil took the baby from Sarah and handed him to Mildred, then helped Sarah down. "Easy now, Mrs. Sax," he told her. "A little walk to the clothing store, then back here to the wagon. I'll be right inside the delivery store. Give me your list of supplies."

Sarah fumbled in her handbag. "You're too kind, Wil. I only hope we'll be going home soon and I'll be sharing these things with Caleb." She handed Wil the list.

Wil Handel was as stern as his wife but he smiled for Sarah, who he thought was a most beautiful woman. He missed Germany and his friends there, but it was good to have neighbors and make new friends. He was glad he had come to Texas, which he considered a great and wild land.

"Not to worry," he told her. "You will need all these things, and the next time you come to town, Caleb will bring you." He gave her a wink and turned, walking inside the supply store while some of his men watched the wagon. Sarah and Mildred walked two doors down to a small women's apparel store. Such stores were a luxury in a place like San Felipe, which was a small, dusty town. Still, a trip to town was a welcome break from the lonely ranches, even if it was such a far cry from the city of St. Louis where Sarah had been raised. It was raw and rugged, and one of the last towns to get the latest fashions, if it ever got them at all. People in Texas cared only about the basic necessities for survival.

But that didn't matter to Sarah. She had come to Texas to be with Caleb. Who cared about the latest fashions? She went inside the store fully aware that all she would find were outdated clothes. She wouldn't buy anything ready-made. She had been a seamstress in St. Louis, and had done very well. She would pick out some pretty material and make her own dress, according to what the fashion had been when last she left St. Louis.

"I don't really need anything here," Mildred told Sarah after they'd been in the store only a minute. "I'm going back to the supply store. I forgot some things from my list, and I can help my Wil find some of the things you wanted there. You just take your time here and enjoy yourself, Sarah," the woman told her, patting her arm.

"Thank you so much, Mildred."

"For a friend, we help," the woman said warmly.

The woman left, and Sarah moved to look through a shelf of material, trying to ignore the shouts of war outside.

"Here, it's in here, Howard," a woman said then, hurrying through the doorway.

Sarah turned to see the woman rush inside, accompanied by a burly, aging, bearded man in buckskins. He was a big man and he followed the woman as though he worshipped her every step. Considering the woman's tiny build, he made an amusing picture, hovering over the woman as she browsed through some material. She wore a plain gray dress and a black, lacy scarf covered her blond hair. One side of her veil was pulled forward as though to hide something. It struck something familiar in Sarah's memory, and it all came into focus when the woman turned and came to the shelf where Sarah stood. She stopped still, suddenly paling when her eyes met Sarah's.

Sarah felt shock move through her own bones, and she scrambled to think. It was Emily Stoner! She knew Emily as a child at Fort Dearborn. Emily had been the daughter of a cruel preacher, and had turned to prostitution at a young age. The last Sarah knew, Emily was working at a house of prostitution in New Orleans. Sarah had discovered the truth when Emily came to visit her in St. Louis to tell her Caleb Sax was still alive, for it was Emily herself who had nursed him back from paralysis after Byron Clawson shot him. What on earth was Emily Stoner doing in San Felipe?

On seeing Sarah, Emily turned away abruptly, as though she wanted to hide. "Howard, you don't need to wait in this place for me. Go ahead and get those supplies you need for the shop."

The man with her looked around the store, where only

women browsed, and appeared relieved at the suggestion. "Sure, honey. You wait right here for me, though. I'll come back for you. I don't want you walking around alone out there."

He patted her shoulder and left, while Sarah watched in astonishment. Honey? He didn't want her walking alone? Emily Stoner had been a prostitute in New Orleans! Why was he so concerned? It dawned on Sarah then that the man surely didn't know about Emily's past. Her mind raced with confusion as Emily turned back to face her.

"Well, they say here in Texas you never know *who* you'll run into." Her eyes softened and actually teared. "You *are* Sarah Sax, aren't you?"

Sarah managed to find her voice. "Emily Stoner?"

The woman held out her left hand, showing off a wedding band. "Emily Cox. Mrs. Emily Cox."

Sarah just blinked, and Emily smiled, then suddenly gave her a quick hug. "Oh, Sarah, I saw you and I knew I had to explain before you met Howard. But that's beside the point at the moment. What in God's name are you doing in Texas!" She pulled away. "The last time I saw you, you were in St. Louis, searching for Caleb." She pulled back, more tears in her eyes.

Sarah could not help being astounded at the change in the woman. She dressed plainly and wore no makeup. She was a married woman! "I . . . I found Caleb," she answered. "It's such a long story—"

"You found him? My God! Is Caleb here—in San Felipe?"

"Yes. He has a ranch northwest of here. Tom is with him. And we've found our daughter, and—"

Emily looked down at the baby in Sarah's arms. "Sarah! Is he yours? Yours and Caleb's?"

"Yes. This is James. I only came here a year ago. Caleb's son Tom went to St. Louis to recruit people to come to Texas. We saw an article about it in the paper and discovered that Caleb was here, a widower. Tom brought us here."

Emily put up her hands. "Wait! You're confusing me. This is all so wonderful! What's this about a daughter?"

"The baby I had by Caleb when I was eighteen. She didn't die. She lived and I found her, Emily. Her name is Lynda, and she's with us here in Texas, married to a Cherokee man."

Emily put her hands to her cheeks, shaking her head. "Whoever would have thought I'd fine you, of all people, here in Texas, or that you and Caleb would find each other!"

"I could say the same for you, Emily. I thought you were in New Orleans."

The woman laughed, a ring of the old, hard Emily in her voice. "Oh, Sarah, we have so much to talk about. I met Howard in New Orleans. He was also recruiting people to come here. I was so tired of the life I was leading. I thought, maybe if I came here, someplace brand new, I could somehow get away from it." She adjusted the black lace shawl, making sure it covered the ugly scar on her face left years ago by a Potawatomi Indian who had captured her, one of the Indians who had killed Sarah's uncle, Tom Sax. Emily would have been a beautiful woman if not for the scar—and a proper lady, if not for her cruel father and for the emotional scars left from being a captive of the Indians.

"I fell in love with Howard right away," she went on. "But I've never told him about—you know." She reddened slightly. "He's such a big sweetie, Sarah. I told him I was widowed in New Orleans." She looked back at the door. "I'll have to introduce you. He'll be back any minute. Please go along with whatever I tell him."

Sarah let out a little gasp of confusion. "Of course. And I'm—I'm so happy for you, Emily. A husband! You seemed so unhappy all those years ago when I saw you. Now you look wonderful."

"I am! And look at you! You were a pretty unhappy woman yourself, you know. At least I was able to tell you Caleb was still alive." She sucked in her breath, her eyes taking on a nostalgic look. "Caleb! Oh, how I'd love to see him again. How is he, Sarah?"

"He's fine, and as handsome as ever. He has quite a large ranch and does well. But right now, I can only hope he's still all right. He's been gone three weeks. Our ranch was raided by Comanche and they stole a son he had by his Cherokee wife. Caleb went after the boy—Caleb, Tom, and a Cherokee son-in-law."

Emily's face clouded. "Caleb went after Comanche?"

"Yes." Sarah held James closer. "The waiting has been terrible."

"Of course!" She put her hands on Sarah's arms. "But remember who he is, Sarah. He's Blue Hawk, at least while he's out there he is. He'll be fine, I'm sure. My goodness, the Lord surely didn't bring you back together just to let something happen to one of you now." She smiled again. "And just think, you found your daughter *and* Caleb. And now you have a new baby! Oh, how I'd love to see Caleb again. When he gets back you must both come and see us. Howard and I live up the street in a little log house. Howard is a blacksmith. We tried farming, up around Viesca. But it's so remote there, and I was too afraid of the Indians." The fear old memories brought moved through the woman's eyes. "I have enough scars from the Potawatomie. I don't care to find out how the Comanche treat a captive. Howard understands. He's so good to me, Sarah. So good. I only hope something from the past won't come up to make him hate me. I'm so happy now."

Sarah smiled. "I can see that. And we will come see you, Emily. I'll explain to Caleb. He won't say anything about your past. Oh, he'll be so surprised, Emily, and so happy to see you. My God, you saved his life all those years ago. If not for you . . . We owe you so much, Emily."

"Nonsense. No one owes me. I'm just glad it turned out the way it did. Imagine! You, me, Caleb—all right here in Texas. What a crazy, wild place this is, isn't it? And all this talk of war! I swear, wherever I go, there's a war. Down in New Orleans it was the war with the British—all those volunteers marching through the streets, including Caleb." An odd pain moved through Emily's eyes. How she had loved Caleb herself once. But she was not the woman for him.

The door opened and Howard Cox walked in. "Emmy, they don't have what I need." He stopped and removed his hat. "Oh, excuse me, ma'am. I didn't realize you and my Emmy was talkin'."

Sarah looked up at him and smiled. "It's all right, Mister Cox." The man had kind eyes that bespoke a gentle good-hearted nature in spite of his tall, burly build. He smiled and reddened when Emily took his arm and squeezed it.

"Howard, this is Sarah Sax. I knew her at Fort Dearborn. Of course, we were just children then. Oh, it's such a long story. I'll explain it all sometime. Suffice to say her husband is Caleb Sax, a man we also knew at Fort Dearborn as a boy. A few years ago Caleb showed up at my doorstep, dying from terrible wounds. My first husband and I had no idea where he'd come from, but he needed help. So we took care of him ourselves, because I had known him as a child." She talked easily about her "first husband," making his existence sound so convincing that Sarah almost believed in him herself. Parts of Emily's story didn't really go together, but she talked fast, and Sarah suspected Howard Cox was not the kind of man who could put things together quickly in his mind. He was perfect for a woman who had something to hide. But it seemed to Sarah a dangerous game for Emily to be playing.

"Caleb got well, then left for parts unknown," Emily continued. "I've never seen him again. And now here's Sarah, in Texas! And come to find out, she's married to Caleb! This is their new baby son."

Cox fingered his hat and grinned. "A fine-looking boy, ma'am. Is your husband about? I'd like to meet any man or woman who was friends with my Emmy."

Emily patted his arm. "Indians raided their place, Howard. They stole a son Caleb had by a Cherokee wife. Caleb has gone to try to get the boy back."

The man's eyebrows arched. "He's gone after Comanche?"

"Now, Howard, don't make it sound so terrible. Sarah is worried enough as it is. But Caleb is part Indian. He can take care of himself. I'll tell you all about him later. This is no place to talk."

"Well, when your husband returns, you folks be sure to come and visit with us," Howard told Sarah. "I'm glad

Emmy run into you. Women friends are hard to come by out here. Seems to be a slight shortage of females." The man laughed lightly and reddened again.

"Yes, I know what you mean," Sarah answered. "At least I have an older daughter at home for companionship. You two will have to come and see us, too."

"I'd like to do that sometime," Cox answered. "But right now I'm awful busy, what with all these newcomers. Seems like San Felipe is growin' like wildfire. And with talk of war and all, I can hardly keep up with the work."

"I can understand that. Perhaps when Caleb returns we'll come to town."

"I'd like that. And I know Emmy would, too."

His use of the name "Emmy" touched Sarah. He seemed to adore Emily absolutely. Sarah could see the hope in Emily's eyes that the man would never find out the truth about her background.

Emily grasped Sarah's arm. "Things will be good for you now, Sarah. I just know it. It's so wonderful, running into you like this. Give Caleb my best."

"I will. And I know things will be good for you, too, Emily. I'm so glad for you."

The woman smiled. "God be with you all, Sarah." She thanked Sarah with her eyes for not revealing anything. "If . . . if things don't go well . . . you remember I'm here, will you?"

Sarah nodded. "I'll remember."

Sarah heard guns outside being fired into the air. She jumped and held James closer as he began to cry. She suddenly wanted only to be home on the ranch, Caleb lying beside her in bed. Where was Caleb? Was he alive? What had happened to make her wake up with that terrible sense of dread? And all the ruckus out in the street only made things seem worse, for Texas was bursting at the seams. Stephen Austin had been arrested, people were angry, and her own husband was somewhere fighting Comanche because the Mexicans had not provided enough protection for the American settlers. All her life she had felt her destiny decided by events she could not control. It was happening again. She could only pray it would not mean losing her Caleb.

She suddenly didn't care about material for her dresses. She wished she had never come to town at all. She wanted to get back to the peaceful Handel ranch, to get back to poor Lynda, who was convinced something awful had happened. More guns fired. It seemed everyone wanted Texas —the Mexicans, the Americans, the Comanche, and the Apache. Where would it all end, and where would she and Caleb and their family be when the questions were resolved?

"I hope things are more peaceful when we meet again." she told Emily, holding James closer to her breast.

Mildred Handel returned and Sarah stumbled through introductions, her mind and heart full of Caleb. It was as though the gunfire had brought it all into focus. Lynda was right. Something terrible had happened. And now Emily Stoner had appeared out of nowhere, someone from a past both Caleb and Sarah would rather forget. It was all strangely foreboding.

They rode hard, all through the night and into late morning, until the horses could no longer keep going. Tom could see his father was pushing both men and animals beyond their limit, as if he were being chased by something terrible. Caleb rode ahead and said nothing, looking back only occasionally to make sure John was all right.

John forced himself to keep up in spite of the fact he had been starved and abused for a few days before being rescued. He knew they had to keep going, to get as far away from the Comanche as possible. One had to be practical in this land. How many times had his father told him that? He knew there was no time even for mourning Lee. That would come later.

Finally, close to noon, heat and exhaustion won out. Caleb headed for a grove of cottonwoods and halted the horses. He dismounted, turning eyes that were shockingly hollow and wild to his sons. He walked over to John, lifting him down and hugging him tightly. Caleb's shoulders shook as he walked under the tree with John in his arms. Tom realized his father was crying.

Tom had no idea what to say to the man. He was suffering his own grief. Lee had been a brother, a best friend, practically Tom's only friend all his life.

Tom's mind raced with questions. What had happened to Lee? Why was his father acting so strangely? He watched as Caleb set John on his feet, then turned away and headed quickly for a huge pile of boulders not far away. He disappeared behind them.

Tom frowned, looking at John, who was wiping at his eyes. He walked up to his young half-brother. This was the first chance they'd had to talk, and Tom needed to know. "What the hell happened back there," he asked John.

"An Indian woman ... she surprised Uncle Lee," the boy answered, sniffing and wiping at a dirty face. He shook with weariness and renewed horror. "She stabbed him with a lance before Pa could get to her. If Uncle Lee ... would have turned sooner," he sniffed, "he'd have seen the woman. But he was ... watching Pa kill those other Indians. Pa just ... sliced their throats. I never ... saw him like that. He ... killed that woman, too. But Uncle Lee ... he was too badly hurt already. I guess Pa couldn't bring him ... 'cause he'd be too heavy to try to carry off with us."

Tom heard choking sounds coming from behind the rocks. "Stay here," he told John. "Get some rest. And give the horses a little water from our canteens." He hesitated a moment, then walked toward the rocks, where he found his father not just weeping, but sick to his stomach. Never in his life had he seen Caleb Sax like this.

"Father, what is it? Let me help you."

Caleb straightened from a kneeling position. He poured some water from the canteen he'd brought with him into the palm of his hand and splashed it on his face, then drank a little and spit it out to wash his mouth. He took a handkerchief from an inside pocket of his buckskin shirt, wet it, and began wiping the white paint from his face. He remained silent, turned away form Tom. Tom walked closer, kneeling down and putting a hand on his father's shoulder.

"Father? Are you wounded or something?"

Caleb shook his head. "No." He blew his nose, then sat down against one of the boulders, closing his eyes and breathing in a deep shudder. "I killed him, Tom," he said quietly. "I killed Lee so the Comanche wouldn't get hold of him and torture him before he died. I killed him." His voice choked again. "What the hell . . . am I going to tell Lynda? I don't even have . . . a body to bring home."

Tom felt a great lump in his throat. He sat down beside his father, rubbing at his eyes. What a horror for Caleb Sax! Lee had been like a son. Tom breathed deeply to keep from weeping himself. For the moment he had to be strong. Life was going to be very lonely and different without Lee, and the loss was beginning to bore into Tom like a bullet. He knew that, for a while, it would get worse before it got better.

"You will just have to tell her the truth," Tom answered.

"No. I don't want her to know it all. That woman . . . stabbed him right between the legs . . . and in the chest. He couldn't have lived, and even if he did . . ." He jerked in a sob, rubbing a hand over his face. "My God." He breathed deeply for control. "He begged me . . . to kill him . . . said not to try to take him . . . he'd never make it. So I . . . cradled him right in my arm . . . and slit his throat." He looked down at his clothes, covered with dried blood, Lee's blood. He shook his head, as though bewildered.

"We can tell Lynda he died right away from the Comanche woman's wounds. We'll say the blood on your clothes is from the Comanche warriors you killed. We couldn't bring Lee's body because he was too heavy and we had to get out of there fast. Does John know what you did?"

"No. He saw Lee stabbed. I'm sure he thinks that's how he died."

"Then don't ever tell him otherwise. We'll explain how hard it would be on Lynda to know he suffered. He'll understand we have to convince her he died right away. It's the most comfort we can give her." He swallowed before continuing, finding it very difficult not to break down. "I hope she doesn't lose the baby over this. It will be very important to her to have the baby. It will help her get over Lee—having his child."

Caleb nodded, then leaned forward and got on his knees again, retching violently. He had never experienced anything like this before. He'd been through a lot of things, killed a lot of men, warred against the Crow, fought in the Battle of New Orleans, struggled to protect his land, lost many loved ones. But never had he taken his own knife to someone dear to him, let alone the fact that Lee Whitestone was one of the finest young men he knew. How would he ever forget this? Surely he had done the right thing—but Lee! Lynda's husband! Marie's brother. Marie. She would understand. Surely she knew right now, and they were together in spirit—Lee and Marie. Yes. He had to think of it that way. He would go home and spill it all out to Sarah. She would understand, too. Only Sarah and Tom would know.

His stomach finally settled and he washed his face and mouth again. He turned to Tom, his first son, the young man who had given him reason to live so many years ago. Tom understood. And surely he, too, was grieving. He had been close to Lee. Caleb reached out and they embraced.

"We'll work it out, Father. You'll see."

"I tell myself . . . I should have let you go instead. Maybe you wouldn't have hesitated. But then if it had been you . . ." He shook his head. "That's what did it," Caleb told him, pulling away again. "The damned softhearted Cherokee hesitated because it was a woman—"

A shot rang out before Caleb could continue, and a piece of the boulder behind them exploded into tiny stones.

"Pa," a startled John shouted from the grove of trees nearby.

Caleb and Tom ducked, hunching down as they made their way back to the trees, where John was hitting at a Comanche warrior with a stick. The warrior was trying to take the horses. Caleb made a growling noise, landing into the man and knocking him to the ground. Tom whisked his musket from its boot on his horse and whirled, quickly firing at two more warriors coming down from the boulders right behind them.

One of them screamed out and fell, while Caleb wrestled on the ground with the first man and John scurried to Lee's horse, taking a musket from that one. Tom ducked and rolled as the third warrior came at him with a tomahawk before Tom could reload. The warrior missed. Tom scrambled back up to face him and swung his musket hard, smashing it into the side of the warrior's face. The Comanche went down under the bone-crunching blow, while three more warriors came down from the rocks.

John took careful aim with Lee's musket and shot one of the oncoming Comanche, while Caleb rammed his knife into his opponent's chest and quickly got up. Caleb pulled his handgun and fired, killing another attacker, while the last man screamed out and lunged for Tom. Caleb wanted to fire but was afraid of hitting Tom. He shoved the gun into its holster and dived into the man, pushing him off Tom. The tomahawk the warrior wielded landed into Caleb's shoulder, more by accident than a deliberate effort. Tom struggled to his feet and retrieved his own pistol from his horse, but it was not necessary. Caleb was already stabbing the warrior. Tom realized the man was already dead, but in Caleb's grief and fury he could not stop. Over and over again he landed the knife into the Comanche man, his shoulder bleeding badly, until Tom came up from behind and grasped his arm, pulling it back.

"Father, stop! He's dead."

Caleb hesitated, staring at the man as though he just then realized what he'd been doing. He dropped his knife and moved wearily off the bloody warrior, panting, forcing himself to his feet. "Were there . . . just the six of them?"

"It looks that way. We'd better get going again," Tom answered. "The horses are about dead, but we have no choice. We are still too deep in Comanche country."

Caleb nodded. He grasped his left arm with his right hand. The blood from his left shoulder was beginning to run down his arm.

"Let me pour some whiskey on that and wrap it, Father."

"Later. Let's get some distance on our heels first."

"You will bleed badly."

"I've bled before." He turned to see John still standing

with Lee's musket in his hand, staring at the Comanche he had killed. John Sax was only twelve, and he had killed a man. His eyes were tearing when he finally moved them to look at his father.

"It feels funny," he told Caleb.

Caleb walked closer to him, his own eyes full of vengeance. "You had every right to shoot him. Out here a man doesn't have a choice, and I guess you're as much man now as Tom here. Your first kill was for Lee. Remember that."

Their eyes held, and John handed Caleb the rifle, then hugged him around the waist. "Don't die, Pa. I don't want anybody else to die."

"I won't die," Caleb answered wearily, patting the boy's head. "God knows I should have many times over. It should be me lying dead back there in that Comanche village, not Lee." He sighed deeply. "Let's get home. Sarah must be having a fit wondering what's happened to us. We'll find a place to hide out better and do most of our riding at night until we're far enough out of Comanche country to make a dash for home."

He looked at Tom, his eyes weary and full of sorrow. Tom knew his father was trying to decide how he was going to tell his daughter her husband was dead. Caleb stumbled to his horse then, his left arm beginning to feel weak and numb.

Chapter
Five

Sarah's knuckles were red from scrubbing clothes on the rough washboard. Mildred Handel insisted she was not strong enough to help with the laundry, but Sarah was determined to do her share. She and Lynda had been with the Handels for nearly six weeks, and Sarah was beginning to feel like a burden, although Mildred seemed genuinely to enjoy the company of the women and the baby.

James lay in a cradle in the shade of the porch overhang, and Lynda was rocking him with her foot.

"Riders coming," one of Handel's men shouted.

Sarah straightened and wiped her hands on her apron. Every time she heard those words she prayed it was Caleb. She walked over to the porch, where Lynda had already risen to watch men approaching on horseback.

There were only three. Sarah's chest tightened. She walked up beside Lynda and put an arm around the girl's waist. The men came closer, and the women could see now that one of them was a young boy. The two men were tall and broad—Tom and Caleb.

"Mother," Lynda whispered. "Where is Lee?"

Sarah just watched as Wil Handel rushed up to greet Caleb and Tom, carrying on with "Thank God's" that they were all right. He reached up to take young John from his horse and hugged him.

Sarah gave Lynda a squeeze. "Lee must be all right," she told the girl. "There will be some explanation."

She let go of the girl and walked down the wooden steps of the porch, hurrying over to John and hugging him. This was not her son, but he was Caleb's, and that was all she needed to know to love him as her own. She leaned back and touched his hair.

"Johnny, are you all right? Did they hurt you?"

He glanced at Lynda and swallowed, then looked back at his stepmother. "I'm okay." He swallowed again. "But Lee's dead," he said quietly so that Lynda couldn't hear.

Sarah paled and looked up at Caleb, who was still on his horse. She was shocked by his appearance: the hollowness to his eyes, the sudden aging of his face. The sleeve of his buckskin shirt was torn and covered with what looked like bloodstains.

"Caleb," she groaned. She glanced at Tom.

"We had more than one run-in with the Comanche," Tom explained. "Father was hurt, but he is healing." His dark eyes moved to Lynda, who came stumbling off the porch, her eyes wide with dread.

Sarah turned to Wil Handel. "Take John inside, will you? Let him get cleaned up. And he's probably hungry."

"Of course, Mrs. Sax." He shook his head. "I am so sorry."

Sarah smoothed her hand through John's dark hair again. "Go with Wil, John. Everything will be all right now. Thank God your father found you." She blinked back tears as the boy walked toward the house. Tom was dismounting, but Caleb seemed frozen in place. He was watching Lynda, who just stared back at him with her father's same blue eyes.

"Lee's dead," Lynda finally said. It was not a question. She knew. Tom moved up beside her, taking her arm.

"He died quickly," he told his sister.

She turned her eyes to Tom. "Where is he? Where is his body?"

Tom glanced at Caleb, who closed his eyes and turned away. Tom sighed and kept hold of Lynda's arm. "We had to leave him. We had to get out and get out fast, Lynda, or they would have killed us all. We never would have got away."

He felt her beginning to shake violently. "No . . . body? I . . . can't even bury him here, where I can be close to him."

"We're so sorry, Lynda. You know we would never have left him if there had been any choice. He was like a brother to me, and a son to Caleb. It's bad for us, too. I grew up with Lee." An aching lump rose in his throat. "We don't need a body. What's a body? It's the spirit that matters, and Lee's spirit will always be with us, alive in this place. Everywhere we look we will see his smile, hear him laughing. He wouldn't want you to look at his dead body. He would want you to remember the Lee Whitestone who left here a few weeks ago."

Lynda barely heard him. Lee! On his last night home they'd made love. His seed was rapidly growing in her womb. This was unreal. Surely he would ride in behind the others any time. Lee was too strong and good to be dead. Not Lee! She needed him. She was going to have his baby. She felt her legs giving way and suddenly Tom was picking her up and carrying her to the house. Someone was screaming Lee's name. Was that anguished sound coming from her own throat?

Caleb watched, his face stricken with alarming desolation. Sarah walked up to him, concerned about his wounds, but also concerned by the look in his eyes.

"It should have been me," he groaned, when his eyes finally met hers.

Sarah reached up and touched his leg. "It shouldn't have been anyone, Caleb. It just happened. There is hardly a settler in Texas who hasn't suffered some kind of loss at the hands of the Comanche—or from the damned weather or outlaws or disease. It all comes with the country, Caleb, and you love this country. You found family here and have built a home here. These things happen. We both know that."

He looked at her wearily. "You don't understand."

She frowned. "What don't I understand? Caleb, please get down. Let me help you."

He wearily dismounted, grimacing with lingering pain. He clung to his horse's bridle and looked down at her. She looked good, thinner again, beautiful as always. But this homecoming was not the joyful event he had hoped for.

"You all right?" he asked. Even his voice sounded weary.

"I'm much stronger."

"The baby?"

"Healthy. Beautiful. He's nearly six weeks old, Caleb."

He glanced at the cradle on the porch, then closed his eyes when he heard Lynda crying Lee's name inside. He opened them to look down at Sarah then, swallowing before he spoke.

"I killed him myself," he told her in a near whisper. "He was . . . badly wounded . . . dying. I had no choice, Sarah, I couldn't . . . let the Comanche hurt him more."

Their eyes held, and he watched the horror in hers. He knew she understood it had been a necessary thing but also understood what it had done to him.

She made an odd choking sound, wilting against his chest and hugging him. "Oh, Caleb, my poor darling Caleb," she groaned.

He moved his arms around her. He needed her strength more than she had ever needed his.

"He was so badly wounded," he repeated, as though he wanted to be sure she understood. "He was dying . . . I was afraid the Comanche would . . ."

She felt him shaking and realized he was crying. "Dear God," she whispered. "Oh, Caleb." She knew full well the hell he was going through. This was something that would haunt Caleb Sax forever. Inside he was so gentle, so loving. But the forces of the outside world had turned him into a man who survived by being practical, sometimes vicious, having to make terrible choices. Those choices were complicated by his two bloods. "Oh, Caleb, I wish I knew how to comfort you."

He breathed deeply, throwing back his head and struggling to regain his composure. "Nothing can. Time, perhaps . . . or someday seeing Lynda happy again."

Sarah reached up and touched his face. "She will be. She's young, Caleb. And she's carrying Lee's baby."

He glanced toward the house again, wet tears still on his cheeks. "I hope she can keep it. It's important she has it."

"She's a strong girl. And she has us."

He looked down at her. "You, maybe. Me she will hate for taking Lee out there. I don't ever want to tell her I'm the one who—" His voice choked.

"Caleb, she wouldn't hate you for that."

"Yes she would. I don't want her to know. Only Tom and you know. John thinks he died from the Comanche lance. It's hard enough facing her without her knowing I slit his throat with my own knife." The words were spoken bitterly through gritted teeth.

Sarah hung her head. "Caleb, Lee went of his own choice. You could never have kept him home. Lynda knows that. John is his full-blood nephew, Marie's son. He had to go. Lynda won't ever blame you for that." She looked up at him. "It's like I said. It was this land that killed him, not you—not even the Comanche."

He looked down at her and touched her face lightly. "And what will this land do to you? What will it do to little James, or perhaps to my Tom, or Lynda?"

"It's no use wondering all those things. We can only take a day at a time. You love it here, and Tom loves it, too. Lynda will stay because she has us. She has lost Lee, but she has her mother and father, and that's so important to her. She loves you, Caleb. She idolizes you. She could never hate you." She took hold of his hand and kissed his palm. "Come inside, Caleb."

She put an arm around his waist, urging him to come with her. They walked to the porch, where Caleb stopped to look down at his son. He'd saved another son, but at a great expense. Yet he'd sacrifice anything for his offspring, even his own life. Right now he wished that was what he had given up for John, not Lee's life. He leaned over and lightly touched James's smooth cheek. He ached over Lee's death, yet he had to be glad he was alive, to come home to this.

"He is beautiful," he told Sarah.

"A little ornery lately. I think he's having tummy pains. This is the best he's slept since yesterday."

He looked back at her, noticing her tired eyes. Delivering and raising a baby in this untamed land was not easy. But Sarah would never complain. She had had the child for him and would do it again. He took a deep breath before entering the house, where Lynda sat in a rocker, bent over and weeping. Tom stood beside her. He looked helplessly at his father, who left Sarah and walked over to Lynda, kneeling in front of her.

"I'm so sorry, Lynda," he told her, his voice gruff with emotion. "He was like a son. We'll make a stone for him, in his memory."

"He . . . didn't suffer?" she asked between sobs. "You wouldn't lie to me? The Comanche didn't capture him? Torture him?"

Caleb looked up at Tom, then back at Lynda, touching her hair. "No. We had snuck into the tipi where John was kept. We thought there were only two drunken warriors inside. But there was a third." What was the use telling her it was a woman? "He stabbed Lee with a lance before he or I had a chance to react. Lee died instantly." He turned and glanced at John, who swallowed back tears and nodded to show he understood that his father wanted Lynda to believe Lee died right away, and not at the hands of a woman.

Lynda threw her arms around her father's neck. "Hold me, Father," she wept. "What will I do? What will I do without Lee!"

He stood up, pulling her up with him and holding her tightly. "You'll do fine. You're a strong, beautiful, good woman, and you're carrying Lee's baby. You will hang on and bear this so you don't lose that baby, you hear? That baby is the most important thing in the world now, a part of Lee you can keep forever. And you have us. You will always have your mother and father. And some day there will be another man for you. You're only eighteen. You will love again."

"No I won't. Not ever! Not like Lee!"

He patted her back. "Yes, you will. I know the feeling, Lynda. I have loved three women, each for her own special goodness. When I lost Walking Grass and Marie, I wanted to die, too. But somehow we keep going. And then God brought Sarah back to me. And He brought me a daughter I never knew I had, and then blessed us with a new son. Now you'll give me a grandchild, and we're still together —still family. You will love again, I promise. And Lee will be looking on and he'll be happy for you. He'll always be with us. Men like Lee never die, Lynda."

She choked in a sob. "I keep thinking . . . he'll come riding in soon. Without a body to bury . . . it's hard to imagine . . . he's really gone."

Caleb's jaw flexed against his own desire to weep again. But for the moment he had to be strong for his daughter. He would save his own tears for a time when he was alone. And there would be many more tears for him, as well as haunting dreams for a long time to come. He could still see Lee's face, his eyes wide with fright and humiliation, his hands reaching for him, hear his voice pleading with him to end his life. How awful was the sting of death. How many more times would he suffer that sting?

Tom carried a handful of fresh biscuits and a bottle of wine to the small hill behind the main house, where the little graveyard for the Sax family was sadly growing. Here lay Marie, her mother, and her son David, as well as the several Cherokee who had died on Sax land, including the fresh graves of those who had died in the fight with the Comanche. And now there was a new grave, only it wasn't really a grave at all. There had been no body to put there. There was only a stone, bearing the name Lee Whitestone.

They had all been home for two weeks. They had quickly left the Handels to get back to their own land, where Tom took over the hiring of more men, helped clean up the burned debris of the barn, and sent men to search for more wild mustangs to replenish the Sax herd as well.

But it was not easy without the help of his father. Caleb was having trouble with his left arm. It was still very sore. But it was not the arm that kept him from taking over his usual position as master of the Sax land. His spirit was gone. He didn't seem to care about getting back to normal, and Tom knew why. Caleb Sax couldn't bear to watch his daughter's agony. Lynda sat at the grave site every day, barely eating, her tears coming unexpectedly. She slept at her parents' house, unable to bear staying in the little cabin she had shared with Lee, but she sat up crying half the night, every night. In spite of all the family support, her grief would not leave her, and she had lost weight.

It was all killing Caleb Sax, and Tom decided it was time for it to end. He approached Lynda, who sat alone under an old, gnarled cottonwood that hung over the little graveyard.

"All right, little sister. It's time to start eating," he spoke up, going to sit beside her.

Lynda looked up at him. She loved this handsome brother of hers, but right now it irritated her that he had intruded on her desire to be alone and she told him so.

"You've been alone too much, Lynda. This is not a time to sit and brood. And if you really loved Lee, you'll start eating and stay healthy so you can deliver a nice, healthy baby for him. You keep this up and you'll lose it."

"Please go away, Tom."

"No. I won't go away." He unfolded the cloth napkin and laid the biscuits in lap. "They're still warm. Now get busy. I brought some wine, too, to relax you better. You know Mr. Handel makes the best homemade wine in these parts. You try some. And I want you to start eating, or I'm going to consider it a disgrace to Lee's memory, the way you are acting. How do you think he would feel if he knew you were neglecting his baby?"

She met his eyes. "Neglecting his baby? I most certainly am not!"

"Yes you are—by not eating. You're thin as a skeleton. You intend to deliver a *baby* skeleton?"

A faint smile drifted over her lips and she picked up a biscuit and took a bite. She chewed slowly and could barely swallow it. "What am I going to do, Tom? There is no one in the whole world like Lee."

"Of course there isn't, just like there's no other you or me or Caleb or Sarah. Everybody is different, with wonderful things about them that people miss once they're gone. Lee was a good man. You think it isn't hard on the rest of us? He was my best friend, you know. I grew up with him. I knew him a lot more years than you did. I'm damned lost without him."

She looked at him sympathetically then, reaching out and touching his arm. "I know. I'm sorry, Tom."

He sighed. "I know the loss is greater for you, but I'm worried about you. Don't add to your sorrow by losing the baby, Lynda. You are a strong woman. Look at all the other things you went through: that orphanage, the factory and that horrible supervisor you told us about, plus falling in love with a gambler and seeing him killed. Now Lee. But at least you had him for a while. He gave you strength and love when you needed it. And think of all the good things—the miracle of finding your mother and father. Now you're having Lee's baby. And you're so young yet, Lynda, and you are by God the prettiest girl in Texas, even if you are my sister. There will be someone else some day."

She shook her head. "Never."

"Never say never when your life has barely begun. Your son or daughter will need a father—and you'll have needs that will wake up again some day."

She reddened slightly, looking down at the biscuits. "Without the right man, the needs fade away. All I feel now is . . . I don't know . . . anger, terrible sorrow."

He pulled the cork from the wine. "The best way to relieve that is by sharing your feelings, not sitting up here all alone letting them fester." He took a swallow. "Here."

She took the bottle but wallowed only a sip, then handed it back.

"I'm hurting—we are all hurting," he told her then. "Especially Father. He thinks he is responsible—thinks he should have gone after John alone. Can you imagine that? He is blaming himself, Lynda. And you aren't helping things any. Lee was like a son to him, you know, and the only thing worse than losing a spouse is losing a child. I don't have either one yet, but I can imagine. Why don't you come down and join everybody again—show Father you are going to get over this. I'm really worried about him. I know you love him, Lynda. But right now you're killing him. Can't you see it?"

She looked at him as though surprised. "No, I . . . I thought Father was getting better."

"Physically, maybe. But inside he is dying, Lynda."

She looked away, staring at the house below. "I kept that blue quill necklace all through my childhood," she said quietly, "trying to envision who owned it. When I first saw Father I felt like I had always known him. And he was so handsome—so wonderful."

"Well, right now I think you need each other. I thought that first day we got back, when you turned to him, everything would be all right. But since then you've drawn up into your own lonely world. Come down and talk to him, Lynda; join the rest of us. If Father doesn't get some of his spirit back soon, I am afraid he'll just sit and shrivel up and die. We—"

He stopped, looking below to see a troop of Mexican soldiers riding in from the south. "Look there!"

Lynda leaned up to look. "Mexicans!"

"Come on." Tom quickly picked up the wine and biscuits in one hand, taking her arm in the other. "Let's get down to the house."

Tom hurried her down while several of Caleb's men moved in to surround the soldiers as they approached the house. Caleb came outside then, his left arm in a sling. He wore cotton pants and shirt, and his long hair was brushed and pulled back, tied into one tail. Sarah stayed inside with James, on Caleb's orders, but John came out to stand beside his father.

The soldiers rode up close to the front of the Sax home, and Caleb eyed them warily. When these men had been badly needed, they had not come to help. Now they came on a peaceful morning, and Caleb suspected their mission was not to help the settlers.

The leader of the soldiers eyed Caleb in return, studying the sling, turning to glance over at the remains of the burned barn. He turned his dark eyes back to Caleb, curious over the fact that he was Indian.

"I am Teniente Leónes. I would like to see the owner of this place, señor. Would you get him?"

Caleb stepped forward. "You are looking at him."

The man frowned. "But . . . you are Indian."

"Half of me is. My name is Caleb Sax. And you're a little late. A couple of months ago my place was raided by Comanche. Where is the protection the Mexican government promised us when we came here, Lieutenant?"

The soldier shifted in his saddle, his grand black horse tossing its head. "There are few of us for such a big land, señor. And you *Americanos* are acting very independent lately. Perhaps you think you do not need us anymore."

"We've done nothing but ask for our rights as Mexican citizens, protection that was promised us. And what does your government do in return for our cooperation? You arrest a man who is very important to us—an innocent man who went to Mexico City in good faith to speak to Santa Anna. You don't seem to try too hard to remain popular with the American settlers. If you don't free Stephen Austin soon, there will be big trouble."

The lieutenant scanned the group of Indians who stood around his men then. He moved his eyes back to Caleb. "You should tell your men to put down their guns, señor," the man replied. "Or you are right—there will be trouble. Only it will not be between the citizens and my government. It will be trouble for you."

"I'm used to trouble. Suppose you tell me just why you're here."

The Mexican nodded. "I am here at the bidding of our great general and *presidente*, Antonio López de Santa Anna, who has declared that all *Americanos* in the Province of Texas must give up their arms to him and promise there will be no more talk against the great country of Mexico, which has been kind to you by letting you come here to settle."

Caleb's men looked at each other, hanging on to their pistols and muskets. Tom and Lynda reached the house, where Tom hurried his sister inside through the back door. A moment later he came out the front door to join John in standing beside his father.

"Your kindness stopped when you began allowing men to rot in prison, and when you failed to give us the protection from Indians and outlaws that you promised, Lieutenant Leónes. Take your men and get off my land," Caleb answered.

Leónes grinned a little. "Everywhere I go, señor, I find such answers. You *Americanos* are asking for much trouble—more trouble than any Indians or outlaws could give you. Santa Anna will not be happy with the things I have to tell him when we return."

"I don't give a damn how happy your *presidente* is! You picked a damned bad time to come, Lieutenant. The mood I'm in, it wouldn't take much for me to order my men to shoot you right off that horse. This sling I wear is from a wound I received fighting Comanche, who killed my son-in-law. You go tell Santa Anna he'll get no weapons from me or my men, and that he had better free Stephen Austin from prison, or he's going to have some very angry Americans breathing down his neck!"

Leónes shook his head, while his men sat tensely on their horses. There were as many Sax men as there were soldiers, and none of them trusted the cockiness of the Americans. But Leónes remained confident.

"Why make things difficult for yourself," he told Caleb. "It is so simple. You and your men turn over your arms. We will allow every third man to keep a handgun. We will not leave you completely defenseless."

"Get out of here!" The words were shouted by Lynda, who surprised them all when she appeared at the corner of the house wielding a musket herself and aiming it directly at the lieutenant.

Caleb turned in surprise.

"Lynda!" Tom scowled at her.

"Put that gun away, Lynda," Caleb ordered.

The lieutenant grinned. "She is a pretty one," he sneered. "It would be a shame to have to shoot her."

Lynda moved closer to her father. "Make them leave, Father, before I pull this trigger," she sneered in return. "They're at fault for what happened to Lee—not you—not even the Comanche! Make them leave before I kill the lieutenant!"

Leónes swallowed, losing his smile and thinking what he'd do to her if he were not surrounded by men with guns.

"I mean it, Father. I'll kill him!"

Caleb smiled a little then, looking at Leónes. "You heard my daughter. You had better go, Lieutenant, or a war with Mexico will start right here. The Americans are doing everything they can to avoid that. Your president seems intent on making it happen."

"No Sax man is going to give up his weapons," Lynda sneered. "To give them up means death. I just lost my husband to Comanche, mister. You and your president are not going to leave us helpless!"

Tom stood with his hand on a gun at his side, while Sarah waited inside with a pounding heart. John glared at the soldiers, and Caleb straightened beside Lynda. "You go and tell Santa Anna that if he wants my weapons, he can come for them himself, and the only way he'll get them then is over my dead body," he told the lieutenant.

Leónes glared back at him, his dark eyes turning to narrow slits. "You have been warned, all of you Americans. Our *presidente* is very angry."

"And so are we," Caleb answered.

The lieutenant jerked his horse back and turned it, motioning for his men to follow. Caleb's men moved behind them. "We'll see that they get all the way off the land," one of them yelled out to Caleb.

"Start guarding the borders. Make sure they stay off," Caleb answered.

Lynda lowered the musket, her hands shaking now. She struggled against tears, looking up at her father. "This is what happens when you don't get out there and take care of your land," she chided. "When you sit around moping, so do the men, and Mexican soldiers ride right in without anybody knowing it! When are you going to stop sitting around feeling guilty about Lee, Father? You got John back. Lee gave up his life for John. He did what he had to do. Now it's time for you to do what you have to do and run this place the way it should be run—the way only Caleb Sax can run it!"

Caleb frowned, reaching out and taking the musket from her and handing it to Tom, keeping his eyes on Lynda.

"What is this all about?"

Their eyes held. "It's about you...and me and Lee. Nobody is to blame, Father. And Lee would hate how you are acting, how I'm acting, too." She looked down, touching her stomach. "Tom made me realize if I don't take care of myself, I will lose Lee's baby." She met his eyes again. "I want this baby more than anything. And I want things to be as normal as possible again. I want to see you out here giving orders and helping round up some new horses and getting the barn rebuilt. And I don't want you feeling guilty about Lee. I have never held you to blame." She looked out at the barn and the disappearing soldiers. "Lee helped you build this place. You've got to get it back into shape." She met his eyes again. "You owe it to those people who are buried up there behind the house."

A faint smile moved over his lips. "Well, by God, if you aren't a Sax through and through. I think you really would have shot that man."

They both smiled. "I never told you how glad I was to see that you and Tom and John at least survived. I feel so selfish. I didn't even seem to care that you had been wounded, that you had risked your own life. But I did care, Father. This would all be so much more unbearable if something had happened to you, too."

Sarah walked out onto the veranda then. Lynda turned to her and they embraced. Sarah looked up at Caleb and saw a brighter look to his eyes, saw a little bit of the old Caleb returning. Caleb turned to Tom.

"Let's go for a ride, son. It has been a long time since I rode the borders and took a look at what needs to be done. And we will hire a few extra men to get the barn built faster."

Tom grinned. "Chester Stone spotted some beautiful wild horses in the northern valley. You want to go check them out?"

Caleb nodded. "Sounds good to me." He looked back at

Sarah, bending down and kissing her cheek, then Lynda's. "I will be back by nightfall," he told them.

"I will be waiting," Sarah answered, her green eyes shining with love. Their eyes held, and she saw a look there she'd not seen in a while. Caleb Sax was healing emotionally. And that meant he would come back to her in spirit—and body. She felt old sexual urges awakening as she watched him walk off, loving the easy gait of his long legs, loving Caleb Sax with every bone in her body. She just then realized she had never told him she had seen Emily Stoner. They had been so wrapped up in their grief over Lee, it just didn't seem important. She would have to tell him, tonight. Tonight they would really talk—be the old Caleb and Sarah. The healing had begun. If only there weren't this worry over Santa Anna and the Mexicans.

Chapter
Six

Caleb stretched out in bed, watching Sarah brush out her long, red-gold hair. There were times when she seemed eighteen again—still slender, her skin soft. Sarah had lost much of the weight she had gained from the baby, and it pained Caleb's heart to realize that part of the reason was the work and worry of living in this land he called home. But Sarah never complained. They were together again. That was all that mattered. Caleb felt joy at the memory of the little girl at Fort Dearborn who, the first time he met her, had taken his hand and led him to the house, eager to teach her way of life to the Indian boy her uncle had brought home. She had not really lost that sweetness. Byron Clawson had tried to destroy it, but it had survived.

"Do you think there will be trouble with those Mexican soldiers?" she asked.

"Most likely. But not just for us—for everybody. When I rode off with Tom earlier we ran into Wil Handel. He told us there is going to be a meeting in San Felipe in a couple of days with that Sam Houston fellow. I intend to go."

Sarah sighed and put down the brush, removing her housecoat as she approached the bed. Caleb turned on his side to watch her climb in. He reached out with a sore left arm and urged her to move closer. She reddened almost like the young girl she had been when he first took her. Neither of them had been able to think about sex in weeks; she had been big with child, then Caleb had left to rescue John, and then their awful grief had come between them.

"I like you this way," he told her, "all soft and warm in a flannel gown, your hair long and loose." He bent down to kiss her, lightly massaging a full breast with his big hand. His lips hungrily met her mouth. Sweet, beautiful Sarah, his best friend in youth, his lover, now, finally, his wife. His lips left her mouth and traveled over her eyes, her cheek. "She'll be all right, won't she? Tell me she'll be all right."

She knew he meant Lynda. "Of course she will," Sarah answered softly. "She's a Sax. We'll all help her through this and when she has the baby it will help. And some day there will be another man for her. She's so young and beautiful. It's just so sad that she had Lee for such a short time. Things like that are so much harder to accept when you're young."

"We both know that," he answered. "Yet if I lost you now, being older wouldn't help much. It hurts at any age." He studied the green eyes. "I just hope I never have to go through losing you again."

She kissed his chest. "You won't lose me."

He nuzzled her hair. "Who can promise anything anymore? This damned Mexican situation—"

She put her fingers to his lips. "Let's not talk about it." She decided to change the subject before all his troubles and grief spoiled the night. "Caleb, I never told you—while you were gone I went to San Felipe with Mildred Handel, and guess who I saw. No, don't guess. You'd never guess in a hundred years. Emily Stoner!"

His eyebrows arched and he raised up, leaning on his right arm. "Emily? In San Felipe?"

"Yes." Sarah grinned. "And would you believe she has a husband?"

He smiled, but he didn't laugh. He rested his head on his hand. "I'll be damned. I would love to meet the man. He must be a saint."

"Oh, Caleb, don't tease. It isn't funny, not when you see the look on Emily's face. She told me he knows nothing about her past. When she first introduced us, she talked about her 'first' husband, how he helped her take care of you.

"She has told Howard, that's her husband, that she's a widow. And she talks so fast around him, I think she keeps him confused enough not to question her. Her husband is a blacksmith and is from Texas. He was in New Orleans to recruit people to settle here when she met him. I really think Emily came here hoping she could start a new life and leave her past behind."

He lay down and pulled her into his arms. "Emily Stoner—married," Caleb said reflectively. "At the time she was nursing me back to health, I could tell she was wishing she could live a different life. But she didn't have much faith in herself. I tried to tell her what happened in her childhood—her tyrant of a father—and being captured by the Indians—didn't have to stop her from being happy. What is her husband like?" he added tentatively.

"He's a big, rather clumsy-looking man in his forties, and I think he all but worships Emily—calls her 'Emmy.' You should see his eyes when he looks at her. His name is Howard Cox."

Caleb grinned. "Imagine that—Emily Stoner settled, and living right here in San Felipe."

"They might come and visit. If they do, you mustn't give anything away. You have to act like it was she and her husband who helped you, not just Emily." She sighed deeply. "We owe her, in spite of what she was, Caleb. She saved you from death, and later she came to see me in St. Louis to tell me you were alive. It helped me so much to know that, even though neither of us knew where to look for you. I at least had some hope. She didn't want to be seen coming into my house that night, but I didn't care who saw. And I'll never forget how lonely she looked. I dearly hope she can be happy here."

Caleb frowned. "How did she explain to him about knowing us?"

"She just told him we had all known each other at Fort Dearborn."

Caleb's heart tightened. He had never told Sarah the reason he had first fled Fort Dearborn in his teens and ended up living among the Cheyenne. Sarah had already been sent to St. Louis to be with her father when it happened. They had all been hardly more than children then. The promiscuous Emily Stoner seduced the then-virgin Caleb Sax into a torrid series of sexual pleasures, until her violent preacher father found them together, at which time a frightened Emily Stoner screamed rape and nearly got poor Caleb hung. He had to flee for his life, and not long after that Fort Dearborn had to be abandoned. In their flight south, Tom Sax and Emily's father were killed by the Potawatomies, and Emily was taken as their captive.

When Caleb ended up in New Orleans years later, during the War of 1812, he discovered Emily living there, working in a brothel. He hated her then, but later when she helped him after being wounded, they came to an understanding, and Caleb learned the horrors of what her life had been like with her crazed preacher father. His animosity left him, and they parted good friends. That had been at least eighteen years ago. And their teenage sexual fling had been even earlier than that. What was the sense of saying anything to Sarah now?

"I'll look her and her husband up when I go to San Felipe," he said aloud.

"You be careful in San Felipe. We're caught between, you know. You're an American settler, with the same complaints as the rest. You're one of them, and yet you're not.

I have heard settlers grumbling about the Indians coming into Texas from the southern states. It would be easy for the talk to turn against all Indians."

Caleb began to unbutton her gown. "I don't want to even think about it tonight."

She reached up and touched his face. "My strong, wonderful Caleb. The past few weeks, I hated watching you suffer so. It's been so hard. I was wondering if you would ever be my Caleb again."

Pain stabbed at him again at the memory of Lee, but he forced it out of his mind. He had to remember the living and their needs. This was his Sarah—so special, so damned special. Caleb pulled her gown off her shoulder, exposing a breast. He bent closer and lightly sucked at the firm nipple, catching a taste of his own son's nourishment. Desire ripped through him as she let out a small whimper. A man could take nourishment from a woman's breast, too—a different kind of nourishment, a kind of security in knowing he was loved and desired.

His touch brought out her own long-buried desires. "Oh, Caleb, it's been so long," she whispered.

He nuzzled his face between her breasts then, eager from so many weeks without his woman. He kissed her slowly as he moved down, taking the gown with him, refreshing his memory on her every curve and shadow, her every secret place. He pulled the gown off her ankles and threw it aside, lost in her, hardly aware of her remarks about hoping she still looked good to him. How could she not look good to him? She was Sarah, and these were her lovely ankles he was kissing, her slender legs, her smooth, firm thighs. This was her secret place, owned by Caleb Sax, the first man to invade her, the only man she'd ever loved.

Sarah was glad Lynda had chosen to sleep in her own cabin that night. She would not want the girl to overhear their sounds of lovemaking. Tom had long ago decided to sleep in the bunkhouse so his father and Sarah could have more privacy. John slept in the loft, and he always slept soundly. James slept in a cradle nearby. The house was quiet. Sarah could not control the whimpers and cries of ecstasy as her husband touched her in all the right ways, exploring, bringing out her every passion, reawakening desires that had not been stirred for a long time. Her pleasure came not just from his touch, but from the knowledge that emotionally he was healing and was her Caleb again.

Caleb moved quickly, and she understood. It had been a long time. She was as anxious as he. His lips moved back over her belly, her breasts, to her throat. He supported himself mostly with his right arm as his powerful legs forced hers apart and that most manly part of Caleb Sax found its way into the nest of love that waited for him.

He pushed deep and hard, groaning her name, needing this as a last step in overcoming his grief, needing to be human again, to know there was still life and love in a world of prejudice and violence. He moved rhythmically but almost frantically, grasping her hair, his body damp against her naked skin. Her own passion rose to greet him with a pulsating climax that sent fire ripping through his loins. He held out as long as possible, to satisfy her own intense needs. Then his life spilled into her, and he relaxed beside her, pulling her into his arms and kissing her hair.

"I love you, Sarah," he whispered. She felt his trembling, and when she reached up to touch his face, she realized his cheeks were wet with tears.

"It's all right now, Caleb," she said softly, curling up against him and kissing his chest. "It's over. Lynda will heal. We all will heal."

Steam poured from the water into which Howard Cox was dunking a red-hot horseshoe. He looked up for a moment, just in time to see a couple entering his small workshed. He grinned when he recognized Sarah.

"Mrs. Sax!" He removed the shoe from the water with hammer tongs and hung it over an iron bar. He then wiped sweat from his brow with his sleeve and dried his hands on a heavy apron. "Nice to see you again."

Caleb studied the big man, whose smile and eyes suggested a very decent, good-hearted person.

"We asked where we could find the new blacksmith," Sarah told him, walking up to him and putting out her hand. "We knew if we could find you, we could find Emily."

"Oh, ma'am, I can't take your hand. I'm too dirty." Cox looked somewhat embarrassed, as Lynda and Tom also came inside, standing near Caleb. He ran a hand through his dark, curly hair.

"Well, not too dirty for another man," Caleb put in then, putting out his own hand. "I'm Caleb Sax!"

"Well, well!" Cox shook his hand heartily. "I've heard so much about you. Emmy has told me all about you folks. Why, you've got to go and see Emmy. She'd be real proud to see you walking so tall and strong, Mister Sax."

Emmy. Caleb was astounded to see immediately that this man seemed to have no inkling of his wife's past.

"Yes. They were very good to me," he replied, letting go of Howard's hand.

"Well, I'm real glad you two found each other."

"And we're glad to see Emily is over the grief of losing her first husband and has found herself a good man," Caleb answered.

Cox just laughed. "Well, I was never one to settle . . . roamed the mountains mostly—trapped, hunted, laid trails. But I always knew smithy work—just never stuck to it. Now that I have a wife to support, and couldn't quite make it at farming, I came to town to do what I do best."

Caleb grinned. "I'm sure you're good at it. I'm here to go to the meeting. I want to get a look at Sam Houston. What do you think of him?"

Cox shrugged. "Seems like a good man."

"Well, I'd like to see Emily and then go to the meeting. He turned to the others. "This is our daughter, Lynda; and my son Tom by my first wife. I guess you've already seen the baby."

Cox nodded to Lynda and Tom and turned to Caleb. "Right handsome family you've got, Mister Sax. And a new baby to boot. You must be a very proud and happy man."

Caleb nodded. "I am. I have another son at home— John."

Cox wiped his hands again. "Well, then, you did get him

back from the Comanche. Emmy said you would—said no Comanche could take on Caleb Sax and win. Is the boy all right?"

"He's fine. But my son-in-law—Lynda's husband—he was killed."

Cox sobered, turning to Lynda with genuine sorrow in his eyes. "Oh, I'm real sorry about that, ma'am. Real sorry."

Lynda gave him a faint smile. "Thank you."

"Well, you've got a fine family to support you and help you—strong parents, an older brother who I'll bet would defend you to the death. Isn't that right, Tom?"

The man looked at Tom and the young man grinned. "Yes, sir. We will take care of her."

"Of course you will." Cox looked back at Caleb. "Emmy and me live in a little cabin up at the left end of the street." He walked out of the small shed. "Right up there. She's got roses all around the front step. You'll see it. Lord knows there's not much in flowers around here, or women, for that matter."

"Thank you, Mister Cox." Caleb shook his hand again. "I really am glad to meet you."

"Call me Howard. And any friend of Emmy's is a friend of mine."

The man's almost innocent ignorance was close to amusing, if it were not for the wonder of what he would say or how he would feel if he knew the truth about his Emmy's past. Caleb was truly glad for Emily. The problem was how sad it would be for her if her husband discovered she was once a prostitute.

"And to you I am Caleb. Bring Emily out to our place some time. Sarah and Lynda don't get much chance to visit."

"We'll do that. I've been kept so busy here, what with so many newcomers, we just haven't had the time to leave town at all. Things are getting pretty busy in San Felipe."

"I can see that. When I first settled here it was peaceful, and there weren't many of us. Now with this offer of more free land, people are flooding in."

"Well, you know how it is. The frontier just keeps pushing west. They'll surge right through to California some day, mark my words."

"I don't doubt that. I'll let you get back to your work, Howard. Don't forget our invitation."

"No, sir, I won't. Have a good visit now." The man nodded and went back inside, and Caleb led Sarah to where they had tied wagon and team, taking the baby from her while she climbed up, then handing James up to her.

"I'll take Lynda to the supply store," Tom told Caleb. "It's been a long time since she's been to town, and your first visit with this Emily should be alone."

Their eyes met. Tom knew all about Emily Stoner, as did Lynda. But none of them knew about the teenage affair that had exiled a young Caleb Sax from Fort Dearborn. Caleb looked at Lynda.

"Go ahead, Father. I'll be with Tom. We'll stay at the supply store and wait for you."

Caleb looked back at Tom. "Make sure you do just that. These newcomers are troublemakers, and Lynda has been through enough lately. I don't want her to have any problems. God knows she's pretty enough to cause a stir and a lot of men around here haven't seen much in the way of women in a long time. And some of them think an Indian woman is anybody's property."

Tom slipped an arm around his sister's waist. "I can take care of her. We'll see you in a few minutes." He whisked Lynda away, determined to keep her busy enough to help her forget her grief. She had argued against coming along at all, but Tom would hear none of it.

Caleb watched them walk off, and again the deep pain of ending Lee's life quickly moved through his chest, stirring lingering sorrow and guilt. He looked up at Sarah.

"Let's go find Emily," she told him. "We've all got to get back to the living, Caleb."

He sighed and climbed up in the seat beside her, nudging the horses forward with a slap of the reins. They headed up the street to look for a cabin with roses around the steps.

* * *

"Caleb!" Emily's eyes widened as she stood in the doorway, looking at him as though he'd been resurrected from the dead. "My God! Look at you! So healthy and..." Her eyes teared. "Caleb Sax." She reached out to him and he embraced her.

"Hello, Emily." No matter what Emily Stoner had been, if not for her Caleb would probably be dead, or at least perhaps still lying paralyzed.

She pulled back, and Caleb studied the thin, scarred face. Even at Emily's age and all she had been through, there was still that hint of her considerable beauty that had been destroyed by an Indian captor, and the hard life of a prostitute. She was still too thin. She had always been too thin, making her seem even taller than she really was, although that was taller than most women. She wore a plain blue dress, and to Caleb, Emily looked prettier without all the paint on her face she used to wear, even though she was actually a couple of years older than he.

"When I saw Sarah a few weeks ago, it was so wonderful to know that you two had found each other again, and you had a new baby! I told her I would pray for your safety. Thank God you're all right. What about your son?"

"He's fine. But my son-in-law was killed—Lynda's husband."

"Oh, I'm so sorry. I've not met her yet."

"She and my son Tom walked to the supply store. They thought maybe this time Sarah and I should come alone. Howard told us how to find you."

Her face colored slightly. "Howard? You've met him?"

He smiled. "He's a fine man. I'm glad for you, Emily. We both are."

She stepped back. "Come in." She reached out for Sarah. "Both of you—or I should say, all three of you!" She took the baby from Sarah. "Oh, how I wish I could have one of these. But the life I led..." She sighed. "How I wish I would have found someone like Howard before then."

"I told you once you should have tried to get away from that damned life, Emily," Caleb told her.

She looked up from toying with the baby's cheek. "I was so sure it was much too late." She reddened slightly, turning away, thinking that there was a time when she'd wanted Caleb for herself. "Well, if we are to be friends here in Texas, we might as well get things in the open, hadn't we," she spoke up. She faced Sarah. "Surely you can imagine . . . nursing Caleb back to health and all . . . watching him struggle . . . feeling all his sorrows . . . I couldn't help but have deep feelings for him." She handed the baby back to Sarah. "But the man was so full of Sarah Sax, there wasn't much hope, let alone the fact of what I was. Lord knows I was never the kind of woman for Caleb Sax."

Sarah struggled a moment with a twinge of jealousy. That was the kind of woman Emily was—open, bold. All of it was so many years ago, and they owed this woman so much. The room hung silent for a tense moment, until Sarah gave her a kind smile. "He's easy to love. And thank God you did love him—enough to work with him and encourage him to walk again."

Emily looked away. "Well, at least I finally did what he told me to do. I got out of New Orleans and I found myself a man—a hell of a man, I might add." She turned to face them both then, smiling. "Oh, but let's not talk about that. It seems so incredible that we're all here together. Texas certainly attracts all sorts of people, doesn't it? I never dreamed when I was a young girl growing up at Fort Dearborn that I'd end up in a wild land like this. But I'd live anywhere as long as it means being with Howard. The only thing I couldn't take was the danger of Comanche. I had to live closer to town."

She put a hand self-consciously to the pink, puckered scar on her cheek, the brand her Potawatomie captor had given her to show she belonged to him. "I told Howard that if the Comanche ever got hold of me he'd better shoot me. I'll not go through that kind of hell again." Her eyes teared again, her conversation nervously fluctuating. "Would you believe it doesn't matter to Howard? I told him about how I got the scar. I just never told him the other—about what I became after that."

She turned away, again going to a coffee pot that sat on a

grate over hot coals in a fireplace. "Sit down. I have coffee. If I had known you were coming, I would have baked something fresh. I do have some cake from yesterday."

James began to fuss. "Coffee sounds good," Caleb answered, inwardly astounded at the change in the woman from when he'd known her. "And it sounds like James could use a meal himself."

His eyes moved over her as she poured coffee into china cups she took down from a cupboard. "It's good to see you, Emily, to know you've found a husband and you're happy. There were so many times I was tempted to come back to New Orleans and check on you—let you know I was all right in return. But I married a Cherokee woman and settled here, and God knows trying to make a go of it here takes every hour of every day. A man has little time to get away."

Emily moved to the table with a tray of cups. She set it down and pulled out a chair for Sarah, then moved around the table to take another chair herself.

"At least we're all alive—and together in Texas," Emily said then, reaching out to touch Caleb's hand. She smiled encouragingly, looking from him to Sarah. "Why, it almost gives me the chills to think of it—the three of us just children at Fort Dearborn—then going in so many different directions, so many miles apart, suffering our own forms of hell, and ending up together again here in Texas. Fate certainly deals strange hands, doesn't it?"

She looked back at Caleb, and he knew by her eyes she would never say anything about their teenage sexual play at Fort Dearborn. "It certainly does," he answered. He gave her a smile then. "We really are happy for you, Emily. Come and see us at the ranch when you can."

She nodded. "Sure." She could not help but feel the old twinge, the desire he stirred in her. He had been a young, and, in many ways, totally innocent Indian boy when she first seduced him; a ravaged, heartbroken man when next she saw him; then a badly wounded, nearly dead man the third time. Now he was close to forty but seemed as fine and strong and handsome as that young man at Fort Dearborn, only more handsome and more desirable in spite of added scars and lines of age in the dark skin around his blue eyes. But he belonged to Sarah Sax. He had always belonged to Sarah Sax, even during the years the two had been separated.

Sarah watched the woman's eyes. Yes, the love was still there. Caleb saw it, too, and watched the two women. "Caleb, why don't you get the sack of vegetables we brought?" Sarah asked her husband.

Caleb quickly scooted back his chair. "That's right. I almost forgot." He let go of Emily's hand. "Sarah keeps a garden," he told Emily. "I don't know how she does it in this soil, but she grows the prettiest vegetables. We brought some for you. God knows fresh vegetables are not easy to come by."

He walked out and Emily turned to Sarah. "Oh, Sarah, that wasn't necessary. With such a big family, you must need everything you grow."

"We can spare some for a friend." Their eyes held, and Emily, who in her profession had long ago learned to read a look, spoke up.

"No," she said quietly. "In spite of what I was at the time I helped Caleb, Sarah, we never slept together."

Sarah reddened. "I never asked—"

"Yes you did. With your eyes. It's all right. What woman wouldn't wonder, considering the circumstances? Caleb was just too full of you. He had no interest in anyone else." She smiled as James began to fuss more. "Feed that poor baby. He looks so underfed." They both laughed, for James Sax was a very healthy-looking baby with fat hands and knees and a double chin.

Sarah relaxed and opened her dress, covering herself with a blanket as James found his nourishment. But she looked nervously toward the door when she heard wild hollering farther up the street. It seemed that her whole life had been constantly threatened by wars and violence. Sarah looked back at Emily. They were two very different people, yet their lives held many parallels, and now here they both were in Texas.

"Thanks for not letting on to my Howard," Emily was saying, as she moved to take a cake from another table.

"Oh, we would never do that, Emily. But we both think you should tell him."

Emily brought the cake over to the table. "I will—some day," she said quietly. "I just have to get up the courage." She breathed deeply, meeting Sarah's eyes. "You're such a lucky woman, Sarah Sax. Why, I feel honored to have you in my house."

Their eyes held. "I don't think we're so different, Emily, you know. Not deep inside."

Emily nodded. "Maybe not."

Caleb walked in then and Emily looked away, picking up a knife to cut the cake. "I'd better eat quickly and get on into town," he told them, plunking a gunny sack full of raw vegetables onto the table. "Sounds like things might be getting out of hand. I'm a little worried about Lynda and Tom." He looked at Sarah. "Why don't you stay here and visit with Emily until I get back. There's no sense you going to that meeting with the baby and all. He'll probably want to nap when he's through eating. I'll go find Lynda and Tom and go to the meeting, then come back for you. I have a feeling it will be no place for you anyway. I probably shouldn't have let Tom take Lynda to the supply store." He sat down to quickly guzzle some coffee.

"All right," Sarah told him. She jumped a little when another shot was fired. "Just be careful."

He swallowed and set down the cup, which looked too delicate for his big, dark hand. "I learned to be careful when I was a very small boy," he answered with a wink.

"Oh, Sarah—Caleb—these vegetables are wonderful," Emily put in, rummaging through the sack. "How kind of you."

"You deserve a hell of a lot more than a sack of vegetables," Caleb told her. "How does a man set a price on being able to walk?"

She looked at him lovingly. "Just being able to call both of you friends—that's all I need," the woman answered.

"Well that's something you'll always be able to call us," Caleb answered.

Horses thundered by then, their riders laughing. Caleb glanced at Sarah.

"I'd better get into town," he spoke up. He moved out of his chair and bent down to kiss Sarah's cheek. "You stay here and visit—and stay inside."

"Caleb, you didn't even have any cake," Emily told him.

"Maybe later." He reached across the table, grasping her hand. "It's damned good to see you again, Emily, and doing so well. We'll talk more when I get back." He hurried out then and Emily looked at Sarah.

"He's restless, isn't he?"

"Always." Sarah patted James's bottom. "He loves his family so much—has so much to protect. It's getting harder all the time and it worries all of us."

Emily folded her arms. "Caleb's a damned good man. I look forward to meeting your daughter and his son Tom when they come back."

Sarah cradled James in one arm, reaching out with the other hand to sip some of her coffee. "Lynda is pregnant. At least she'll have Lee's child to comfort her. We're all praying she'll carry to full term and have a healthy baby. She had a miscarriage about three years ago by a gambler she'd been living with." She met Emily's eyes. "She had a pretty hard life before she found me, after Byron put her in that orphanage. Poor Lynda learned about life the hard way, at a very young age. She's been through so much."

"Well, thank God she did find you. And it's good that she's pregnant. It's too bad about her husband." She glanced at the doorway. "Caleb still harbor thoughts of killing Byron Clawson?"

Sarah felt her blood chill. "Yes. He doesn't talk much about it, but I know it's as fresh in his mind as it was twenty years ago."

Emily nodded. "That's the way it is with men like Caleb. I had a feeling time hadn't eased his hatred of the man. Hate can be a very powerful force, maybe even more powerful than love." The woman sipped her coffee thoughtfully. "Trouble is, that could apply to my Howard, too. If he ever found out about me, maybe hatred would win out over his love for me. I live with the fear of it every day." She put on a false smile. "Come on. Have a piece of cake," she said then, feigning a casual attitude and hoping to keep Sarah's thoughts off the noise and hollering outside. San Felipe—Texas itself—was changing, perhaps growing too fast. Sarah felt something intangible slipping away, but she could not name it.

Chapter
Seven

Lynda examined some cloth for baby clothes. The expertise she had developed through seamstress work with her mother in St. Louis and in the clothing factory she'd worked in as a child gave her an eye for good cloth, and an ability to envision a finished product. She held up a soft flannel, studying the tiny flowers.

"That's very pretty," came the voice of a young girl behind her.

Lynda lowered the cloth and turned to look into the deep brown eyes of a beautiful girl who could not be more than a year or two younger than she. Her chestnut-colored hair swirled up tidily under a green feathered hat that matched an attractive green dress and cape of the latest fashion. Her skin was fair, her face stunning. Lynda couldn't help being glad just to see someone her own age. "Hello," she said.

"Hello," the girl replied eagerly. "I'm Elizabeth Hafer." She twisted a tiny purse nervously, glancing around the dusty store. "Everyone calls me Bess. I'm new here. You're the first woman I've seen who's nearly my age—I think. I'm seventeen."

"I'm eighteen. My name is Lynda Whitestone."

The girl smiled and nodded. "Do you live here in San Felipe?"

"No. I live on my father's ranch. His name is Caleb Sax."

The girl's eyes widened. "Sax?" She searched Lynda's eyes eagerly. "Then we might be neighbors. My father bought some land near someone named Sax, up along the Brazos River." It was obvious the girl was eager to talk. "We're from St. Louis," she went on. "My mother died and my brother—" She hesitated. This young woman facing her looked Indian. Her own brother had been killed by Indians, but her brother had been a bully and a drunk. Her father never saw that in his son, nor did he see it in himself. He even blamed her mother's death on what had happened to her brother, but Bess knew it had been caused by her father's neglect of the woman.

Her mother was sorely overworked on the old farm. Now, suddenly, her father was living the life of a rich man, a life her mother should have been able to lead. Why had he waited until the poor woman's death to sell the farm?

Bess loved her father. She didn't like facing some of his bad traits. She loyally overlooked them most of the time. But she couldn't understand his actions sometimes, and ever since her brother's death there had been hard feelings between them.

"My brother is dead, too," Bess finished. "The farm wasn't doing well, so we came to Texas to start over."

Lynda picked up the bolt of cloth. "I'm sorry about your mother and brother. Welcome to Texas. It's a little wild, but I guess it isn't where we live that counts. Being with loved ones is all that really matters. Your father must be lonely. Are there other children?"

"No. Just me." The girl looked at the cloth again. "Is it for a nightgown?"

Lynda smiled. "No. It's for baby clothes."

Bess brightened. "Oh! Are you going to have—" She reddened. "I guess it's not nice of me to pry that way. I'm sorry."

"It's all right. Yes. I'm having a baby. I just don't show yet."

The girl smiled again. "You and your husband must be very happy."

Lynda's smile faded. "My husband is dead. He was killed by Comanche."

Bess looked devastated. "I'm sorry. I seem to be saying all the wrong things, don't I?"

Lynda could see the loneliness in the girl's eyes. She clearly wanted a friend. "It's all right." She set the cloth aside. "How long have you been here?"

"Only a few days. I was so glad to come to town. Back on the land my father bought, it's so lonely—no women at all. I hope we come here often."

"Sometimes the weather or the general chores of ranching can keep you away from town for weeks at a time," Lynda answered. "I agree it's a lonely life. At least I have my mother. If you really do live close, you should come and visit."

The girl swallowed, and Lynda was surprised to see that her eyes seemed to be tearing. "I would dearly love that."

"Then we would love to have you."

Bess looked relieved. "Oh, thank you!" She looked at Lynda closer. "Are you . . . are you Indian?"

Lynda sensed nothing but curiosity in the question. "I'm part Cheyenne, on my father's side. My mother is white."

"White!" Bess looked her over like some kind of unusual object. "I've never known someone with mixed blood. You're very beautiful."

Lynda suppressed laughter at the girl's almost childish curiosity. She was only a year younger than Lynda but seemed much younger than that. Lynda reminded herself she had been through things this girl probably knew nothing about. In attitude and her knowledge of the world's realities, she was years beyond this girl staring at her now.

"Thank you—I think," she answered.

"Oh, I didn't mean—I meant that as a compliment," the girl told her. "Back home there are very few Indians left, except a few Osage. I have seen a lot more since we got to Texas." She couldn't help still feeling sorry for the young Osage men who had hung for her brother's death. She had seen her brother drinking and provoking them earlier that day, calling them names and making fun of them. They had only come there looking for work. And she had seen Billy Parker, a boy who had always hated her brother, follow him into the barn the night Charles Jr. died. She had told her father, but the man was so against Indians he would not believe anyone else but the Osage men had murdered his son. The whole farming community was quickly up in arms and had the Indians arrested. Her father had forced her to watch the awful hanging, and she would never forget their constant protests and pleading, and the way one of them cried before being hung. Nor would she forget the look on Billy Parker's face—one of victory. She had never been able since then to hate the Indians the way her father did.

"I've never known any Indians who owned land and had money," she went on.

Lynda frowned. "Well, we're just like anyone else. My father owns thousands of acres. He was one of the first settlers here. And he raises some of the finest horses in these parts."

"Oh, I'm sure he does, ma'am," the girl answered quickly.

A faint smile passed over Lynda's lips. "Call me Lynda."

The girl breathed deeply, looking relieved. "And you can call me Bess." She laughed nervously then. "I guess I already told you my name." She twisted the strings of her purse more. "I'm going to ask my father if he'll let me come and visit you. I mean, if you don't mind. It's just so nice meeting someone my age."

"Yes, it is for me, too. Since my husband died, I get so lonely, even with my family around. I would like it very much if you visited." Lynda picked up the cloth again and moved to a nearby rack of ribbons. "Maybe you could help me pick out a nice ribbon that I could use to decorate this cloth. I sew a lot. My mother and I make most of our own clothes, and I'll make my baby's clothes."

"Oh, I don't sew much at all. Maybe you could teach me."

"That would be fun." Lynda ran her dark, slender fingers through the ribbon, studying the colors.

"A pretty ribbon for the squaw's hair?" a male voice spoke up behind her in a slow drawl.

Lynda felt a tinge of fear as she turned to look into the grinning face of a man of perhaps forty. He smiled through brown teeth, and a stained scarf hung limply around his dirty neck. His blue cotton shirt bore perspiration stains under the arms, and his pale blue eyes moved over her appreciatively. "What's a squaw doin' in a white man's store?"

"I am not a squaw. I am the daughter of a Texas landowner, and you had better get away from me or you will answer to my brother," Lynda replied firmly, refusing to show any fear.

The man only laughed. "That so? Well, I'd look forward to it." His eyes moved to Bess Hafer. "What you doin' talkin' to an Indian, little girl? Don't you know nice white girls don't talk to squaws? It's the same as talkin' to a whore."

The storekeeper looked in their direction, then looked away. He would not stick up for an Indian, nor for a white girl who would let herself be seen talking to one.

Bess reddened with anger. "You get away from here," she answered, trying to sound brave. "I'll talk to whomever I want. And some of my father's men are outside waiting for me. You'd better get away from both of us. We haven't bothered you any, so why are you bothering us?"

The man reached out and jerked the bolt of cloth from Lynda's hands, throwing it on the floor. "Any man can bother a pretty squaw any time he wants. Ain't no law against that." He came closer. "And this is the prettiest piece of Indian woman I've ever set my eyes on."

He grasped Lynda's wrists suddenly and jerked her arms behind her. A couple of men who were standing nearby only laughed as he tried to kiss Lynda's neck while she twisted away from him and kicked him hard in the leg. The man howled from the vicious kick and let go, bending down to rub his leg, while Bess picked up a bolt of heavier cloth and slammed it over the man's head, the unexpected blow catching him off balance and knocking him to the floor.

The men who had been watching laughed even louder as the two women stepped back. "You get away and leave her alone," Bess said angrily. She thought how angry her father would be if he knew about this, but she didn't care.

Lynda watched the man with dark, hateful eyes. He got to his knees, then stood up. He glowered at Bess, incensed that two women had hurt him and knocked him down in front of the other men.

"You stupid little bitch!" He came closer and pushed Bess away with a swing of the arm, making her stumble against another counter, then reached for Lynda again; but she had quietly grabbed up a pair of sewing shears while he was bent over. She raised her hand, threatening to stab him if he came closer.

The man hesitated, grinning. "Well, well. The squaw bitch is a fighter, is she?"

Suddenly he felt a pistol in his ribs. "Get away from these women," a hard voice warned.

The man froze as someone behind him moved away.

"Step back," came the voice. The man slowly turned. He looked into the dark eyes of Tom Sax. Bess Hafer watched in surprise, taken by the tall, handsome Indian, knowing instantly this must be the brother Lynda had mentioned.

"You're lookin' for bad trouble, boy."

"I'd say it's the other way around. You make a move toward them again, and you won't need a mouth to breathe through. I'll open a hole right in your lungs!"

The man swallowed, seeing the determination in Tom Sax's eyes. "Just havin' a little fun, boy. You Indians shouldn't be in a place like this. This is a supply store for white folks."

"My father was here long before you ever stepped foot in Texas, mister. And we aren't too crazy about the trash that's coming in these days! You get your smelly body away from my sister!"

"Sister?" The man grinned. "Sure, boy. But you'd best keep a better eye on her. Everybody knows Indian women is for the takin', and when they look like that, it sets a man's desires kind of rushin' on, if you know what I mean."

Tom waved the pistol and spoke through gritted teeth. "Get the hell out of my sight before I open up your gut!"

"You want some help, Lou?" one of the onlookers asked Lynda's attacker. "The boy can't take all three of us."

"Maybe I can even up the odds," said another voice behind them. They turned to see a menacing Indian man in buckskins towering over them, his hand resting on the handle of a huge knife.

Both men swallowed and one of them scowled. "Come on. Let's get out of here. I'm not fightin' two Indians," one of them grumbled. "Indians fight dirty." Both onlookers quickly moved past Caleb, whose steely blue eyes moved then to the first man, who was still held at gunpoint by Tom. The man put on a grin, trying to be casual and look unafraid.

"I give up," he said kiddingly. "Just have trouble controllin' myself around pretty women," he added. He moved his eyes to Lynda and Bess. "Sorry, ladies." He turned and quickly darted past Caleb, wanting nothing more than to get away from the two Indians. "Damned savages," he muttered on the way out.

Tom looked at his father and shoved his pistol into his belt. "Bastards. What kind of people are coming to San Felipe? We never had this kind of trouble before."

Caleb walked up to Lynda. "Are you all right?"

Lynda blinked back tears, bending down and picking up the cloth. "Just angry," she said in a shaking voice. "I wanted to kill him!"

Bess stood aside, nearly in tears herself. She felt like an outsider—one of the new people the younger man had complained of. Lynda turned to face her. "Thank you, Bess, for sticking up for me."

Tom's eyes moved to the young white girl, truly noticing her for the first time. His cheeks suddenly felt hot, and pleasant urges rushed through his body. She was beautiful. She filled out the bodice of her green dress in a most enticing way, and her eyes were large and tender as a young doe's.

"This is Bess Hafer," Lynda was telling them. "She tried to help me. She even hit that man over the head with a bolt of cloth." She laughed lightly then. "It seems funny now." She reached out and grasped Bess's arm, drawing her closer. "Bess, this is my brother, Tom. And this other man is my father, Caleb Sax."

Bess tore her eyes from staring at Tom to glance at Caleb. "How do you do, Mister Sax. I'm new here, too, but I'm not like those men."

Caleb grinned in amusement. "I have no doubt of that. Thank you for trying to help my daughter."

The girl shivered. "That man was terrible. I was embarrassed at the way he talked to Lynda." She looked back at Tom then, as though he were some kind of hero, "But your son stopped him from hurting us."

"Oh, he shoved you, didn't he?" Lynda said then. "I just remembered. Are you all right?"

The girl put a hand to her chest. "Yes." Her eyes were still on Tom. "I'm glad to meet you, Mister Sax."

Tom nodded. "You, too." Their eyes held. Tom's experience with women had been primarily with a Mexican woman named Rosy back at the ranch. Rosy was a widow who welcomed anyone to her bed, especially the handsome Cheyenne *patrón*, the Spanish word for "boss." She knew the extent of his commitment to her did not go beyond the sexual pleasures she afforded him, and she didn't mind. And there had been a couple of prostitutes in town he favored. Tom knew a great deal about women, or at least he thought he did. But this one . . .

He raised his chin, angry with himself for letting this girl make him feel so uncomfortable and nervous. "Where do you live?" he asked her.

Bess twisted at the purse strings again. "I could never find it by myself. It's somewhere north of here, on the Brazos. I was just telling your sister that I think we're

neighbors. My father said something about buying land
that joins land owned by someone named Sax." He was
beautiful! How she would love to know him better. Her
father would think it wrong, but Tom Sax was so handsome, so brave but so soft-spoken. Bess began to redden
under his dark gaze, and she looked over at Caleb, suddenly feeling exposed. "My father will be at the meeting.
You can meet him then." She wondered why she had said
that. Her father hated Indians! Maybe with these people for
neighbors, her father would discover they were not all bad.

Caleb nodded. "I would like to, if it's true we'll be
neighbors."

She looked back at Tom. "Thank you for stopping that
man."

Tom Sax had never seen such a pretty girl in his life.
"You and my sister seemed to be doing very well on your
own. It might have been interesting to see how much he
would have suffered just answering to you two," he told
her, breaking into a winning smile.

Bess reddened more, and laughed nervously. "Actually I
was scared to death." She looked around the store. "Isn't
there any law here?"

"Not much."

"It's certainly not like St. Louis."

"St. Louis? Is that where you're from?" Caleb asked.
"My wife is from there."

"Well, we all have something in common," Bess replied
with a bright smile. "But we are not really from the city
itself. We had a farm a few miles from town. My father
sold it and came to Texas when my mother and brother
died."

"I see. I'm sorry about your loss."

The girl's smilé faded. "It's kind of lonely for me. There
aren't any women at our place. I was telling Lynda that I
would like to come and visit."

"I would like that," Tom spoke up, still grinning.

Bess reddened and Caleb subdued an urge to laugh, but
Lynda raised her eyebrows and shifted the bolt of cloth in

her arm. "I bet you would, big brother. She's the prettiest girl in these parts and you know it."

Tom gave her a look of brotherly anger, and his dark skin did little to hide the color that came to his face. He shifted, putting on a manly, uncaring air. "I agree it must be lonely for her," he answered. He looked at Bess again. "You come and visit any time." He turned to his father. "We had better go to the meeting."

Caleb looked at Lynda. "Did you find what you want?"

"I didn't have much time. Give me a couple more minutes."

"The meeting is starting. Why don't we go and come back here after it ends? I don't want to leave you here alone."

"All right."

Tom looked at Bess again. "Is there someone supposed to be watching after you?"

Her heart fluttered with the realization that he was concerned for her safety. Tom Sax looked like a man who could protect any woman, a man of skill and bravery. She was sure of that already. "Some of my father's men are outside, but those terrible men in here weren't any of them. I'll be fine. In fact, my father will be here any minute. All of you go ahead. I'll look for you at the meeting."

"Are you sure we can leave you?"

"Oh, yes. No one will bother me anyway. It was just because your sister is In—" She reddened again. "They bothered her because she's Indian."

Tom noticed her eyes moving to his own long, dark hair that hung from beneath his leather hat over the shoulders of the checked shirt he wore. He wondered what she thought of Indians herself, but this was neither the time nor the place to ask.

"Tom, we have to go," Caleb spoke up.

Tom's eyes moved over Bess Hafer again, drinking in her perfectly rounded beauty. "I guess maybe we'll see each other again."

The girl nodded. "I am glad to meet all of you. I feel

better already about being here in Texas." She looked at Lynda. "Good-bye, Lynda."

Lynda took her hand and squeezed it. "Good-bye." She moved to Caleb and he took her arm. Tom looked at Bess a moment longer, then turned to follow them.

"We have got to be more careful—and you watch your temper, Tom," Caleb said when they got outside. "A lot of these newcomers are from the South, where they're forcing all the Cherokee and the Choctaw out. They don't like Indians owning land."

"Bastards," Tom muttered. "That son of a bitch had no right putting his hands on Lynda. I wanted to shoot him."

"Take it easy here in town. Some of these people would love to see an Indian hang."

Caleb, Tom, and Lynda moved through a crowd that kept growing as they approached the platform. "There's Sam Houston now," Caleb heard someone in the crowd say, pointing to a tall, stately man on the platform.

"He'll help us figure out what to do," another put in. "Jackson himself sent him here."

Tom hardly heard. His mind swirled with thoughts of Bess Hafer. Not only was she pretty, but she was also kind and brave. She had stood up for Lynda. A man didn't have to know a girl like that long to realize she was good—a quality woman in the making. He had trouble making himself think about anything else as they moved through a rowdy crowd, keeping Lynda between them.

Caleb saw that Sarah had been right. San Felipe was fast growing into a meeting place for war talk, and these new volunteers coming in were not the kind of people he would like to see settling in the area. But not only was he disturbed by the kind of people filtering in and rumors of war; Caleb found the consequences such a war could have on all settlers disturbing. Compared to Mexican forces, there were very few Texans; and in war it seemed even the winning side had its share of losses, both in lives and in finances. Caleb had seen war before. Now that he had a family, it was the last thing he wanted, and he was sure a lot of the other settlers felt the same way. But some kind of confrontation was inevitable.

"Who is this Santa Anna?" someone shouted. "The bastard wants to take away my weapons—leave me helpless against the Comanche!"

"We agreed to settle this part of the country for them, and they turn around and take away our weapons so we can't defend ourselves against Indians," someone else shouted. "Where's the protection they promised us? They don't even send the soldiers who are supposed to help us. Then they try to take our guns."

More shouting picked up until no one could be heard individually. Fists were raised and Caleb put an arm around Lynda's waist, keeping her close.

The man on the platform above the crowd waved his arms for them all to be quiet.

"Shut up so we can hear Mister Houston," someone yelled, joined by others.

"They say Andrew Jackson has a strong interest in Texas's value to the States," came another voice.

Caleb had always had mixed feelings about Andrew Jackson, under whom he had fought at New Orleans. As both a fighting soldier and a leader, a man would have to go far to match "Old Hickory." But the man seemed two-faced, calling the Indians friends on one hand and using them in war; then turning on them, as he was doing now with the Cherokee, giving them no support in their efforts to remain in Georgia. He was allowing Indians to literally be kicked out of their homelands all over the South so the whites could have their valuable land. Caleb wondered if Sam Houston was any different. Perhaps. He had lived with Cherokee—had a Cherokee wife, so people said. If this man became an important leader in Texas, perhaps it would mean hope for the Indians living there peacefully.

"Santa Anna is just trying to bluff you right now," Houston shouted then when the crowd finally quieted. "He wants us to march down to Mexico City and take Stephen Austin."

"Then let's do it," someone retorted.

"No. You would be playing right into his hands. He wants you to make the first move, so that he can accuse the Americans of being the aggressors. He is hoping you will come, as well as hoping that when his soldiers come here and try to disarm you, one of you will fire on them, fight with them. We must remain calm, show Santa Anna and the world that we are not the aggressors, that our intentions are completely peaceful, that all we want are a few rights that would bring no harm to Mexico and would not necessitate a break from Mexico. The time may come when you have no choice but to fight, but the longer you hold out the better."

There was more shouting, but Tom paid little attention. He was too busy thinking about Bess Hafer. He liked the name. He scanned the crowd, looking for her, finally spotting her at the edge of the crowd surrounded by several men. He figured one of them must be her father. He was relieved to know she was so well protected, yet he wondered why he was so concerned about this girl he hardly knew.

His height helped him see her past others. Bess in turn spotted his floppy leather hat and checkered shirt. He saw her pointing, and she pulled at an older man with a broad build. He scowled and held her back, seeming to admonish her for something. Tom could see the man meant for her to stay put for the moment, and it was difficult for him to keep from turning and staring at her whenever he could while the meeting continued for several more minutes. Houston managed finally to calm those in attendance and convince them they must continue to be peaceful and cooperative with the Mexicans for the time being, to show the Mexicans and the world that they were living up to their end of their agreement with Mexico.

Tom looked down at Lynda as the crowd began to disburse. "How old is she?" he asked.

Lynda grinned. "Who?"

Tom scowled. "You know who."

"Bess?"

"Come on, Lynda."

"Seventeen. Pretty, isn't she?"

Tom just grinned, moving his dark eyes over to where Bess stood to see the girl tugging at the big man again.

They headed in Tom's direction then, the bigger man looking slightly irritated for some reason. But as they came closer, he put on a pleasant look when Bess introduced them.

"These are the Saxes, Father. This is Mister Caleb Sax, and this is his daughter, Lynda, who I told you about. This is Tom Sax. He's the one who stopped that terrible man."

"Well, I guess I owe you a thanks, Mister Sax," the man said to Tom, putting out his hand. "You did what my men should have been doing. They were outside and didn't know anything was happening."

Tom shook his hand but did not feel the firmness of a man who was being truly friendly. "I was in another part of the store myself and happened to come back to check on my sister just then."

Hafer let go of his hand and turned to Caleb. "I'm Charles Hafer. Even without what happened earlier, I would have looked you up, Mister Sax. We're neighbors now, you know. I had intentions of meeting you."

Caleb nodded, taking the man's outstretched hand. "I didn't know we were neighbors." He studied Hafer's brown eyes, which held a look that reminded Caleb of the way Sarah's father used to look at him. His defenses were immediately awakened. "The last I knew, the land north of me was still unclaimed. That's the only unclaimed area that borders me. I take it that's the land we're talking about."

Hafer let go of Caleb's hand. "It is. I've settled several thousand acres just north and west of your place. I was hoping you would be at this meeting today. At any rate, I've come to Texas to sort of start over. Too many memories back home, what with my wife and son dead and all, plus I had a farm that was becoming worthless."

"I'm sorry about your family. Your daughter is very lovely, but it must be lonely here for her." He looked at Lynda. "This is my own daughter, Lynda. I have another son, John. And my wife and I just recently had a baby boy. John is home tending to a favorite mare of his that is about to give us a new foal."

"Well, it sounds like you have quite a large family. And I hear you raise fine horses."

"I try to breed the best. I did have a lot more, before Comanche stole them a few weeks ago—took my son John, too."

Hafer's eyebrows arched. "My God, man, what did you do?"

"I went after the boy and got him back. But I couldn't get the horses."

"You went after Comanche?" Hafer felt a twinge of apprehension. He had been sent here to harass this man, perhaps enough to make him leave Texas or even cost him his life. But Caleb Sax was not only a commanding man physically, he also was apparently the brave sort who did not back down easily. Few men went out on the trail of Comanche, no matter what the reason, and even fewer lived to tell about it. Even more than that, this Caleb Sax was bold and Hafer already sensed he was intelligent. He was different from any Indians he had known in Missouri.

"I couldn't let them keep my son. But we are deeply grieved because it cost the life of my son-in-law, Lynda's husband."

Hafer looked at Lynda, but not with the genuine sympathy she had detected in his daughter. She liked Bess, but she already did not like the girl's father. "I'm so sorry, ma'am," he was saying, tipping his hat slightly.

"Thank you," Lynda answered, no more fooled by the man's words than was Caleb, who also watched suspiciously.

"Did you go with your father after the Comanche?" Bess asked Tom.

He straightened more. "Yes," he answered, angry that she was again making him feel awkward and uncomfortable. If only she weren't so damned pretty.

"But—you're Indian, too."

"Not even another Indian carries much feeling for the Comanche. Even the Apache hate them. And Indian or not, we couldn't let them have my brother."

"Oh, of course not—"

"Bess, mind yourself," Hafer told his daughter, irritation in his voice. "Don't be so forward."

She looked at him in surprise. "But I've already met him, Father. Tom and Lynda both."

The man scowled at her, and neither Caleb nor Tom missed the real meaning behind the man's irritation. He didn't like his daughter associating with Indians. Hafer put on a smile and looked at Caleb. "As I said, I'm very sorry about what happened, Mister Sax. I hope the Comanche didn't do too much damage to you financially. Are you getting along all right?"

Caleb thought the question too probing. "I do fine."

"Well, my opinion is that down here in Texas the money eventually will be in cattle—and perhaps cotton. I intend to look into both. So, if you find any stray beef on your land, I'd appreciate it if you would send them hightailing back to my place."

Caleb held his eyes. "And you will do the same with my horses?"

"Oh, certainly. Out here we will have to help each other out, right?"

"Oh, Father, we should invite them to our barn raising," Bess put in.

Hafer reddened slightly, giving her a chastising look, angry that she had brought it up. But she was his daughter and knew nothing of why they had come to Texas. Try as he might, he couldn't make her understand about Indians. Even her brother's death had not convinced her. Still, before he could go up against Caleb Sax, Hafer had to know the man better, and get a feel of his weak points, if indeed he had any. Perhaps it *was* a good idea to invite the Saxes to his barn raising.

"Of course," he answered. The last thing he wanted was to have Indians there, but the best way was to be friendly first. There would be several others there who were not fond of Indians. It would be a good way to hint to Caleb Sax that he was up against some power, so that when Hafer's men moved in for the "kill," Sax would understand he might as well give up without a fight. There was a lot of money in this venture. Hafer meant to win. "We're having a barn raising next Saturday. You're welcome to come, Sax—you and your family. God knows, in this territory people have little enough to celebrate; and all are starving for a chance to visit. Just bring a dish to pass, and be ready to do a little work."

Bess looked up at Tom again, her wide, dark eyes gleaming with hope. "Do say you'll come," she almost pleaded.

For Tom there was no argument, and no reasoning about alternative motives. Elizabeth Hafer wanted him to come, which meant she wanted to get to know him better. He was not going to argue with that. "Sure we'll come," he told her.

Now it was Caleb who gave his son a chastising look. Tom had not even given him a chance to answer, but considering the charming looks of Elizabeth Hafer, Caleb could hardly blame the young man. Still, he smelled danger as strongly as if someone were waving smoke up his nose.

"Apparently my son has decided for me," Caleb told Hafer.

Lynda turned and looked up at Tom, nodding her head knowingly and making him smile bashfully. "Yes. Apparently he has," she added.

"And do bring Mrs. Sax," Bess told Caleb. "I would love to see the baby." She glanced again at Tom, a tiny smile at the corner of her mouth at the mention of the baby. Tom gave her his most winning smile in return. She seemed so genuinely sweet. He held her eyes, and for an instant, each read the other's thoughts. It was the old, unexplainable, instant attraction—the magical drawing together of two spirits as though some being above was directing their emotions beyond their control.

Hafer cast an irritated look at Tom Sax, struggling to control the sudden fear that gripped him. The handsome young Indian man! That was why Bess had spoken so suddenly about the barn raising. It wasn't the women or the baby, or the incident in the supply store. His chest tightened with the dreadful thought that his daughter might become interested in an Indian—a Sax, no less. That would present monumental problems to his plans. He quickly tore his eyes from Tom, but not soon enough to keep Caleb from reading his very thoughts. Again, Hafer put on the friendly smile.

"Well, this wild meeting is no place to talk. We'll look forward to seeing you next Saturday," he told Caleb.

Caleb nodded. "I look forward to it also." Yes, he thought, it would be a good chance to see what this man Hafer was all about. He wanted to get an idea of his spread, how many men he had, and all the other things which, Caleb had a feeling, might be important to know later on.

"Mister Hafer, there's a feed supplier over here wants to talk to you," said a young man just approaching. He had thick, sandy hair, sky blue eyes, and skin tanned deep by the Texas sun. He was perhaps five foot ten, broad-shouldered, and rock hard, walking with slightly bowed legs. He had the look of a man who lived outdoors more than inside, and Lynda was surprised and angry with herself to realize she was slightly taken by his rugged, handsome looks.

"Thank you, Jess." Hafer nodded to Caleb. "See you in a few days. Glad to meet you, Sax."

Caleb nodded. "Sure. Same here."

Hafer turned, taking his daughter's arm and hurrying her away. The man called Jess lingered a moment, pushing back his hat and flashing a brilliant smile at Lynda, who immediately caught his eye with her voluptuous looks. "Jess Purnell," he spoke up. He eyed them all then. "I work for Mister Hafer." His eyes moved to Lynda again. "Might I have the pleasure of knowing your name?"

Lynda stiffened, reading the man's look but too full of Lee to feel comfortable. "Lynda Sax."

Purnell glanced at Tom. "This your husband?"

"I'm her brother," Tom spoke up defensively. "And you can save your fancy smile, mister. My sister is recently widowed."

Purnell frowned, his gentle blue eyes showing genuine concern. "I'm very sorry, ma'am. Excuse my rudeness."

Lynda wanted to be angry, but his eyes unnerved her. "It's all right," she answered. "You couldn't have known."

"Have you worked for Hafer long?" Caleb spoke up.

Purnell shrugged. "He hasn't been in Texas very long."

"What kind of man is he?"

Purnell stole one more appreciative look at Lynda, then looked back at Caleb. "Seems fair. He's okay, I guess. I just take orders and get paid better than most. Nothing to complain about. I'm sort of a roamer. I've helped work a lot of ranches—go where the money is—hope to have a place of my own some day."

Caleb nodded. "We'll see you next Saturday, I suppose. We're coming to the barn raising."

Purnell grinned. "Good." He put out his hand. "Till then."

Caleb took the hand and shook it firmly. Purnell returned the firm hold, as though to try to assure Caleb he was a decent person.

"I didn't mean to offend your daughter, Mister Sax."

Caleb managed a grin then. "I'm sure you didn't."

Purnell looked at Lynda again and nodded. "Good day, ma'am."

Lynda only nodded in reply. She could appreciate his wonderful looks and genuine apology. He seemed a nice man but surely unstable if he was such a roamer. But nothing about him could stir her as he apparently had hoped. Right now the most handsome man in the world could not stir her. All she wanted was Lee—her precious, loving, devoted Lee.

"I have a feeling Saturday will be an interesting day," Caleb spoke up, watching Hafer in the distance. "Let's go get those supplies."

As they left, Tom's thoughts were whirling, not with thoughts of a war, the Comanche, or buying supplies, but with thoughts of a pretty girl with dark hair and eyes and a wonderfully enticing shape. He glanced back to get one more look at Bess Hafer, but she was gone.

Chapter Eight

Caleb watched Tom rope the wild mustang and bring the spotted horse under control. The broad-shouldered stallion with its strong back and perfect lines would make a good stud horse, but Caleb could already see that it would not be easy keeping this one corralled. He took off his hat and waved it as a signal of a job well done. Tom dismounted, the rope tied to the pommel of his saddle, and followed the rope to the whinnying, rearing animal. Its eyes were wide and wild, and it snorted and tugged as Tom came closer.

Caleb rode down, his old instincts of being overprotective of his firstborn still with him. He knew Tom really needed no help. His son was good with horses and had been riding since a small boy.

"Be careful," he called out as Tom came closer to the animal. He moved his own Appaloosa closer, holding the reins loosely in one hand. Caleb Sax needed hardly more than his legs and gentle commands to handle a horse. He used only the small, stuffed hide saddle that most Indians used, except on days when there was considerable roundup work to do and pommels and other gear came in handy. His Appaloosa gelding snorted and pranced as it came closer to the wild, spotted bronc that Tom now spoke to softly. The young man held the rope in one hand and carefully reached out, petting the wild horse's nose.

Caleb patted his horse's neck to soothe the animal before dismounting and dropping the reins. The animal bent its head to nibble at scrubby, yellow grass, while Caleb slowly approached Tom.

"He's a good one," Tom said quietly, sensing his father was close behind him. "He'll make a good stud."

Caleb slowly walked around the animal, studying its power and the shine of its coat. It was a lovely sand color, dotted with black, white, and brown, with a white mane. "He's wonderful," Caleb said.

"I told you. I knew I'd find him again. It took three days and nights of camping out here, but he finally came along."

Caleb nodded. "You've got a hell of an eye, Tom. He'll sure be a help in replenishing the herd."

Tom grinned, still getting a boyish satisfaction out of pleasing his father. "That is what I figured." The animal suddenly reared and whinnied, but Tom kept hold of the rope and spoke to the animal again. "Now I can really enjoy myself at the barn raising Saturday," he said then, "knowing I finally found this one." He moved back along the rope toward his own horse. "We'll let him stand there and get used to our smell for a few minutes before I try to get him to go back with us."

Caleb nodded, taking a tobacco pouch from his belt and a pipe from the parfleche on his own horse. "You're really looking forward to Saturday, aren't you?"

Tom grinned. "Sure I am. I'll get to see Bess Hafer again. I've never seen a girl that pretty in my whole life."

There was a moment of silence while Caleb stuffed the pipe. "She's also white," he told the boy carefully.

Tom took his eyes from the mustang and faced his father in surprise. "So?"

Their eyes held. "You met her father. I know his kind, Tom, too well. And I know the hurt going against his kind can bring." Caleb kept his eyes on his son as he raised the pipe and lit it. His jaw flexed as he puffed on it several times to get it burning.

Tom smiled nervously. "It wouldn't be that bad. It's different here. We own land. We have money. We live like everybody else."

"We're Indian."

"So what? We live just like they do."

Caleb lowered the pipe. "Men like Hafer don't give a damn about that," he answered. "It doesn't matter if you're worth a million dollars, Tom. You're Indian. That's all men like that see. You saw how he acted. He doesn't want his daughter talking to us, associating with us. He wouldn't even have invited us to that barn raising if Bess hadn't spoken first."

His heart ached at the hurt and anger in Tom's eyes. The young man looked away, holding the rope and watching the wild horse he had just roped and captured. "Well, I'm going," he answered. "Whether Hafer wants me there or not, I'm going. And if I want to talk to Bess, I'll talk to her. She's a nice girl."

"And you're at the age a man starts thinking about family, children, marriage. You think I can't read your mind?"

Tom looked back at his father. "I would be crazy not to look at her that way. A man doesn't often see women like Bess Hafer out in these parts."

"And there are probably about five hundred other men who are thinking the same thing."

"Well, she doesn't look at them the way I saw her look at me. She likes me, and she's lonely. I feel sorry for her. I'm going to talk to her Saturday and nobody is going to stop me."

Caleb puffed the pipe for a moment. "I never said I would try to stop you. I'm only trying to help you avoid a lot of hurt—both you *and* Bess. Don't forget what Sarah and I went through. It still affects us, Tom. When you love somebody, it kills you to see them hurting, and Sarah is still hurting."

Tom ducked under the rope to come to the other side and face his father fully. "And she wouldn't have had it any other way. You knew it was wrong, but you went after her anyway, right?"

Caleb lowered the pipe again and sighed deeply. "Be careful, Tom. Going after Comanche could prove to be easier than going after a pretty white girl whose father hates Indians. And that man hates Indians. I know the look."

"I don't care. Bess is the prettiest thing I've ever seen. And she'll grow to be a good woman."

Caleb forced back an urge to grin. "I don't doubt that in the least. Sarah, too, was the sweetest girl a man could want. But her father was another story, and I still suffer a great deal of physical pain because of what he and Byron Clawson did to me. I love you, Tom. I don't like the thought of you suffering or going through any of the hell I went through. Life here is hard enough with problems like the elements and Comanche. But a woman can be more dangerous than anything this land can throw at you."

Tom tossed his head, throwing back some of the long, dark hair that he wore loose. "And if you could do it over, would you change anything? Would you leave Sarah and never see her again?"

Caleb smiled sadly. "You know I wouldn't."

Tom nodded, holding his father's eyes. "I want to know her better, Father. It's like—like a pain that won't go away unless I see her again."

Caleb put the pipe back into his mouth and puffed it a moment, looking over at the wild horse. "Then be damned careful," he answered. "Remember how important you are to me. I will help you all I can."

"You're still going to the barn raising, aren't you?"

Caleb met his eyes again. "You bet I'm going." He lowered the pipe again. "I have a lot of things to check out, and I have a feeling Hafer is checking me out in return. I like to know the odds. I intend to see what kind of place he's got—how much manpower."

Tom laughed lightly. "Father, I think you're being too serious. He's just another settler."

Caleb shook his head. "No. There is more to it than that. I have been through enough to read the eyes of a man like that. You watch yourself." He started to turn away.

"Father."

Caleb turned.

"You understand, don't you?"

Their eyes held. "I understand. Come on. Let's see if we can get that mustang home and penned up." He remounted his horse, his heart heavy for his son. Memories painfully pressed against his mind and heart. He would not want such hell for his son. But a pretty girl with a sweet smile and soft curves had a way of keeping a young man from thinking clearly. He should know. It had happened to him twenty years ago. He had no doubts about going to the barn raising now. He was not about to let his son go alone.

Sarah sat in front of a mirror and brushed out her hair. It still hung thick, long, and reddish-gold. Caleb turned from the washbowl, drying his face and hands, then walked up behind her, laying the towel aside and grasping her shoulders, massaging her gently along the shoulders and neck. She closed her eyes.

"That feels good."

He smiled lovingly, watching her in the mirror. "Have I ever told you you're as beautiful as the day I set eyes on you in St. Louis? You never change, Sarah."

She laughed lightly, looking at him in the mirror. His frame was dark and muscular standing behind her. And scarred. So many scars he had, inside and out. "You're looking through the eyes of love," she told him. "It gives a man a distorted view. I, on the other hand, can look at you and set all love aside. And you still come out more handsome than ever. Aging only seems to make you better, Caleb Sax."

He grinned again. "Let's face it. We'll each always see the other the same way." He leaned down, crossing broad, hard forearms over her breasts, which felt soft and warm through the robe she wore. He kissed her hair. "Tom brought back some memories today, talking about that Hafer girl. Made me remember how I felt when I first fell in love with you. I wanted you so bad I hurt all over. Sometimes I still feel that way—like tonight."

She turned her face and he met her lips hungrily. She reached up and he picked her up from the stool, carrying her to the bed and laying her down on it, crawling onto it beside her.

"I remember, too," she spoke then, studying the handsome face, the blue eyes that she loved. How strange that this man could be so wild, that he had once gone on a mad rampage against Crow Indians and his Indian name still struck fear in them. How strange that he could be so gentle with a woman. "I wanted you the same way. When I saw you standing there—my Caleb." She traced a finger over the lines of his face and down over the thin, white scar. "You were so handsome and wild—so beautiful."

He took her hand and kissed her fingers, then bent to kiss her chest where the robe had slipped down. He gently pushed the robe open, exposing her breasts. Sarah thought about Emily. Was the woman telling the truth when she said Caleb never touched her? It really didn't matter anymore, Sarah concluded, ignoring the childish jealousy such a thought brought to mind. They were together now. They had found each other and nothing else mattered.

"Make love to me, Caleb," she whispered.

His lips moved up to her throat and met her mouth, his tongue searching inside. He pushed open the robe the rest of the way, his fingers searching secret places that belonged only to him, touching her in light, circular motions that drew out her deepest passions. He had a way of relaxing her that erased all the hard work and rushing of the day. This was their own special time—a time to set aside problems and chores and children and give only to each other, and take from each other. Now they were not just friends or husband and wife, or mother and father. They were lovers, in the most beautiful sense of the word.

She ran her hands over the hard muscle of his arms and shoulders, and grasped his dark hair as he moved down and kissed her belly. She never tired of this, never turned him away. He seemed to know when she was simply too tired or not feeling well, never insisting on having his way with her. But then she didn't take much prompting. Not from Caleb Sax.

She bent her knee as he kissed her thighs, then moved his lips over her belly again, his fingers searching her silken depths until she gasped with the wonderful pulsations that told him she was ready for him. Caleb moved quickly then, realizing he had been so engrossed in her he hadn't even removed his underwear. She opened her eyes and grinned as he pulled them off and threw them aside. He saw her smile and grinned back.

"You laughing at me, Sarah Sax?"

"Just having fun watching you try to hurry."

He moved on top of her, laughing lightly himself and kissing her eyes, pressing his hardness against her belly. "I don't like to keep a beautiful lady waiting."

Their eyes held boldly as he moved inside her and she arched up to him willingly. Her eyes closed then in ecstasy, and he watched her take him, enjoyed the pleasure on her face. He moved rhythmically, taking his time, and taking his own pleasure in return. He moved his hands under her hips and pushed, forcing her to meet him even harder, feeling the mixture of power and weakness that mating with her brought him. He could force this if he wanted, but he would never do that to his Sarah, nor did he have to.

His release came in strong thrusts that brought groans of pleasure from his own lips, and he let out a long sigh then, reluctantly pulling away from her and lying down beside her, pulling a light quilt over both of them.

For several minutes neither of them said a word. Then he swallowed, rubbing his eyes. "My God, Sarah, I hope it doesn't turn out like it was with you and me and your father."

"What are you talking about?"

"Tom and that Hafer girl."

"Caleb, he hardly knows her."

"You didn't see how he looked at her in town. He's so excited about going to that barn raising he can hardly stand it. But if you had seen Hafer's eyes, you'd know what I'm talking about. He's Terrence Sax reborn."

She shivered. "Don't say that, Caleb."

He pulled her close. "I'm sorry. I know I shouldn't dredge up old memories. I just—I love him so much. Why couldn't he fall for some Cherokee girl?"

She pulled back and arched her eyebrows. "I do believe he's his father's son. Did his father use such common sense?"

Caleb smiled sadly. "I guess I didn't."

"If he chooses to love this girl, you can't do a thing about it, Caleb. You know that."

Their eyes held. "I know. I just don't want him to go through what we went through."

"We will be here to help him. That's more than you and I had."

He kissed her cheek. "You're right." They hugged tighter, their own memories flooding in and making them cling to one another to again remind them that this was real and they were together now, and no one would ever separate them again. Sarah fell asleep thinking that at least for Tom there was no Byron Clawson in the picture. That was one thing in his favor.

Bess adjusted the bow on the soft yellow checked dress she decided to wear for the picnic. The wide cotton sash made her waist appear even smaller. She leaned into the mirror, pinching her cheeks for color, wondering how a girl with such fair skin looked to an Indian. Did they prefer dark-skinned women and joke about white women?

Tom wouldn't. She just knew it. And his father was married to a white woman. What was the woman like? Was she pretty? Her father had cruelly joked that the woman couldn't be much—"probably loose and ugly," he had said. It pained her to hear him insulting Indians all week. He wouldn't leave the subject alone. But she would never think less of Tom Sax, or of his sister. They were clean and friendly and well dressed. Their father owned a huge horse ranch. They spoke well and seemed as intelligent as anyone else she had known.

Her heart fluttered at the very thought of seeing Tom again. Bess worried he wouldn't come at all. Maybe he didn't even care about seeing her again. But she couldn't believe that. She could still feel the magnetism of his dark eyes, and she shivered with the memory of how he looked at her. Never had she been so attracted to someone as she was to Tom Sax, seeing him standing there with the pistol so steady in his hand, ready to protect not just his sister, but herself as well. She was certain he would have done the same thing even if his sister were not involved. The name alone was masculine and handsome—Tom Sax. He had grown up in this land, knew everything about it, knew how to handle himself, had even fought Comanche!

Bess touched her hair, which she wore long and loose today, except for tying back the sides with a yellow ribbon that matched her dress. She turned and walked out onto the porch of the small cabin she shared with her father. She looked over at the great stone house the man was having built. Her father had assured her she'd feel better once she had a fine house, but what good was a big house if she still had no one to talk to? She would just be even more lonely, with so many rooms in which to wander. She wanted to visit the Saxes, but her conversation with her father on the way home from San Felipe had made her afraid even to ask.

"The Saxes seem like fine people," she had told her father. "We should get to know them better. We might need their help sometime."

"We won't need their help. And I do not appreciate your inviting them to the barn raising without saying something tst."

Bess frowned. "Why? They're our closest neighbors."

"They're Indians."

"But . . . they're not *Indian* Indians. I mean, they're just like us. And Mister Sax and his son know about Comanche. It might be important—"

"Bess, I want nothing to do with Indians. You know that! Look what they did to your brother! And no decent white girl even *speaks* to Indians. Surely you know that."

Bess reddened still at the memory of the cruel remark from her own father. She stared at the partially finished stone house, then moved her eyes to the foundation for the barn, feeling a fierce pain in her chest at her father's words, as though he was insinuating she was not decent. It angered her, and his attitude didn't seem Christian.

Her father was approaching now, the rising sun behind him. People would be coming soon. A barn raising was an all-day affair, and a chance for lonely settlers to gather together and visit.

"You look very pretty, Bess," Hafer told her as he came

closer. "You be careful of the young men. Of all the men, as far as that goes," he added. "A girl pretty like you doesn't go long without a husband in places like this. But there are plenty of untrustworthy gents out here, no doubt about that. You stay close. And stay away from that Sax boy."

She felt the lump rising in her throat again. "He's not a boy. And they were very nice," she answered. "It doesn't seem Christian to hate them just for the fact that they are Indian."

Hafer sighed with frustration, but in fact he was more irritated with Byron Clawson than anyone. He had not counted on this catch in his plans. Clawson never told him about the handsome young Tom Sax. Perhaps he didn't even know about him. And he hadn't warned him of the intelligence and power of Caleb Sax.

"Bess, believe me, Indians are trouble. They all have a wild streak. Indian men beat their women, and they all drink and steal. They'll kill a man as easily as looking at him."

"You don't know that the Saxes do those things. Lynda certainly doesn't look like an abused woman, and you haven't even met Mrs. Sax. I can't judge people that way, Father."

"You are young and innocent and ignorant of reality. Do you think I'd get angry with you if I didn't love you? My God, didn't you learn about Indians when your brother was killed? You're all I have left now that your mother and brother are gone, and I want the best for you. Maybe I should send you to that boarding school in St. Louis we considered before we left. Maybe I shouldn't have brought you here at all. But I'm still lonely for your mother and I wanted you with me."

She blinked back tears, putting her arm in his. "And I wanted to be with you, Father. Don't send me back. But don't ask me to hate people for no reason. And don't say I'm not decent."

He sighed deeply, looking into her beautiful dark eyes. "I never meant that, Bess. I know the fine girl my daughter is. I just don't want the men talking, thinking other things about my Bess, that's all."

She made no reply. If she could find a way to talk alone with Tom Sax today, she would do it. And she didn't care what anyone else would think, not even her father.

Chapter Nine

The Sax wagon clattered toward the picnic area, where several people had already gathered, including the Handels. Caleb drove and Sarah sat beside him holding the baby. Lynda rode in the back, cushioned by lots of quilts to keep the jolting to a minimum. The family's goal now was to make sure Lynda did not lose the baby, and they were pampering her to the extreme.

Lynda was nearly six months along, but she hardly showed under her full-skirted dress. Sarah fretted secretly that she was still so small, but she said nothing to Lynda, not wanting to alarm her. Lately the girl had been plagued by sickness that came not just in the mornings but sometimes in the afternoon or at night. Ada Highwater assured her it would end soon, and that not all pregnancies were alike. "With one I was sick all the time, with another not at all," she had assured Lynda.

Lynda felt ill the day they left, but she couldn't bear the thought of staying home alone. The pain of Lee's memory still stabbed at her in aching spasms, and at times it still seemed impossible he could be dead. He had been a young man so full of life and love and fun, and she was more sure than ever that his spirit still walked with her and slept with her. She wondered how she would ever get over the terrible depression that enveloped her deep in the night.

It was a day's ride to the Hafer ranch. Rather than arrive late at night, the Saxes had left the day before and camped overnight. Tom rode his horse, the finest golden gelding he could pick, and Caleb knew exactly why. Tom Sax intended to make as grand an impression as he could on Bess Hafer. Palominoes were rare in Texas, and Caleb had paid a trader dearly for the animal. Tom wore new cotton pants and a bright red shirt with rolled-up sleeves that exposed his muscular forearms. The shirt was open at the neck, revealing a silver and turquoise necklace that made his dark skin look even darker. A wide silver bracelet decorated his solid wrist and he wore his hair in two tails, with a red band around his forehead. He was determined to show he was proud to be an Indian. If Bess Hafer was going to be interested at all, she had to care about all that he was, not just how much he acted like a white man. The palomino pranced proudly as Tom rode in, seeming to sense that it was supposed to put on a show. People turned, commenting quietly to each other, not only about the horse, but also whispering about the Indian who rode it and wondering what Indians were doing at the barn raising.

Young John rode beside Tom, his own long, dark hair flying in the wind, a bright blue band tied along his forehead. He wore cotton pants and a blue calico shirt. Both John and Tom wore Indian moccasins. John all but worshipped his older brother, who spent more time with him now that Lee was gone. John had changed since the Comanche raid. He did a man's work, and he yearned to be as grown up as Tom and his father. He would never forget his father's quick skills the night he was rescued, and he often tried to visualize some of the adventures his father told about in the days he rode against the Crow. There was an Indian spirit in both John and Tom that all the living like a white man would not quell, and both often talked about how much fun it would be to ride free on the plains.

The Handels hurried over to greet Sarah and Caleb. A few men were already busily hammering pegs into holes in order to connect beams to the corner posts of the already-rising barn. Men on the beams turned to stare.

"I'll be damned," one of them muttered. "Indians. I wonder who invited them."

Jess Purnell turned to look, feeling a little flutter in his chest when he realized it must be the Saxes. "They're neighbors to the south," he told the man who had made the remark. "Hafer invited them."

"He did, did he? Now that's damned strange."

Jess faced the man. "What do you mean?"

The man shrugged. "I done heard him tell one man he intended to do something about Indians who owned land in Texas—said it wasn't right. I tend to agree with him, and so do most folks in these parts. You got a partiality to Indians, Purnell? You'd best tell him if you have a soft spot for redskins."

The man sneered the words and Jess returned to his hammering. "I've got no soft spot for them—not the ones who make trouble anyway. But there's no reason to stir up the peaceful ones. Texas has enough trouble right now."

Sarah handed Mildred Handel several loaves of potato bread and a deep kettle of *frijoles*, flavored with salt pork and her own choice of spices that enhanced the flavor of the *pinto* beans. Lynda offered three cherry pies made from wild cherry trees that grew near the river on Sax land.

There were a few other people there Caleb and Sarah knew and many they did not know. Most were friendly but cool. Sarah knew why but it didn't bother her. She proudly showed off three-month-old James, a fat, smiling boy who was more beautiful than any white baby there as far as she was concerned. James had his father's blue eyes, and skin that was a lovely pale brown but not as dark as Caleb's. His sandy hair was a mass of thick curls, totally unlike his father's and brothers' straight, black hair.

It was the baby who warmed the situation and brought other women flocking, some out of curiosity, wondering how a white woman could sleep with an Indian man, but many secretly understanding. Even though they whispered about the "odd" marriage and the fact that Sarah Sax seemed genuinely happy, none could deny the handsome looks of Caleb Sax, nor the stirrings any woman felt in his commanding presence. But, the other women whispered, wasn't it true Indian men were cruel to their women? Still, Sarah Sax certainly didn't look abused. Whenever she looked at her man, love shone in her eyes like the sun.

Some of the men grumbled among themselves about the fact that Caleb Sax was harboring Cherokee refugees from Georgia. Texas didn't need any more Indians than it already had. Some thought he should send them to Indian Territory where they belonged, but none had the courage to tell him so. Even better, they would like to see Caleb himself go with them.

Caleb, wearing buckskin pants and a deep blue calico shirt that matched his eyes, walked on long legs toward the barn, leaving Sarah with Mildred Handel. Lynda stayed with her mother, and John was soon playing with other boys his age and younger—children who still did not carry all the hatred and prejudice of their elders. But there were a few who were already on their way to such feelings and who would not play with John. They were boys slightly older, who stood off to the side, some of them smoking pipes and feeling very grown up, especially when they occasionally made remarks whenever John was near, joking about the "Indian bastard." John struggled to pay no heed. He had been ordered by his father to start no trouble.

Tom rode near the food table, his eyes scanning the group of people who had gathered, some coming for many miles just for the chance to visit and picnic. He finally spotted Bess. She was watching him and she blushed and smiled when he caught her eye. She looked delicious, filling out the bodice of her yellow dress with full, firm breasts Tom was sure had never been touched by man. It only made her all the more attractive to him, let alone the bright smile she gave him now, dimples showing in her fair but blushing cheeks. He rode closer.

"Hello," he said.

Bess wondered if she would faint. One word and she felt weak. All her father's warnings immediately meant nothing to her. She paid no heed to some of the women who turned to stare when she said hello to the young Indian man.

"I have to go help with the barn awhile, but I will be back. Can I talk with you?" Tom asked.

"I'd like that."

His grin grew wider, and his dark eyes scanned the array of food. "That all looks pretty good. What did you make?"

She twisted her fingers nervously. "I baked a cake—and I made a potato salad."

"Then that is what I will eat first." His horse whinnied and pranced nervously, and Tom yanked on the reins, patting the animal's neck and talking to it soothingly. Bess's skin tingled. What a mannerly and handsome young man he was. There was so much she wanted to know about him, about Indians, about his parents. "I'll be right here," she told him.

He nodded. "I will look for you."

It was understood—so quickly.

He didn't have to know her well to know she was the most wonderful girl in the whole world. And she did not have to know him well to be sure he was the most wonderful man. The attraction was instant and powerful—as natural as breathing.

Tom rode past her and she watched after him. She would be glad when the men all came down for their meal later in the afternoon. The hours beforehand would seem like days.

Caleb set a beam in place, with the help of Jess Purnell. He held it steady while Purnell drilled a peg hole carefully, turning the auger with a strong arm, then removing the shavings and shoving in a peg partway, then pounding it hard.

"This is good oak," Caleb commented. "Hafer must have brought it in from the East."

"Yup. Only the best for Mister Hafer," Jess answered. "That's what they say."

"Any idea where he gets the money?"

Jess shrugged. "Damned if I know. Some say it's from the sale of his farm back in Missouri, but I never knew a farm that brought this kind of money. Some think somebody is backing him. Others say he was a wealthy man on his own. He's kind of vague about it. I think someone is backing him myself. There's plenty of men with money back in the States who are watching Texas, you know—waiting to see what happens, figuring this territory could be valuable some day."

"Well, that's what white men are best at, sizing up the value of land and moving in for the kill."

Jess turned to look at him. "Not all of us."

Their eyes held, and Caleb studied Jess Purnell's intently before returning to his work. There was an open honesty about the man that he liked.

Purnell picked up the auger. "How is your daughter holding up?"

Caleb was immediately wary. "She's fine."

"How long has her husband been gone?"

"Three months. Not long enough for her to be interested in anyone else, especially not someone who works for an Indian hater."

Purnell stopped drilling and looked at him again. "Look, Sax, I'm no Indian hater."

"You work for one. That's the same thing in my book."

"You don't know he's an Indian hater."

"I've been through enough to know an Indian hater when I see one."

"Why did you come then?"

Caleb lifted another beam with strong arms. "To give my wife a chance to visit—and to check out Hafer." He laid the beam in place.

More Hafer men moved closer then with still another beam and Purnell said nothing more. He had gotten off on a bad foot with Caleb Sax, something he had not wanted. Why shouldn't the man think him an Indian hater when he worked for a man who apparently was? But then it didn't much matter. Sax's daughter was apparently far from ready to take an interest in any man. It was a source of irritation to Jess Purnell, who had not been able to get her off his mind since first setting eyes on her in San Felipe. She had a savage beauty about her that stirred needs in a man seldom satisfied in this desolate land.

By late afternoon the men had most of the barn up—enough that Hafer's men could finish it within a couple of weeks. Charles Hafer made the rounds introducing himself as the men climbed down from their lofty perches, thanking each of them with a handshake and a ten-dollar note. His eyes took on a challenging look when he slapped the money into Caleb's hand.

"Well, well, you really came. Glad to see you, Sax."

He was almost as tall as Caleb, but not quite. Both had broad shoulders, but Caleb was more slender and solid, whereas Hafer was a balding, barrel-chested man.

"Appreciate the money, Hafer. But I didn't come here expecting to get paid. A barn raising is a neighborly get-together. I'd rather have the use of some of your men in return—to rebuild the barn the Comanche burned down on my place."

Hafer put on a patronizing grin. "Oh, I'd oblige you, Sax, but I've got my hands full here. I really can't spare any men. There's an awful lot of work to do getting a place going. You surely know that. We've started a house, too." He nodded toward a partially finished stone structure. "I want to get my Bess out of that closet of a cabin we're living in. You understand."

Caleb shoved the bill into his pocket. "Sure. And we both know hardly any of these people would come to any barn raising I might hold, except maybe the Handels. But then they're good, honest people who appreciate a man for what he is, not for his money or the color of his skin."

Hafer frowned. "Oh, now, you misjudge me, Sax."

"I don't think so."

Hafer's grin immediately vanished. Caleb Sax was smarter and more cunning than he'd figured.

"I'm told you're harboring quite a few Cherokees on your place, Sax," he said defensively. "I'd be careful doing that, if I were you. You're walking on eggs already, being part Indian yourself."

Caleb lit his cigar. "That so? You think you're telling me something I don't already know, making a friendly suggestion, or giving me a warning?"

"Oh, a friendly suggestion, I assure you. It matters hardly at all to me. But if we're going to be neighbors, I'd hate to see you having a lot of troubles, and it does make me a little uncomfortable having so many Indians right next door. You're perfectly welcome, of course, but how do I know I can trust those newcomers who have nothing?"

Caleb puffed the cigar. "You can trust them. They're probably more honest than any white man you've ever dealt with." His eyes moved to Tom, who was standing near Bess Hafer drinking a glass of water. He could almost feel the sparks flying, and he well knew the trouble that was brewing. But he couldn't have kept Tom away without tying him to a post. Tom was man enough to make his own decisions, and Caleb suddenly didn't care if Tom took an interest in the girl.

"At any rate, I'm still grateful, Sax, for your coming today," Hafer was saying. "I met your wife, by the way. Beautiful woman. Beautiful woman." Caleb knew the man was wondering why on earth Sarah had married an Indian. "And a fine-looking baby boy you have there." Caleb started to answer but the man interrupted him. "Sorry I can't supply any men to help with your barn."

Hafer immediately and rudely turned his back on Caleb and began talking to the next man. Caleb was glad. It kept Hafer from noticing that his daughter was walking off with Tom Sax. Caleb just grinned to himself and left to find Sarah, as men began to line up for food.

Chapter Ten

Bess leaned back against the stone wall of the unfinished house, which sat on a hill overlooking the crowd that had gathered for the barn raising. Below, everyone ate and visited. Here, she and Tom Sax were alone and unseen, where they could talk without whispers and stares. Still, the whispers and stares didn't much matter to her. She barely noticed. Tom Sax had come straight to her when he came down from the barn and asked her to walk with him. He didn't even want to eat first. She felt light-headed, almost dizzy. His arm had brushed hers once and a wonderful tingle moved across her skin.

"It's such a beautiful story—terrible but beautiful," she told him. He had been telling her about Caleb and Sarah, and how they had found each other again after thinking each other dead. Tom stood near her, almost too near, his hand resting against the wall behind her so that he leaned close. "And your stepmother is so beautiful, Tom. I met her while we were preparing the food table. She's so—so elegant for a woman out here. I found it easy to talk to her. She makes me miss my mother."

"She is a good woman." His eyes moved over her. "I hardly know you, but I think you are much like her. And you are very beautiful yourself."

She smiled and looked down. "Thank you." She swallowed, every nerve end, every part of her body feeling so alive. "I'm glad you decided to come today. It has been so lonely out here. I love having all the people here. It's too bad we can't do these things more often."

"It would be nice. But there is so much work to do that most people don't have much time for these things. We don't even get into town very often. Life out here is very hard. It must be hard for you, coming here from St. Louis. I know it was hard for Sarah, but then she had my father and that was all that mattered. You came out here with only your father, and no friends."

She looked up at him again, meeting his eyes. "I'm making a friend right now, aren't I?"

He grinned, fighting a terrible urge to kiss her. "I hope so. When I saw you back in San Felipe, I couldn't forget about you. I wanted to see you again, talk to you more."

"That's why I came up here. We could never talk down there."

Their eyes held again, speaking without words. "What will you do here now?" he asked.

She shrugged. "I don't even know. I've been kind of lost ever since my mother died." She kept trying to explain about her brother but was afraid to bring it up. Still, he had a right to know before their friendship went any farther. "I left some good friends back in Missouri, but I just couldn't let my father come here alone," she continued. "He needs me right now. He is very lonely. He has been wanting to get away from the old farm, where everything was too familiar. He . . . he had been drinking a lot because of my . . . my mother's death. I thought it would be exciting coming here, but father is so busy all the time, and the only woman around is an old Mexican woman whose husband works for my father. She is usually busy with her own family. I just sit in the cabin reading, waiting for Father to come home to eat. I don't dare go running about too much. Father says I should stay away from the hired help."

"That's a good idea. You're very beautiful, and some of those men haven't seen anything but their horse's . . . I mean . . . sometimes they can be pretty rude. You should be careful. Now I am going to worry about you."

She held his dark eyes. "You are?"

"Yes, I am."

"But why? You hardly know me."

"You're easy to know—and to like. But my father says I should stay away from you."

She studied the dark eyes. "Why?"

Her blood raced when he took hold of her hand. He put it up against his cheek. "See the difference? That is why."

He lowered her hand but kept hold of it.

"You mean . . . because you're Indian?"

"You know that's what I mean. I don't think your father cares much for Indians. And my father has been through some pretty terrible things because of men like that. He thinks it would be wise for me not to become friendly with you."

Their eyes continued to hold. "And what do you think, Tom?"

"I think I don't care about what's wise. I think I'd like to see more of you, if you will let me."

He squeezed her hand and saw her visibly tremble.

"Yes. You may come and see me any time you wish."

"Perhaps your father will let some of the men he trusts ride you to our place, so you can visit with my mother and my sister. It would be good for you—get you away from here—give you something to do."

"Oh, I'd like that." Perhaps now that her father had met Sarah Sax today, she could approach him again. After all, Sarah Sax was white, and a beautiful, refined woman. Surely her father would let her visit.

Tom grinned. "Good." He sighed deeply then. "We had better go back before people talk. I don't think your father even knows we're up here."

"I know. But I hate to leave."

His eyes sparked and his jaw flexed in reaction to painful desires that swept through him. "So do I."

He still had hold of her hand. He drew it to his chest and leaned closer, kissing her cheek, then waited for a slap. It didn't come. But she did redden and pulled her hand away.

"You must think I'm terrible, letting you do that." She looked down at the ground. "I don't know what got into me. I'm just so lonely—"

"I could never think of you as terrible. I know better, Bess."

She looked up at him then. "You wouldn't fool me, would you? Do you really want to come and see me again?"

"Sure I do. You know I do."

"I mean . . ." She looked away. "Father says young Indian men like white girls . . . for bad things."

She could almost feel him stiffen without even looking at him. "Is that what you think?"

She looked up at him again, seeing the hurt in his dark eyes, and also seeing the gentleness there. "No. I don't even know for sure what he's talking about." She reddened again. "I mean . . . I sort of do. But . . . I'm not afraid with you. I feel very safe. You make me feel good . . . happy. It's just that Father says Indian men are cruel to women, and they drink—"

He turned away. "We better go back down. I think you listen too much to your father, who apparently doesn't know much about Indians."

"Tom, I'm sorry. I wasn't speaking for me. I'm just telling you what he feels. I truly do want to see more of you."

He met her eyes with his own proud look. "My father almost never drinks. And *I* don't drink. My father would die before he would hurt his wife. He won't even spank his children like white men do. He can be ruthless when it is necessary—against his enemies. But *never* has he raised a hand against anyone in his family! Nor would I. Your father is a fool to say such things."

Her eyes teared. "You don't understand, Tom. He has reason to feel the way he does."

"Reason? What reason?" He stood watching her defiantly, his hands on his hips. She let out a sigh of resignation, folding her arms and turning away.

"I . . . I didn't want to tell you. I was afraid you wouldn't like me at all anymore."

Tom could not help losing some of his anger. She looked so small and pretty standing there. "You don't have to be afraid to tell me anything."

She breathed deeply for courage. "Tom, my brother . . .

he was killed by Indians. At least that's what my father and most of the neighbors believed. I didn't believe it and I still don't."

There was a long moment of silence while Tom tried to weigh the news in his mind. Allowing himself to like this girl seemed even more stupid and hopeless now. When a man lost a son, his bitterness and hatred lived on forever. Caleb was right. Her father *was* an Indian hater, and for the best reason, at least for a white man. For an Indian to kill a white man made all Indians bad in their eyes. "What happened? Why don't you believe it yourself?"

She wiped the tears on her cheeks and turned to face him. "My brother drank a lot. He was a bully. He even used to push me around sometimes. I loved him because he was my brother, but I didn't like him very much." She turned away again and began pacing nervously in little circles. She had no choice now. She might as well tell him and get it over with.

"There are only a few Indians left where I live—Osage. Charles Jr., that's my brother's name, he used to make fun of them, for no particular reason. He just didn't like Indians. He thought they were inferior. One day a boy named Billy Parker had come over. I stayed in the house because I hated Billy. He was always trying to get me into a corner and saying dirty things to me. I didn't see everything that happened, but the next thing I knew Billy and my brother were fighting over some money my brother had made selling homemade whiskey. They used to get into fights all the time. Billy left, and later three young Osage men came looking for work on the farm. My brother started calling them names and making fun of them. He pushed one of them, and the Indian pushed back. They got into a tussle but nothing serious. The other two Indians pulled their friend off and they left. I watched all of it through a window. Mother had been sick a lot and she was lying in bed asleep. Father was out in the fields and didn't see, but he did see the three Indian boys leave. He came rushing back and my brother gave him an exaggerated story about their being drunk and that they bothered me and tried to rob us. None of it was true. I tried to tell my father that later, but he thinks that I'm just a naive girl who doesn't understand about men."

She looked at him almost pleadingly. "Maybe I don't, but I know what I saw! My brother provoked the whole thing, and he lied to my father." She lowered her eyes. "And my father was the kind who was always ready to believe the worst about Indians."

"What happened then?"

"That night after father went to bed my brother went out to the barn. I was still up finishing chores my mother couldn't do. My brother said he was going out to the barn to sit with a favorite horse of his. He did that sometimes— just sat and drank. Father never cared that he drank. He drank right along with him sometimes and they went to taverns together on Saturday nights."

She walked farther away. "Later I went to the screen door to call out to my brother to bring in some wood. But I didn't say anything when I saw Billy Parker walking toward the barn. He didn't live far and usually walked over instead of riding. He knew very well that my brother sometimes sat out in the barn drinking at night. He walked right in. I knew they'd probably get in another fight, but they always fought, so I just went back to my chores. I wasn't about to go out there near Billy Parker with my brother drunk."

Tom felt his protective instincts growing again, and a fierce jealousy of Billy Parker burned in his chest. He would like to meet the young man and give him a taste of his fists.

Bess shook her head. "The next thing I knew, the barn was on fire. I shook my father awake and we ran out there, but there was no stopping the fire by then. My father rushed inside and found my brother, stabbed to death. He dragged him out just before the whole barn was consumed in flames. We lost a lot of equipment, and a couple of horses. But none of that mattered to my father. His son had been killed. Those Osage boys had camped not far away that day. My father remembered seeing them when he went into town later in the day. He was sure it was they who had killed my brother and set our barn on fire. I tried to tell

Father I'd seen Billy go into the barn, but he just waved me off. He said Billy and Charles were always fighting, but Billy would never kill Charles. He rode straight into town and brought back the sheriff and had the Osage boys arrested."

She blinked back tears. "I felt bad about my brother, but I also know Billy killed him—not those poor Indian boys. I felt so sorry for them. Nobody would defend them. It was more like a lynching than a fair trial. The town had them tried and hung within two days, and all the while they begged and pleaded and swore their innocence. I kept arguing with my father about Billy, but he just grabbed me and shook me and told me I'd better never bring it up again. He just wouldn't believe it could be anyone but those Indian boys. My mother died not long after, and he blamed it on the trauma of Charles's death. But it wasn't that. She was simply worked to death. That left a lot of the work to me, and it also left me alone against Billy Parker. That was part of the reason I was glad Father decided to come to Texas. It got me away from Billy."

She sniffed and wiped at her eyes, then turned and looked at Tom. "Life has been easier here as far as work. I don't have to do any. But it's harder in so many other ways. I miss my mother terribly, and I still feel guilty about those Osage boys."

"Guilty? Why should *you* feel guilty?"

She shrugged. "I don't know. I keep thinking I could have done something more. But I was afraid to speak up publicly in defense of Indians." She reddened and looked down again, wiping at tears on her cheeks. "I'll never let that happen again. I guess maybe that's part of the reason I defended your sister last week. I don't blame you if you hate me now. But suddenly. . ." Her shoulders shook and she sniffed and wiped her cheeks again. "Suddenly this whole day is ruined."

She turned her back to him, and in the next moment his hands were on her shoulders. "None of the things that happened were your fault," came his voice. She sensed no anger or animosity. "I can understand why you were afraid to say anything, Bess. You're just. . . you're so young.

How can somebody like you know what to do? The important thing is you believed those Indian boys were innocent, when nobody else would believe it. I am glad to know that."

She turned and looked up at him. "You are?"

He took a big finger and traced it over her cheek, wiping the tears, then placed both hands on either side of her face moving a thumb over her chin and lips. "It would be easier to treat you casually and tell you good-bye right now for good—if you were not so pretty," he told her then, "and if I didn't know inside you are a good person."

She closed her eyes, shivering at the wonderful sensation he aroused deep in her body when he touched her. He resisted another surge of desire to pull her close and kiss her like the savage she thought he might be. But he wanted her to know that was not all he wanted from her, nor all he had on his mind.

"I'm so sorry, Tom," she told him, putting her hands on his strong wrists and meeting his eyes again. "My father . . . hates Indians. I shouldn't be up here with you, but I couldn't resist. I . . . I like you very much, and I hope that . . . somehow we can see each other again. I know my father would be against it, but maybe somehow I can reason with him."

She saw the look of disappointment in his eyes. He moved his hands to grasp both of hers. "I have a feeling that will be impossible. But somehow I will see you again. You can't let his personal hatred spoil your own life, Bess. And you can't hate just because he tells you to hate."

"I know. But . . . he's all I have now. Let me talk to him. Give it some time before you try to see me again."

"That will not be easy. I would like to stay here longer and talk more, but we have to get back down before your father suspects. Having him find us up here would not be a very good way of starting to change his mind." His eyes glittered with warm friendship. "I'm sorry about your brother. It must have all been terrible for you."

She squeezed his hands tightly and hung her head. "Father made me watch the hanging. He said people would wonder if I didn't. I'll never forget it—never, never,

never." She started to cry again and he could not resist pulling her close and holding her for a moment.

"Don't cry, Bess. Come on now. You have to go back down. You don't want anyone to know you have been crying."

It took her a moment to compose herself. Sheaway then, blushing at the realization she had let him hold her. Tom felt an intense desire at the feel of her full breasts against his chest and the scent of her hair. An overwhelming need to comfort and protect her nearly brought pain to every part of him. He waited while she blinked and wiped her eyes again, smoothing her dress and taking a handkerchief from a little pocket near her waist. She blew her nose, then smoothed her hair and looked up at him. "Am I all right?"

"You look fine," he told her with a gentle smile. "You had better go down first. I'll come down from another direction. That might be best today."

"No." She held up her chin. "We'll go down together. I don't care what anyone thinks or says. And I don't even care right now if Father sees us."

Tom smiled. "You are not only beautiful and good, but also very bold, Bess Hafer. You are just the right kind of woman for Texas." He put a hand to her waist and led her toward the path, realizing his father had most certainly been right about Charles Hafer.

Below, Jess Purnell was handing Lynda a glass of water. She sat away from the others, wiping perspiration from her forehead and looking pale.

"Why are you sitting here all alone?" he asked.

Lynda looked up. "Hello," she said quietly, taking the water. "Thank you." She drank it eagerly.

"You all right? You don't look well."

She lowered the glass. "It's just the heat."

"Yeah, it stays pretty hot here in September. Makes a man long for the mountains. Did you eat? Can I get you something?"

"No. Thank you."

He sighed, feeling awkward, wanting to strike up some

kind of friendship. "I . . . I really am sorry about the other day . . . half flirting with you like that. I didn't know about your husband."

"It's all right." She looked up into kind blue eyes and handed him the glass. "But I really am not feeling well right now." She suddenly rose and hurried over to an outhouse, going around behind it. Jess followed, concerned. He found her vomiting. "Go away," she pleaded, spitting and choking.

"Do you need help? Do you want me to get someone?"

"I'll be all right. I'm just—it's my condition." She spit again. She breathed deeply, wiping her face with a handkerchief and leaning against the outhouse. "I'll be all right now."

Jess took a piece of peppermint candy from his shirt pocket where he'd put some earlier in the day. "Here," he told her. "Suck on this."

She stared at it, then looked up at him and smiled faintly. "Thank you." She took the candy and put it in her mouth.

"You, uh, are you pregnant?"

Lynda nodded. "I'm so embarrassed."

"Embarrassed? Because you're having a baby?"

She put a hand to her stomach. "Women don't usually talk openly about such things."

"Well, I think it's real nice—I mean . . . you've got something of your husband left. You must be real happy about that."

"I am."

"What was he like—your husband?"

She stared at a distant cottonwood tree. "He was wonderful—good, gentle, devoted." She looked up at him then. "He was Cherokee."

Jess Purnell's eyes moved over her appreciatively. "Well, he was a very lucky man. You're a very beautiful woman."

She looked away. Just talking to another man was like a betrayal to Lee. Still Jess Purnell seemed nice enough. And he had a rugged handsomeness to him that under normal circumstances would turn any girl's head. But he was not

Lee Whitestone, and she had no feelings for any other man.

"I'm all right now," she said. "I'm going back to find my mother."

"She your real mother?"

"Yes. It's a long story."

He took her arm. "You need some help?"

She pulled it away. "No." She hurried away from him then and Purnell watched after her, imagining her long, dark, willowy body lying next to his in the night. Surely she was wild and wonderful in bed with a man she truly wanted. He wouldn't mind being that man.

Tom lay awake in his bunk thinking about the day before. Most, including the Saxes, had stayed so late that they decided to stay all night, sleeping in wagons or on the ground, and return home the next morning. All that night he had lay staring at the Hafer cabin. Bess was in there lying in a bed in her soft flannel gown. Now it was the second night and he was home. He had left her behind, had not seen her at all that morning. She had not even come out of the cabin. He could not help but wonder if it was at her father's command. The man had been standing with a group of women staring and pointing as Tom and Bess came toward them, and Hafer's face had been almost purple with rage. But the man had said nothing, greeting Tom with a fake smile.

"I see you've been watching after my daughter, young man," he said. "She has a habit of wandering off for walks alone."

Their eyes held. "Yes," Tom answered, realizing the man was quickly trying to avoid gossip about his daughter. "I saw her walking away and told her she had better come back here where it was safer. With the Comanche, one can never be sure when they might be around. Tom had accented the word Comanche, trying to point out that not all Indians were to be feared. But Hafer had only given him a sneering look, then led Bess away, introducing her to some other women. She looked back at Tom apologetically and he gave here a smile. But his heart was heavy.

Perhaps his father was right. To try to see her would only bring a lot of trouble. It was best to leave her alone and not stir up a powerful man whose property adjoined his father's. It made so much sense just to let it go, to forget her.

Tom turned over in bed. He felt torn, remembering the softness of her cheek when he kissed it; the sparkle in her dark eyes when she looked at him; the full firmness of her untouched bosom. It seemed impossible to let some other man be the one to make a woman of her. It should be himself who did that. The thought of some other man invading such innocence and maybe hurting her or being mean to her brought a jealous rage to his soul. And there were plenty of available men on the Hafer spread.

Yet there was his own father to think about. He loved Caleb Sax as much as his own life. They had always been close. How could he do something that would bring his father trouble? There had been enough problems in the man's life. Now Lee was dead, and Caleb Sax was still struggling with the horror of his death. No. He never should have gone to the barn raising and let himself see Bess Hafer again. He saw it all in the eyes of Bess's father. He had missed it the first time he met the man—not completely—but he had missed the intensity of the man's hatred. Not only would pursuing Bess bring problems to his father, but it would surely bring bigger problems for Bess. She was too nice to put her through all that. Perhaps if Tom left her alone there would be no problems with Charles Hafer. He owed his father that much. He hadn't even told his father yet about Hafer's son, but he knew he had better do so soon.

Forget her. He would forget her. He closed his eyes and there she was, smiling, soft, beautiful. He could smell her lilac perfume and feel the soft skin of her cheek against his lips. He sat up, flinging back his blankets angrily. He rose, wearing his pants but no shirt.

"You better get some sleep, Tom," one of the men spoke up. "Lots of work to do tomorrow."

"I'll be ready," Tom answered, pulling on a shirt.

"Where you going this time of night?"

"To Rosy's."

A couple of the others made panting sounds and another whistled, while the first man hooted.

"Hey, she's a wild one, that Rosy," one man yelled from a dark corner. "You won't have any energy tomorrow. Better save it for another time, young lover."

"Shut up, Dan. I can't save it."

"Hurts that much, huh?"

They all laughed and Tom was glad it was dark. He pulled out his moccasins and went out the door.

Rosy cooked for the hired help who had no families. The men who had families lived in their own cabins on another section of Sax land. But to those single men in the bunkhouse, Rosy sometimes served more needs than their hunger for food. . . . She would let Tom in. Rosy always let Tom in.

The next morning Tom rode with Caleb and several others to Blue Valley, Caleb's favorite spot on his land. He had named the place Blue Valley because of the blue look to it at dusk. It was actually green, greener than any other spot in what was mostly a land of browns and yellows. The green came from a stream that was fed by the Brazos River about ten miles north of the valley, its beginning actually not even on Sax land. That had never bothered Caleb before, but it did now. The beginnings of the tributary were now on Hafer land. The stream drifted south into Blue Valley, creating soft ground and wonderful grass for grazing horses. It was a natural feeding area, and Caleb kept several men camped there on shifts constantly to guard some of the finest horses in Texas from Comanche raids.

Caleb slowed his horse, letting the others go by and signaling for Tom to slow up with him.

"We'll cut out a couple of those roan mares," he told Tom. "I want to mate them with Apache and Painter. Those two are itching for a female, and I think those two mares mated with them would produce some damned strong horses."

Tom nodded. "I agree."

Caleb took off his hat and wiped perspiration. "You care to tell me what happened with that Hafer girl?"

They rode slowly to talk. Tom shrugged. "Nothing special."

Caleb turned to look at him, seeing hidden feelings. "If it was nothing special, why did you feel you had to go visit Rosy last night?"

Tom looked at him in surprise, then turned away. "How did you know?"

"Men talk. They like to joke about it."

Tom sighed with irritation.

"They like to rib you a little, that's all," Caleb added. "God knows they've probably all had a turn at Rosy."

Tom grinned a little then. "She likes me best."

Caleb laughed lightly. "Come on now. What about Bess Hafer? That's why you went. I have been around a long time, remember? You can't fool your father."

Tom sobered. "All right. I like her a lot. She walked with me. We talked. We didn't have a lot of time, but enough for me to know she's easy to talk to; and she's nice—and beautiful—and untouched. But it was just as you said. When we came back her father was waiting, and if looks could kill, I would be a dead man. I never saw her the next morning, and I think I know why. I decided last night that even though I promised her I would come and see her again, I had better not. Maybe if I don't go and she gets mad, it will be easier on her."

They rode along quietly for a moment. "Do you really think you can stay away, Tom?"

"I have to. I love you too much. It's not like giving up a woman with whom I've fallen madly in love and have already had an affair, or someone I have always known like you knew Sarah. And I could see by Hafer's eyes that if I tried to see her there would be trouble. I don't want to make trouble for you, Father. I thought it would be easy, but after learning *why* Hafer hates Indians . . ." He halted his horse. "I might as well tell you you were more right than you know about Hafer."

Caleb drew up beside him. "How's that?"

Tom met the man's eyes. "I didn't say anything on the way home because of Sarah. You know how she worries about everything."

Caleb smiled softly. "I appreciate that. What is so terrible that you didn't want to tell me in front of her? She sensed Hafer's feelings toward Indians as much as I did. That wouldn't surprise her."

Tom hated having to tell him, but it was important his father be alerted to everything. "Hafer had a son, Father. He was killed a couple of years ago back in Missouri—supposedly by Osage Indians. At least that's who was blamed."

Caleb's gentle smile turned to a look of grim concern. "A son!"

Tom nodded. He turned his eyes to gaze at the distant mountains, telling the man everything Bess had told him about her brother. "Bess was the only one who believed the Osages' innocence."

Caleb shook his head and sighed deeply, suddenly sounding and looking weary. "Damn," he muttered. "This all looks bad, Tom. Not just you and Bess."

Tom turned to meet the man's eyes again. "I know. It leaves a lot of questions: why Hafer didn't say anything right away, why he tried to act friendly at first, and why he bothered to invite us at all to that barn raising. The way Bess talks, he hates all Indians."

"Lord knows I'm well aware of what it feels like to lose a son. But I'd never judge all men by those who killed him. Hafer was an Indian hater before his son was ever killed." He crooked one leg over the top of his horse, hooking it around the pommel of his saddle. "There's something not quite right about any of this, Tom, but I can't figure it. I talked to one of Hafer's men—that Jess Purnell. He says nobody is quite sure how Hafer got his money. He thinks somebody is backing the man—some investor who is looking at the possible value of Texas land. That could mean whoever it is thinks some day land belonging to Indians will be up for bids."

"Not our land! They'll never get our land!"

Caleb looked back at him. "Don't be too sure, Tom. You still don't understand just what lengths whites will go to get what they want. You should have some idea from all the Cherokee who have been filtering in from the South."

He put his hat back on. "At any rate, this is all very strange. Hafer is from the St. Louis area. There are a lot of land hawkers, investors, bankers in that—" He stopped short, a look of sudden knowledge moving through his eyes, followed by hatred.

"What is it, Father?"

Clawson. Byron Clawson. Could it have anything to do with him? That was impossible. Too many years had gone by, and Clawson wouldn't dream of crossing him. Still, before Sarah had left for Texas, Clawson had threatened her against telling anyone about their failure of a marriage —a tale that would certainly taint his public image. But surely he knew if he crossed Caleb Sax again he was risking his life.

"Never mind," Caleb answered aloud. "I think I'm making something out of nothing. Maybe Hafer isn't up to anything in particular. But I find that hard to believe. At any rate, whatever it is, Bess apparently is too innocent to figure it all out. She must be a pretty confused and lonely little girl. It's obvious that she, at least, is untouched by all her father's hatred and prejudice, which brings me to my next question. You be honest, Tom. How do you really feel about the girl, aside from not wanting to make trouble for me?"

Tom held his eyes. "She's wonderful. When I'm around her I feel . . . I don't know . . . not like I ever felt around any other girl." He looked out over the valley. "I mean, she's too important to touch or kiss without feelings and respect. A man could never bed that one and just walk away from her."

Caleb smiled in understanding. "And you really think you can forget her?"

Tom shrugged. "I thought you would want me to."

"All I want is your happiness, Tom." The boy looked back at him as he spoke. "I just wanted to protect you from the hurt I know loving a girl like Bess can bring, not just to you, but to her, too. And I also want you to be sure. I don't want you blaming me a couple of years from now if Bess Hafer is gone or married. I appreciate your not wanting to stir up trouble, but I have had plenty of that before and I can handle it. You're free to go wherever your heart leads you and free to see her more if you want. I wouldn't be angry, but I would be damned worried."

Tom sighed deeply. "You have enough worries. I won't give you any more for a while. I'm going to give it some time. Maybe after awhile the feelings will go away."

"The feelings you tried to get rid of last night through Rosy?"

Tom laughed. "Yes. Those feelings. But much more than that."

"I know what you mean. And I think you have a problem, Tom Sax."

"It will go away. Right now my biggest problem is to beat you to Split Rock up ahead." He whipped his horse into a gallop and Caleb charged after him.

Three months passed and Bess moved into the stone house. To her it seemed more like a stone prison. How could a person live in such a big land and still feel so confined? Just a day's ride south lay Sax land—and Tom Sax. Why hadn't he come back? Did he know how terribly her father had spoken to her after the barn raising? Did he know how ugly her father had made her walk with Tom sound, how bad the man had made her feel, how he had forbidden her to ever set eyes on Tom Sax again? Surely he did, for she had not even been allowed to come out the next morning to say good-bye to anyone.

"I've never been so ashamed in my life," he'd told her. "And in front of all those women! You know how women gossip! I didn't bring you here for that, Elizabeth Anne Hafer. Your mother would turn over in her grave if she knew. *And* your brother!" He stormed up and down the room. "I ought to send you back to St. Louis right this minute! What's got into you? Are you that lonely? Do you want me to bring in some other families? And look at all the other young men around here. You could have your choice of any of them, except for the fact that you're too young for any of them—white or Indian—and too damned *good* for them, too. You'll marry better than any of that scum out there."

On and on he had raged. "Why do you talk of marriage?" she had sobbed. "I took a walk with him. That isn't exactly something to compare to marriage."

"You wouldn't have walked with him if you weren't interested. If you're going to get to know them, why didn't you pick his sister or his mother? Anything but an Indian man!"

He had broken her down into sobs, mixing her up, breaking her heart. He had always been a blustery, overbearing man, but since selling their farm he had taken on an arrogance that made him more a stranger than her father. Where was her father getting so much money? It seemed to be more than her brother's death that bothered him; more, even, than her walking with Tom Sax, as though she was spoiling some grand plan he had for his new land. The stone house was finished. It was much cooler than the old cabin, and finer than anything they ever had at home. It even had a second floor, with two bedrooms there, and a kitchen and very large living area below. It seemed a waste somehow, for no one came to visit. It was as though Charles Hafer built it simply to flaunt his sudden wealth.

She sat down in a rocker on the front porch, staring to the south, toward Sax land. They were a real family. It was so obvious. Perhaps they also found little time to visit, but at least they had each other. Her heart hurt so bad she rubbed her chest. It all seemed so hopeless. Between her father's hatred of Indians and his new wealth, he would never let her see Tom again.

Bess pulled a sweater close around her against the early morning chill, surprised it could actually get cold in Texas. Some of the men even said snow might come soon. Her mother had knitted the sweater for her, so long ago. She missed her mother terribly, longed for her companionship.

But most of all she longed for Tom Sax. Surely he knew her father's feelings and that was why he hadn't come back as she had hoped. Maybe he was even still angry over what she had said to him about her father's opinion of Indians. It embarrassed her, and never had she felt so alone and lonely. She could not stop thinking about him, dreaming about him. She could not forget the touch of his lips on her cheek, his hand so gentle on her face. He was so utterly handsome—beautiful was a better word for it . . . so strong and brave and skilled. How many times had she dreamed about being kissed by him—really kissed—on the lips? Her heart surged with jealousy at the wonder of how many other girls he might be interested in. She wanted to be the special one—the only one.

Perhaps he was only staying away to avoid trouble, or perhaps he thought she didn't care because she had never come out to say good-bye. If there were only a way she could see him again. She would tell him she did care, that it was all her father's fault she did not come out that morning.

One of the hired hands rode by, halting his horse in front of her and looking her over. "Mornin', Miss Hafer. Your pa around?"

"Not right now, Stu."

Stu was handsome in his own way but never seemed to be able to keep himself shaved.

He grinned. "Long as he's gone, there anything I can do for you, little girl? All of us are ready to help you out any time you need it."

The idea entered her mind quickly, unexpectedly. Her father had become so stern and quiet around her that the hurt he had brought her only made her more determined to prove him wrong, and more determined to have her own way. If nothing else, it would be a great adventure—better than sitting here hour after hour with nothing to do and no one to talk to.

"Now that you mention it, I've been wanting to visit Sarah and Lynda Sax," she told the man. "Father says he doesn't mind," she lied. "But he says all you men are too busy to accompany me. As long as father is gone—he's at another ranch trying to make a deal for some winter feed —maybe you and some of the others could take me to the Saxes. I'm so bored and lonely. I'm sure Father wouldn't mind."

Stu frowned. "You sure? The Saxes are Indians."

"I know. But they're very nice, and Father doesn't mind

my making friends with the women, especially Mrs. Sax.
She's white, and a very fine woman. I'd love to go visiting
before the weather gets any colder."

The man looked her over. The way he'd heard it,
Charles Hafer was off studying the water supply on Sax
land, not seeing about feed. If possible, he would cut that
supply. There had been no rain for six weeks, and this was
the dry season anyway. For some reason Charles Hafer
wanted to make it even dryer for Caleb Sax. Stu didn't
mind helping out. He had no use for Indians.

"I could lose my job if your father doesn't approve,
missy."

"Oh, but I wouldn't lie to you, Stu."

He looked her over. Maybe it was worth the risk. In
fact, if he got her far enough away, he could even have at
her and get away before either of them was ever found. By
the time she was found, the first ones to be blamed would
be the Saxes. Everyone figured Indians good for rape and
murder. This could work out just fine—and having a turn
at the beautiful young Elizabeth Hafer was worth leaving
his job with her father, even if the man did pay him well.
He would just move on to the next job afterward.

"All right, missy. I'll take you. I'll go saddle a horse for
you. Just be sure to dress warm."

"Oh, thank you, Stu!" She jumped up from her chair.
"Just give me a minute to change."

He watched after her. "Sure," he answered with a grin.
"I'll wait. It's early enough that if we don't waste time I
can get you there by dusk, long as we ride horses and don't
take a wagon. You can stay over a night or two and then
I'll bring you back. Be sure to leave your father a note."

"I will." She went inside. She wouldn't really leave a
note. Her father would be furious, but if she left a note, he
would come for her right away, and Bess wanted some
time to visit. If she kept him guessing . . . She shivered.
Perhaps this was all wrong, but she didn't care. All that
mattered was to get away from the stone house . . . and to
see Tom Sax.

Chapter
Eleven

Tom sat alone on the ridge above Blue Valley, looking out at the vast and seemingly endless stretch of Texas flatland that was spread out before him to the north. Try as he might, he had not been able to forget about Bess. He had found all kinds of excuses to come to the Valley to help out the Cherokee there who tended the horses, but his real reason was always to ride on and try to see Bess.

But always he changed his mind. He had told his father he would not go and had stuck to his word, even though Caleb had told him it was all right. Too many things were happening now to give his father problems. There had been some skirmishes between Americans and Mexicans; and Sam Houston was talking of forming a stronger militia. There had been a drought in Texas and Blue Valley was about the only truly good grazing spot left on Sax land. Lynda's stomach had suddenly blossomed huge and she was still sick a lot. She could deliver any time. And little James, close to six months old now, had just got over a bad fever. It seemed there were so many things to think about, so many dangers lurking, not the least of which was the continuing threat of Comanche raids. How could he add to the family problems by bringing Bess into the picture?

He shivered against a chilly late November wind, wondering if he should take his wool jacket from his bedroll and put it on. He smelled snow in the air, and dark clouds hung in the west. He decided against the jacket for the moment and moved his horse down the ridge and through the valley up the other side, where he could gaze across the flat land to the north.

Hafer's land was out there, but the endless horizon all looked the same from where he sat, especially at dusk. It was strange how such vast expanses of land could trick the eye. Sometimes things seemed to be moving that were not, and things moving were actually stationary. Now he watched two objects that seemed to be moving. At first he figured them to be two rocks, or perhaps cacti that only looked to be moving because of the shifting winds or odd movements of sand. But after several minutes of watching them, he realized what he saw were two figures riding toward Sax land.

He continued to watch curiously, for they seemed to be riding hard. As always in this land, it seemed to take forever for them to get closer. What looked like two miles could be twenty. But finally he could see them better. The horse in front was slowing, surely overheated by now, in spite of the cold air. No horse should be ridden so hard for such a distance. Was someone coming to warn them of some kind of danger?

He eased his horse down the slope, working his way around rocks and heading down a sandy escarpment. Tom let his skilled palomino find its own way while he kept his eyes on the two riders. His keen eye soon deciphered that the one in front was a woman. His heart quickened. What woman could be coming from the north, except perhaps Elizabeth Hafer?

Neither rider had seen him yet. The one behind the woman seemed intent on catching up to her, but the woman apparently was a good rider. Suddenly there was a gunshot and the horse in front stumbled and fell. The woman screamed and landed hard, tumbling away from the animal, which kicked out for a few seconds before lying still. The second rider reached the woman and dismounted. The woman got up and started to run, but the man tackled her down and hit her.

Tom turned his stallion into a hard gallop. He took out his pistol from his belt and fired it once into the air. The man the woman was struggling with jumped up and looked around. Tom let out a war whoop and rode right toward them. The man ran for his horse, grabbing his flintlock and aiming it. Tom ducked to the left side of his horse, hanging from it in the way Indians did when dodging bullets. The palomino kept up its hard run as a shot went off but missed. The man started desperately reloading, but Tom brought his stallion to a tearing halt, jumping down and pulling his own flintlock from its boot, but the gun jammed on him.

The man got off another shot, barely missing Tom, and the girl screamed his name. Tom turned to see Bess standing there, her dress torn, her hair tumbling down from its original bun. Tom quickly pieced together what was happening, and he pulled a knife, holding it out toward the man and crouching.

"I wouldn't try to reload if I were you," he warned. "I'd just get on my horse and ride out of here."

The man fidgeted with his rifle, then threw it down with a curse. He met Tom's eyes. "Get the hell out of here, Indian! You've got no business here!"

"You're on Sax land, mister. I've got *every* right to be here! And you're trespassing. Now get going!"

The man glanced at Bess. He had not counted on her being such a good rider, nor on her being so ungrateful. If she'd have let him have his way, she'd have discovered soon enough the fun he could have shown her. This was not how he had planned it at all. He looked back at Tom.

"Look, Indian, why miss out on a good chance? Put the knife away and we can both have at her. Wouldn't you like to get inside a white girl, especially one as pretty as that one? Why fight when you could be havin' a good time with that pretty girl?"

Elizabeth broke into sobs.

"This is my last warning, mister," Tom growled. "Get going before I kill you!"

Stu Clements was not about to be outdone in front of Elizabeth Hafer, especially not by an Indian. He pulled out a hunting knife he wore tied to the side of his leg. "Like hell I will, you red-skinned bastard! I was guttin' and skinnin' men with this thing while you were still pissin' in your cradleboard!" He waved the knife and Tom came closer. "You'd better think twice, Indian," Stu warned. "We could take turns and say Comanche did it. But if you kill me, they'll say you stole that girl and killed me for her. You'll hang, boy!"

"They'll know the truth—from her!"

"No they won't—because you'll rape and kill her. I know what Indians do!"

"It's white men who understand raping and killing! You were going to do the same."

Stu lunged at Tom, who darted back. Bess whimpered and watched, her heart pounding with fear for Tom. Stu lunged again, but Tom was quick. He grasped the man's wrist with his left hand, pushing upward with a powerful arm while Stu in turn managed to get hold of Tom's right arm, trying to push it down and back. They struggled muscle to muscle for a few seconds until Tom managed to swing a foot around and catch Stu behind the ankle. He jerked his foot hard, causing the man to fall onto his back. Stu's knife went flying and Tom leaped on top of him.

Dirt and rocks tore their clothes as they rolled on the ground. Stu kept a firm hold on Tom's wrist with both hands and dust billowed around them as the two men scrambled and wrestled. Tom finally managed to get a firm hold of Stu's throat then with his left hand, pressing hard and squeezing until the man began to choke and turn beet red. Stu let go of Tom's knife hand in order to pry Tom's left arm, but his energy was spent from lack of air. Tom pressed his knife near the man's eye.

"Now you will go," he sneered. "Or I will cut out your eye!"

Stu lay there panting. "I'll go," he muttered.

Tom slowly moved off the man, his buckskins scraped, one arm bleeding where his shirt had torn and rocks cut into it. His dark eyes gleamed with a desire to kill. Stu slowly got up, grabbing a fistful of sand and rocks when Tom glanced over at Bess. When Tom looked back Stu flung the pebbles in Tom's face. Tom bent over, shaking his head and rubbing his eyes, and Stu lunged for his own knife.

"Tom, look out," Bess screamed.

Tom could see only a blur coming at him. He dove for the ground, rolling away and coming to his feet again, his eyes clearing slightly. Stu came at him then, slashing with his blade, catching Tom just lightly across the belly. Tom kept backing up, blinking, waiting for the right moment. Stu made a lunge with his knife then and Tom caught his arm, quickly turning so that Stu was behind him and yanking the man's arm over his shoulder, then hoisting him, flipping him over his head to land hard on the ground in front of him. He made no hesitation then. The man had been warned. Tom's knife came down hard, scraping into Stu Clements's chest and piercing the heart. Blood spurted onto Tom, and Bess turned away in horror, feeling sick.

Tom yanked out the knife with a sneer, wiping the blade on Clements before putting it back in its sheath on his belt. He stood there bent over the man a moment, panting, still shaking sand from his eyes and hair. He turned then, stumbling to his horse and canteen, opening the canteen and pouring some of the water over his face. He waited another moment, breathing deeply to regain his composure before walking over to where Bess stood, still turned away.

"He is dead," he told her. "Here." He held out the canteen. "Do you need some water?"

She only sniffled. He put a hand on her shoulder. "How bad did he hurt you?"

She wiped her eyes with a trembling hand. "He tried . . . to attack me. I got to my horse . . . and just started riding this way . . . hoping I'd find people . . . anyone."

He gently stroked her hair, pulling out the scarf that had held it and running his fingers through its long tresses. He knew already that this time there would be no forgetting. He had seen her again, and worse, he had felt rage at the thought of her pursuer hurting her, perhaps raping her.

"I will take you to our home and my mother and sister can help you clean up. I can't take you back to your father, Bess, not this way . . . not alone. God only knows what they'll accuse me of. We'll have to clean you up and take you back with some extra men. Besides, it would be too dangerous for me to take you back alone." He ran a hand over her shoulders. "I am sorry you had to see me kill him. I had no choice. What the hell were you doing out here anyway?"

"I . . . hired him . . . to ride me here so I could see you," she sniffed, shivering then from the wind.

His heart filled with love and sorrow and he gently turned her, taking her chin and forcing her to look up at him. He felt torn at the dirty and bruised face. "Me? You rode through dangerous country with only one man for a guard, just to see me?"

Tears traced over her cheeks. "Why didn't you come back to see me? You promised you would."

He frowned, realizing just how young and trusting she was. "Bess, considering the circumstances, I thought it best—"

"You broke your promise. You said you liked me. You said we were friends. You said I could come here and visit. Tom, I'm so lonely. I hate it there. I feel like I'm going crazy. And most of all I missed you."

He sighed, drawing her close. Desires pulsed through her at his embrace. "You stupid girl. Why didn't you send me a message or something? You shouldn't have tried to come yourself. If Comanche had ever spotted you—" He hugged her tighter. "I don't think you even know what a brave thing you did. Young women don't go into this country with just one man to watch out for them, Bess. Come on. I'll take you to the house."

He led her toward his horse. "What about Stu?" she asked.

"Is that his name?"

"Stu Clements."

Tom looked at him and sneered. "Let the buzzards have him. He deserves no burial for what he was going to do to you." He lifted her then, easily, as though she weighed nothing. "Your horse is dead and his has run off. You can ride in front of me on my horse." He took his wool coat from his gear, then eased up behind her, draping the jacket around her shoulders. She turned to look into his dark eyes.

"Tom, you're hurt. He cut you."

He looked down at himself, putting a hand to the blood. "Not deep. My stepmother will take care of it. First I have to get you off this flatland and closer to places where we will be safer."

She was so close—right there—inches from him. And she did not turn away. "I'm afraid I have to tell you I'm damned glad to see you, Bess. You have been on my mind every hour of every day." He lightly met her lips and she let him, shivering when his tongue gently traced the corners of her mouth. He pulled back suddenly then, as though hit by a quick pain. She supposed it was his wound, too innocent to realize it was for him something much more painful. He leaned over her then, enveloping her in his arms as he picked up the reins of his horse, then kept one arm around her tightly as he rode off toward home.

Sarah bathed Bess's face while Caleb paced nervously, and Tom removed his shirt so Lynda could wash the wound on his abdomen. It was well after dark when they arrived at Caleb's house. Caleb's shock had quickly turned to near panic.

"You could be in a lot of trouble, Tom, a lot of trouble," Caleb fumed. "Couldn't you have just wounded him? Don't you remember what Hafer did to those Osage boys?"

"What would you have done," the boy retorted. "If a man hurt Sarah and then tried to kill you, what would you have done?"

Caleb met Sarah's eyes, then ran a hand over tired eyes. "I would have done the same damned thing."

"This is all my fault," Bess sobbed. "I just . . . wanted to go visiting. I didn't know what that man would do. I didn't mean to get anybody in trouble." The words were squeaked through tears.

"It's all right, Bess," Sarah soothed. "That man took advantage of you. You couldn't help it." She looked at Caleb. "I'm sure once Bess explains it will be all right."

"An Indian killing a white man—and one of Hafer's

men no less?" Caleb let out a disgusted sigh. "They won't care about why it happened."

"We'll go over there with most of our men," Tom put in, wincing as Lynda splashed whiskey on his cut. Bess watched, totally in awe of Tom Sax now. He was her hero. He could have been killed. Now he stood there shirtless, wearing only buckskin pants and moccasins. His stomach was muscled and lean, and she reddened when she realized she was staring at a dark-skinned, shirtless man and remembering his kiss. She looked down, hoping no one had noticed. "We'll ride there with plenty of protection and we will tell them the truth. Hafer can't do anything if we go over there willingly and take Bess with us so she can tell them the truth."

"I don't want to go back," the girl sniffled. "I never asked Father. He'll be furious. He'll send me back to St. Louis!"

Tom's heart quickened at the thought. He didn't want her to go, ever.

"We have no choice," Caleb spoke up. "If we don't take you back, they'll say we attacked you both, killed Clements and stole you away. It's impossible to keep you here."

"I've made a mess of everything. None of you will ever want to call me friend again," Bess sobbed. "What will I do if something happens to Tom?"

Sarah pulled the girl close in a motherly way, so that Bess's head rested against Sarah's stomach. Sarah stroked her hair. "Nothing is going to happen to Tom," she said firmly, watching her husband, knowing his agony. "You are all going to do like Tom said and ride over there in force and tell the truth."

"Except that I'll say I killed the man—not Tom," Caleb spoke up.

The room quieted and they all looked at him.

"No," Tom spoke up, moving away from Lynda before she was through. "You can't do that."

"I can do whatever I please when it means protecting my son! You're the one Hafer would just as soon hang if he had a good enough excuse. You're the one who has shown an interest in his daughter."

Bess reddened and closed her eyes.

"If I say I went to Bess's aid and killed Clements, it will be better accepted than if they know it was you," Caleb said in a determined voice. "They might say you did it on purpose, out of jealousy or something. We'll go over there and we'll take Bess back, but under *my* terms. I will have no arguments about it!"

Tom swallowed back a lump in his throat. "I can't let another man take the blame for something I did, especially not my own father!"

"You have no choice in the matter. In fact, you aren't even going. They might see your bruises and cuts. If they ask about you, I'll say you weren't even around through any of this. You were at the Handels. I can get Wil Handel to vouch for that. He'll understand."

"Father, you can't——"

"No arguments! I'll go with several other men, and Bess can explain what happened. The only way Hafer will be really furious is if he sees your face. Then he'll know the truth just by looking at you. Without you there's a chance we can get away with this. Nobody here is going to get arrested and sit in a Mexican prison for six months before getting a hearing! Stu Clements got what he deserved. Surely some of Hafer's men know the man wasn't trustworthy. But I want you completely left out of the matter."

"I'll go with you," Sarah spoke up.

Caleb looked at her with a frown. "You'll do no such thing. Who knows what Hafer will do? They might shoot at us as we come in, for all I know."

"I am going with you and this time I am the one who will have no arguments. I can testify as to the condition of Bess when she came here, and a show of friendship between myself and Bess will only prove none of this could have had anything to do with us. Bess wouldn't befriend someone who tried to hurt her. And maybe the presence of a woman—and, I'm sorry to add, a white woman—will help keep the entire situation calm."

"I could go, too," Lynda spoke up.

"No," Sarah told her. "You've been too sick, and we should ride horses so we can get there more quickly. You stay here and watch after James. Feed him on cow's milk until I return. Tom, you stay with Lynda."

"Don't take me yet," Bess begged. "I'm so tired. I have to get my composure so I can lie about Mister Sax."

Sarah let go of her. "We certainly can't start tonight. We'll leave first thing in the morning. If we ride horses we'll get there before dark. I'll fix you a bowl of soup, Bess. I just made it fresh this morning. You eat some and rest for a while." She held Caleb's eyes as she spoke. "All of you will rest tonight and get your stories straight."

Tom sighed and strode over to the wall where some of his clothes hung on a hook. He took down another buckskin shirt. His savagelike presence filled the room, and made him seem even bigger to Bess.

"I'm not through dressing that wound," Lynda told him.

"It's all right. It will heal," he muttered. He looked at his father again, almost pleadingly. "I'm sorry, Father. I told you I didn't want to bring trouble. It just happened. But you should let me go myself."

"I can't let you do it. I killed the man. You might as well all start thinking that way right now. I'll tell my men the same story." He looked at Sarah again, wanting to scold her, tell her she couldn't go. It was too dangerous, and yet it did make sense. Hafer would have to be grateful to the woman for being the temporary mother Bess needed. He loved her for thinking of it and for volunteering.

"All of you sit down," Sarah told them. "We ate very late and there is still some soup left. Tom and Bess should eat. Surely you're hungry, Bess."

The girl wiped at her eyes. "I'm too upset to eat."

"I insist that you get something in your stomach—you and Tom both."

The girl looked up at her. "Thank you so much for everything you're doing. I really didn't mean to make trouble for the family. It's all my fault—just mine. I'll make my father understand that, even if it means having to leave Texas."

Sarah patted her shoulder. "Well, maybe that won't happen." She looked at Tom, scanning the scraped and wounded body. "Thank God you're all right. Come and sit down, Tom—and calm down. You remind me of a wild animal on a chain—you and your father both."

The young man sat down reluctantly, but he made sure to sit beside Bess. He reached over under the table and took her hand, squeezing it. It gave her a warm, accepted feeling. She was overwhelmed that they were all being kind to her and not blaming her for what had happened, even though it was all her fault as far as she was concerned. If only she had not decided to come. And yet if she hadn't, she wouldn't be sitting here now next to Tom.

"They probably haven't even figured out Clements is missing yet," Tom spoke up, taking a biscuit then that Sarah handed him. She handed him a jar of homemade jam. "They're probably running around trying to figure out what could have happened to Bess."

"Hafer will send men out in every direction. The first thing they'll suspect is Comanche," Caleb put in, still standing.

"Hafer might not even know yet. Bess said he was off someplace seeing about winter feed. He didn't even know she left. The men don't mess around the house. They'll think she's inside and won't think much about it. When they find out, they'll have to ride for Hafer first, to see what he wants them to do."

"Good. That means we'll get there well before Bess's father is worked up and frantic. That will help." He glanced at Bess. "I'm amazed Clements waited as long as he did. He must have wanted to get onto Sax land before he attacked you so he could say one of us did it. He had it all figured out."

She reddened at the thought of what Clements had intended to do to her. He had been very graphic in his explanation, laughing the whole time, terrifying her. Was that what all men did to women? Why did it seem so horrible with someone like Clements, yet bring fire to her blood at the thought of Tom Sax doing that to her?

Caleb's eyes moved over her appreciatively. Yes. She was certainly beautiful. And he had no doubt that Tom's seeing the girl again would only lead to a situation the young man had tried to avoid. He wouldn't let her go this time—wouldn't forget her. He would never be able to keep his promise to stay away from her.

Bess could only pick at her food.

"This will all get straightened out, and you will come and visit us often, Bess," Sarah was telling her. "I was a seamstress back in St. Louis. Lynda helped me. We'll teach you how to make clothes. Would you like that?" she added.

The girl nodded, her eyes tearing again. She could hardly stand them being so nice to her. Besides, her father would never let her come back. What was she to do?

"Take one day at a time, Bess," Sarah spoke up, as though to read her thoughts. "That's all any of us can do. That's how Caleb and I get by without going crazy. There is never a tomorrow—only a today." She looked at Caleb and he saw the fear in her eyes. How she feared losing him again! But she didn't dare show it in front of poor Bess. She didn't want him saying he'd killed the man, but she knew it was the right choice.

Tom scooted back his chair. "Excuse me. I want to walk with Bess before everybody goes to sleep."

He met his father's eyes. Caleb nodded. "Go ahead. Take her over to Lynda's cabin. But don't keep her long. She's been through a lot and needs her sleep before she leaves tomorrow morning."

"Do you need anything, Bess?" Lynda asked. "I have some dresses at my cabin that might fit you, although they'd probably be a little long." She put a hand to her swollen belly. "I'm so big with child I can't wear any of them."

Bess shook her head. "No, thank you. It might be better if I go back like this—with my dress torn and all—so my father sees."

"But if you put on one of my dresses, he'll know we helped you. You can show him the torn one. Besides, that one has Tom's blood on it."

Bess put a hand to a ripped sleeve, feeling awkward and embarrassed. "Yes. Maybe you're right."

Lynda rose. "Give us a few minutes, Tom. Come with me, Bess. We'll find you something to wear."

Bess looked at Tom, who gave her a supportive smile. "Go ahead."

The girl backed away. "I really am sorry—for all of you," she told them again. "I'll just die if anyone gets hurt over this."

"It will all work out," Sarah assured her.

The girl left with Lynda, and Sarah met Caleb's eyes. "We'll go together. Hafer won't be able to do a thing."

He sighed. "I don't like you going."

"Nor do I," Tom put in. "Let me go, Father. This is all wrong!"

"The worst thing you could do is go there yourself. I told you that once."

His eyes showed a desperate look. "But he'll send her away!"

"Maybe not," Sarah answered, "if we can convince him she only did it out of loneliness for a woman's company—not for you. But it *was* for you, wasn't it?"

Tom toyed with a biscuit. "Dumb, crazy girl," he muttered.

Sarah glanced at Caleb again. "Yes. We all do dumb, crazy things at times. I know a young girl who once ran off with a young Indian man against her father's wishes." A lump rose in her throat at the memory and she looked away, picking up some of the food. "Poor Bess hardly ate." She looked at Tom then. "Let's hope nothing as disastrous as what Caleb and I went through happens to you."

Tom rose and went to the door. "I'm going to the bunkhouse to clean up a little before I see Bess."

Sarah looked at him in concern. "Your wound should be wrapped."

"It's all right." He turned and left, and moments later young John looked down from the loft.

"Can I go with you to the Hafer's, Pa?"

Caleb looked up. He'd forgotten the boy had gone to bed and probably heard everything. "I guess so, son. Just don't say a word, and do everything I tell you, understand?"

"Yes, sir. Will there be a lot of people there like last time?"

Caleb felt his chest tighten. "Only Hafer men this time, I'm afraid."

Tom walked to Lynda's cabin. Bess opened the door to his knock. She wore a pink flowered dress and her hair was brushed out long. His eyes moved over her with admiration shining in them, but the bruises on her face aroused his anger again. He checked it, giving her a soft smile.

"You look nice."

She smiled, but her eyes were red and her bruises ached. Her arm was badly scratched and it hurt under the sleeve of the dress. "The dress is too long. I'm so short, and Lynda is taller than most women." He took her hand and looked past her at Lynda.

"She's feeling better," Lynda told him. "Don't worry about Father, Tom. He can take care of himself. You know that." She saw the concern in her brother's eyes. He loved his father—worshipped him. He didn't like the man covering for him. But Caleb was not going to have it any other way. "I'll leave you two alone for a while." Lynda moved past them and out the door to walk back to her parents' house. Tom stepped inside the cabin. He had changed into a blue calico shirt when he went to the bunkhouse. He wore no jacket, and wondered if it was pure anger that made him feel warm in spite of the cold air. He had washed off the dirt from his struggle with Clements, but he walked slowly, and Bess knew his wound hurt him.

"I'm so sorry, Tom," she could not help saying again. "It all seems so unnecessary. I never should have been so forward as to try to come here anyway, not even knowing if you wanted to see me. I should have left well enough alone."

He looked down at her. "Bess, I told you I'm glad you came. Every day I tried to decide if I should go see you, but I thought if I avoided seeing you, I could forget you. It didn't work."

Their eyes held and he finally tore his away to walk her to the bed in the little one-room cabin. He sat down on the edge of it and urged her to do the same. She felt embarrassed, but she obeyed.

"Whatever happens, Bess," he told her, "I don't regret what I did today. That man deserved to die. And I'm glad you came to see me. Don't ever blame yourself for any of it."

"It's so hard not to. I . . . I care about you so much, Tom. I wanted so badly to see you again that I did a stupid thing."

He shrugged. "It's not so stupid or bad—not when all you wanted was to see a friend."

"But we hardly know each other."

He met her eyes, leaning close. "Out here in this land people don't have to know each other long. Things happen fast. People get lonely."

"Are you lonely?"

He put a gentle hand to her face. "I am surrounded by family—parents, brothers, a sister. And still I am lonely. I miss my brother-in-law, Lee—my sister's husband who was killed by the Comanche. He was my best friend. But it's more than that." His voice lowered to a near whisper. "I'm lonely for a woman."

He came closer and she closed her eyes, whimpering slightly when his mouth met hers in a lingering kiss. His tongue lightly tasted her lips, sending flames through her blood, and a light, tender kiss began to turn into a more demanding one, as both reacted to the intense passions of youth and newfound love.

She should pull away. Yes, she should pull away. But she did not want to. Tom Sax was a man. He kissed her like a man, not like the boys back home had kissed her—not that there had been many—only a couple of playful romances—nothing like this. Tom Sax was a man who knew what he wanted and knew how to take it. She was helpless against him, and she gasped and returned his kiss when he put a hand to her back and gently laid her onto the bed, consumed with a need to touch her more, feel her against him. He still had not left her mouth when he moved on top of her, kissing her in heated passion now, groaning slightly, loving the feel of her firm breasts against his chest, the feel of his own hardness against her belly.

Finally he left her mouth, breathing hard, moving his

lips to her neck. "You make me feel crazy," he whispered. "I want to forget you but I can't."

"I can't forget you either," she whispered in return, feeling weak and dizzy and consumed with fiery desires she'd never felt before. Tom! This was Tom Sax! He wanted her! He'd kissed her! He was lying against her. Was she being bad? Surely not. Surely if a girl loved someone . . . love. How could she be in love so soon, so quickly? Oh, it was easy. He was so handsome, so strong and good and kind and brave. He had saved her from Stu Clements's scheming. So what if he was Indian? None of those things her father had said could possibly be true about Tom Sax.

"I think I love you, Bess," he was whispering now. "I know it sounds crazy." He raised up slightly, studying her eyes lovingly, his face only inches away. "It's like they say. Things happen so fast out here. It's a dangerous land, and there isn't time for fancy courting and those things. It's like every day could be the last. Do you know what I mean?"

"Yes," she whispered. "I think I love you, too."

How easy it would be to take her right then and there. Oh, how he wanted to try! But she had been through too much this day. It was all wrong. There would be a right time, a right place. She would be his wife first. Was that possible? A desperate fear engulfed him. Would he never see her again? He'd never let Hafer send her away. If he sent her away, Tom would follow and bring her back. He would never let her go. Never!

He met her lips again, savagely, hungrily.

Wonderful sensations swept through Bess Hafer's innocent body. This was so different from the ugliness of Stu Clements. This was Tom. He made her want to please him, made her feel totally under his control, and she was, for he knew everything and she knew nothing. She had never had these feelings before—never wanted a man in the physical sense, never dreamed she could abandon her "proper" ways and let some young man kiss her the way Tom Sax was kissing her, hold her against himself in such a sinful way. But was it sinful, if there were feelings of love involved?

"I'll see more of you," he whispered in her ear. "Somehow I'll see more of you, Bess. That's a promise I'll keep this time."

He kissed her more gently then. Oh, how she loved his lips, his touch, his smile. He moved off her reluctantly, lying beside her then and pulling her into the crook of his arm.

"You rest now," he told her. "Rest right here beside me."

"But there's so much to talk about. I want to know more about you and your family—about your Indian heritage—"

"Hush. You've got to rest. Somehow we'll be together another time when there's more time to talk about those things. My father will leave early. You've got to rest."

She sighed, nestling into his shoulder, astonished that it was so easy for her to do.

"You're crazy to have feelings for me, you know, Bess," he told her then. "It will make things hard for you. You had better think about it once you're home. When I see you again, if you say I shouldn't come back, I'll understand."

"Never. I'll never change my mind. But it would be so much easier if my father would understand and let us be friends."

He moved his hand to lightly stroke her hair, and his arm brushed against her full breasts as he did so, making her breasts ache with an arousal unlike anything she'd known. "I think we will be more than friends, Bess Hafer," he told her.

Chapter Twelve

They rode onto Hafer land, Caleb and several Cherokee in front, men on either side and behind of Sarah and Bess. Caleb wanted the women in the middle where they would not be easy targets. When they first left, Cherokee scouts who rode ahead had found the body of Stu Clements. Caleb had ordered it buried. Now it was late, the sun beginning to set. They were nearing Hafer's house. Sarah prayed there would be no violence, not just because of Caleb, but also because young John rode right beside his father. Anyone could tell the boy rode in that position very proudly, puffing his chest out and thinking himself fully a man, proud Caleb had let him come along.

She looked over at Bess and smiled. The girl seemed stronger and more determined today. Perhaps it was because of her feelings for Tom, which were so very obvious. The girl all but worshipped him and considered him nothing short of a hero. Sarah could not blame her. She well remembered her feelings for Caleb when he had first visited her in St. Louis, and how his savage masculinity overwhelmed her. It still did.

Sarah hoped Bess understood that the best thing she could do right now was not to mention Tom in any way, and not to grow too impatient if she did not see him for a while. They must be cautious until Hafer got over the incident with Stu Clements, and Bess must approach her father carefully on the subject of Tom Sax. But young love was usually not patient.

Sarah shivered. The sun had done little to warm the cold November wind.

Caleb looked back at her. "You all right?"

"I'm fine, Caleb. Don't worry so much."

He knew her well enough to know she would never let on if she was uncomfortable or hurting. He knew her breasts were sore and tender from not feeding James and wondered if he should have let her come at all. The stone house was finally in sight, and several men were riding toward them now. Caleb raised his hand for everyone to halt. Sarah retied her warm scarf, her heart pounding.

Bess moved closer, looking worried. Sarah reached out and took her hand as Hafer men came closer, wielding long rifles.

"Sax!" one of them shouted.

Caleb recognized Jess Purnell.

"Hello, Purnell. We're here to return Bess Hafer safely home."

Purnell frowned. "What the hell happened? We didn't realize till last night she was even missing. Hafer is frantic."

"She's been at our place. She got lonely for a woman's company and hired one of your men to ride her to our place to see my wife and daughter."

Purnell's eyes moved to Bess. "That was a damned fool thing to do. You didn't even tell your father."

Bess looked down, unable to speak.

"She was going to send the man back to tell him," Caleb put in. "His name was Stu Clements. You know which one he is?"

Purnell nodded, while other Hafer men moved around the Cherokee threateningly. "He's sure not the one I'd pick to accompany a young girl that far."

"I'm glad you realize that, Purnell. I killed him."

Purnell stiffened.

"What the hell are you sayin', Indian?" one of the other men said.

"You heard me. I killed Clements."

"He had to, Jess," Bess blurted out. "Stu tried to attack me. He was going to do something bad to me. Mister Sax tried to stop him, but then Stu tried to kill him."

Purnell's eyes moved from Caleb to the girl. He suspected more but said nothing.

"Clements is buried near the border where our land connects," Caleb told him. "He waited till he got on Sax land. Must have figured on blaming it on one of us."

"We ought to hang him," one of the other men said. "He had no right killin' the man—an Indian killin' a white man!"

"Should he have let Clements kill him instead? And then rape and murder Charles Hafer's daughter?" Sarah asked, angered. "I suggest you get your priorities straight, sir."

The man's eyes softened somewhat. "This is no place for a woman, ma'am."

"Bess has had a bad experience and was frightened. I came along as a friend."

"Please take us to my father, Jess," Bess spoke up. "These people have been kind to me. Don't keep them sitting out here in the cold wind."

The man looked them all over, sighing and pushing back his hat. "Come on."

They all rode in together, and before they reached the house a man rode out toward them. Bess recognized her father. Her heart pounded, and she reminded herself not to mention Tom. Oh, how it had hurt to leave him this morning, knowing it might be a long time before she saw him again. But at least she had the memory of his kiss, the hope of knowing he cared very much for her.

"Bess!" Her father rode closer. He halted his horse before going to her, realizing she was surrounded by Caleb Sax and his men. "What the hell is going on here? Sax! What are you doing with my daughter?"

"He saved her life, Mister Hafer," Jess Purnell said. "Your daughter got lonely for some company and asked Stu Clements to ride her over to the Saxes to visit with the women there. Stu attacked her and Sax killed him."

Hafer stiffened. "*Killed* him! You killed one of my men?"

"It couldn't be helped. He was attacking your daughter.

Last night at dusk I happened to be riding the north range and saw her riding away from him. He shot her horse from under her and attacked her. I broke it up and he tried to kill me. I stabbed him. We buried him on our way here. We have the saddle with us from the dead horse, and your daughter's torn dress. Bess was very upset, so I took her to our place first so Sarah could help her clean up. My daughter gave her a clean dress and she stayed the night with us. We left this morning to bring her back."

Hafer frowned at Caleb, scanning the rest of them then as though looking for someone. "Where's your oldest son, Sax?"

Caleb held his eyes steadily. "He's at San Felipe ... been there a couple of days now seeing about winter supplies and looking into possibly volunteering for the militia."

Hafer studied him a long time, then nudged his horse forward, moving through Caleb's men to Bess, his face red with anger. "I'm glad as hell to see you're all right, young lady, but I want an explanation! You've just about given me heart failure!"

The girl swallowed and her eyes teared. "You're never home, Father. I get so lonely and bored. I just wanted to talk to another woman. I know now it was wrong, but I felt like I was going crazy, sitting around day after day without even you to talk to. Stu Clements rode by and I got the idea all of a sudden to go visiting. I knew you wouldn't be back till this morning. And I knew you'd never let me go—"

"There are Mexican women around here for companionship," he interrupted.

"That's not the same as somebody like Mrs. Sax. I can't even understand them when they talk. Mrs. Sax is more like ... like a mother ... somebody I can really talk to. And Lynda Sax is only a year older than I."

The man sighed deeply, visibly shaken. "If you ever do a thing like this again, you'll go back to St. Louis. Is that understood?"

She blinked back tears, glad that he at least talked as though he wouldn't send her back immediately. Apparently he believed it was just for the women. But then came the disappointing words.

"And you are to stay away from the Saxes," he added. "Is *that* understood!"

She reddened. "Father! Mister Sax saved my life! You can't blame them for what happened back in Missouri."

He glowered at her. "Don't bring your brother into this. I am grateful Sax helped you, but that doesn't give you license to be friendly with Indians. Mister Sax has my gratitude—" He turned to Caleb. "If this whole story is true."

"Father! How can you be so mean and ungrateful—"

"Be still and get to the house," he ordered.

The girl jerked in a sob and looked at Sarah, who reached out and took her hand. "It's all right, Bess. We understand. Do as your father tells you."

The girl broke into tears and rode off, and Sarah looked angrily at Charles Hafer. "Your daughter is very lonely, Mister Hafer. She needs a mother and a friend. Surely you can let her come and see me occasionally. After all, I am *white*." She sneered the word. "Or do you think I will contaminate her because I am *married* to an Indian?"

The man reddened, moving his eyes to Caleb, who met his look challengingly. He looked back at Sarah Sax, figuring it would be wise not to insult her in front of her husband. "I appreciate your concern for my daughter, Mrs. Sax. But you have to understand my own concern. She is very young and as you can see sometimes foolish. We both know your oldest son has eyes for her. It would be very unfortunate if out of pure loneliness my Bess allowed herself to become friends with him. I cannot believe that you and your daughter are the only reasons Bess tried to come and see you." He turned to Caleb, riding closer. "I'll be blunt, Sax. I don't ever want to see your son skulking around my land and my daughter."

"My son doesn't 'skulk,'" Caleb sneered. "If he came around here he'd ride straight in like the man that he is. And in spite of your ungratefulness, your daughter is still welcome at our place any time she needs a woman's company. My son had nothing to do with this. He doesn't even know yet that any of this happened."

Hafer's eyes narrowed. "Maybe not. But you warn him anyway."

"I'm sorry about what happened to your son, Hafer. I have lost a son, too, and by violence, just like yours. *White* men killed him. That makes our experiences pretty even. But I don't hate all white men for what happened to my son."

"I don't need your sympathy, Sax, *or* your sage advice!" Hafer reddened. "I'll let this one go, Sax, because you apparently helped my daughter. It wouldn't take much for me to turn this on you and get you hung for killing a white man, and you know it! I could have you sitting and rotting in a Mexican prison, or hanging in the main street of San Felipe. You took a great chance killing Stu Clements."

"I saved your daughter from being raped, you bastard," Caleb sneered. "I don't know what your problem is, Hafer, but this is more than what happened to your son or to Bess. And whatever it is, you shouldn't bring your daughter in on it."

Hafer stiffened. "You don't fool me, Caleb Sax. Your son had something to do with this. He came for her, didn't he? He came for her and Stu Clements tried to stop them. Stu would never let her ride off with an Indian."

"My son had nothing to do with it," Caleb growled. "Your daughter came to our place of her own accord. You try to lay this on my son and you'll regret the day you were born!"

Hafer backed his horse. "I'll get the truth out of my daughter. She's covering for him. He came for her like the sneaking Indian he is and rode off with her. If that's the way it happened, you and he will *both* hang!"

Caleb jerked his horse's reins, moving the restless animal closer to Hafer. "Why don't you and I settle this right now," he said boldly. "Man to man, Hafer! I don't need other men around me to be brave. How about you? We'll go someplace and have it over with."

Sarah's heart pounded as Hafer's men moved closer to Caleb and Caleb's own men pulled guns and knives.

Hafer just grinned then. "Oh, no, Sax, it won't be that easy. I'm not fool enough to fight hand to hand with the likes of you. But I owe you one for helping my daughter, *if* your story is true. I'm paying you back by letting you go free even though you killed one of my men; besides, your woman is along. I wouldn't want any females getting hurt. But I think you're covering for your son."

"How about physical proof your man tried to kill me," Caleb hissed through gritted teeth. He pulled off his buck-skin jacket, then raised his shirt, showing Charles Hafer an ugly gash across his stomach. "That's from Stu Clements's knife," he snarled. "That proof enough?"

Hafer's men gasped, and Sarah looked away, her heart aching at the sacrifice Caleb was making for his son. He had deliberately slashed his own skin the night before to make his story more authentic, and to explain the blood on Bess's torn dress.

Even Charles Hafer looked shocked, and some of the animosity left his eyes. "All right, Sax. You've made your point. But this doesn't change the fact that your son took an interest in my daughter at the barn raising. I'll not have my Bess gossiped about and looked down on. So keep Tom Sax off my land."

"My son makes his own decisions," Caleb sneered, putting his jacket back on. "Thank you for your hospitality and gratefulness, Hafer. It tells me all I need to know."

Caleb whirled his horse and signaled his men to follow. He rode on the left beside Sarah and John rode on her other side. Sax men followed behind for a couple of miles, then rode ahead, leaving Caleb and Sarah to themselves.

"Oh, Caleb, I hate to leave her there," Sarah said sadly.

"Right now it's her or Tom. You see what would have happened if we'd tried to keep her with us, or if Tom had tried to go back with us and told them the truth. It was just as I thought. And there's more to this than that man not wanting his daughter to get interested in Tom, or that he's lost a son. He's here for another purpose, and Bess has messed up his plans. I can't put it all together yet. It's just something that eats at me. I don't like any of this."

He gave her a reassuring smile then. "I don't want you fretting over it, though. Thank you for today, Sarah," he told her. "You were right. I think it helped having you there. I'm sorry about the insults."

"It doesn't matter. All that matters is that you got out of there safely and Tom is all right."

"Nevertheless I wish you were home. You tell me the minute you need to stop and rest," he told her. "We'll hurry back, but only at a pace you can handle. I'm afraid we'll have to camp somewhere overnight before we make it all the way home." He looked back toward the Hafer home, small now on the horizon. How was he going to keep Tom Sax away from this place? He smelled trouble, lots of trouble.

Caleb and Tom herded the horses toward Blue Valley. The air had the cold snap of December to it now. But their lips and skin felt dry, dry as everything else in the Valley. All they could hope for was some winter rains to bring life back to the parched land for spring. There had been barely any rainfall all summer. Most of the decent grazing land was eaten bare and grass was not growing back for lack of water. The only good grazing land left was Blue Valley. Now Caleb had to worry about over-grazing there. But at least the stream that still filtered in from the Brazos kept the Valley alive.

The horses before them were some of Caleb's finest. In the spring he would get good money for these horses when he sold them on the coast for shipment to the States. But they had to be kept well fed in the meantime, and winter feed was in short supply. Caleb had sensed a very deliberate attempt to keep him from getting his own supply the last time he'd been to San Felipe. Winter feed was needed now for militia horses, let alone the tremendous influx of new settlers. And Caleb was Indian. He came last. It angered him. He was one of the first settlers in this land, had lost several family members to the elements and the Comanche and outlaws. But that didn't seem to matter much to the outsiders and new suppliers.

Things did not look good. Stephen Austin still languished in a Mexican prison. Texas was filling up with a lot of undesirables who came in response to a promise of free land, and there was still talk of war. There had been a bad drought that still lingered, and the Comanche were more active again. And Lynda was great with child, ready to deliver any time, overdue by her count.

Then there was the problem of his own son, who was like a wild animal in a cage. It was not easy for him to stay away from Bess Hafer. Caleb had urged him to lay low, but staying away from her had only made the young man want her more. He was not the happy, joking Tom Sax now. He was always serious, too quiet, consumed with love. Neither of them knew quite how to resolve the situation, and Caleb worried that Tom would be foolish enough to ride right onto Hafer land and demand to see Bess.

Tom veered to the right, yipping and calling, turning some stray mares. Caleb studied the land as he rode. He had grown to love it here. This was home, the only real home he had ever had. But he felt it being threatened from every side. To some it was barren land, but to him it was beautiful in its stark nakedness and intense quiet. No wonder the Comanche loved it. They were bred for it, and deep inside Caleb Sax was bred for it. But there was always that white blood in him that drew him to settling, to keeping one woman and having a place to call his own.

He was a man torn between two worlds. He had lived in both of them, understood both of them. He didn't fully blame the Comanche, in spite of what they had done to his family. In a sense they were no different from the Cherokee coming into Texas. The only difference was the Cherokee were fighting by peaceful means, and the less educated, more savage Comanche chose a more violent means to keep what was theirs.

The white man was doing what he knew how to do best, pitting Indian against Indian. Now he did it by shoving the red men together into new lands, forcing the more advanced Eastern Indians to cohabitate with the wilder plains and mountain Indians.

In these times of trouble the Indian side of himself would take over. It would be so simple just to leave and join his red brothers who were still wild and free, shake off all the responsibilities he had taken on. But he had a family now, and a commitment to Marie, who had given her life helping him settle this piece of land; and to Sarah, who could not live the savage life. Sarah came first. She would always come first.

Two Cherokee rode toward them from Blue Valley, thundering up to Caleb with alarm in their eyes. "We have been waiting for you, Caleb," Jake Highwater told him. "We were going to come and get you. The water is gone."

Caleb frowned. "What are you talking about?"

"It's gone! Yesterday the stream all of a sudden got smaller and smaller, and today it quit running all together."

Caleb looked at Tom. "Part of that stream runs through Hafer's land," the young man told his father.

Caleb gripped the reins tighter. "Let's get the horses down there and check things out."

They whistled and shouted, running the herd into the Valley, where Caleb rode to the low spot that had carried water into this place even in the worst of droughts. Now there was nothing but wet stones and mushy grass.

"Sons of bitches," he muttered. He looked at Jake. It had to have something to do with Hafer. "Keep a few men here. Round up the rest. We're going to check this out, even if it means riding onto Hafer land!"

"Yes, sir."

Caleb, Tom, and eight Sax men were soon riding north, looking more like a small tribe of Indians on the warpath, many of them with long hair flying and wearing buckskins, including Caleb, who also wore a wolfskin coat Sarah had made for him. Horses snorted as they moved in a rhythmic slow run, their breath coming out from their nostrils in little white clouds in the cold air. Tom said nothing to his father, whose anger was evident. He relished a chance to ride onto Hafer land. Maybe he would see Bess. He must see her soon. He had to be sure she had not been sent away. But even after riding several miles onto Hafer land, the house was still a considerable distance ahead of them, yet already they spotted Hafer men.

They had followed the tributary out of Blue Valley, and it remained dry for a good six or seven miles into Hafer land, until they came upon a host of Hafer men digging small canals leading from the stream deep into dry land covered with parched grass—Hafer land.

"What's going on here?" Caleb demanded, riding hard up to one of the men.

The man shrugged. "We're diggin' irrigation ditches, Indian. What's it to you?"

"You're running off badly needed water from my land. Without this water, the only water left is along the river, where my horses are more open to Comanche attacks and where all good grazing land is used up. This water flows into my best grazing land! Where's Charles Hafer?"

The man nodded toward the house, which was still just a dot several miles distant but visible across the wide, clear horizon. "Up to his house."

Caleb turned his horse and a Hafer man standing near him raised a musket. "You'd better think twice about goin' over there," the man warned.

Caleb kicked out, knocking the musket from the man's hands. "And you'd better think twice about threatening me, white man," he snarled. "This is between me and Hafer. Stay out of it!" He rode off, signaling his men to follow. Horses thundered across the plains and it seemed to take forever to reach the house, which remained just a dot for another hour before finally taking shape. Tom's heart quickened. Would she be there?

More Hafer men rode out, shouting at Caleb to stop, but he kept going. They hesitated, not sure what Hafer would want them to do. Most knew this was some kind of deliberate act against Caleb Sax, so they guessed Hafer was actually waiting for confrontation and would want his men to let the Indian ride in.

Caleb and the others approached the house, and Charles Hafer himself came strolling out calmly, a smirk on his face when Caleb drew up his mount in front of the man. Inwardly Hafer felt very proud and happy. Clawson would love to see this. He was earning his money.

"Well, I can't say as I'm surprised to see you, Sax," he spoke up. He looked up at Tom and reddened with anger. "What's that boy doing here? I told you he'd better never set foot on my land!"

"He's with me," Caleb sneered, a warning look in his eyes.

Hafer swallowed, some of his arrogance leaving him. Caleb Sax had the look of a wild Indian in his blue eyes, and he presented a commanding appearance when angry.

"What the hell are you doing with my water?" Caleb growled.

"You can see what I'm doing, and it's not your water. On this end it's mine. It's been a dry fall and winter, Sax. I need to get that ground worked up. I'm thinking of planting cotton. The way I see it, this territory could be one of the biggest producers of cotton in the world. Why, the ground is perfect, and we're close to the Brazos—just ship the cotton down—"

"You know what I'm talking about, Hafer," Caleb interrupted. "You deliberately picked that particular stream to cut off my water!"

Hafer frowned. "Oh, come now, Sax, you do carry a chip on your shoulder, don't you?"

"I know deliberate destruction when I see it, and you're destroying my best grazing land—which could mean destroying my best horses! Get rid of those canals, Hafer, or I'll do it for you!"

Hafer shook his head and clucked. "I wouldn't try that if I were you. It could be awfully dangerous."

"You think I'm worried about that?"

Tom looked toward the door as it opened. He straightened and felt a surge of desire when Bess stepped outside. Their eyes met and she smiled. Their look said it all—"I love you." "I've missed you." "I want to see you again."

"That part of the stream runs through my land, and I'm using it as I see fit," Hafer told Caleb.

"There's another stream not much farther up from that one."

"It isn't as practical," Hafer answered.

"Why not? Because using it wouldn't give *me* problems?" Caleb dismounted, walking up to face Hafer threateningly. "I'll go to the council at San Felipe. I've got first rights to that water, Hafer. I've been here longer—sacrificed blood for this land! You have no right to take that water."

"Go ahead and tell them. And I will tell them how your

son tried to steal away my daughter a few weeks ago—
tried to rape her, in fact. They'd love to find out you Indians are making trouble. There are any number of men in
Texas now who would love an excuse to get rid of you."

Caleb grabbed the man's shirt and jerked him. "You
stinking liar!"

Hafer men leveled guns at Caleb and his men.

"Let it go, men," Hafer told them. "He doesn't dare hurt
me." He smiled at Caleb. "Do you, Sax?"

Caleb gave him a shove. "I'll get my water back,
Hafer," he hissed. "Even if I have to go over your dead
body!" He turned and mounted, leaving a pale Charles
Hafer to watch him back away.

Again Caleb Sax was proving to be more man than
Hafer had bargained for. He had to make this work. He
needed the money—wanted the money. But Caleb Sax was
not an easy man to fight, physically or intellectually. He
noticed Tom linger as Caleb and the others turned to ride
off. Tom was still watching Bess.

"Get out of here," Hafer growled at him. "Get out before
I shoot you."

Tom turned his horse. "You're a bastard, Hafer—a bastard and a thief."

He rode off, and a Hafer man raised a gun to Tom, but
Jess Purnell reached out and pushed it down. "Don't be the
first to fire," he told the man. "Mister Hafer said to let
them be first. You know that. Then we can say they started
it."

He watched after the Sax riders. He didn't like this dirty
work. It sure wasn't any way to get on the good side of
Caleb Sax's daughter. He hadn't forgot her. How did a man
forget that one? He wondered if she'd had the baby yet—
how she was doing. And he wondered how much longer he
could go on working for Hafer.

"Get in the house," Hafer shouted at his daughter.

Bess scurried inside, going to her room and throwing
herself onto her bed, breaking into tears. Tom! She'd seen
Tom! But her father was being so mean to them. How
could they ever, ever be together?

Hafer followed her inside. "How *dare* you come out of

the house when that boy is here," he yelled. "You know I forbid you to see him. Why did you encourage him by going out there?"

She looked up at him with tear-filled eyes. "I don't understand you any more, Father. He's nice. The Saxes are all good people. Caleb Sax saved me from that awful man. Why are you so mean to them?"

He clenched his fists in frustration. "Damn it, Bess, you don't understand. You just don't understand. You're ruining everything! If not for you I could—"

He stopped and walked to his desk, sitting down and taking out a quill pen and a piece of paper.

"What, Father? You could what?"

He turned, glowering at her. "I could do what I came here to do."

Their eyes held. "Came here to do? I thought you came here to settle and start over—to forget Mother and Charles's deaths—enjoy the money from selling the farm and—"

"Oh, you're so damned innocent, Bess—and ignorant! Haven't you noticed how *much* money I have now? I could buy you anything, send you to the best schools, give you anything you want. You didn't have to come to this godforsaken place with me. You could have stayed in St. Louis and had the best of everything. You still can, and you will. I'm sending you back. I saw how that boy looked at you. I've got to get you out of Texas. Besides, there's going to be war around here soon—and not just with the Mexicans. It will be with the Saxes."

Her heart tightened. St. Louis! "Father, don't you want me here with you? I thought you loved me—needed me."

"You know I love you," he answered, his back to her as he wrote. "That has nothing to do with it—on second thought, it has *everything* to do with it. I want what's best for you, and Texas and Tom Sax are not it." He kept writing. "Damned Indians," he grumbled.

She sniffed and fought an urge to sob uncontrollably. She had to tell Tom. But how could she? "What . . . what did you mean about the money, Father? Where did you get it?"

He sighed and stopped his writing. "From a man who is paying me to settle right here. I won't tell you any more than that. But it's a lot of money, and I am finally out of debt—for the first time in my life."

She shook her head. "But why would he pay you?"

"Never mind that."

"Father, give them their water back. Give it back and I'll go home without complaining."

"I can't do that. And you will go home, complaining or not. I'm writing a letter to that school, and another to the man I'm working for. I want you to give his letter to someone at the school and have them deliver it. It's very important."

"Is he rich? Who is it?"

"Never mind. In a week or so there will be a boat leaving San Felipe for the coast. I'll take you to San Felipe myself and see that you get on it and pay the captain well to make sure you get on the right ship to take you through the Gulf waters to New Orleans and on up to St. Louis. I'll send a couple of my men along for protection—men I know I can trust, not someone like that Stu Clements. He was the worst choice you could have made. That's what I mean about you, Bess. You're too ignorant and trusting. That Sax boy is an Indian and once he got to you he'd hurt you, cheat on you, abuse you—God knows what all. I won't have that kind of life for you. It was a mistake to bring you here. I thought it could work, but you aren't happy and my own job here is not getting done."

She turned away, crying quietly. "And what is that job, Father?" she asked, weeping. "Hurting the Saxes? Killing Mister Sax? I don't understand ... how you can be this way."

"When you're older you will. You'll know the importance of money—and the worthlessness of Indians."

He kept writing then, saying nothing more. Bess just stared at him, amazed at his coldness, wondering at the way money could make a man change. Her mother would never put up with this. But she was a daughter and had no say. Tom! If only she could get to Tom! She'd never come back to this place and to this man who was like a stranger to her now. She broke into harder crying and Hafer gritted his teeth, wondering if he ought to just kill Caleb Sax outright. He had to consult Byron Clawson about all this right away.

Chapter **Thirteen**

It was December 28, 1833, when Lynda went into labor in the middle of the night. Eighteen hours later she still lay groaning in labor, her cries of agony mixed with weeping for Lee. Every time she sobbed his name, pain ripped through Caleb's heart. He kept watching the curtained doorway, where Lynda lay in his and Sarah's bed, Sarah and Ada Highwater helping with the birth.

Tom, who waited in the outer room with his father and young John, knew how difficult the situation was for Caleb, who spoke little while he paced nervously and smoked his pipe. Tom knew his pacing was not all because of Lynda. Caleb Sax wanted his water back. He had planned to ride directly to San Felipe to complain about what Hafer was doing, try to get something done legally before taking the law into his own hands.

But that would all have to wait now. He would not leave until Lynda delivered. He fumed over the fact that once he did go to town, he would have to spend money on feed. The good, green grass in Blue Valley was not going to last unless he got his water back. The river was too far away in that section to try digging canals like Hafer was doing, and the grass wasn't nearly good enough in any other section.

Tom sat by the fireplace, lost in his own thoughts, his fondest of which was the best way to kill Charles Hafer. Yet how could he bring harm to Bess's father? The whole situation seemed hopeless, and seeing Bess for that brief moment and then leaving had been torture for him.

"You gonna get the water back, Pa," John asked Caleb, interrupting the man's thoughts. The boy stood at the table cutting himself a piece of bread. Caleb took his pipe from his mouth.

"I will get it back, all right. I will try it the right way first, and if that doesn't work, I'll take every Cherokee settler on this place and all the men who work for me and get it back by force. I've got plenty of help if you count the Cherokee I have let settle on the southern range."

John grinned. "Can I go when you do?"

"I don't think so, John. It will be too dangerous."

Another groan came from the bedroom, followed quickly by another. "Push now," he heard Ada tell the girl.

The baby must be coming. Caleb waited nervously, watching little James crawl to John to be picked up, and then beg him for a piece of bread. James was six months old now, a fat, happy baby who showed little trace of Indian, nothing like Tom and John. John gave the boy a piece of bread and picked him up.

"You're getting heavy, little brother," the boy told him. "Hey, Pa, James is really growing."

Caleb nodded. Family. Another addition was coming. A grandchild. He and Sarah had a six-month-old child of their own, yet soon would have a grandchild. It didn't seem so long ago that he was only nine years old himself, wandering alone deep in the woods of the north.

Caleb was nine years old when Tom Sax found him and adopted him, teaching him the white man's ways. What a different world his Indian life had been.

Where were those Cheyenne now? They had been pushed westward by white settlement, but were still no doubt riding the plains where he had found them and lived with them after he left Fort Dearborn. They had played a significant part in the war against the British, with both British and American fur companies bribing the Indians to help them. The Cheyenne had been used then and would be used again, then cast aside the way Andrew Jackson was now doing to the Cherokee.

He heard a baby's cry and his heart swelled with pride. He looked at John, who grinned. Tom stood up, going to the curtained doorway. "What is it?" he asked anxiously.

"A boy," Sarah answered. Caleb could hear the joy in her voice and he smiled. "Just give us a minute," Sarah told them from behind the curtain.

They all waited anxiously, then heard weeping again. Caleb's heart filled with fear until Sarah came out with a smile on her face. "You are a grandfather, Caleb Sax. How about that for a man who had hardly any family at all a couple of years ago?"

Caleb frowned. "Why is she crying? Is the baby all right?"

"She's crying because she's wishing Lee could be here to see his son. He's beautiful, and strong. I think he's going to look just like Lee. She wants to see you first."

John wrinkled his nose. "I want to see it," he complained.

"You'll get your turn. Let your father go in first."

Caleb put his hands on her shoulders and bent down to kiss her cheek. "Thank you, Sarah."

Their eyes held. "Thank Ada. She helped Lynda most. Just remember when you go after Charles Hafer that you have a big family back here. Be careful, Caleb."

She saw the bitterness in his eyes at the mention of Hafer. "I'm always careful. He's the one who will have to be careful." He left her and went inside the bedroom, where Lynda lay cradling the baby beside her. Ada tucked blankets around her and moved toward the door.

"Not too long, Mister Sax. I have to come back in a while and check for more afterbirth. And she needs lots of rest now."

"I know. Thanks, Ada. You go get some rest yourself."

She smiled and left, and Caleb moved his eyes to meet Lynda's.

"Oh, Father, look at him! He'll look just like Lee."

The sight tore at the old wound of Lee's death. How he

wished Lee could be here for this. Lynda had had him for such a short time, suffered so much before finding her mother and then Lee. It wasn't fair.

He sat down carefully on the edge of the bed, studying the baby. "He's beautiful, Lynda. Lee would be proud."

"He *is* proud. He knows, Father. I'm sure of it."

Caleb nodded. "Yes. I think he does, too." He took her hand. "Does it help—having the baby?"

"Yes," she whispered. She sniffed and spoke louder. "I am going to name him Caleb, after his grandfather. Caleb Lee. We'll call him Cale, so you won't both come running every time I call for him."

Caleb frowned and looked away, squeezing her hand. "You sure you want to name him after me?"

"Of course I'm sure. Why shouldn't I? Don't you want me to?"

He turned and met her eyes. "Lynda . . ." He swallowed. "Now that the baby has come and we're over the risk of losing it . . ." He hesitated. "Damn," he whispered.

"Father, what is it?"

His eyes grew watery as they held her dark ones lovingly. "Lynda, I have to tell you something . . . you naming the boy after me and all . . ." He took a deep breath. "Maybe you won't want to do that when I've told you."

She smiled nervously. "Father, that's ridiculous. What on earth could change my mind?"

She saw the sudden anguish in her father's eyes and grew alarmed.

"Father, you can tell me. It's Lee, isn't it? There's something more to what happened to him."

Caleb closed his eyes and swallowed, squeezing her hand.

"I knew it. I knew by the look in your eyes when you first returned. Was he captured? Tortured?"

Caleb shook his head. "No." He met her eyes again. "Lynda, when we went after the Comanche, they didn't kill Lee . . . not outright."

She frowned. "What do you mean?"

"He was badly wounded, just the way we said—from a lance. He was dying. No one would have doubted that.

And we were right in their camp. We had to get out of there or all four of us would have been slaughtered. If I had thought he had a chance . . ." Her eyes widened and he kept hold of her hand. "He was dying, Lynda. He was in horrible pain, and he was dying," he stressed again. "If I had tried to carry his body, we never would have got away fast enough. He knew that. But he also knew there would be a worse horror for him if the Comanche discovered him before he was dead. I couldn't . . . I couldn't . . . leave him there . . . like that . . ." His voice choked. ". . . dying but . . . alive enough to be aware of what they might do to him." He kept squeezing her hand. "He begged me . . . to leave him there and get away . . . but not to . . . not to leave him there . . . alive."

He rose then, letting go of her hand and turning away. A tear slipped down his cheek, and he stood breathing deeply for self control, waiting for shouted words of hatred from his daughter.

"My God," she whispered. "You killed him. You killed Lee!"

He struggled to find his voice. "Quickly. It would have been crueler to let him die slowly . . . of the awful wounds he had . . . even if we could have got him out of there."

"Oh, Father." She almost groaned the words. "What a terrible thing for you to have to do. Why didn't you tell me before?"

He turned and looked at her in surprise. "I didn't want you to know he had been wounded first . . . that he had suffered. And I was afraid of what you would think of me if I told you I'm the one who actually ended his life."

"I know you well enough to know you must have done the right thing. You loved Lee like a son. You never would have done it if you thought there was a chance he could live. It must have been so terrible for you. It must haunt you in the night."

He held her eyes, astounded, then nodded. "I have killed so many men—in my war with the Crow, British soldiers, Comanche. I killed my first white man when I was only sixteen. But none of them haunted me like Lee does."

She studied her very Indian father, a man who could be

as vicious as any Comanche, a man who moved about with an animal grace but who could be so gentle, who inside was so good. This was the man for whom she had searched for so many years, the mysterious father who had left her the blue quill necklace. Now he was taking off the necklace. He untied the leather ties and loosened it, laying it beside her.

"This necklace helped you find your mother and me. I gave it to your mother all those years ago as a love gift. You brought it back to me—a daughter I never knew I had. You keep it now—my love gift to you and Cale. Give it to him when he's old enough to understand its meaning. It will bring him luck."

She touched the necklace, tears in her eyes. "But it's so important to you. Your Cheyenne mother gave it to you."

He bent over and took her hand. "I'm sure she meant for me to keep passing it on."

"Then you should give it to Tom."

Caleb shook his head. "No. I'm giving it to my first grandson. Tom would understand."

She held his eyes. "Will you teach Cale the Indian ways—teach him about the Cheyenne?"

He nodded. "I'll teach him. But he should learn about the Cherokee, too. His father was Cherokee."

Her eyes teared more. "I miss him so," she cried.

"I know. I know damned well how it feels, Lynda, and there isn't anything anyone can say to make it any better. Only time makes it better. Now you have Cale. And you always have us. You will be all right, Lynda. And someone will come along who will love you just as much as Lee did."

She managed a half smile. "You will be careful about Mister Hafer, won't you? I don't want anything to happen to you."

She saw the determination in his eyes. "Nothing is going to happen to your father, Lynda. Don't you worry about that. You just lie here and rest now. Tom and I are going into San Felipe to see the Council there. I might have to take this all the way to the *ayuntamiento* at San Antonio. We'll see. Otherwise there is only one way to settle the matter, and that's to ride over there and fill those canals and tear down the dam he built."

Their eyes held. Both knew what that would mean.

"What do you hear about Sam Houston?" Caleb asked Wil Handel, who accompanied him into San Felipe. Their breath made white vapors against the crisp December air. Their horses snorted thicker clouds of vapor as Tom and John rode thier own mounts next to Caleb and Handel.

"Ah, they say he has claimed some land over along the Trinity River. And he has set up a law practice." Handel laughed. "What good is a law practice if there are no laws but Mexican laws, I say."

Caleb grinned. "I met the man a few weeks ago. He is very sympathetic toward our problems with Mexico, and he is also very supportive of Indians who want to settle. He is going to try to form a militia, and thinks we'll need one before too long."

"He is probably right," the man said in his clipped manner of speaking.

"Maybe he can help me with my land dispute," Caleb told the man.

Handel shook his head. "Maybe. Maybe not. I think he is a pretty busy man with all these problems with Mexico. To you your problem is very great. To others—" He shrugged. "I am sorry to say I think you will have to settle that yourself, Caleb. Right now they will not think it is very important. If there is anything I can do, you come and tell me."

"Thank you, Wil. I'll do that."

They rode into town. Several Sax wagons lumbered behind Caleb to be used to carry bags of feed—feed he could not really afford but had to buy. Tom and John rode beside Caleb as they moved past the little cabin on the outskirts of town in which Emily lived. There would be no time for visiting today.

Caleb wondered if things were still all right. They rode past the blacksmith's, and Howard Cox stood outside. He waved. Caleb stopped a moment to talk to Howard, telling the man to say hello to Emily. Yes. Things were still all right.

Their backs were turned to the street as a fancy buggy clattered by. They drew up in front of the supply store. Wil said his farewells and rode on, but Tom's eyes had caught sight of the buggy. It looked familiar. He was sure it was Hafer's. His heartbeat quickened. Maybe Bess was in it. But there had been luggage tied to the back and a couple of men following behind. Why the luggage? Was Hafer making her go back to St. Louis?

"Father, I have some things to do myself. Can I leave for a while?"

Caleb frowned, looking around. He didn't see the buggy. "I suppose. I'm going to the Council while the men load up the wagons. Meet me back here in an hour or so."

The young man nodded and turned his horse, riding on down the street. Caleb frowned with a gnawing worry. Tom had said nothing earlier about having "other things" to do. But Caleb had too much on his mind to be concerned at the moment. He gave his men instructions and told John to stay with them, then headed for the building where American settlers took their complaints to their own appointed leaders. At one time that was Stephen Austin. But Austin still languished in prison in Mexico. Others had taken over for the time being.

Caleb approached the building and dismounted. The town seemed to be teeming with men he didn't even know. There was a time when he knew most people around here, a time when he was one of only a few. That had all changed. Apparently even a place as big as Texas could gradually fill with people, especially when whites smelled free land. He unbuttoned his heavy wolfskin jacket and walked inside, feeling the stares of a few who he knew were wondering why an Indian was here. He was finely tuned to such looks, knew the prejudiced ones in a moment. He walked through the door.

"We're gonna have to do somethin' about all the Indians comin' to Texas some day," a man outside said to another. "What do you figure him for? Cherokee?"

"Hell no. Cherokee dress different. He's almost too big

for any kind of full-blood Indian. Maybe he's a breed. Looks a little like Sioux or Cheyenne."

"Down here? Looks right civilized for any kind of Indian. Nice horse he rides."

"That's Caleb Sax," someone nearby spoke up. "He's been here since Austin first came. Owns a big spread north of here—raises those horses."

"Yeah?" The first man looked the horse over. "Wouldn't mind liftin' a few off him."

"I wouldn't try it," the third man told him. "He's not one to mess with. I hear tell he rode right into a Comanche camp to take back a son they'd stole. In my book, that's not the kind of man I'd want to go up against."

The first man backed off but put on a cocky smile. "Well, the day's gonna come when him *and* the Comanche is gonna have to leave. You'll see."

Piano music spilled from a nearby tavern and several men rode up then. "Where is it we go to claim our land?" one of them shouted.

The third man who had spoken nodded toward the door. "In there," he told them.

The men dismounted and laughed and pushed each other around as they went inside.

"Yeah," the man muttered to himself. "I don't expect the Indians *will* be here much longer."

Tom rode through the town, scanning both sides of the dirt street in which old ruts had hardened in the cold weather. He saw no sign of the carriage anywhere in town, and decided to try the docks along the river. If the luggage tied to the carriage meant what he thought it did, Charles Hafer was sending his daughter away. And most people heading East left this place by the river to the Gulf.

His suspicions proved to be right. His heart quickened when he spotted the carriage tied at the docks. He quickly dismounted, tying his horse out of sight and cautiously moving closer, scanning the several people who stood about until he spotted a young woman standing between two men.

There was no mistaking the slender form of Bess Hafer.

Her back was to him as all three of them looked out over the river, standing near a small, flat-bottomed steamboat used to carry passengers to the Gulf.

All his senses came alive. He couldn't let her leave! Surely seeing her, coming here the very day her father was sending her away, was a sign from God that he must not let her go. He looked carefully about for Charles Hafer but couldn't see him, then made his way even closer, wanting to call out to Bess but not daring to do it. He waited impatiently until finally she turned.

He could see as she looked around that she was hoping, searching desperately for help. Her father had probably watched her like a hawk to make sure she found no way to let him know she was leaving. Finally she spotted Tom, looking ready to cry out at the sight of him. Tom waved his arms and shook his head, signaling her to say nothing and putting fingers to his lips for silence. The men with her still watched the river and did not notice. Bess's eyes were wide with surprise as Tom pointed to the other side of the shacklike building that served as headquarters for the docks, then moved in that direction.

Bess quickly turned around, talking to the men casually for a few minutes, keeping their attention while Tom ducked around behind the building and waited, praying Bess could get away. Finally she appeared, walking along the dock as though taking in the sights, then turning and walking quickly to where Tom stood out of sight of the others.

"Tom!" She broke into tears and rushed to him, and he embraced her tightly.

"Tom, he's sending me back to St. Louis. I didn't know how to get a message to you. I was going to write you when I got to St. Louis. Oh, Tom, I don't want to go! Take me away with you."

He kissed her hair, on fire for her, wanting her more than ever. She couldn't go away! She couldn't!

He grasped her arms and gently pulled away. "Those men could come any minute."

"I told them I wanted to walk alone for a minute.

They're along for protection. They're supposed to accompany me all the way to St. Louis."

"Where's your father?"

"Right inside that building talking to the attendant," she said in a near whisper, indicating the very building behind which they stood.

"All right. You go back right away, and don't let them see you crying."

"What are you going to do?"

"You watch for me—all the way downriver. The boats always stop to let people off to relieve themselves. Be ready. That's when I'll come. Try to walk a little bit away from those men. Don't worry about your baggage or anything. I can get you new clothes. The important thing is to get away and get you to the ranch. I'll wait till the boat is several miles downstream so it will take a while to get the word back to your father. By that time we'll be married and there won't be anything he can do about it."

Her eyes widened. "Married!"

He frowned. "You *will* marry me, won't you?"

She gasped and smiled, hugging him again. "Oh, Tom, you know I will."

He kissed her cheek. "There's an old mission not far from where we live. I know the priest there. He'll marry us. Go on now. Get back there, and don't let on you're all excited, girl. You look too happy. You're supposed to be sad, remember?"

He gave her the smile that melted her and quickly kissed her lips lightly. "It will be all right," he told her. "You don't have to be a wife right away, Bess. I'll understand. We'll just get it legal on paper."

Her blood rushed with wanton desires, and her face turned crimson, yet her heart pounded with apprehension. She must trust him completely, and to actually let him make a woman of her frightened her, yet thrilled her at the same time. She had never felt so confused and had that confusion be so exciting. And she was sure by his tender, dark eyes that he truly wouldn't touch her if she wasn't ready.

"I'll be watching for you," she whispered. She darted

away then and he waited a moment before moving around the other side of the building, being careful again that no one who knew him saw him. He moved along with a crowd of newcomers then to his horse, mounting up and riding back to the supply store.

"You do what you have to do," a man in charge told Caleb. "Mister, we're so thick with new people claiming land and all this business with the Mexicans and trying to raise an army that we don't have time for a neighborly fight over water."

"There could be violence. I intend to get my water back," Caleb warned. "I want it known that I came here for help the legal way first. Some men might get killed and I don't intend to hang for it or for one of my men to."

The man leaned back, scanning Caleb. "You're a big landowner, one of the first settlers here. I'd say you're free to do as you wish."

"I am also Indian. That's getting to be an issue around here."

"Not as far as I'm concerned. I've got nothing against the settled ones. We run things here the way Mister Austin would want them run, not the newcomers." The man studied a map, then opened a book that had names written in it. "What I don't understand is why this Hafer is giving you trouble, Mister Sax. It isn't even his land."

Caleb frowned. "What are you talking about?"

"Didn't he tell you he's settling it for some big investor in St. Louis?"

Caleb was fully alert. "He doesn't own it himself?"

"No. It belongs to . . . uh . . . Clawson. A Byron Clawson. Says here he's some banker from St. Louis."

Every nerve end came alive in Caleb Sax. Byron Clawson! He should have known; when for that one brief moment weeks ago Clawson had come to mind, Caleb should have come to town right then to check it out. It all made so much sense now! It was all he needed to know, the final blow. Hafer would pay for this! And Byron Clawson's fears of Caleb Sax would be strongly reawakened.

"Thank you," he said aloud, his eyes shining with revenge. "I'm free then to settle this any way I can?"

The man closed the book. "Sax, this is still a relatively lawless land. We sure don't have enough militia men to do anything about it, nor any specific laws to cover it. Until Texas is more settled and civilized, men are still going to have to make their own laws and settle their own disputes."

"You record it in that ledger you keep. Write down that I was here for help, and sign it."

The man sighed impatiently. "You can count on my word, Sax."

"Maybe so. Maybe not. I know the sentiment that's building around here against Indians. I want my visit and my request in writing. And put your name on a piece of paper and give it to me so I'll remember it if I ever need a witness."

The man shook his head and began writing the visit into his ledger, then handed Caleb the piece of paper.

Caleb nodded. "Thanks for your time." He quickly left.

Byron Clawson! His mind reeled with the meaning of it. The thought of what the man was up to made Caleb more determined to find a way to kill him some day. So, after all these years, Clawson was still trying to do him in, only in a cowardly, subtle way. That was like Clawson. He would make the man shake in his shoes. He would destroy Charles Hafer, and Clawson would find out about it and know he was a marked man.

He eased up onto his horse and rode to the supply store, where John waited for him. "Tom was here, Pa." The boy took Caleb's reins and tied them to a hitching post. "He said to tell you he has something to do and might be gone a few days and not to worry about him. He'll talk to you when he gets back."

Caleb's heart tightened with alarm. He dismounted and looked around the crowded street, seeing no sign of his eldest son. He turned back to John.

"How long ago was this?"

The boy shrugged. "About twenty minutes ago, I guess."

"Did he look upset, like something was wrong?"

John pursed his lips. "Nope. He acted kind of happy and excited."

All of Caleb's instincts were alert. It all rang of Bess Hafer. "Damn," he muttered. "Which way did he head?"

John pointed down the street toward the docks. "He said to please trust him and just wait till he comes home."

Caleb was tempted to ride to the docks, but just then Jake Highwater came out with a problem about the feed.

"We can't get all we need, Caleb. Not enough," the man told him.

Caleb tore his thoughts from Tom. "Not enough? Or is it just that we're Indians."

"My guess is the last, but what can we do?"

"We'll take what we can get, and then we're going to pay Charles Hafer a visit," Caleb answered.

The man grinned. "Right. We're all ready when you are."

"Help load the feed, John," he told the boy.

"Yes, sir." John obeyed immediately. He was a good son, always eager to please.

Caleb turned to watch for Tom again, but the young man was nowhere to be seen.

Chapter Fourteen

Tom followed the river, keeping to rough brush and stands of cottonwood and mesquite whenever possible, holding far back from the flatboat when the land cleared. She was on that boat. That he knew for certain, for he'd watched her father hug her and bid her farewell at the docks. That was yesterday. In order to keep up with the boat, he had ridden all night. He only hoped his horse would have enough energy left to run when the time was right.

There were moments when he wondered if he and Bess were both crazy. They still knew very little about each other, and yet Tom felt he knew her so well. That was the kind of woman she was. She exuded goodness, and he could see beyond her youthful fears and excitedness enough to know she would be a good, strong woman some day.

His heart pounded with anticipation. He would make her his wife and that was that. Both their fathers would be upset. It didn't matter. It would surely cause his own father problems, but Caleb understood. He had been through this himself. At least Bess would belong to Tom legally and no one could take her away. He would not touch her, if she wasn't ready. Just to know she was his and they could stay together was all that mattered. He wanted Bess Hafer and he was going to have her.

He rode for several more miles before he decided it was time to make his move. There were enough miles now between the boat and Charles Hafer. He waited until the boat finally clanged its bell, slowing to let people off to tend to personal needs. Tom nudged his horse to move a little faster, heading for a stand of cottonwoods closer to the boat where it had finally pulled up next to the river-bank. Several people moved about on board. It looked as though Bess and one other woman were the only females. The two men who had originally been with Bess walked behind her along a plank to shore, followed by several other passengers.

Bess headed for some bushes, turning to the men and saying something to them in an irritated voice. Tom knew she was telling them she didn't need them to follow her all the way behind the bushes to watch her lift her skirts. He dismounted, leaving his horse in the stand of trees. He crept closer, watching her kneel behind the bushes but not relieve herself. She was waiting, hoping Tom would come this time. Tom waited while the two men took care of themselves, then headed back to the boat.

"Let's go, Miss Hafer."

"I'm going to need longer," she answered. "Please give me some privacy. Go back on the boat. I'll be along."

The two men looked at each other and shrugged. "You call out if you have a problem," one of them answered. They shook their heads and headed back for the boat. Tom waited until they were on board, then darted closer.

"Bess," he said in a loud whisper.

She turned and smiled with delight. He held out his hand and she ran to him.

"Come on," he told her. "My horse is nearby. They can't catch us. They have no horses."

He pulled her along to his mount, lifting her onto it.

Someone had spotted them.

"Hey!" It was a man's voice, probably one of her guards. There was no time to turn and see. Tom leaped onto the horse in front of Bess.

"Hang on," he told her, kicking the animal into a dead gallop.

"Hey! Come back here!"

Shots were fired into the air.

"My God, an Indian rode off with that girl," someone yelled.

"Oh, no," a woman wailed. "The poor child has been kidnapped by a Comanche!"

"That wasn't any Comanche," one of her guards muttered. Tom and Bess were already out of sight. "There's no Comanche this far east! If my guess is right, that was that son-of-a-bitchin' son of Caleb Sax." He looked at his partner.

"Jesus," the man answered. "We're in a lot of god-damned trouble."

The first man sighed. "We gotta go tell Hafer. He'll want to get her back."

"We'll lose our jobs."

"Let's hope that's all we lose." The man turned to the boat's captain. "How close is the next settlement?" he shouted. "We've got to get some horses and get back to Mister Hafer."

"About another hour, mister."

"Well get this thing moving!"

The captain nodded, and the small boat started off down the river.

They rode hard for a few miles, until Tom was sure they were safely away from anyone who might try to stop them. He slowed his horse, realizing that if he kept up the pace he'd kill the animal. He would be in enough trouble with his father without overworking one of his best mounts. He slowed the gelding to a walk to let him cool down a little before halting him completely.

"You all right?" he asked Bess.

"I think so." Her own heart pounded, not so much with the daring thing they had just done, but also because she was entirely alone now with this young Indian man who intended to marry her. She had trusted him. But truly being alone with him was a little frightening, until he stopped the horse and threw his leg over in front of him, sliding down. He reached up for her then.

"We'll rest," he told her.

Their eyes held a moment.

"It's all right, Bess," he told her. "Don't be afraid of me. You don't even have to marry me if you don't want. I'll just take you back to our ranch and we'll keep you there."

She leaned down and he grasped her about the waist, lifting her down with strong arms. "I'm so nervous," she admitted.

He smiled, a warm, understanding smile that took away some of her fear. "Hey, we are not going to do anything you don't want to do. Now, you tell me, do you want to go to the ranch, or to the mission?"

She studied the handsome face. He had just risked his life for her, and it was not over yet. Surely he knew how angry her father would be. But he didn't seem to care. Surely he did love her and was most wonderful and brave to do what he had just done. She swallowed.

"Do you love me, Tom?"

He sobered, studying her with dark eyes of passion. "How can you ask that after what I just did? Yes. I love you. It sounds crazy, I know. It's so soon But I love you." He put a hand to the side of her face. "And I want you." He bent down, meeting her mouth gently, sending shivers of desire through her innocent body. Oh, yes, he loved her, and he would be gentle with her. He drew back, holding her eyes. "Don't be afraid of me, Bess. I won't hurt you. I want to take care of you for the rest of my life. I want you to live with me, be my wife. But only when you're ready. You decide."

She trembled with the excitement of what it all meant. And yet it seemed so right to want to let this man have his way with her, to enjoy her. She wanted to please him, to show him she was a woman. She had been so lonely, and he was beautiful, and strong. She never dreamed anyone could cause her to defy her own father so blatantly. But the deed was done. Her father would never forgive her now. There was no going back.

"I want to get married," she told him. "I truly do—right away—so Father can't take me away from you. But . . . it scares me a little."

He smoothed back her hair. "We will do only what you want to do. You will be my wife. Whether you are my wife physically doesn't matter. We don't have to tell anyone that we have not been one. Let them think it. That's all that matters."

The wonderful desires rippled through her again. She wanted him so. It was a strange sort of fear, an excited, almost wonderful fear. She nodded. "Let's get married then."

He smiled, then hugged her tightly, whirling her around in his arms. "I love you, Bess Hafer. Soon you will be Elizabeth Sax."

She smiled, hugging him tightly around the neck, catching his long, dark hair in her arms. He lowered her slightly until their faces were close. They kissed again, her breasts pressed tightly against him. "I love you, too," she told him. "I love you, Tom Sax."

* * *

They rode the rest of the day. Bess felt free and alive again, happy for the first time in months, except for the stabbing pain of knowing she was defying her father, and at the realization that her father was so different now from what he once was. Things would never be the same between them again, but that couldn't be helped. She couldn't bear the thought of going back to St. Louis and never seeing Tom Sax again.

They had to make camp for the night. It was over a day's ride to the mission, and it had already been afternoon when Tom rode off with her. Bess was losing all her apprehensiveness. When they stopped to relieve themselves, he never came near her. And that night he slept beside her, his arms around her to keep her warm. Yet he never touched her rudely or suggested they do something they shouldn't. It was as though he understood she would have to be his wife first, respected her for it.

In the morning they were off again, and by the next afternoon they reached the mission. The old priest there, Father Raphael, married them quickly out of the kindness of his heart. He was an old man who knew the Sax family well, and although he suspected parental approval had not been given, he saw the deep love in their eyes, and felt their eagerness. Better to legalize that which they were going to do anyway, than to let them fall into sin. He blessed them several times over, telling them he would pray there would be no trouble for them.

Father Raphael made the ceremony lovely. A nun helped Bess bathe first and gave her a pretty white robe to wear, promising to wash the clothes she had worn on the long, dusty ride. She brushed her hair out long and put flowers in it from indoor pots that were kept alive at the mission in winter, tended to by the nuns.

When Tom saw Bess then his blood surged hot. She was beautiful, and all in white, just as she should be. He had bathed himself and wore clean pants and a shirt, wishing he had taken the white buckskins along that his father had given him. They were made of beautifully bleached doeskin with a splendid Indian design woven from beads right into the garment. It was a stunning set of Indian clothing, given to Caleb by the Cheyenne, passed on to Tom. He had always planned on wearing the clothes for a very special occasion, such as his marriage, but this had all happened so fast. He was not prepared, nor was he prepared for the way Bess looked now, a vision of innocence and beauty.

She stood beside him, and they said their vows with enthusiastic sincerity. Soon it was over, and Tom thanked Father Raphael.

"You must stay the night here," the priest told them. "It is too late to try to leave tonight, too dangerous to be out there alone. There is a room at the back of the mission; a small one, but it has a bed and a fireplace. You are welcome to stay there."

Tom put an arm around Bess's waist. "Thank you, Father. We might stay an extra day or so. We have to stay in hiding for a while. If you could keep my horse out of sight, I would be most grateful. Don't tell anyone you've seen us."

"Of course not. Come." The old man led them down a long, dark hallway and opened a heavy oak door into a small room where a fire was already burning. Fresh biscuits sat on the table and a pot of coffee hung over the fire, as well as a deep kettle of stew. A wooden cabinet held a washbasin and a pitcher of water, as well as some towels and soap, and in a corner behind a curtain was a chamber pot.

"There. You see? The nuns have provided everything you need. They are excited about the young newlyweds." The priest eagerly led them inside. "No one will disturb you and we will tell no one that you are here." He put his hand on Tom's arm and held his eyes. "Be good to her, son. She is hardly more than a child."

Tom nodded. "I love her, Father. I won't hurt her."

The old man smiled and nodded, taking Bess's hand and patting it before leaving. Bess's face was crimson with the realization of what they had been talking about. She watched the door close and suddenly felt weak. It had all happened so quickly. She was Mrs. Tom Sax. She liked the sound of it, but felt almost faint from nervous anticipation.

Tom seemed calm and sure as he walked over to the pot of stew and sniffed it.

"This was very nice of them." He looked at her. "You hungry? We haven't eaten since this morning."

She stood rigid and shook her head. "No," she said quietly. "I don't think I could eat right now."

He smiled. "Hey, there is no reason to be afraid." He walked over to her, taking her arm and leading her to the bed. "You look ready to pass out." He knelt in front of her and took her hands. "You are going to eat whether you want to or not, and then you are going to sleep. Surely the night before last, when you knew you were going away, you didn't sleep well. Last night we slept little, and that was on the cold ground. You'll be sick. Now sit right there and I'll get you a dish of that stew and a biscuit."

She watched him with wide eyes as he did just that and insisted she eat. She managed to swallow some of it and chew the biscuit, as well as drink some coffee. He pulled back the covers of the bed then. "Get in," he told her. "Get some sleep. I don't want my new wife getting sick." He began unbuttoning her shoes.

Her eyes brimmed with tears then. "I'm sorry, Tom. I'm a terrible wife, aren't I? This isn't what you wanted."

He smiled resignedly. "If you had come at me like a wanton woman, I would have been disappointed. That isn't my Bess." He pulled off her shoes. "Go on, now, get some sleep."

She wiped tears. "Are you sure?"

He leaned forward and kissed her cheek. "I'm sure."

"What will you do?"

"Eat, and sleep."

"Where?"

He laughed lightly. "Right beside you in that bed, that's where." He kissed the other cheek. "Don't worry. I am just as tired as you are. You won't be disturbed. I at least deserve to get to sleep beside you, don't I?"

She smiled through her tears and nodded. She suddenly hugged him then. "Thank you, Tom. I love you so."

He patted her back, feeling already the pain of abstinence. She turned and moved under the blankets, curling up into the pillow and letting him tuck the blankets around her still-clothed body. He quietly got his own food and ate, sitting down in a chair and watching her. In moments she was fast asleep.

Tom finished his meal and stood up, watching her sleep for several minutes, studying her beauty; the long, thick, auburn hair, and the fine bones of her face. He longed to do with her the things he had done with Rosy, explore every part of her, claim every inch of her, invade her, possess her. But he had to be patient. He began removing his clothes then, stripping down to the nude. He always slept that way. It was the first step. She might as well get used to it.

He crawled in beside her, pulling the covers over him and pulling her close. She slept so soundly she didn't even realize what he was doing. He nestled his face into the thick hair, smelling its sweet scent, and fell asleep wondering how long it would take Hafer to find out his daughter had ridden off with an Indian. It wouldn't take the man long to figure out who the Indian was.

Tom only hoped his own father wouldn't be too angry for doing this without consulting him first. Caleb was probably wondering right now what had happened to him. But a messenger had been sent right away and should reach his father by morning with the letter letting Caleb know he had married Charles Hafer's daughter.

Caleb gathered his men. Two full days had passed since the day he'd left town without Tom and his son had still not returned home. Something was wrong. He would check things out at San Felipe first, then ride directly to Hafer's if Tom was not there. If anything had happened to him, the first place to look was Charles Hafer's ranch. Sarah came out the door, Lynda behind her, holding her new baby. None of them thought she should be up walking around, but she was worried about her brother and couldn't lie still.

"Caleb, be careful," Sarah called out to him as he mounted his horse.

"Father, he told you he had something to do. Maybe he's all right."

"He's never done this before," Caleb answered. "Something is wrong."

John rode up beside him. "I'm going, too, Pa. He helped find me. Now I'll help find him."

"You stick close to me and do what I tell you," Caleb told the boy.

"I will, Pa."

They both hesitated. Jake Highwater came riding hard toward them. "A rider is coming, Caleb," he called out, while still at a distance.

"Who is it?"

"Don't know. Looks like an Apache Indian."

Caleb frowned, looking at Sarah. "You and Lynda had better get inside. It's too cold out here. I'll be right back."

He turned his horse and rode out to meet the intruder, too anxious to wait for the man to reach the house. John and Jake rode beside him and the women waited at the house, watching out a window as the men met far in the distance.

Caleb jerked his mount to a halt in front of the stranger, who had already been surrounded by more Sax men.

"He says he has a message for you, Mister Sax," one of them said.

"Message—just for Caleb Sax," the Indian told Caleb.

Caleb studied him warily. "Who are you?"

"Fast Wolf. I am Christian now," the man said with a grin that showed two teeth missing. "Be good Indian now —help Father Raphael at the St. Matthew mission. He gives me written message for Caleb Sax; say I give only to him."

Caleb frowned. "Father Raphael?"

The man nodded.

The mission! Was Tom hurt? "I'm Caleb Sax," he told the Apache. "You can give me the message."

The man handed the piece of paper to Caleb. "You are welcome to come to the house for something hot to eat and drink before you go back, Fast Wolf," Caleb told the man.

Fast Wolf nodded. "Fast Wolf is grateful. What Indian are you, Caleb Sax?"

"Half Cheyenne," Caleb answered, opening the note.

"Cheyenne—they are good horse Indians. But your eyes. They are not Indian."

Caleb was reading the note and didn't answer. He felt his blood chill at the words.

> *"Father. Forgive me, but I could tell no one. I have married Bess. Her father was sending her away. I couldn't let her go. I took her from the boat and came to the mission, where Father Raphael married us. Bess must rest for a couple of days. It has all been hard on her, but she loves me and I love her. I couldn't let her get away from me. We will be home soon and explain more. Please welcome her. She has been through so much and needs your friendship. I know there will be trouble. Now you will be ready for it. I'm sorry. Love, Tom."*

"Jesus Christ," Caleb muttered. He refolded the note and put it in his pocket.

"Is Tom all right, Caleb?" Jake asked.

Caleb paled, then smiled sarcastically. "He's fine—having a good time, in fact, breaking in a new wife."

"Wife! Tom? But who—"

"Elizabeth Hafer," Caleb finished.

Jake's eyes widened. "Miss Hafer?" He shook his head and pushed back his hat. "That's going to be big trouble, Caleb. What about the water?"

Caleb looked northward toward Blue Valley. "We are still going to raid those canals and get rid of them. We have enough men," he answered. "We'll wait until Tom gets here."

"My brother is married?" John asked in surprise.

Caleb rubbed his eyes. "Yes, son, I'm afraid so. I can't fully blame him. But there is going to be big trouble over this one." He looked at Fast Wolf. "How long has my son been there?"

"Come yesterday."

Caleb nodded. "Yesterday then." He turned his horse. "Come on," he told Jake and the others. "I'm not quite certain how to break this to Sarah." He rode back toward the house and the others followed, including Fast Wolf.

Caleb was lost in thought, both glad and angry with Tom. He had been all set to raid the Hafer ranch. This only made it all the more dangerous. And the danger would upset Sarah. He hadn't even told her about Byron Clawson owning the Hafer land. He wanted to put off her knowledge of that for as long as possible. He always hated bringing up that man's name to her.

He told himself he had no call to be angry with Tom. Caleb had to remember what it was like for him and Sarah: how he felt, how he'd tried to run away with her in spite of her father's protests. The only thing he could do now was make sure none of the terrible things that had happened to them would happen to Tom and Bess. His heart tightened with the awful fear of losing his son. Hafer would be after Tom's hide now. He had to protect him.

Tom and Bess spent the day walking in the crisp air around the ancient stone porticoes of the mission, sometimes sitting inside the large sanctuary, talking quietly in the high-ceilinged, echoey chamber painted with Biblical scenery. It seemed as though they were the only two people in the world. Bess was never more sure who she loved. They had slept the night together and he hadn't touched her, even though he lay naked beside her. She awoke to find him still asleep but with the covers thrown off, and he was beautiful and intriguing in his raw splendor. Yet it had been frightening also, until he awoke and pulled on his long underwear.

Somehow Tom knew her every instinct, her fears, her anticipation. He knew she had to talk, and he wanted the same—to get to know better this young woman who was his wife. When they walked outside the next day she cried about her dead mother, and about the whole mess over her brother's death. He held and comforted her. He revealed to her his longing to have known his own Cheyenne mother and reminded her she was lucky to at least have known her own mother. She told him about the farm and her friends back in Missouri. He talked of boyhood days, of growing up in Texas with a father with whom he was very close, raised by a Cherokee woman who died in an outlaw raid. He told of his father's great agony during those dark times, for he had also lost a son. And he told her again of how Sarah and Lynda had found them, of the reunion between his father and Sarah. He expressed his love of Texas, where he had lived most of his life. She talked of her fear of war with Mexico and her fear he would have to go to war himself.

"We won't think about that now," Tom told her. "We'll just think about us."

There had been the kiss then, the beautiful kiss, the daring but gentle fondling of her breasts through her dress, the marvelous joy of realizing she liked it. It was easy to let him touch her. Her skin was suddenly on fire and she nestled her face against his neck.

"Take me back to our room," she whispered.

He said nothing. He stood up and picked her up in his arms and carried her there, kicking shut the door and capturing her mouth with his own as he laid her on the bed. What fears she had left were kissed away, shoved aside with gentle words of love, rubbed away by his expert touch in all the right places. Her clothes were coming off and she did not resist. His movements were deliberate, his attitude gentle but demanding in the sense that he knew what he was doing and she should relax and let him show her the path to ecstasy.

Then they were lying naked together. The room swirled around her, and she was enveloped with a dark-skinned, muscular body, dark eyes, long dark hair that fell into her own auburn hair. She shuddered with the thrill of feeling his lips move down, caressing her neck, her shoulders, tasting her breasts with a gentle sucking that made her feel wild and free, made her want to abandon all inhibitions and give herself to him.

Surely it was not wrong. This was her friend, now her husband. He had a right to take his pleasure in her, but never did she dream that by giving him that pleasure she could receive so much pleasure in return. Nor did she imagine she could ever be so bold for any man, allowing him to kiss, taste, touch, explore with such intimacy, until suddenly her insides rippled with the most wonderful pulsations, making her cry out his name and arch up to his lovemaking.

"Don't be afraid if it hurts," he told her gently, moving his lips to her cheek then, sliding his body over her own, pushing his knees between her legs. "They say it almost always hurts the first time. But it will get better, Bess. I promise it will get better."

It didn't matter. There had to be a first time if there were going to be the more pleasurable times. She closed her eyes and the pain hit her hard, surging into her belly and making her cry out in surprise. He held her tightly, moved rhythmically even though he felt her stiffen. It had to be done. There was no going back for him. But she was so beautiful and he loved her so much that it didn't take him long to spill his life into her and have it over with. He wanted this first time to be quick.

He relaxed on top of her then, shuddering with the total ecstasy of finally having been one with Bess Hafer—no, Bess Sax. That was her name now. And if they made love together often enough, there would soon be a little Sax, a child of his own. He kissed her eyes, her cheeks, her mouth, her hair, his heart aching for her quiet tears of pain and surprise.

"I'm sorry, Bess, if I hurt you." He raised up slightly. "Are you all right?"

She sniffed and managed a smile. "You said it gets better. I believe you."

"I'll see if maybe we can get a tub in here and some hot water. Maybe you'd feel better if you sat in a nice hot bath for a while. Would you like that?"

She smiled, but more tears spilled from her eyes. She hugged him tightly around the neck. "Oh, Tom, thank you for being so good, for not being mean to me on our wedding night."

He pulled the covers over them and held her tightly. "How can I be mean to the woman I love?" He ran a hand over her bottom. "Thank you, Bess, for letting me have you. You could have waited longer. I would have understood."

"No," she whispered. "I started thinking about my father, and I got scared." She clung to him. "It's like there's so little time. I'm so scared he'll do something terrible to take me away from you."

"Don't you worry about that. Everything is going to be all right, Bess Sax. You'll see."

He lay there holding her for several minutes, deciding not to voice his own concerns about Charles Hafer. They would enjoy this short respite from the outer world. The time would come soon enough when they would have to face the consequences of what they had done. But he didn't want to yet. It was so beautiful and peaceful at the mission. They would stay a few more days. They would enjoy their new-found love and share that love through their bodies many times over before leaving this sanctuary to face the real world.

Chapter Fifteen

Sarah covered the fresh-baked bread and removed her apron. James slept soundly, and John had chosen to sleep in the bunkhouse with the men that night, as he was often doing lately, thinking himself quite grown up now and enjoying the "man talk." Caleb let him go, understanding that the boy also liked talking to the Cherokee men and learning about his own roots on his mother's side.

Caleb sat near the fireplace, brooding over Tom's marriage and the complications that would arise from it. Sarah walked over to where he sat, kneeling in front of him.

"Lynda will sleep at her own place tonight." She looked up at him. "We're alone, and James is sleeping so well."

He frowned teasingly. "Is all that supposed to mean something?"

She blushed. He loved the way she blushed, as though she were seventeen again. "Caleb Sax, you know what I mean."

He smiled, touching her cheek with the back of his hand. He had to tell her about Byron Clawson owning that land. He had put it off long enough. But he would not spoil the moment. "Something you want?"

She lay her head in his lap. "You know what I want. I was just thinking about Tom and Bess. It reminds me so much of when you and I ran off together. I'm so glad they were able to actually marry and nothing went wrong. I just hope Charles Hafer doesn't do anything drastic to spoil it for them. Oh, Caleb, I don't want them to suffer like we did."

He sighed, undoing the pins in her hair that held its long tresses into a neat bun. "They won't suffer. I won't let them. That is part of the reason I'm not going after them right away, now that I know they're all right. We might as well give them some time alone." He set the combs and pins aside, ruffling his hands through her hair with his hands and shaking it out, enjoying its soft thickness. "Does it bother you a lot, Sarah, that we never found a preacher, that we never married before we were found?"

She looked up at him in surprise. "Oh, no, Caleb, I didn't mean it that way! Neither of us could help how it happened. Besides, we . . . when we stayed in that cave together . . . we were as much as married in our hearts. I always thought of it that way. We weren't married only a year and a half ago, Caleb. We were married nineteen years ago . . . in that cave." She reached up and touched the scarred cheek. "Tom and Bess make it all come back so clearly, Caleb."

He took her hand and kissed her fingers, then rose with her, putting an arm around her waist and walking with her into the bedroom. "Far be it from me to let this mood of yours slip by. I never argue with a beautiful woman who wants to make love," he teased, turning her and unhooking the back of her dress.

"And how many have there been?" she quipped.

"Oh, dozens. You know how Texas abounds with beautiful, delicate belles." He laughed lightly, pulling the dress over her shoulders. "Actually, you're the one to be watched. The shortage of females in this land makes you pretty damned valuable."

"Oh, there are a lot of women here now."

He turned her, looking down at her full breasts as the dress fell to her waist. "Not women who look like you."

She felt her cheeks flush, and her nipples peaked under his gaze. She smiled bashfully and looked down, pulling her dress the rest of the way off. "Well there aren't many men who look like you, either. It can go both ways. Don't think I didn't notice how some of those women looked at you the day of that barn raising. They might gossip about you being Indian, but I'm a woman and I can read other women's eyes. They were saying one thing but thinking another. I felt their envy, and I loved every minute of it."

Caleb chuckled and began removing his own clothes. "You're in a humorous mood tonight, considering the gravity of the situation with Tom and Bess."

The lamp in the bedroom was dimly lit, and excitement surged through him as she removed the rest of her clothes and quickly got under the covers. He removed the rest of his own clothes and joined her.

"But they have us, Caleb. It's different for them. We didn't have anybody to help us."

She snuggled closer and he moved on top of her, resting on his elbows. "True. But you're right. It does remind me of you and me." His eyes glittered with love. "And you don't look one bit different than you did that first time I made you my woman."

She smiled, touching his dark hair. Perhaps their love was made more intense by the fact that they had been such good friends before ever becoming lovers. For so long they were brother and sister, yet both had sensed something more the day Sarah had to be sent away from Fort Dearborn. Now, in mid-life, that love and the sexual attraction were enhanced by years of struggle that brought a wisdom and satisfaction not enjoyed by younger lovers. Their love seemed to grow more intense with age.

"I've been thinking about this all day," she said quietly.

His eyebrows arched. "What kind of wanton woman have I married?"

She ran her hands over his muscular shoulders. "The most wicked, shameless kind there is."

He sighed deeply. "Well, I suppose I have to oblige you. You're taking advantage of my manly weaknesses tonight, woman. I'm tired."

"Oh, I think you have enough energy left to satisfy your woman's needs. You can draw on that inner strength of yours that helps you force yourself to do the impossible."

He grinned, meeting her lips. That was all it took, for the memory of those days of youth, those magical moments they spent together in a cave and discovered one another sexually, was vivid for both of them tonight. A passion not unlike the passion they shared then surged through both of them, so that their breathing quickened, their kisses hard and searching. Her legs parted, and he entered her quickly, discovering that already her satiny juices of desire were flowing full force, welcoming him inside with soft caresses. He felt on fire for her. He pushed with a sudden possessiveness, remembering those days, remembering how he had so quickly lost her again. He would not lose her this time.

"I love you so much, Sarah," he groaned. She felt him moving in circular motions inside of her, bringing out the boldness she saved only for him, a desire she had never had for anyone else. She arched up and moved with him, so beautifully and so passionately that he had difficulty holding himself back so that she could enjoy the moment as long as possible.

He felt the glorious pulsations of her climax and raised to his knees, grasping her bottom and burying himself in the magical depths of her. He made sure she enjoyed every bit of him, taking his own pleasure in return and holding out for several more minutes until release was impossible to contain. His life surged into her in hard throbs that made her cry out his name. Even when he was through there was a certain pleasure remaining inside of her, and he lay down on top of her again, holding his weight off her by resting on his elbows, kissing her tenderly about the face for several seconds before finally pulling away from her.

He pulled the covers over them and lay there for several quiet minutes. Sarah sighed deeply.

"I don't know why, but I just . . . I need you more than usual tonight," she told him then. She faced him in the dim light of the lamp. "It isn't just Tom and Bess, Caleb. It's something else—an urgent feeling. I think it's partly from a sense that something more is wrong than Tom and Bess. You've had something on your mind ever since you came back from San Felipe."

He raised up, resting his head on his hand and frowning down at her. "You're too damned smart, you know that?"

"What is it, Caleb?"

He sighed, lying back down and pulling her close. "The trouble with a really good woman who is smart besides, is that a man can't hide one damned thing from her."

"And usually when you're hiding something it's because you're trying to protect me from something. I'm a big girl, Caleb. You can tell me."

He lay there saying nothing for several long seconds, then held her even tighter. "Promise me you won't worry. Believe me, there's nothing to worry about this time. I'm in my own territory and things are completely different now. I've got plenty of help and I am now a much wiser man than I was years ago."

She frowned. "What on earth are you talking about?"

He sighed deeply. God how he hated to tell her. But she had to know. "I discovered something when I was in town at the Council the other day, Sarah. I went to report the trouble with Hafer, like I told you. But I found out—" He swallowed, keeping a firm hold on her. "I found out he doesn't really own that land. He's a front man for someone in St. Louis who's backing the whole thing—paying him off to give me trouble."

She lay there several seconds saying nothing, as though mulling it all over in her mind. "Oh, my God," she suddenly whimpered. "Byron! It's Byron, isn't it?"

He hugged her tightly, kissing her hair. "Yes."

"Oh, Caleb, he's doing it again."

"Stop it, Sarah," he said sternly. "There isn't anything for you to be fretting about, you hear me? That man can't do a thing to us here. He'll find that out when I'm through with Hafer. You told me yourself the man is terrified I'll come after him. This must be his way of trying to make sure I don't do that. But it won't work, and when I'm through with Hafer, Byron Clawson will have a lot of sleepless nights."

She broke into furious tears. "Damn him! Damn him!" Her fists clenched and she began to shake. She always did when she got extremely upset, a lingering ailment from the drugs Clawson had fed her after she gave birth to Lynda, drugs that had left her a vegetable for nearly three years after.

Caleb jerked her closer, holding her tightly against the shaking. "You listen to me, Sarah Sax. You are here in Texas with me, right in bed with your husband. We have our daughter, and our new son is sleeping right here in this room with us. Byron Clawson can't reach us here, and even if he tries, he is playing a whole different game now—a very dangerous one. You're my wife, and I'm ordering you not to give it another thought. I mean that. If you let this get you down, I will be all-out angry with you, and very disappointed in your lack of trust in me."

"You know . . . I trust you," she sniffed.

"Then trust me when I tell you I don't want you worrying about this. It's good that I found out. That makes everything very clear for me now. I know what I'm fighting; I understand Hafer's motives. That makes all the difference in fighting him, Sarah. And you know Byron Clawson is going to stay right there in his safe little office in St. Louis, well away from Caleb Sax. I'm a far different man from the one he shot down all those years ago. The next time he and I meet, it's going to be a whole different story."

"But you'll get hung."

"Oh, no I won't. I'm a lot wiser now and a lot more powerful." He kissed her hair. "I want you just the way you were before I told you, Sarah. I'm sorry I had to tell you, but it needed telling. It's done now and it's good that you know. But you are a lot stronger yourself now. That man can't hurt you anymore, Sarah. You just be the strong, courageous woman you've become since you came back to me. Don't you dare let that bastard make you crumble again. You're made of better stuff than that. And don't you let him come between us again."

She wiped tears with shaking hands and turned to face him. "How could he come between us?"

"In spirit. Don't let that happen, Sarah. Don't go back to being the frightened woman he tried to make you into. You're proud and strong and beautiful, and you have to trust in my own strength and abilities. You're here with Caleb Sax. That's all that matters. Put Byron Clawson out of your mind. You've spent years struggling to get over what he did to you. Don't let it all come pouring back in on you." He kissed her tears.

The thought of Byron touching her brought on a feeling of fierce possessiveness, and he felt a renewed need growing: to prove to Sarah and to himself who she really belonged to, and to erase all the ugly things Byron Clawson had done to her.

He met her lips then, almost savagely, and she returned the kiss with the same passion, her own sexual arousal still alive, her body still warm, secret places still moist and ready.

He never left her lips as he moved on top of her again, his tongue searching deep into her mouth in a commanding way that made her want to give herself all over again to this virile man who owned her. Yes, Caleb Sax owned her, not Byron Clawson. For years, when they were apart thinking each other dead, she had gone without a man, lost all sexual desires. Those desires had lain dormant, waiting . . . waiting for Caleb Sax. The moment she found him they had stirred awake, and she knew they would never sleep again as long as she belonged to this beautiful man.

She would do as he asked and try not to worry about the fact that Byron owned Hafer's land. After all, this was Caleb. Why should she worry about anything as long as she had this man to possess and protect her? Her legs parted, and they were making love again.

It was late morning when Caleb opened the door to Jake's pounding. "Hafer men coming," the man said excitedly. "We're letting them come on in, but our men are keeping a close eye."

It was the sixth day since Caleb had left Tom in town, time enough for Charles Hafer to get the news and piece it together.

"He knows by now," Caleb said. "There is no doubt why the man is coming. Watch yourself. I'll be right out." He closed the door and turned to Sarah. Lynda sat near the fireplace breastfeeding little Cale. "You two stay inside."

Sarah watched him take his flintlock down from the mantel and load it. She felt sorry for him—torn between his love for his son and the problems Tom had given him. The door burst open then.

"Pa, come on," John shouted. "They're almost here. Mister Hafer looks real mad."

"Of that I have no doubt," Caleb answered, pulling on his wolfskin coat and walking out the door. He stood in the frosty air then with John beside him, both waiting in front of the house while Hafer and his men rode closer. There were eight men besides Hafer, all of them well armed. Caleb waited until Hafer drew his mount to a halt only a few feet from the steps of the veranda, where Sarah's rosebushes sat stiff and barren, waiting for warmer weather to bring new blossoms to their thorny stems.

The horse had barely halted when Hafer was out of the saddle and storming up to Caleb. "Where is she?" The words were belted out in a threatening tone.

Caleb frowned. He knew he had to buy Tom a little more time, keep Hafer in doubt. "Where is who?"

"You know damned well who I mean! My daughter! Turn her over to me this minute!"

Caleb set his weapon aside and folded his arms. "Your

daughter isn't here. And if she were, I'm not sure I'd let you have her, considering the look on your face. Why don't you tell me what's wrong."

Hafer's eyes narrowed. "Some young Indian man rode off with my daughter six days ago! She was on a boat headed for the Gulf to go home to St. Louis. She got off to tend to personal matters and the next thing my men knew, she was riding off with an *Indian*! And considering the fact that she didn't even scream for help, I can draw only one conclusion. It was your son, Sax! He has taken her away somewhere! The poor girl is innocent and trusting. God only knows what he's done to her by now!"

Caleb's face darkened with anger. "My son would never hurt a young lady, Hafer. And if it were Tom, then it must have been because you were sending her away. They're in love."

"Love! Indians don't love! They *lust*, especially when it comes to white women!"

Caleb winced as though someone had hit him in the gut. He lowered his arms, clenching his fists. "Get off my land, Hafer, before I kill you," he growled then.

"Not without my daughter!"

"I told you she isn't here. I'm sorry something has happened to her, but you won't find her here!"

"And where is your son?"

"He's off hunting."

"Hunting," he sneered. "Let me tell you something, Sax. If that boy of yours has soiled my Bess, I'll *kill* him!"

Caleb grabbed his coat front in a flash, startling the man, shoving him backward. A Hafer man pointed his rifle and a shot rang out. The rifle flew from his hands, knocked away by a Sax man's bullet, and the rest of the Hafer and Sax men faced each other off while Caleb slammed Hafer against a porch post.

"Touch my son, and you're a *dead* man, Hafer! I don't know if he's the one who rode off with your daughter or not, but if he is, then you've got to accept it! Let the girl be happy!" He let go of Hafer, shoving him toward his horse. "I've done nothing against you, Hafer, but you've stolen my water, and now you come here insulting my family! And I know about Byron Clawson, so you had best get out of my sight damned quick. I've got no use for any man who deals with trash like him!"

Hafer paled with shock. He knew! He had to act quickly now against Sax, but at the moment he couldn't think what to do. He forced himself to look unaffected by the news and glared back at Caleb. "This is just the beginning, Sax. So you figured it all out. Fine! Now we both know where the other stands. Even if my daughter hasn't run off with your son, I came here to do a job and I intend to *do* it!"

Jess Purnell was among those who had come with Hafer and his men. He felt uncomfortable with the whole matter and, in fact, had secretly come along only in the hope that he could help keep things from getting out of hand. He really saw nothing wrong with Tom Sax. After all, his father was a big landowner and a respected horse breeder. He had watched Caleb Sax enough to sense the worth of the man and felt embarrassed to be with Hafer.

His eyes moved to the window. Lynda was looking out. Their eyes met for a moment, and he saw the hatred and anger in her dark look. Surely she had had her baby by now. He wished he could talk to her again, see the baby and see if she were well and happy. But the way things were going, it all looked even more hopeless. Charles Hafer had become the enemy, and Jess worked for him.

"I intend to get my water back," Caleb was warning Hafer. "You'll regret selling yourself out, Hafer. It's too bad your daughter got in the way, isn't it?"

The man reddened. "I intend to do my job, daughter or no daughter. I'll find her and I'll send her back to St. Louis where she belongs."

"Not if she has married my son. That makes her a Sax!"

"Sax!" The man spit the word. "No daughter of mine will carry the name of a half-breed."

Hafer mounted his horse.

"What's more important to you, Hafer, money and position, or your only living child?"

The man turned and said angrily, "I'll have *both*. And when I'm through, you'll have nothing!"

"I don't go down easy, Hafer. Get off my land, now! If you're so concerned about your daughter, I suggest you ride into San Felipe and ask around. And don't ever come onto my property again."

Hafer reined his horse backward slightly. "It won't be your property for long, Sax. And if your son shows up with my daughter, I suggest you send her to me if you value your life."

"If they show up here, they'll get shelter. I will not go dragging your daughter to your home against her will."

"How do you know she's with him willingly in the first place?"

"I don't know she's with him at all! And you're the one who said she didn't scream out. That sounds pretty willing to me."

"He could have threatened her life!"

Caleb put his hand on the handle of his knife at his waist. "You're pressing your luck, Hafer. The Council advised me to handle you any way I choose. I can certainly think of one good way to settle this whole thing."

Hafer grinned, trying to hide his fear of the man. "The Council won't be on your side much longer, Sax. Men are taking over who know what's really best for Texas. In the meantime, I suggest you keep a close watch on your property and your family." He sneered the words. "If I ever come back here, it won't be announced." He whirled his horse before Caleb could reply, half expecting to feel a blade in his back and anxious to get out.

Caleb stormed into the house, slamming the door. "I should have killed him then and there!"

"Father, you can't just kill him outright," Lynda warned, laying Cale in a cradle as she spoke.

Caleb walked to where his parfleche hung on a wall. "There are ways," he grumbled. He handed the parfleche to Lynda. "Pack me a little food. I'm going to that mission to accompany Tom and Bess back here. I'd hate to see Hafer men come onto them by accident. We've got to get them back here where they're safe."

Lynda took the parfleche and Caleb walked over to

Sarah, grasping her shoulders. "They've had enough time alone. I'll feel better if they're here with us."

"Be careful, Caleb."

He leaned down and kissed her cheek. "Don't you worry." He walked to a hook to get his leather hat. "And when we get back, we're all riding onto Hafer land and filling those canals."

"Caleb—" She started to protest but knew it was useless. He turned to face her then.

"Byron Clawson won't win this one, Sarah. That's who we're really fighting. He's too much of a coward to come down here and show his face. So I'll send his front man running back to St. Louis with his tail between his legs! That should make him think twice. And with all the trouble down here, he is hardly likely to show up himself."

"But it will never end. After Hafer there will be some-one else."

"And we'll be ready for them!" He came over and gave her a hug. "You stay calm. It's all going to be all right. Hafer and his men should be headed for San Felipe. That will keep them well away from the mission and give us time to get there and get Tom and Bess back here safely." He kissed her hair and let go of her.

Lynda handed him a parfleche packed with a few pota-toes, some salt, bacon, and biscuits. He looked at Sarah once more.

"I'll be back day after tomorrow," he told her. He flung the parfleche over his shoulder and gave Lynda a quick kiss, then left.

Sarah watched the door close. She had to be strong for him now. He had enough troubles without her falling apart. She took a deep breath and looked at Lynda.

"If you don't mind, Lynda, perhaps you should sleep in our house for a few weeks, in the loft. John can sleep out here on the floor. That way Tom and Bess can sleep at your cabin until we get another built for them. They should have some privacy."

Lynda smiled. "I think it's wonderful—snatching her right off the boat," she said proudly. "That sounds like my brother! Isn't it romantic? I can't wait until they get here. Please watch the baby. I'll go get some of my things."

She hurried out and Sarah sank into a chair. "God be with them," she whispered.

"There is someone in the sanctuary to see you," Father Raphael told Tom, who sat in the kitchen with Bess eating lunch. "He says he is your father."

Tom looked at Bess in surprise, then looked back at the priest, caution in his eyes. "What did he look like?"

The old man grinned. "About like you. If he was not wearing white man's clothing, at least mostly, I would have wondered if I was safe. Tall, very Indian looking."

Tom smiled. "That's him." He grabbed Bess's hand. "Come on."

She hesitated, pulling back. "Tom, what if he's angry? What if he tells you I have to go back?"

He pulled her again. "Never. He'll never do that. Come on now."

She followed him reluctantly, reddening when they entered the sanctuary, feeling awkward as a new bride, realizing everyone would know what they had been up to. And what they had been up to had been the most beautiful experience of her life. She was no longer a young girl. She was a woman.

Tom stopped, staring at Caleb, trying to read his eyes. Caleb's own eyes moved from his son to Bess's crimson cheeks. She looked at the floor. He looked back at Tom. "You two happy?"

Tom grinned, pulling her close reassuringly. "We're very happy, Father. I'm sorry . . . the way I did it. But she was leaving. There was no time to explain."

Caleb sighed deeply. "You both are going to have to be pretty strong, and Bess is going to face some hard times. Bess, your father has already been to the ranch, literally threatening Tom's life."

Bess gasped, looking up at Tom. She hugged him tightly.

"If he thinks he's going to get her back——"

"I told him I knew nothing about any of this and told

him to try looking for Bess at San Felipe. I wanted to give us some time to get you safely back to the ranch. But it's obvious nothing is going to change his attitude toward this marriage, and I intend to go and get my water back, which means fighting—the worst kind of fighting—feuding over land and loved ones. Bess has to face the fact that people could get hurt, including her father. I'll not stand back and let my family be threatened."

Bess's eyes teared and she looked up at Caleb. "I love Tom. I wouldn't want to see anything bad happen to my father. I love him, too. But he's changed, Mister Sax. I don't know him anymore. He got so mean."

Caleb studied the beautiful face and lovely form of her. No wonder Tom couldn't keep away from her. "Did you know your father doesn't really own that land, Bess?"

She looked first at Tom. Then they both looked at Caleb. "No," she told Caleb. "I mean, I knew it was strange that he suddenly had so much money, and I knew he was supposed to look into some more land for some investor in St. Louis, but I thought the land we're living on was his."

Caleb looked at Tom. "It belongs to Byron Clawson."

Tom's eyes widened. "Clawson!" He looked at Bess. "I told you about him—the man back in St. Louis Sarah used to be married to."

She looked up at Caleb. "He tried to kill you once."

The bitterness was evident in his eyes. "He did. And if I didn't have so many responsibilities here I would repay the favor. I still might. I have no doubt your father's orders are to give me as much trouble as possible, to get rid of me if he can. I don't know how much he's getting paid for it, but if he's going up against me, it had better be a lot."

She looked down. "I'm so sorry. I didn't know. I had no idea there was any connection." She shivered.

"Well, you've upset your father's plans, to say the least."

Bess looked up at Tom. "I didn't know. Truly I didn't."

He kissed her forehead. "I know that." He looked at his father. "Does Sarah know about Clawson?"

Caleb nodded. "She does now. It all only makes it more necessary for me to ride against Hafer and knock down that

dam he built and fill those canals. I just want to be sure
you two are real sure of your love and realize the trouble
you've caused. You being married makes it all a lot more
complicated."

Bess put her arms around Tom's waist and rested her
head against his chest. "We know. We don't care. We want
to be together."

Caleb looked at his son, then stood up and put a hand on
his shoulder. "Then let's go home. She all right to travel?"

Tom smiled. "Sure. She's fine. A little tired, maybe.
I've been keeping her busy."

He laughed lightly and Caleb grinned while Bess put a
hand over her face. Caleb touched her hair. "Welcome to
the family, Bess. I will do my best to see your father
doesn't get hurt."

She nodded, wiping tears.

"We'll sleep here the night and leave early in the morning. I don't want to camp out on the plains in case Hafer's
men are about. We can get home by nightfall." He gave
Bess a smile. "Sarah and Lynda will be very happy to add
another woman to the household."

"Will they truly," she asked. "They don't hate me?"

"You love Tom. And you are part of the family now.
Why should they hate you? You're a Sax."

She smiled and sniffed. "I am, aren't I?" She looked at
Tom. "I'm a Sax."

He gave her a kiss, embarrassing her in front of his father. "You bet you are," he replied. "Nothing can change
that now. I won't let it."

It was a virtual Sax army that rode onto Hafer land,
spreading out on both sides of Caleb himself. Most of
the men were Cherokee, some who worked full time for
Caleb, and some who were living with families on Sax
property. All together, Caleb took thirty men with him. He
had made one last effort at doing this the right way, sending Hafer a note via messenger to tell him his son and Bess
were indeed married, very happily, and were living at his
ranch. He had called for a truce, a discussion of how to use

the water; told the man his daughter loved him and wanted to see him.

The reply had been an attack on Caleb's men at Blue Valley. Several of Caleb's best horses were killed senselessly, one man killed and two more wounded.

There was nothing left to discuss, and Caleb's anger left no more room for reason. Men had been murdered, and prized horses had also been lost. Blue Valley was drying up from the loss of its water. The remaining horses would have to be driven closer to the house for the winter and water carried from the well there, adding to the chores, let alone the fact that feed would have to be bought for them. This all would create a terrible drain on Caleb's monetary supply. Caleb Sax intended to replenish the natural arroyo that ran through Blue Valley, and there was only one way to do that.

The hooves of Sax horses made a rumbling sound as Caleb and his men rode onto Hafer property. Tom rode beside Caleb. John had been left behind, but not without a flurry of protests from the boy.

They rode hard and fast once they got closer to the canals. Their purpose must be accomplished quickly. Perhaps Hafer would repair whatever damage they did, but they had to try anyway, to give Charles Hafer as much trouble as Hafer had given Caleb Sax.

Hafer men looked up in surprise from their guard posts around the canals. One scurried behind a large boulder and others also began running for cover, all aware on sight of the Sax men that they were outnumbered.

"The dam goes first," Caleb shouted to his men. Several of them headed for the dam that blocked off the water feeding Blue Valley, Jake Highwater in the lead. A Hafer man fired at them, and one of Caleb's men fell from his startled, rearing horse, a hole in his back.

That first shot was all Caleb wanted to hear. The Cherokee circled and took cover, while more headed for the dam and another rode over to the man who had been shot.

"He's dead, Mister Sax," the man called out.

"Fire at will," came Caleb's shouted order in reply.

Sax men opened a volley of shots, and Caleb saw a

Hafer man go down, then another and another. He and his men had taken cover behind boulders, some behind mere brush. So many musket balls flew from Sax guns that several of Hafer's men began running for their own horses. Some of those went down under a new hail of fire. They fired back, and a piece of rock shattered near Caleb's head, a piece of it striking him on the forehead and creating a deep cut that bled profusely. Caleb just wiped it and kept firing.

Hafer men kept returning the fire until three more went down and they realized they had no chance. Those remaining ran for their horses, some riding off bareback, leaving saddles and camp equipment behind. Caleb yelled out to his men to stop shooting, running up to one Hafer straggler who was having trouble getting his horse under control so he could mount it. The man froze when he saw Caleb approaching him, musket in hand.

"Don't shoot," he called out, his eyes wide.

"I'm not going to shoot you," Caleb answered. "I want you to give Hafer a message. Tell him I'm waiting here for him. We're going to finish this here and now. You tell him if he wants to fight this, he can come right back to this spot and we will settle this water thing once and for all."

The man swallowed. "I'll tell him. Just don't shoot me."

Caleb lowered his musket. "Get going."

The man nodded, turned, and finally managed to mount his horse. He rode off at a fast gallop.

It had all taken only minutes.

"Father, you're hurt," Tom exclaimed, running up to Caleb then.

Caleb put a handkerchief to the wound. "Just a piece of rock. Not a bullet." He tied the handkerchief around his forehead, covering the cut. He walked to his horse and mounted again, dried blood on his face and clothes. The wound brought out his old fierceness, reminded him of his days of warring with the Crow.

"Fill the ends of those canals," he shouted to Jake. "Just enough so water can't get through. Then dig some trenches. Hafer will be back before nightfall! We've got to dig in and take cover."

In the distance men finished tearing down the dam, and water rushed back through its original bed, headed for Sax land. Caleb grinned triumphantly. "Isn't that a pretty sight," he told Tom. Tom watched proudly but frowned when he looked at his father.

"You didn't see Hafer anyplace, did you?"

Their eyes held.

"No," Caleb answered. "The men said they would watch for him and try to spare him, but I can't make any guarantees when the shooting starts again. And you know what I would do if I had my choice."

Tom nodded. "He deserves killing. But he is her father."

"I know the feeling, Tom. But a man has to do what he has to do. Come on. Let's go help fill those canals."

When the ends of the canals were filled, Caleb and his men dug trenches. The horses were secured far behind the lines, out of the range of fire. The waiting began. Caleb knew Hafer's men would be back. He intended to show Charles Hafer he meant business. The dam would not be rebuilt, and the canals would not be redug.

"This could go on forever," Tom said, as night fell. "We attack them, they attack us, we attack them, they attack us. They'll come back and try to take the water again."

Caleb leaned back against the dirt inside the trench. He took out a thin cigar and lit it. "It could happen that way. But I'm betting that Charles Hafer isn't a true fighting man. Bess said all they did back in Missouri was farm. He's all mouth and bluster. If I push him enough, he just might give up. It really depends on how much he's being paid. Bess says he's never actually killed anyone himself. Everything has backfired on him. He came here to get rich but lost his daughter. And Clawson must have figured that we were more civilized in this state than we are; he figured the law would be on us, especially since we are Indian. He's sitting in his fancy office in St. Louis expecting to hear Hafer has had all of us arrested and hung, or at least run out. It's not that easy. Not in Texas."

Tom sighed. "I hope you're right—about Hafer giving up. I sure wouldn't want to have to go back and tell Bess anything happened to her father."

"She will be all right as long as she remembers this would have happened even without you and she getting married. Hafer has had this planned for a long time." He puffed the cigar and Tom watched it glow red in the dark. "You really love her, don't you?"

Tom felt an ache at the desire to be sleeping with her tonight. He could never quite get enough of her, and this was the first time they had been apart since getting married the week before. "Yeah. She's so sweet, and stronger than she knows. It feels good to be married. I want to get back and get a cabin built just for us. If we're real lucky, Bess will have a baby before the year is out. All of a sudden, I want sons."

"Every man does eventually. But she is young, and birthing is hard on the young. Don't be too anxious."

"Lynda did okay."

"And she lost one before that, by that gambler. Just remember that out here in this country every successful birth is something to rejoice."

Tom sighed. "I miss her already."

Caleb smiled. "I know." How well he remembered that young passion. He still felt that way about Sarah. Finding her was like being young and starting all over again. "Get some rest," he told his son. "I have a feeling we'll be busy tomorrow."

Dawn was not really dawn, for there was no sun. The morning brought only a cold rain, and as daylight came the Sax men were greeted by a long line of Hafer men who had ridden to within several yards of them during the night. Caleb quickly counted about forty men.

"Caleb Sax!" Charles Hafer scanned the creek, noticing as the morning got lighter that Sax men had dug trenches in which they hid. Only a few heads and several musket barrels could be seen through the cold drizzle.

"Say your piece, Hafer," Caleb called out from one of the trenches. He stayed hunkered down, a poncho draped around his shoulders, water dripping from his leather hat.

"Give me back my daughter and I'll let the water go. That will be the end of it," Hafer answered.

Caleb looked at Tom, whose sorrow at bringing his father this additional trouble was evident.

"Never," Caleb yelled back. "She's a Sax now. We have given her the choice. She wants to stay with us."

"She's too young to know what she wants."

"They're legally married, Hafer, and not just on paper."

Silence hung in the air for a moment.

"How long do you think you can stay there?" Hafer called out then. "You'll starve in those holes before we let you out."

"It's real simple. We just shoot down your men." Caleb gave out a whistle that they all recognized. It was the signal to start firing. Muskets reported, and several Hafer men fell from their horses. Other horses reared, and Hafer's remaining men scattered to take cover and began returning fire, but their targets were difficult to see. More Hafer men cried out as bullets struck them. Several of them scurried to move the horses farther back, and a period of silence fell during which men reloaded and got their bearings, passing signals back and forth.

It was a bitterly cold day. Rain began to turn to snow and Caleb threw off his wet poncho, pulling his wolfskin coat closer around his neck. He took out a piece of beef jerky and shared it with Tom.

"We can't stay here forever," Hafer called out to Caleb.

"You've lost more men that I. You had better get the wounded ones back and get them some help, Hafer."

Behind Hafer's line Jess Purnell worked desperately bandaging a badly wounded man. But the man died before Jess could finish. Jess was angry and cursed under his breath. He was fed up with the whole useless mess. Why should he and these other men die just because Hafer wanted to make trouble for Caleb Sax, for no other reason than the fact that the man was an Indian . . . or just because Hafer's daughter had married Sax's son? He could think of a lot of better things to fight about. Some of these men he called friend and they were getting hurt and killed. Even at that, this would all be easier if he could get the vision of Lynda Sax's beautiful and lonely blue eyes out of his mind. It had been roughly seven months since first he set eyes on her, and he had seen her only twice since—talked to her only that one time at the barn raising. That was all it took for her to get right under his skin and into his blood. How many women were that beautiful, and needing a man besides?

"Damn," he muttered. He lay down the dead man and ducked down, crawling to where Charles Hafer had taken shelter.

"Hank just died, Mister Hafer," he told Hafer. "And it looks like a good snowstorm is coming on. There's no sense trying to do any more until the weather warms again. We've got to get the wounded out of this cold and back where they can get some help."

"Keep your mouth shut. You're getting paid well."

Jess stiffened, his pride stinging. More shots were exchanged and there was no time to answer Hafer. The snow came down so hard then that no one could see what he was shooting at. Suddenly Hafer's men heard literal war cries, as though a swarm of Indians was upon them. And it was true—Cherokee and a couple of Cheyenne came running out of the snow wielding rifles, tomahawks, and knives.

"Jesus Christ," one of Hafer's men swore. He ran for his horse. Some fired back, but the Indians ducked and rolled and darted around in the blinding snow. A tomahawk came down into a Hafer man's arm while a knife sunk into another's chest. More shots were fired. A couple of Caleb's men went down, but it was Hafer's men who took the worst of the beating. Their screams filled the air.

Jess shot at a Cherokee, then went for his horse, disgusted with the fighting. He was not one to run from anything, but this made no sense. He waited beside his horse, then, unsure of what to do. It was his job to stay with Hafer.

Suddenly things quieted, and Caleb's men disappeared as quickly as they had appeared.

Hafer stared into the snow to see them retreating. "By God, they're on the run," he shouted. But then a strong arm suddenly came around his neck from behind, and a blade flashed in front of him. "End it now or you're a dead man," Caleb growled.

Hafer started to struggle, until the knife nicked his cheek. "Do it!"

Hafer froze. Caleb Sax meant business.

"We're going back, men," he shouted. "Too many losses—and too cold. Pass it on."

One of his men came into view, looking startled when he saw Caleb. He started to raise his rifle.

"Your boss will be dead before you pull the trigger," Caleb warned him.

"Don't shoot, Gus," Hafer said, his voice sounding strangled. "Tell the others. Pick up the wounded and head back."

The man lowered his rifle. Tom and several of Caleb's men came into view then, Tom stepping close to Hafer. "Your daughter is fine, Mister Hafer. She would like very much to see you—to tell you she still loves you and hopes you still love her. There is no reason for what you are doing. Why don't you just let her be happy?"

Caleb slowly released the man, shoving his knife into its sheath. "Happy," Hafer sneered. "With the likes of you?"

Caleb whirled the man, landing a big fist into his face. Hafer sprawled backward. Most of his men could be heard riding off, but Jess Purnell appeared, helping the man up. For a moment they all thought that was the end of it, as Hafer wiped at a bloodied lip. But Hafer then dove into Caleb, pushing him to the ground. Men stepped aside as both Hafer and Caleb rolled on the ground until Caleb managed to get to his feet and yank Hafer up with him. Hafer kicked hard at Caleb's legs, making Caleb's grip weaken. Then he knocked Caleb's hands away and hit him hard in the chest and jaw. Caleb stumbled back, but only slightly, coming back and ducking a punch, then landing a fist hard into Hafer's middle, then backhanding him with brutal force when he bent over. Hafer's big frame slammed to the ground and stayed there.

"I've killed plenty of men in my lifetime," Caleb panted. "You had better consider yourself damned lucky to be alive, Hafer! If it weren't for Bess, your guts would be freezing in the cold wind right now! They still will if you give me any more trouble! If that creek dries up again, we'll be back! And if I lose one more man, or any more horses, you're a *dead* man!" He looked at Purnell. "Take your boss home," he sneered. "And take a good look at the kind of man you're working for."

He turned, disappearing into the snow. The wind began howling, blowing new snow over bloodstains on the ground and in the snow that had already fallen. Sax men picked up their wounded men and left, and by the end of the day, water again began trickling into Blue Valley.

Chapter Sixteen

Sarah watched as Caleb undressed, never tiring of looking at his magnificent physique, which seemed to harden with age rather than get softer. She could not forget how he looked when he first got home, his face covered with dried and frozen blood from the wound on his forehead, and his ribs bruised. Yet he was jubilant. He was sure it would be some time before Hafer could get his men organized to give him any more trouble. A heavy snowstorm would keep the man at bay, at least for a while.

"What about Byron?" she asked.

He turned to bend over the cradle and gently pat little James's bottom. The boy lay sleeping peacefully. "This kid is getting much too big for this cradle, even though I built it big," he answered.

"Caleb, I wasn't talking about James. I was talking about Byron Clawson."

He leaned closer and kissed James's soft, fine hair. Then he stood up, coming over to the bed and unbuttoning his long underwear. "Byron has lost this one, and he'll lose every time. Don't even think about it."

She closed her eyes and sighed. "I have to think about it. He's desperately afraid of you, you know. A frightened man will do anything to get rid of that which frightens him, especially a coward like Byron."

"Let him try." Caleb moved under the covers. "My fondest hope is that Byron Clawson will give up hoping someone else can do his dirty work for him, and will come down here himself. Then he'll be in *my* territory, and all the money and power in the world won't help him." He turned on his side, facing her.

She studied the incredibly blue eyes. "What would you do?"

He thought about Byron Clawson pawing her, literally raping her, beating her. His eyes glittered with vengeance. "It's very simple. I would kill him. If I could get away from here, I'd go do it anyway. But places like St. Louis and I don't mix. We both learned that the hard way. Out here, in untamed country, this is where I can be more powerful than someone like Byron. But if I have to, I will go to St. Louis and do it."

She reached up and touched the gauze around his forehead. A spot of blood still showed from the wound. "Caleb, my Caleb. All your life you've been fighting and killing, haven't you? The Indian wars, that horrible man at Fort Dearborn, all those Crow Indians, then the British. And here in Texas the Comanche, outlaws. Yet deep inside you're a gentle man who never wanted any of it."

He grasped her hand and kissed it. "Trouble has a way of following a half-breed, Sarah." He nestled down beside her. "Sometimes I think I never should have let you stay here. I should have told you that after all those years I didn't love you anymore—made you go back. Maybe I'm asking too much of you to stay here. Maybe I should give it all up and take you to more civilized places."

She smiled sadly. "I am happy right here. I'm happy where my man is happy. Don't make any moves for me, Caleb. Do what you need to do. And I know you'd never be happy in a city. What on earth would you do with yourself, you, a man who likes to ride free and raise horses and be in the sun, who lived as an Indian for years and who would do it again if not for his wife. I don't need civilized places to be happy. All I need is you. If I died out here tomorrow, it would all have been worth it."

They faced each other, and he traced a finger around her lips, always amazed at how she had retained her beauty. It seemed so strange that this could be the little girl he had grown up with at Fort Dearborn, the happy, inquisitive child who took his hand and taught him English and the white man's ways.

"Then be happy in that," he told her, "and don't give Byron Clawson another thought. He'll never hurt you again. And I don't think Hafer will be giving us trouble for a while."

He leaned closer and kissed her lips, moving a hand over her full breast.

"I hope poor Bess is all right. It was all so hard on her," she said when his lips left her mouth and he began pulling her gown over her shoulder.

"Bess will be fine. She has Tom." He kissed her throat. "No more talking, woman. Put all your worries aside."

"Caleb, you're wounded," she reminded him as he pulled her gown down more.

"Don't you know that after a fight, a man's sexual desires come alive, especially when he's the victor?"

She laughed lightly as his lips found the tender nipple of her breast. He pulled the gown away from it. It had taken them all night and a day to get back home, for the wind howled around them, and snow nearly blinded their way. Caleb was elated that only one of his men had been killed, only a few wounded; and that Hafer's men had literally run from them. Water was again flowing into Blue Valley, and he'd had a chance to land his own fist into Charles Hafer. To Caleb it was a victory over Byron Clawson, and he was riding high on it. Tom and Bess were together and things were going to be better. He was sure of it. They had made it through a bad blizzard and found home, a warm hearth, their women waiting. What more could a man ask for?

He moved over her more deliberately then, and she gladly welcomed him. She was glad that none of her loved ones had been seriously hurt. Sarah closed her eyes as he pushed up her gown and moved a rough but gentle hand over her bottom. She wore nothing under the gown, hoping when she came to bed that he would want her, needing this just as much as he did. It was the ultimate proof that her man was alive and well and safe in her arms.

His lips kissed her belly, her thighs, the warm crevice of her inner thighs, making her open up to him in daring abandon, losing her natural modesty and allowing her husband whatever he desired, for she was not just giving. She was also taking—selfishly enjoying this beautiful man who belonged only to her. She reached up and grasped the posts of the brass bed, groaning in the absolute ecstasy of Caleb Sax's tender exploration of her, until she felt the wonderful pulsations that meant she was ready for his invasion, the contracting muscles that asked for something to consume and caress.

He moved on top of her then. Moving his mouth back over her belly, he made his way to her breasts, exposed where he'd pulled the gown from the top. It was still on her, lying in disarray about her middle. He moved between her legs and entered her, bringing a little gasp that told him he was indeed filling her to her satisfaction. Two babies hadn't changed his ability to give her full pleasure. He reached under her bottom and pushed into her in glorious rhythm, his chest pressed against her full breasts, his lips caressing her throat, her eyes, his own groans telling her she could still please him in return.

She arched up to him, whimpering his name then, and the bed rocked with the rhythm of their intercourse. She felt his own pulsating release, and heard her name whispered lovingly as Caleb sighed and relaxed beside her, his exhaustion from the raid finally catching up to him. He was soon asleep in her arms.

In the outer room young John had heard nothing. But in

the loft Lynda lay awake, feeling her own needs, quietly crying because Lee was not with her. She could not help but hear the sounds of her parents' lovemaking. Now the house was quiet, and her loneliness intense.

How she missed him still! How she needed a man. But all she wanted was Lee, and he was gone forever. She turned over and curled up, sighing with the near pain of needing to be a woman again that way. But whenever she felt this loneliness, Jess Purnell kept coming to mind. It upset her, for Jess was a Hafer man. He had been with Hafer when he came demanding his daughter; and he had been present at the fighting. But there was something in his eyes the few times she had seen him that suggested a man who was someplace he didn't want to be.

Still, what did it matter? The fact remained he was a part of Hafer's dirty deeds and therefore a man she could never even consider calling friend, let alone anything more.

Caleb halted his horse in front of Emily's cabin. The weather had cleared and what snow they had gotten had melted, giving him the opportunity to ride into town. He intended to continue keeping everything as open and legal as possible with the Council and had come to San Felipe to tell them exactly what he had done about Charles Hafer. Besides that, Wil Handel had stopped by to tell him a meeting of settlers was being held this very afternoon to discuss their desired laws and a constitution. Delegates would be picked to attend a convention in San Antonio de Bexar, where a final constitution would be drawn and some decisions made about their rights and about their problems with Mexico. This would include another plea to Santa Anna to free Stephen Austin. They would show Santa Anna that they won't tolerate a dictatorship, which was exactly what his rule was becoming.

This time Caleb could not come to town without seeing Emily again. He knocked on the door. "Who is it?" came her voice.

"It's me—Caleb."

The door opened seconds later. "Caleb!" Her face

brightened and her pale blue eyes shone with delight. "I thought you had forgotten about me."

"Now how could I do that?" He grinned and stepped inside so she could close the door against the cold. "Howard here?"

She turned away. "No," she answered. He sensed a defensive ring to the reply. A warm fire crackled in the fireplace of the one-room cabin and the bed was neatly made.

"I . . . I just thought I'd say hello, Emily—tell you everybody is fine. We've had some trouble out at our place—neighbor who has no love for Indians. About a week ago I took the law into my own hands and solved a little dispute over water. Thought I'd talk to the Council about it. I would have brought Sarah with me, but it's so damned cold."

She turned to face him, smiling. But her eyes looked troubled. "I understand. The last thing you want to do is expose Sarah to the elements. You've got to take good care of that one, Caleb, so you'll have her a good, long time. She's a wonderful woman."

Their eyes held, and he saw a strange sadness there. The first time he had seen her in San Felipe, she radiated joy and happiness at her new marriage. "What's wrong, Emily?"

She stiffened, talking on the air of the old, hard Emily he'd once known. "Oh, I'm just . . . thinking how undeserving I am of all this." Her eyes teared and she quickly looked away.

He frowned. "What the hell is the matter?"

She shrugged. "Nothing really. It's just me . . . inside. I was getting ready to walk to town and do a little shopping. I feel so cooped up in this little place when it's cold." She shrugged. "Anyway, I . . . I saw some men riding down the street." She swallowed. "I recognized them, Caleb. They didn't seem to notice me close enough to know me, but I remember them." She shivered. "God, Caleb, they were customers of mine once. I just . . . ran inside and closed the door."

She sniffed then and turned. "What if they had recognized me? What if they came back later, when Howard was home, asking me if I'm still in the business of prostitution?" Her voice broke, but she refused to break down. "I thought . . . here in Texas . . . I could get away from it. But every day, with all these new men coming in, any time someone who knows me from New Orleans could call out —say something in front of Howard. I just . . . don't know what I would do if he found out."

He sighed, coming over and putting a hand on her shoulder. "That's not too likely to happen, Emily. But even if it did, I think after he thought about it awhile, Howard wouldn't even care. He's a hell of a nice man. He would understand why you were afraid to tell him. You love him and he knows that."

She reached up, touching the hand on her shoulder. "Do you really think so?"

"I do. It might take him a little time, but you'd never lose him forever. And if he gets ornery about it, you come to me. I'll have a damned good talk with him."

She wiped her eyes and looked at him, forcing a smile and tossing her head like the old Emily. "Here I am moaning about my problems, and there are so much more important things going on. Are you here about the meeting?"

He nodded. "Partly. I want to report what's happening at my place, too."

"How bad is it?"

"Bad enough. You know well enough how some people think about Indians. I've got one of the worst living right next to my land, and have come to find out that he's a front man for Byron Clawson, who is the real owner of the land."

"Clawson! Are you sure?"

"I'm sure. To make matters worse, my son Tom fell in love with this neighbor's daughter and rode off with her and married her in secret. They're at our place now. Needless to say, her father is less than happy about the whole thing."

She smiled and shook her head. "Young passions. They don't stop to reason much, do they?"

Their eyes held a moment, both remembering the wild sexual encounters they had had as mere children at Fort

Dearborn. "No, I guess not," Caleb answered. "But she's a nice young woman and they seem to be very much in love. All the fighting has been hard on her, but her loyalty lies with Tom now."

Emily smiled and wiped some remaining tears. "Well, that's good. That's the way it should be. A girl leaves the nest and turns her trust and faith from her father to her husband." She smiled sarcastically, going to a coffeepot hanging over the fire. "I never had the kind of father I had to worry about hurting. I hated him all my life." She took up a heavy pad and used it to wrap around the handle of the coffee pot. "Want some of this black stuff? It's strong."

"That's the way I like it. Sounds good. I need to warm up a little. But I can't stay long. I don't like being away from the ranch, but I need to find out what's going on at this meeting."

She poured two cups and sat down at the table. He took a chair across from her. "Life's crazy, isn't it?" she said. "Seems like we're led more by fate than by our own wills, Caleb."

"Not completely. You decided to change your life—of your own free will. Fate didn't do that. You are now a married woman living with one man—living the kind of life you were always meant to live."

She stared at her coffee. "Perhaps. And it's true I made an effort to change my life. But fate could take it all away from me, Caleb. Seeing those men today reminded me of how delicate our lives are, how dictated they are by outside factors we can't control."

She met his eyes. "I hope it doesn't happen to you," she added. "You don't deserve any more unhappiness. But me . . ." She shrugged, putting on the old, hard smile. "I deserve everything that happens to me, except Howard and happiness. I don't deserve that."

"You have every right to it. Your father stole all your happiness in childhood, and Potawatomies took away any last remnants of pride and dignity. Considering what you went through, I admire what you've done. You have risen above it, Emily."

She laughed lightly. "Have I? Once a whore always a

whore, that's what most men think. And that's what Howard will think if he ever finds out." She sighed deeply, rising. "I guess I should have told him right at the beginning. He either would have married me or told me to go to hell. At least I'd have had it over with before I became so emotionally involved. I didn't really love him at first, you know. I just married him so I could live like other women for once in my life. But he's so...so damned good to me...so kind and considerate...and so trusting. That's the part that really bothers me. He's so trusting."

Caleb drank more coffee, then got up himself, going over and putting his hands on her shoulders. "Quit worrying about things that haven't happened and probably never will."

She smiled. "How about that old injury? You ever have trouble with the paralysis?"

He let go of her. "Not in years. Just some stiffness in my legs, especially in this cold weather. But I still live with the fear of it happening all over again and lying helpless." He walked to the table and sipped some more coffee. "I have Byron Clawson to thank for that."

She rose and put her hands on her hips. "He still gets to you, doesn't he?"

He finished his coffee. "I still plan to kill him somehow, if that's what you mean. He will live to regret what he's doing now and what he has done in the past." He set down his cup.

She studied the powerful physique, which seemed to fill the whole room. "He probably will regret it—probably does already. You watch yourself, Caleb."

"Don't worry about me. And thanks for the coffee. I've got to get going. I just wanted to say hello again."

She nodded. "Thanks. We have a way of landing in the same places. Considering how big this land is, and how much you've roamed it, that seems like quite a miracle." She sobered. "I can't help but think there's a reason for it, Caleb—something that brought me here—something more than wanting to change my life. It's as though there's something more I'm supposed to do for you, but I can't imagine what it could be now."

"Quit thinking you owe me for Fort Dearborn. You paid that back many times over when you got me walking again. Fort Dearborn was a century ago, and we were kids." He patted her scarred cheek. "You've got to learn to relax and enjoy your new happiness, Emily Cox. I think you should put on a coat and go into town like you planned. You can't hibernate in here forever for fear of seeing someone you know."

She smiled sadly. "Yeah, maybe I'll go after all."

"Good. And I'll try to see you the next time I come again. Maybe Sarah will be with me." He walked to the door and turned. "Go on into town. That's an order."

He left and she stared at the doorway. "Sure," she said quietly, a lump coming into her throat at the thought of Howard's total love and trust.

Lynda looked out the window at the sound of approaching horses. To her surprise, her heart quickened at the sight of Jess Purnell, accompanied by Sax men. What on earth was he doing here? She turned and looked at Sarah and Bess, who stood at the table kneading bread dough.

"It's that Jess Purnell," she told them.

Bess paled. "Maybe something has happened to my father."

Lynda frowned. "I just wish Tom or Father were here. Did Tom say how far he was going this morning?"

"He's down at the south end seeing about a sick colt. One of the men came and told him about it this morning. He said he'd be home for supper, though."

"And Father won't be back till day after tomorrow. He's got so much business in town, he won't get any farther home than the Handel place before dark tomorrow." Lynda looked around the room. "Don't tell this man Father is that far away."

Purnell was at the door by then with Jake Highwater. Lynda opened the door and her eyes met Jess Purnell's, an unnerving attraction moving through her, something she hoped went undetected. His eyes moved over her appreciatively. "Hello, ma'am."

Lynda refused to smile. She looked at Jake. "What is this man doing here?" she asked him. "He's a Hafer man!"

"Yes, but he insisted on coming here. We took his weapons. He's alone. He wants to talk to Caleb. I told him Caleb was in San Felipe, so he said he'd talk to you, and you could tell your pa what he wants—then he'll be back."

Lynda's irritation was evident in her eyes. "You shouldn't have told him that, Jake," she snapped. She felt a pang of guilt at the hurt pride in Jake's eyes then and was even angrier with Purnell, who made her so nervous she had taken it out on Jake.

She moved her eyes to Jess. "What do you want?" she demanded sternly.

"Lynda, let the man in," Sarah spoke up. "It's so cold."

Lynda stepped back. "You come in, too, please," she indicated to Jake. "Tom is someplace south of here and we are alone."

"You don't need to tell me that. I look out for your best interest, Lynda. You know that." The proud Cherokee still looked disturbed as he came inside behind Purnell, removing his hat.

Jess followed suit, and John came bounding in behind them, taking off his own hat and gloves and staring at the Hafer man. Lynda refused to offer Jess a chair. Jess's blue eyes moved to Bess and he nodded. "Miss Hafer? You all right?"

Bess bristled. "The name is Mrs. Sax. Yes, I'm just fine —very happy. You tell my father that. You tell him I love him in spite of what he's done, and he's welcome to come and see me here any time he wants."

Purnell sighed. "He'd like you to come home, Miss . . . I mean, Mrs. Sax. I'm supposed to tell you—" He sighed and looked at Lynda. "Look, my name is Jess Purnell, in case you don't remember." He looked around at all of them. "Look, I'm not supposed to be here at all. I came on my own. I know Hafer is planning something, and I wanted to warn you. I don't know just what it is because he has only let a certain few of his men in on it."

"How sad," Lynda said sarcastically. "You can go back

and tell your boss to give up. He'll not get Bess away from here."

Purnell sighed, fingering his hat in his hand. His blue eyes drilled into Lynda's. "Look, I came here to warn you, and to tell you I don't go along with what the man is doing. I really don't. You've got to believe that."

"Why?" Lynda asked coldly.

Sarah watched from the table, seeing under all Lynda's challenging and hardness that her daughter was attracted to the handsome Jess Purnell.

Purnell reddened some and shrugged. "Well, because . . . because it's just wrong, that's all."

"Then why do you work for him?" Lynda asked pointedly.

He held her eyes. Yes, she was strong, and smart, and not easily conquered. It only made him want her more. "Because all my life I've done ranch work and this was a good job. I did not know all the things the man had planned." His eyes hardened slightly. "What I do is really none of your business, ma'am. But now I have come here to warn you to be careful, and to ask if I could work here, for your father. It might pay less, but I've had it with Hafer!"

Lynda's eyebrows arched, and she suddenly smiled, but it was more of a sneer than a genuine smile. "You? Work here! That's ridiculous! Do you really think I believe you've suddenly changed sides? You're spying!"

"Lynda!" Sarah spoke up then. "Let the man have his say."

Lynda turned. "Mother, he's lying, can't you see? He's a Hafer man. That's all we have to remember. Father would *never* hire him on here! At the least, we can't do it without his say."

"Well, what about your brother? Will he be back soon?"

"Yes. He'll be back by supper," Lynda answered.

"What about your father?" Jess asked the questions.

"Jake already told you—" She stopped and bristled. Why was he asking? "I suggest you leave, Mister Purnell. And don't come back. Hafer men are not wanted around here."

"I wish you'd believe me. I'd really rather work for your father, if he'd have me."

"Well, he won't. You get off our property."

Their eyes held.

"I'll be back to talk to your father. You tell him I was here—and that I warned you about Hafer," Jess said firmly.

"We'll tell him," Sarah spoke then. "And thank you for telling us, Mister Purnell. We realize you didn't have to, and Caleb wasn't expecting Hafer to do anything more until spring."

"Mother—" Lynda started to object, but Cale began to cry. She quickly looked over to where he lay in a cradle in the corner of the room.

"Yours?" Jess asked.

She looked back at him, her eyes softening just a little. "Yes. I had a son."

He grinned. "Good. That's good. I'm glad for you."

Lynda blinked, caught off guard by his seemingly genuine concern.

"Thank you," she managed to say, before turning away.

"Would you like a hot cup of coffee before you go, Mister Purnell?" Sarah spoke up. There was something in the man's eyes that made her believe him, and she already knew Caleb liked the man. He had mentioned him once or twice.

"That's all right, Mrs. Sax," Jess returned. "I'll get going. I'll come back another time."

"And where will you go, Mister Purnell?" Lynda asked sarcastically. "Back to Hafer?"

"For the time being. It's too cold to be riding alone looking for other work." He nodded to her. "Good-bye, ma'am."

She folded her arms and said nothing.

"Good-bye, Mister Purnell," Sarah answered for her.

Jess gave her a smile and left, totally unaware that Hafer men were headed for Sax land that very day—to take back Elizabeth Hafer and get rid of her husband.

* * *

Hafer's men came in the night. Many of them were newly hired volunteers who had come to Texas to fight a war that had not yet started. So they had turned their energies to help fight this smaller battle instead.

Their goal was simple. Strike quickly while everyone slept. Take the girl. Kill Caleb Sax, and the son who had "violated" Bess Hafer. There would be guards at the Sax place. A man always kept guards in Comanche country. But Comanche seldom struck at night, and enemies would not be expected.

They rode in a circle around the northeast rim of Sax land, coming in through the more mountainous country, a route Caleb's men would never expect to see Hafer men use. The regular trail was well guarded, but this route was not. Scouts moved ahead before nightfall, seeing only two lookouts, who were killed with knives to keep things quiet. Then the forty men rode in slowly and quietly, to a point from which they could see the houses—the main adobe house, a smaller cabin and another cabin only partially built.

"She has to be either in the main house or in that finished cabin," Hafer told his men. "Bart, you and your bunch take the bunkhouses. Hold them at gunpoint and anybody who resists gets killed. As soon as the bunkhouses are secure, we'll move in on the main houses. All of you —anybody gets in the way, kill him. But nobody kills Tom Sax. He's mine. You can kill the father, but that boy is going to suffer for defiling my Bess."

The men nodded. Hafer waited until two o'clock in the morning, when all would be in their deepest sleep. Even though Jess had warned them, Caleb's men did not expect any trouble so soon. Hafer's men left their horses at a distance and moved in on foot so their horses would not wake anyone.

But Tom Sax was already awake. He had never been a man to sleep soundly all night, just as his father was not. In this land a man had to sleep with his eyes half-open. But this night he was unable to sleep at all. He sat by dim lamplight, trying to make sense out of a book of poetry that Bess had given him. But Tom could understand none of the fancy writing and shook his head at the strange things women thought were important.

Suddenly his skin tingled and all senses came alert. He could not explain why. Perhaps it was his Indian instincts that told him something was amiss. His first thought was Comanche. He quickly blew out the lamp and darted to the bed, shaking Bess. She moaned and rubbed her eyes. "Tom?"

"Be still," he whispered. "Something's wrong."

She gasped, sitting up.

"Come on," he told her, pulling her out of bed. He took down two pictures and removed two logs sliced through the middle. They comprised the fake wall that served as a hiding place.

"Get behind here, and don't come out unless it's me who comes for you—no matter what you hear. Understand?"

"But, Tom, what about you?" she whispered as he quickly tugged away at the logs and lay them aside. Behind them was an enclosure big enough for a woman and a couple of children. He was already worried about the main house. He had to get there in time to hide Sarah and Lynda.

"Don't worry about me. Just get in there, and damn it, if you come out for anyone but me or because you hear someone else in trouble, I'll . . . I don't know. Just get in there."

She crawled inside. "But, Tom—"

"Stay there," he almost growled. "Promise me, Bess, no matter what!" He heard her sniff, then heard a scream from the main house. "Goddamn it! Get in there!"

Bess hovered inside, terrified now. Tom quickly put back the logs and the pictures, then went for his musket, but not before something crashed through the window. "Out of there now, Sax, if you value the lives of your mother and sister," someone growled from just outside in clear English. "And bring the little woman with you!"

Tom froze. It wasn't Indians at all! Hafer! It must be Hafer men. He hesitated. There were probably a lot of them, and there was only one of him. They had apparently already invaded the main house. He glanced at the fake wall, which he could see in the moonlight, and prayed Bess would have sense enough to stay put.

"She's not here," he called out in the darkness.

"You expect us to believe that? Open the door, Sax."

Tom walked cautiously to the door, dressed only in his underwear. He heard several gunshots from the area of the bunkhouse, and he knew Sax men were dying. He opened the door and several men burst in, one carrying a lantern.

"She's not here," one of them said after searching the one-room structure. "Let's get him over to the main house and see what Hafer wants to do."

"He ain't got nothin' but his underwear on," another spoke up.

"So it's a little cold out. So what? Won't be long before he won't feel the cold at all." The man who had answered walked up to Tom and rammed a rifle butt into his back, sending him to his knees. "Drag him over there."

They all left and Bess shivered behind the logs, trying to decide what to do. Tom had ordered her not to come out. It seemed the only way to save him was to go out and go to her father, and yet perhaps that would be the worst thing she could do. Once he had her, he would kill Tom for certain. Tom's only chance of living was for the men to be unable to find her. But what would they do to Tom to make him tell where she was? Which was the worse decision? She shivered in the shelflike enclosure and quietly wept, hating her father more than ever.

At the main house Tom's fury raged when he saw Lynda's face was bruised. Sarah stood near the table. Both wore only their nightgowns, and Charles Hafer was growling at Sarah, telling her she'd better tell where Bess was. She said nothing, meeting his eyes boldly.

Tom jerked at the men who held him, but another kicked him in the groin. "Like the white women, huh? You filthy rapist!"

Hafer came over to Tom then, his eyes lighting up with hatred. He grabbed Tom's hair and jerked back his head. Tom grimaced and panted from the pain between his legs, needing to bend over but unable to do so. "Where's my daughter, you son of a bitch! What have you done to her!"

"Your daughter . . . is fine . . . and happy. You're . . . the son of a bitch! She'll . . . hate you now."

"Where is she?" Hafer shouted.

"You'll . . . never get her back . . . not now."

Hafer landed a fist into his belly.

"Maybe if we had at his sister, he'd tell," one of the men spoke up. "She's a looker."

Lynda was still reeling from a stunning blow from a Hafer man, delivered during a quick skirmish for a musket that stood in a corner of the room. Lynda had tried to reach it. The invasion had been so sudden there had not been time for Lynda and Sarah to get into the hideaway under the floor. Tom knew that if Caleb were home, he'd have been just as alert to something wrong as Tom had been.

"She's got to be around here somewhere," Hafer roared.

"We searched the cabin, boss. It's only got one room."

"Look harder!"

Men began tearing things out of closets and cupboards, and a few returned to the cabin. Tom looked over at Sarah. She would know where Bess was, but she would never tell either. She looked back at him with eyes that told him not to tell, eyes that reassured him that Caleb Sax would most certainly do something about this.

"Where's your husband?" Hafer growled at Sarah then, walking close to her. His eyes moved over her in an effort to undo her by making her think she might be raped.

"He isn't here either. He's in San Felipe," she answered calmly.

Lynda jerked away from a man who had grasped her arm to make her stay put. She looked at him with a wild look.

"Touch me or my mother, and you'll die slowly at my father's hands," she hissed.

Tom again struggled to get free, suddenly jerking one arm loose and landing a fist into the second man who held him. But there were too many. Instantly five men were on him, pummeling him to the floor.

"Tom," Lynda screamed, running into the pack to futilely try to pull them off. One of them hit her again, sending her flying against a wall. Sarah started to go to her, but Hafer grabbed her arm.

"I'll ask you once more, Mrs. Sax. Where is your husband, and where is my daughter?"

"I told you my husband is in San Felipe. He . . . he took Bess with him. She wanted to go into town, but Tom couldn't go. He has been nursing a colt that is special to him. So Caleb took her."

Hafer grinned, shoving her toward the others. She knelt down to where Tom lay groaning on the floor.

"You two are going with us," Hafer told them. He looked over at Lynda, who stood staring.

"No! Don't take my mother," she told him. "What kind of man are you?"

"A man who wants his daughter back. You tell your father that if he wants to see them both alive again, and his woman untouched, he had better bring my daughter to me. If I don't get what I want in three days, the boy gets his head blown off, and the wife enjoys the pleasures of any of my men who needs a woman. You tell him."

"You goddamned son of a bitch," Tom roared, struggling to his knees.

"Take one of their horses and tie him to the back of it, Gus," Hafer ordered. "Let Mister Sax try to keep up with the gallop while you take him to where our horses are tied. Leave him half-naked like he is. The cold air and the rough ground will wake him up."

"No!" Sarah cried out, reaching out for Tom. But the men dragged him out. Sarah turned to Hafer. "You've lost your daughter's love forever," she told him in a voice filled with sorrow. "You could have had her back so easily, just by loving her and accepting her husband. You're a fool, Charles Hafer, and a coward! My husband will *kill* you for this!"

The man just grinned. "He's the one who's going to die —the minute he steps foot on my land to return my daughter. And he will come . . . for you and his son. Then my job here in Texas will be complete. Get yourself a coat."

"I will get dressed first." She turned, but he grabbed her arm. "Get your coat."

Whistles and whoops could be heard outside and horses galloped off. "He bounces real good," someone hollered. Sarah closed her eyes and walked to a hook near the door where her woolen cape and hood hung.

"You bastard," Lynda sneered. "My father will carve you up like a gutted pig!"

"He'll be humble enough when he finds out I've got his wife and son."

"I need some shoes," Sarah said wearily.

Hafer looked around, spotting some furry Indian winter moccasins in the corner. "Wear those."

"They're my husband's. They're too big for me."

"Put them on. You've stalled long enough."

Sarah looked at Lynda. "It's all right, Lynda. Keep James fed for me. It's best that I go. Tom will need me."

One of the other men still in the house snickered. "That's a fact. All that dark skin will be scraped off by the time they're through with him. Maybe we'll make a white man out of him after all."

Sarah felt ill, and Lynda shook with rage. Sarah looked at John as she pulled on the moccasins. "Don't be afraid, John," she told the boy. "Tell your father exactly what has happened." She looked at Hafer. "He'll know what to do. Mister Hafer has made a great mistake. All the money in the world isn't worth what will happen to him for this."

Hafer paled slightly at the calm confidence in her eyes. He grabbed her arm and pulled her outside. There were a few more gunshots and shouts as Hafer and his men rode away with Sarah and Tom.

Lynda ran outside and watched them go, whispering her mother's name as the figures faded in the distance.

Chapter
Seventeen

Caleb brushed down his horse, grateful for Wil Handel's friendship. The Handel place was a good halfway point to and from town. He had stayed the night before on his way into town and would stay tonight and return home in the morning. It was not yet dark, but too late to go any farther.

Everyone at the meeting in town that day had been urged to join the Texas militia. The man Caleb had talked to about his problems with Hafer had suggested that any continued lawlessness would be more easily "tolerated" if he pledged himself to the militia.

It still angered Caleb that they thought they needed to bribe him into joining. If it came down to a war with Mexico, he would not hesitate to take part, nor would Tom. Of course he would join the militia, and he flatly told the man so, reminding him that he was one of the first settlers in Texas, that several members of his family were buried on his land. But Caleb had not missed the look in the man's eyes, as though to tell Caleb that because he was an Indian he was going to have to try harder than any white man to keep what he owned, including proving his loyalty by joining the militia.

"When we declare war against Mexico, I'll be riding with the militia," Caleb told the man. "Right now you've got plenty of free men coming in to help. I have a ranch to run and a family to watch after."

The looming fear of losing both ranch and family haunted him again. He didn't like the attitudes developing in Texas and was glad that Sam Houston was still in charge. Houston's popularity was growing every day, especially with Stephen Austin still in prison in Mexico City. Caleb liked Houston, knew by his eyes he was an honest man and by his past record he was a friend to Indians. Still, the changes in Texas only added to the uneasy feeling that plagued him since leaving San Felipe.

He walked out of the barn to see a rider coming. As the man came closer he recognized Jake Highwater, and his heart quickened with the urgency of the man's hard ride and the way he paid no heed to Handel men who waved to him, except to stop and ask one of them if Caleb was there.

"Jake! Over here," Caleb called out, walking quickly toward the man.

Jake rode up to him, his horse pushing dirt into little piles in front of its hooves as Jake drew it to a quick halt. The animal snorted and tossed its head, lather showing along its neck. "I hoped I'd find you here, Caleb. Bad trouble! A lot of the men have been killed and wounded. They took Tom—and Sarah!"

Caleb's face visibly darkened with rage. "Who?"

"Hafer and his men. They came last night. Actually it was about two this morning," the man panted. "They planned it out well, Caleb. We didn't expect them to come so soon, or at that hour. They were looking for Bess, but Tom hid her behind the logs in the fake wall. They dragged Tom out—beat him and took off dragging him behind a horse. They took Sarah, too. They didn't even let her get dressed first—took her in her robe and gown."

Caleb's blue eyes turned to a wild look the man had never seen in them. "Lynda? John and the babies?"

"The boy is okay, and the babies. They hit Lynda. They never found Bess. She's okay, but she's awful upset— thinks it's all her fault—thinks you'll blame it all on her." The man's eyes teared. "Goddamn, Caleb, they caught us sleeping. I never thought they would come back at us so soon. Some of them held Ada and my sons at gunpoint. There was nothing I could do."

"Don't blame yourself, Jake. We'll get them back. There's only one person to blame, and that's Charles Hafer," he hissed. "He will die for this!" He walked back to the barn to get his horse. "Go tell Wil what happened. We'll leave right now—ride all night if we have to. Borrow a fresh horse from Wil. We'll pick yours up later."

Jake rode up to the house and Caleb went to the stall where his horse was bedded down. His thoughts spun wildly. What had they done to Tom? And Sarah? If any man touched her, he would die a slow, agonizing death.

Caleb reached home by noon the next day, nearly half the time it should have taken him. He jumped off his horse before it even came to a complete halt, ordering a man to take care of it and get a fresh horse ready.

He ran into the house. Lynda looked up from slicing some bread, and Bess sat in a rocker near the hearth holding Cale. Her brown eyes showed terror and sorrow, deep circles under them. She looked away quickly when Caleb entered, and Caleb went directly to Lynda, who reached out for him.

"They took him—dragged him," she told him, breaking into tears. "And they took Mother."

He hugged her tightly. "I'll get them back."

He pulled away, studying her bruised face, his fury almost unbearable. He put a hand to her face. "Sons of bitches," he hissed. "Did they hit your mother?"

"No," she sniffed. She held his eyes. "They said if you want Tom back alive and don't want anything to happen to Mother, you're to bring Bess to them by Friday noon. That's the day after tomorrow. What should we do!"

"Don't you worry. We'll get them back." He turned to look at Bess, who sat with her head hanging, rocking Cale.

"I should have come out," she said quietly. "Tom told me . . . not to." Her words broke as she also began crying. "They're going to kill Tom. And it's . . . all my fault."

"You did the right thing," Caleb told her. "If they had got you right away they would have killed Tom then and there. You're our insurance."

She met his eyes. "I'm sorry," she wept.

"It isn't your fault, Bess. You love Tom. There's nothing wrong in that. And I'll get him back—and Sarah."

"Are you . . . returning me to my father?"

His eyes glittered with rage. "Never. I don't need to trade you to take back what's mine. But your father's life isn't worth much right now, Bess. I'm sorry."

She sniffed and cuddled Cale closer. James came crawling toward his father, taking on a bright smile. Caleb went to him, picking him up and hugging him tightly. At least they hadn't harmed the babies.

"That's the first time he's smiled this morning," Lynda told him, wiping her eyes. "He's been crawling all over the house looking for his mother."

Caleb kissed the boy's cheek, a lump in his throat. "She'll be here holding him in no time at all," he answered. He set the boy down. "Pack me a little food. I'm going to check on the men and see how many I can muster up." He turned to leave.

"Father."

He stopped and looked at Lynda.

"They're waiting for you. Hafer wants you dead. He said since the Council doesn't care how this is handled, he has free license to get rid of you."

Caleb smiled bitterly. "Let him try. I'm sure there is a big bonus in it for him from Mister Byron Clawson if he succeeds. But Clawson is going to be sweating in his sleep for a long time when he finds out Hafer failed!"

John came rushing in then. "Pa!" He ran to his father and hugged him. "Pa, they took Tom! They beat him up bad. And they took Sarah—"

"I know all about it, John."

The boy looked up at him. "You'll get them, won't you, Pa? You'll get all of them for what they did."

Caleb gently pushed him away. "That's right, John. I'll have Sarah and Tom back here in no time at all."

"Can I go with you, Pa?"

Caleb shook his head. "Not this time. There will be too much shooting going on."

"Rider," someone shouted from outside.

Caleb and John went out, and Lynda went to the doorway. The day was going to be unusually warm for late January, but that sometimes happened. The early thaw was usually followed by more cold weather before the sun brought back the shimmering heat of a Texas summer. Lynda went to the open door and watched the rider approaching. Two of Caleb's men rode beside him, and Lynda recognized Jess Purnell. Her eyes turned to cool slivers of hatred as she marched outside to face him.

"Liar," she shouted at him. "Spy! You're a stinking spy and a man who takes money for people's lives!"

Caleb grasped her arm. "Get back inside!"

"He was here the day before yesterday—asking questions! He said he wanted to work for you, but he was only spying! He knew you were gone. Hafer sent him, I know it! They were all waiting to hear what Jess Purnell told them! They raided us that very night because Jess Purnell told them you were gone!"

"That isn't true," Jess shouted. "I came here to help you, Mister Sax. I can help you get your wife and son back. I know where they're being held. Don't ride in there blind." The man looked weary and his horse was lathered, but Lynda failed to notice. Jess halted in front of the steps.

"You'll lead my father into a trap," Lynda shouted.

"I'm not doing any such thing!" Jess turned to Caleb, taking off his hat. "You've got to believe me! I'm here to help. I didn't even know about the raid. I wasn't there when Hafer left with his men. But I was already back by the time they rode in with your wife and son late yesterday. I left again right away to come and offer my help, but not before I saw where they put your wife and son. Can't you see how hard I've been riding? My horse is about dead and so am I! I got here in half the time it should have taken."

"It's all a trick," Lynda insisted.

"Lynda, get in the house," Caleb repeated. "Now!"

She pressed her lips together in anger, glaring at Jess Purnell, who could see that a future with Lynda Sax looked dim indeed. She looked up at her father then. "Don't trust him," she glowered. She stomped inside and slammed the door. Caleb turned his attention back to Purnell.

"Explain your presence, Purnell. The mood I'm in right now, your life isn't worth much!"

Purnell shifted in his saddle uncomfortably, as though he thought he might be shot. "I don't like Hafer's ways," he told Caleb. "I came here day before yesterday to talk to you, but you were gone. I wanted to work for you, even if it was for less pay than Hafer's."

"Why?"

"I told you why. I can't work for a man like Hafer any longer."

"Any other reason?"

The man reddened slightly, then turned defensive. "Yeah," he answered, straightening. "I didn't like your daughter thinking I was an Indian hater. I'm not."

"What do you care what my daughter thinks?" Caleb's eyes drilled into him. He knew. The man was very discerning and Jess knew the best way to deal with Caleb Sax was straight on.

"I care because I care about her personally. I could see that would get nowhere as long as I worked for Charles Hafer. So I came to work for you. I really didn't know anything about that raid. Hafer doesn't even know I came, and he doesn't know I'm here now. I can work both sides, Sax. I can go back and help you from the inside, don't you see? You need a man who knows where they are and knows the layout of Hafer's place. I'm that man. Let me help you. After I help you get back your wife and son, you can give me a job, or you can kick me out, whichever you choose. But I want to help."

Caleb studied him intently. There had always been something in the man's eyes he liked and trusted. "Get down off your horse."

Jess obeyed, stepping up closer to Caleb, feeling a shiver at the look in the man's eyes.

"You cross me, Purnell, and your guts will be greeting the sun but your eyes won't because you won't have any! You understand what I'm saying?"

The man swallowed. "I damned well do."

"Don't trust him, Caleb," Jake spoke up. "It's a trick."

"We don't have a hell of a lot of choice," Caleb returned. "The man is right. We need an insider." His eyes never left Purnell as he spoke, lowering his voice again. "If you prove yourself, you have a job. But my daughter is off limits to even a grin if she doesn't want you near her. You understand that, too?"

Purnell nodded. "You didn't have to tell me that."

Caleb's hand fidgeted nervously with the handle of the big blade he wore on his belt. "We don't have much time. What's Hafer's layout?"

Purnell looked relieved. "He's expecting you to come charging in there with an army. Why not sneak in quietly, you and I, in the night with just a few men. I can take you straight to where they're holding your son and wife."

"It's a trick, Mister Sax," another of Caleb's men spoke up. "It's a good way to get you over there alone. Then they've got you."

"I say we string this one up right now," still another put in. "Hafer's payin' him to do this."

"I think your daughter is right, Mister Sax. Don't trust him," Jake said.

Caleb held Purnell's eyes through all of it. "All right," he told him. "But before we leave, we set Hafer's nice new barn on fire. That would distract their attention and buy us a little more time."

"All right then. We get Tom and Mrs. Sax away, then set the barn on fire. That will obviously attract their attention, and confuse them. They won't know right away your son and wife are missing. When you spot Hafer, he's yours. The rest of the men we bring with us will take care of the others. The key is to get your wife and son out first so they won't be in danger. I can help there. I can go back first. I'll get there by tomorrow afternoon. I'll try to get Hafer to let me keep guard tomorrow night. If he won't, I'll wait till dark and take care of whoever is put on duty so that I can be there myself. Take me inside and I'll draw you the layout so you know where to come in. The most important thing is to be as quiet as possible and to get Mrs. Sax and Tom out of there before all hell breaks loose. Like I say, they'll be looking for a mob of men, not just a few."

Caleb's blue eyes looked him over carefully. Purnell was

a handsome man, strong and hard, shorter than Caleb but powerfully built. Again he saw only sincerity in the man's eyes. "Come inside." He turned and the two went inside.

Lynda's eyes widened in surprise, then turned to blue pools of hatred. "Why are you letting that man in our house?" she demanded.

"He's going to help us get your mother and brother back."

"Help us! Father, have you gone crazy? He works for Charles Hafer."

"He did. Now he works for me."

"Father—"

"I trust him, Lynda," Caleb interrupted. "You've been through a lot. Don't make me raise my voice to you."

Her eyes teared and she turned away. Caleb handed Purnell a piece of paper and a quill pen. "Show me the layout," he told the man.

Purnell took the paper and started drawing, and Caleb looked at Lynda. "Why are you doing this? You'll be killed," she said in a shaking voice.

He shook his head. "I have been through too much to be easily fooled, Lynda. I think Purnell is telling the truth. Besides, I don't have much choice. If I ride in there blindly, I might not find your mother and Tom. They could be in any of the buildings. It could be a wasted raid, and by then Hafe would know I don't intend to return Bess and he'd go ahead and kill Tom—maybe Sarah, too, if not something worse. Mr. Purnell knows that either way his life is in danger. If he's actually against us, his life is on the line from our side. If he's helping us, then it's Hafer who will be after him. But if we handle this right, there won't be a Charles Hafer to worry about."

He heard a sniffle from the fireplace where Bess still sat. His heart went out to her. She was a tenderhearted girl, whose heart was badly bruised by the conflict between her love for her father and her husband.

"Here you go," Purnell spoke up. He handed Caleb the paper and Caleb took it over to Bess.

"Does the drawing look right to you?" he asked the girl.

Jess met Lynda's eyes while Bess studied the drawing.

Again, in spite of her sureness that Jess Purnell was only tricking her father, Lynda felt the odd magnetism, the strange stirring as his gentle blue eyes seemed to plead with her to believe him. But how could she? It all made so much sense, him being there just before the raid. And everyone knew how well Hafer paid his men. She stiffened, glowering at him.

"How much are you being paid by Hafer to trick my father into coming over there alone?" she sneered.

Purnell rose, sighing deeply. "Ma'am, I wish I knew how to make you believe me. I guess the only way is to come back with your mother and brother." He could not help scanning her sultry beauty once more. "If it had been you they took, I might have been crazy enough to try to get you out on my own."

She felt color going to her cheeks and it only angered her more. "And why would you do that, Mister Purnell?" she sneered. "To rape me and then sell me to outlaws? Indian women don't bring a lot of money, Purnell, even the young ones." She tossed her head. "When this is over and my father realizes you've tricked him, you'll be a dead man!"

She whirled and stormed through a curtained doorway into the bedroom. Purnell turned to look at Caleb, who took the drawing from Bess.

"In case you haven't noticed, my daughter speaks exactly what is on her mind," Caleb told him, walking back over to the table.

"I noticed."

Both men grinned a little as Caleb laid the drawing on the table. "Bess says this looks right to her. Where are they holding Sarah and Tom?"

Jess pointed to a shed not far from the barn. "There. It's locked and a man stands outside it. I'll try to be that man."

Caleb folded the paper. "How bad is my son hurt?"

Purnell's eyes showed their concern. "Pretty bad. They beat him pretty good first, then dragged him. He's torn up real bad. I don't think he can walk. We'll have to carry him out."

Bess broke into renewed tears at the horror of it. Poor

Tom! All for her! She should have stayed on the boat and gone to St. Louis. Then none of this would have happened to him.

"All right," Caleb was saying. "I'll take him on my back. You help my wife if she needs it."

Purnell nodded. "If it helps any, I reckon Hafer's not a rapist, Sax. He's nothing more than a once-peaceful man whose head has been turned by money. He won't really hurt your wife, but he'd have Tom killed if he got Bess back. As far as the other men, I don't know."

The room seemed close with anger and revenge. "We have no time to waste. I'll have my men fix you up with a fresh horse. You leave right away. Can you manage a ride back?"

"I'll have to. But I can't be seen on one of your horses."

"I have a couple that aren't branded yet—some mustangs we've trained but never branded. Take one of those. Just mix it into Hafer's remuda when you get there. In the short time this will all take, the horse won't be noticed. But won't they wonder where you've been?"

"Yesterday and today were my days off. There's a Mexican camp not far from us where the men go sometimes." He glanced at the curtained doorway to see Lynda peeking out at him. She quickly turned away and Jess grinned to himself. "I'll tell them I was over there and was with a woman I didn't want to leave. They'll believe that."

Caleb nodded. "Good excuse." He would have joked about it if the situation were not so serious, but right now he could find no humor in anything.

Lynda came walking back into the main room, looking at no one as she went to the kitchen area, her back to them. Jess sensed he had just stirred something in her.

"I appreciate how hard this has been on you, Purnell," Caleb told him. "If you're on the up and up and this plan works, I will pay you well, and you've got a job here."

Lynda slammed down a spoon and whirled. "Father, why are you trusting this man?"

"Because I've been around long enough to know who to trust and who not to trust," Caleb answered. "And right now I don't have a whole lot of choice."

She turned cold blue eyes to Jess Purnell.

Jess picked up his hat. "I think I take back what I said about rescuing your daughter if she had been the one taken, Mister Sax," he said, his voice sounding his irritation and his eyes never leaving Lynda's. "I think in that case it would have been *Hafer* men who'd needed rescuing. Pity the poor man who crosses that one!" He put on his hat and exchanged a look of understanding with Caleb, who had to smile then in spite of the situation.

"I'm inclined to agree with you, Purnell."

"Father!" Lynda pressed her lips together in anger and turned back around.

"Let's go," Caleb told Jess. They walked outside. Caleb was tired—bone tired from his ride back from San Felipe, and he knew Jess Purnell had to be just as tired. But there was no time for resting now. Tom and Sarah were in trouble. They were depending on him, and on Jess Purnell.

The night was cold but Caleb wore no heavy coat. He wore only his buckskins to give him more freedom of movement. He was too full of hatred and vengeance to feel the outer elements. Silence, stealthiness, timing—that was all that was important.

Purnell should have arrived at Hafer's place earlier in the day. Caleb and his men had taken their time, coming in from several different directions and at different times all through the day and night, each man taking a post out of sight, hiding as only Indians could hide.

There would be no "Sax army." There would be only Caleb and five Sax men, who would silence what guards they spotted with quiet arrows. That was Caleb's advantage. Most of his men were Cherokee. He chose only the ones who still knew how to use a bow so that no shots would be fired. One by one guards went down without a sound as their predators crept ever closer, secretly surrounding the stone house and the outbuildings by nightfall.

They were blessed with a dark night. Clouds covered the moon. A few lanterns were lit around the outbuildings. Caleb kept to the shadows, his moccasined feet making no sound as he made his way toward the shed, where another lantern hung. He was relieved to see that Jess was standing at the door. This was the moment of truth. He gave out a call that sounded like a night owl. Purnell turned at the sound of it, cradling his musket in his arm. He removed his hat and scratched his head, the signal he was to use to tell Caleb it was all right to come in. He turned and unlocked the door to the shed.

"You all right, Mrs. Sax?" Caleb heard him ask. He carried the lantern inside so that it was dark outside the shed. Caleb made his move, darting through the darkness, then scratching on the door. It opened, but Caleb could see nothing. Purnell had blown out the lamp.

"Damned lamp went out," he said loud enough for anyone close to hear, so no one would wonder why there was suddenly no light. He quickly pulled the door shut as Caleb ducked inside. Purnell lit the lamp again and Sarah gasped when she saw Caleb. He put fingers to his lips, then rushed to her and grabbed her up, hugging her tightly. "Tell me they didn't touch you," he whispered.

"I'm all right," she answered. "Mister Purnell kept away one man who's been bothering me."

Caleb released her and turned to Jess, who gave him a steady look. But the rescue wasn't complete yet. Caleb would save his judgments for a more convenient time. His eyes moved to a cot on which Tom lay moaning.

"Jesus Christ," he groaned. He left Sarah, bending over his son, whose skin was torn like old cloth that had become too thin. Blood stained the sheets around him, and his face was grotesquely swollen, his ribs showing purple and black bruises. The long underwear he had been wearing had been ripped off when he was dragged and a sheet was draped over him. His legs and buttocks were bloody and scabbed.

"There was nothing I could do for him but talk to him and assure him you'd come," Sarah whispered, tears wanting to come again. "It was so horrible, Caleb. They wouldn't bring me any water or salve or bandages."

Caleb looked at her with watery eyes, and she could see him shaking with rage. He swallowed before speaking. "We're getting both of you out of here. Purnell is helping us. You can trust him. I'll carry Tom. When we move, move fast and don't ask questions. Can you run if you have to?"

She nodded. He looked at Purnell. "Let's go." He leaned over Tom, gently wrapping the sheet around him. The young man groaned when Caleb lifted him. The last thing Caleb wanted to do was hurt him more, but there was no choice. He hoisted Tom over his shoulder and Jess blew out the lamp and grasped Sarah's hand.

"Hang on to me," he told her.

Both men ducked outside, then ran into the darkness, Tom grunting and groaning in agony, barely aware of what was going on. Caleb stopped and let out several coyotelike yips, and minutes later one end of the brand new barn began to glow with fire. Sarah followed Jess Purnell blindly through the darkness, while behind them the barn fire grew bigger, and more Hafer men went down with silent arrows in them.

"Stop here," Caleb told Purnell. He laid Tom down gently in the grass. "Watch them. I'll be back."

"Caleb," Sarah gasped. "Where are you going?"

"I have some unfinished business with Charles Hafer."

"No! Caleb, don't go back there!"

"I'm just going to give him a good warning," he told her quickly. "He'll never bother us again after tonight."

He disappeared. Now a few shots could be heard, as well as a lot of shouting, as men rushed to stop the barn fire. Sarah held her stomach, whispering Caleb's name.

"Don't worry, ma'am. Those men will be right busy with the fire," Purnell told her. "Mister Sax will be all right. The horses aren't far from here. I'll take Tom now. We fixed up a sort of hanging bed between two horses—tied a blanket between them to lay Tom on. If the man waiting for us and I can ride in rhythm, we can give him a more comfortable ride home than trying to put him on a horse." He bent over and picked up Tom, who cried out with pain. "Come on. There's a horse for you, too."

Sarah stood frozen in place. Purnell could see the look of panic in her eyes, lit up by the growing barn fire. He knew she was terrified to leave Caleb.

"We've got to get moving, ma'am. That's why we set fire to the barn—to distract them."

"I can't leave yet."

"You've got to, ma'am. Come on now. It's your husband's orders. If you want to help him, do like he says. Every minute you wait, the more dangerous it is."

Sarah turned reluctantly. She couldn't prolong Tom's chance for help. She followed Purnell into the darkness, her heart aching for poor Tom who groaned with every step. Suddenly Purnell halted. "Get down," he told her. Sarah ducked and Jess laid Tom down on the ground again. Sarah could hear voices.

"Who the hell are you?" someone shouted.

"Hafer men," Jess said quietly to Sarah. "Must have missed them in the dark. They've found my partner."

"I'm just camping here," she heard a man reply.

"Camping? You a Sax man? What the hell is going on?"

Purnell charged forward and Sarah could hear scuffling and a muffled gunshot, then two more shots. Moments later Jess returned. "Come on." He picked up Tom and seemed to be grunting as though in pain himself.

"Are you all right?" Sarah asked.

"I've been shot. No time to stop and see how bad. Let's get you and Tom the hell out of here."

She followed, stumbling over a body when they reached the horses. She fought an urge to cry out. Here she was riding off into the darkness with a wounded Hafer man and her husband was behind them and in great danger. Now she was tripping over dead bodies. She shivered with the cold.

"Come on, Mrs. Sax," a man told her, lifting her onto a horse. He draped a blanket around her legs. "It's me— Jake."

She recognized the voice and felt more relieved. "Jake! Are you all right?"

"Yes, ma'am." He moved to help Jess lay Tom on the special blanket. Jess mounted up with great effort. Jake mounted his own horse. "We can't go too fast," he told Purnell. "But faster than if he was on a travois. Let's get out of here. Boss's orders."

"Right," Purnell replied.

"You gonna make it?"

"We'll find out."

"Hey, thanks, Purnell," Jake said. "You weren't lying."

"Yeah. Tell that to Lynda," Jess gasped in pain.

They rode off.

Between the main house and the barn, Hafer men were running in every direction, some trying to rescue horses and cattle inside the barn, others trying to form a bucket brigade from the well to the barn to try to put out the fire. But all could see it would be useless. Most suspected a Comanche raid because their men had been killed with arrows.

Charles Hafer ran around cussing, yelling something about "goddamned Comanche" with every other word. He fumed that they had "got the woman," and how the men had better get that fire out.

"I don't think it was Comanche, sir," one man hollered back. "I think it was Caleb Sax."

Hafer's eyes widened and he looked around. Sax! It couldn't be! Where were all the Sax men? He had expected a major fight.

Several yards away two men approached Caleb from behind as he neared Hafer's house. Caleb turned at the last minute, kicking a rifle from one man's hands and lashing out at him with his knife.

"Hey!" the other shouted, able then to see Caleb by the light of the roaring barn fire. "He's here! Caleb Sax is here!"

But there was too much confusion for anyone to notice. Caleb lunged into the second man before he could fire his rifle, knocking him to the ground. He quickly rammed his knife blade into the man's stomach.

The first man got to his feet then. Unable to get to his rifle in time, he kicked Caleb in the ribs while Caleb was still bent over the second man. Caleb rolled over with a grunt, his knife still stuck in the second man. The first man came at him and Caleb kicked out from a prone position, catching the man hard in the chest and knocking the breath out of him. He fell backward and Caleb stumbled to the second man, yanking out the knife.

The first man found his musket and fumbled with it, turning it on Caleb. But Caleb slashed out with the knife again, cutting deeply into the man's arms, desperate to keep the gun from being fired. The man cried out and dropped it. Caleb shoved his knife into its sheath and picked up the rifle, slamming its butt across the side of the Hafer man's face to silence him.

He crept closer then, praying Sarah was well on her way away from Hafer land. He watched Hafer from the shadows. The man was fuming, telling in graphic detail what he intended to do to Caleb Sax when he got his hands on him—and what he should have done to Sarah and Tom.

"We'll get your daughter, Mister Hafer," one of the men assured him.

"Over the dead body of every Sax family member," the man growled. He headed for his house. "I'm going to finish dressing and we're riding to the Sax ranch." He stormed inside, wearing only his long underwear and a robe. He kicked over a chair in anger, unaware of the dark shadow that followed him inside.

The door was suddenly kicked shut, and the house was lit only by the glow of the barn fire. Hafer whirled at the sound of the slammed door, his eyes widening at the sight of Caleb Sax, standing there looking like a true savage, half-naked, painted, his eyes cold and wild. His hand rested on his knife.

"Just a neighbor come to visit," Caleb sneered.

Hafer's eyes moved to a musket resting nearby in a corner. "What do you want, Sax? My God is this—*you* planned this!"

"That's right. Now maybe you understand you can't get away with hurting my family, and you know how easily I can sneak up on you and kill you. I would dearly love to do that, Hafer. Ordinarily your life would be worth nothing right now. It's only because of Bess that I'm not going to kill you, but you'll by God remember never to come near my place again!"

He landed into the man, knocking him back against a chair. The chair flipped out from under Hafer and went flying as the two big men tumbled on the floor. In Caleb's rage, Hafer didn't have a chance. Caleb's fist pummeled into him over and over—into his stomach, his chest, his face, his kidneys. Every blow was stunning, and it was all Caleb could do to keep from taking out his blade and doing what he really wanted to do, which was to let his Indian side loose and cut the man from his belly to his throat. Tom! The memory of how his son looked, how horribly he'd been tortured, it all brought extra force to his fist as again and again he battered Charles Hafer. They crashed about the room, while the men fighting the fire outside had no idea what was happening in the house.

Finally Caleb managed to force himself to stop the beating. He pulled out his blade, holding it against Hafer's cheek as he shoved the bleeding man up against a wall. "This is the last warning you'll get, Hafer! There won't be a second chance. You come near my place or any of my loved ones again, and you'll die—slowly! It's as simple as that!"

Caleb let Hafer loose and Hafer slid down the wall to the floor. Caleb stood staring at him, fingering the knife. His hands ached and bled and some of his knuckles were alread swelling. He backed away then, and the house glowed from the fire outside. He turned to leave the back way when he heard a click. He whirled to see Hafer pointing a small pistol at him. A little table lay overturned nearby, its drawer open.

"*You're* the one who's going to die, Sax," Hafer slurred through bloody, swollen lips.

Caleb quickly ducked aside as the pistol was fired, its orange flame showing bright in the dark room. The ball whizzed past Caleb, and it was all the provocation Caleb needed. His knife was still in his hand. Hafer scrambled to try to get up and run, realizing he'd missed. But a strong hand grabbed his arm, and quickly Hafer felt the knife's thrust in his chest and knew what a grave mistake he'd made agreeing to work for Byron Clawson. All the money in the world wasn't worth this.

"It could have been so easy, Hafer," Caleb sneered as the man's dying body slipped away from him. "All you had to do was give up, come and see your daughter, and give her your blessing. You sold yourself out, you fool!"

The man fell to the floor. Caleb jerked out his knife and wiped it off on Hafer's robe, then shoved it back into its sheath and left the back way. No one saw him.

Chapter
Eighteen

Tom opened his eyes slowly. The first thing he saw was Bess, who was carefully applying more salve to deep lacerations on his stomach. He looked around the room.

Home. He was home. His father must have come for him. He vaguely remembered someone carrying him, but that was all. He didn't know when that was. He didn't really remember anything beyond the horror of being dragged until he was unconscious. Surely he had been at the Hafer ranch, but he had no recollection of it, other than Sarah talking to him soothingly—somewhere, as though in a dream. Sarah! They had taken her, too, hadn't they?

"Bess," he managed to whisper.

She looked at him in surprise. "Tom! You're awake!" She bent over him, bringing her face close to his. "Oh, Tom, I was so afraid you'd never come around!"

"Sarah," he groaned. "What happened? My . . . father."

"They're all right. My father never found me, so they took Sarah with them and said they'd give you and Sarah back when your father brought me to them. But Caleb wouldn't do it. They never hurt Sarah, Tom. Jess Purnell, one of Father's men, he came here and helped your father rescue you. He got hurt bad, too—gunshot. But your father is all right." She kissed his forehead. "Oh, Tom, my father . . . is dead," she told him then, her voice breaking. "Caleb had to kill him. He . . . he tried to shoot Caleb."

She sat down on the edge of the bed, breaking into tears. "Oh, Tom, tell me you'll be all right. And tell me . . . you'll forgive me."

He frowned, managing to move an arm to reach out and take one of her hands. "Forgive you? For what?"

She kissed the scabs on his hand. "It was my father who did this to you. You've . . . been in so much pain . . . and your family has been through so much, all because of my father."

"Not . . . to blame," he muttered. "I love you, Bess. We'll . . . be okay now. I'll be all right."

She clung tightly to his hands, her tears falling onto the bed covers. "Oh, Tom, I know I should weep for my father . . . but I only weep over what he became . . . what he did to you." Her shoulders shook.

Now he wished he could hold her. "What about me?" he said then. "You should . . . hate me, too. My being Indian . . . that's what started it. My own father . . . killed your father."

She met his dark eyes with her own tear-filled eyes. "Oh, Tom, I love you so much. I could never blame you or your father. It wasn't your fault. I'm just so sorry for what happened to you. I don't want this to ruin what we had. I don't want . . . to lose you."

He managed a half grin, then winced with the pain of it. "You won't ever lose me. But you better . . . be a good nurse. The sooner I get well . . . the sooner I can hold you . . . and more."

She held his hand tightly, crying harder, kissing the hand again. Somehow they would get through this terrible time. Their love would see them through, for she did love him, more than life itself.

In the main house Lynda pulled down the blankets to Jess Purnell's waist to check the bleeding from the wound in his side. Caleb had repaired the wound himself, giving no guarantees he'd done it right or that Jess would live. That had been two nights and a day ago. It was noon, and soup was cooking on the stove, where Sarah stood stirring it, watched by Caleb, who could still feel the terror of thinking he might have lost her again.

She turned and set a bowl of soup in front of him and he looked up into her beautiful green eyes. "You think Bess will be all right?"

She understood his worry over having killed Charles Hafer. She ran a hand over his shoulders. "She'll be fine. She has Tom, and this won't change his love for her."

He set down a pipe he'd been puffing on. "I have a way of doing things that could make the people I love most hate me." He glanced over at Lynda, who was gently re-covering Jess Purnell.

"I don't think that's likely. Bess understands. And I have a feeling Lynda is going to be just fine, too."

Lynda looked over at them and seemed to be blushing as she moved away from Purnell. "And what is that supposed to mean, dear Mother?" she asked, putting on independent airs. She walked to the kettle that hung over the fire and dipped out some of the soup into a bowl from the table.

"It means that Mister Jess Purnell expressed to your father a very keen interest in you—enough to risk his life to prove he was not your enemy."

Lynda set the bowl on the table and sat down in front of it. "That was his decision. I never asked him to prove anything to me." She stirred the soup, feeling both of them eyeing her intently. She looked up, first at her mother, then at her father.

"I'm grateful for what he did, Father, but please stop looking at me that way. I have no room left for men in my life, and if I should decide otherwise, it will be a man of my own choosing."

"Of course it will. Who ever said it shouldn't be?"

She blushed slightly. "You know what I mean."

"The only thing I know is you've got to get back to being a woman, and Cale needs a father. I can't be his father, Lynda. Lord knows I hardly have enough time to be the proper father to my own sons. All I'm saying is don't be so against Jess Purnell. I know people, and he's a damned good man."

Lynda suddenly lost her stubborn look, suddenly looking ready to cry. She looked down at her bowl of soup, stirring it absently. "To think of any other man . . . it seems so disloyal to Lee," she said quietly. "I just don't think I could ever love again, Father."

"It's not being disloyal, Lynda," Caleb returned. "Lee would want you to be happy and fulfilled, loved and cared for the way only a husband can do. He wouldn't want you being lonely the rest of your life. A lot of people love more than once, especially in places like this. There is danger and death all around, but people keep on going. I lost two wives to death, but I loved again, and you will, too. You're still healing, that's all."

Lynda wiped her eyes, looking down at her lap. "This is a ridiculous conversation—talking about an absolute stranger!"

Caleb grinned. "Go ahead and eat your soup." He glanced over at Jess then, concern in his eyes. "If he doesn't make it through this, our discussion won't mean much anyway."

Lynda felt her heart tighten. She was not interested in Jess Purnell, yet she felt a strange sorrow at the thought of him dying. She had said some terrible things to him. She hoped she would have a chance to apologize.

Bess watched Tom herd prize horses into Blue Valley. Nearly four months had passed since the terrible raid. It was spring, and water flowed through the Valley again. Everything was green and beautiful and alive, and after weeks of healing for both Tom and Jess, both men were whole again. The joy of spring and temporary peace caused Caleb to make a picnic affair out of the spring herding to that area, and the women sat on a grassy rise above the Valley watching the herd of magnificent horses: spotted Appaloosas, roan-colored mares and geldings, and golden palominos. Caleb's prize studs were kept in separate pens closer to the house, to be used for breeding only when

Caleb knew the time was right, and only with exactly the right mares.

The men returned after an hour of racing through the Valley, showing off their riding skills to the women. Bess never dreamed she could be this happy again after the awful violence involving her father and Tom. But the Saxes had treated her like one of their own, and she felt surrounded by love. Tom Sax had proved to be everything she knew he would be—gentle and loving, a young man of strength, both physical and emotional. Their lovemaking only seemed to get better and better, and she prayed daily that his seed would sprout in her womb, but so far she had been unable to get pregnant. How she longed to give him a child!

He was riding back now, heading up the rise toward her, looking grand and happy, his dark skin healed. The mutilation of his skin from being dragged had left some scars, most of them on his back, belly, and legs. But he had healed much better than any of them believed he could.

Lynda forced herself to look away from Jess as he, too, rode toward them. She had hardly spoken to him since he stayed on and started working for her father. Their words had been confined to those first several days he recovered from his wound. She had apologized for her mean words, but she had remained aloof, struggling to show him she had no interest in him as anyone more important than the other men who worked for her father. He came close then, dismounting. "Caleb invited me to join in on the picnic. You mind?" he asked.

She looked away. "I suppose not. What would you like me to say?"

"Oh, you could say you're glad to have me, something like that."

She looked up at him and shrugged. "All right. We're glad to have you."

"We. Not you in particular?"

She shook her head, unable to prevent a smile at his persistence. "Not me in particular." She reached over and rubbed Cale's belly, feeling a little sorry for her cool attitude toward Purnell, sometimes hating herself for it. He was indeed handsome, a prize catch for any woman. If only she didn't always feel so guilty thinking of him as anything but a ranch hand. If only she weren't so desperately afraid to ever love again.

He remounted his horse. "You're a cruel woman, Lynda Whitestone, and a man's pride can take only so much." He turned his horse.

"Jess, wait," she called out.

He turned back around, and a sudden wave of passion moved through her with surprising force as their eyes met. She actually blushed, turning away to lift Cale and hold him close. "I really am sorry. Don't ride off. I'd like you to stay. We have apple pie. I made it myself."

He smiled warmly, seeing a ray of hope but reminding himself to tread carefully. Lynda was scared to death of caring about anyone again, and she would run away like a frightened deer if he made the wrong move.

"Well, I'd ride a hundred miles for good apple pie." He dismounted again, glancing at Tom and Bess, who were hugging and kissing. He cleared his throat and turned away to lead his horse to better grass. "Thanks for the invitation. I'll be right back."

Caleb had returned and was walking with Sarah, leading her to higher ground where they could get a good view of the Valley.

"It's so beautiful, Caleb," she told him, looking out over the Valley, watching the horses run wild and free. "All of this fits you—such big country, so wild."

He sighed, putting an arm around her shoulders. "A little too wild sometimes for a family man. I'm sorry about all the hardships, Sarah."

She put an arm around his waist. "We're together. That's all that matters. Tom is healed and he and Bess are so happy."

He glanced over at Lynda, who sat playing with Cale. "I just wish our daughter could find that same happiness."

"She will. She's slowly coming around, Caleb. And I've seen her watch that Jess Purnell when she thought no one noticed. She'll be fine, in time."

"Jess is a good man. I'd like to see those two together."

"Well, don't tell her that. She'll just get even more stubborn about it."

"How well I know."

She turned and looked up at him. "It's such a beautiful day! It feels so good—spring, life, love."

He leaned down and kissed her lightly, then ran the back of his hand over her cheek. "You're my strength, you know. I might look big and strong, but that's only on the surface. With you at my side I feel like I can do anything, without you—"

She touched his lips. "We won't talk about that. It will never be that way again—for either of us."

Both felt the old pain of separation. He hugged her close then. She was right. He would die before he ever let it be that way again.

"Let's go enjoy that food," he said, leading her to where Jess Purnell was sitting down near Lynda.

The situation between Texas and its mother country remained stagnant. Texans were anxious to lash back at Santa Anna for squashing their every effort to have their own laws, courts, and constitution; and again there were rumors that Santa Anna meant to disarm all of them, this time by more forceful means. The only thing that kept the Texans from revolting was the pleading of Stephen Austin himself, through letters he was allowed to write from his prison cell, in which he urged the settlers to remain peaceful.

In his absence, Sam Houston was gaining more and more popularity, looming forward as the most important leader of the Texas colonists. It was Houston who wrote letters to President Jackson, hinting that the purchase and annexation of Texas to the United States should be considered. But Jackson wanted no war with Mexico, and it was obvious to Houston that if there should be one, Texas was on her own and, if she should win such a war, would be an independent republic.

The odds in favor of winning seemed small indeed for a handful of American settlers to go up against Santa Anna's Mexican army. It was a disturbing thought, and like Austin, Houston believed the only thing to do for the moment was to tolerate Santa Anna's constant threats and abide by his tighter ruling. But the Americans were a proud, independent people who would not tolerate dictatorship.

It seemed only a matter of time until it would all surely come to war. Already there was a dangerous division growing between the settlers who opted to continue trying to keep the peace, and those who were eager to go to war.

But for several weeks all the shouting grew dimmer, and the influx of even more volunteers halted almost completely when the cholera epidemic swept through Texas. Suddenly the problems with Mexico seemed, for the time, secondary, as the ugly hand of death moved through the settlements taking, in some cases, entire families.

It visited the Sax family in June 1834. For weeks they had lived in fear as the disease swept through the Cherokee first. All they knew about preventing the disease was rumor—boil drinking water, burn everything the victim touches, including his or her clothing and bedding. No one really understood the disease, except that it was a terrible way to die—diarrhea, vomiting, loss of body fluid that often led to shock and death. Why the ugly disease visited some and not others was perplexing and frightening, and when Caleb and Sarah were sure they had been spared, Bess came down with the awful vomiting.

To Tom it was as though someone were standing her up and holding a gun to her head. There was nothing he could do but watch her suffer. Never in his life had he felt so helpless. He insisted on caring for her himself, and Caleb lived in terror that Tom would also get the disease. But it was not Tom who came down with it. Two days after Bess contracted the disease, young John also woke up sick.

The silence of impending death hung over the Sax ranch. Not only was there the agony of trying to save two loved ones from death, but also the waiting and watching to see if little Cale might come down with it, or baby James.

Tom could think of nothing worse than watching his new, young wife shrivel with each day of diarrhea and vomiting, watching her scream with the pain, hearing her beg him to help her end it all quickly. But there was always that hope, that chance she might survive. She was young. Sometimes the young lived through this.

On the fifth day of Bess's agony she seemed somewhat better, her color better as she lay lovingly watching Tom while he again changed her bedding, carrying the old bedding outside and burning it. How she loved him. How patient he had been, so kind and understanding, by her side every minute. She could not have picked a better husband. How sad to leave him behind all alone.

He came back inside to see her watching him, her eyes looking brighter. He smiled for her, forcing back his fear and worry. She would be all right. He came to her side, kneeling next to the bed.

"Are you feeling better, Bess?"

She touched his hand with her own weak, bony hand. His was so big and strong, and so dark. She managed a smile. "Promise me something, Tom," she said in a near whisper.

He leaned closer. "Anything you ask."

"Be strong, Tom, like your father. He . . . lived through . . . so much loss. He . . . loved again. Promise me you will love again, Tom."

Tom frowned. "I don't have to promise that. I have you, and you're going to make it, Bess."

She studied him, her eyes glittering as though full of some free, new spirit. "No, Tom." She swallowed at the horrible sorrow in his eyes. "Don't feel . . . sorry for me. I'll be someplace . . . peaceful and happy. It's you I'm worried about. My beautiful . . . Tom. You've been . . . so good to me. My handsome . . . Indian man." Her eyes teared. "I'm just . . . so sorry . . . I never gave you a son. I wanted to do that . . . more than anything."

"Stop it, Bess," he almost growled. "You stop that talk! You've made it through the worst. You'll be okay now."

She closed her eyes and sighed deeply. "Thank you, Tom. For . . . taking care of me like you have . . . for loving me. I prayed . . . you wouldn't get this too . . ." Her voice broke and she swallowed before going on. "I just know . . . God will spare my Tom. Many wonderful things . . . are waiting for you, Tom Sax. Go . . . and find them."

Tears were streaming down his face then. "Bess, I wish you wouldn't talk this way. I love you. I need you. I can't . . . I can't live without you now."

"Yes, you can. Just like your father did . . . when he lost your Cheyenne mother . . . and when he lost Marie. I was just . . . your first love." She felt the ugly pain moving through her bowels again and she gasped and shuddered. "Let me go, Tom," she groaned. "Tell me . . . you'll be strong . . . you'll be all right. Tell me you'll . . . love again . . . so I can go in peace. I have to be free . . . of this pain."

He just sat there trembling, holding her hand and shaking his head. She met his eyes again. "Tell me, Tom."

He swallowed, hardly able to find his voice "I'll . . . be all right. I'm a Sax, aren't I?" he tried to say kiddingly.

She smiled. "Yes. That's why I know . . . you'll be just fine. You're so strong, Tom."

He forced a smile through his tears. "Sure. Don't you worry about me, Bess."

She just watched him then, a strange light in her eyes. "I . . . love you so much," she whispered, before her eyes closed and her body suddenly jerked, then began shaking violently.

"Bess!" Tom stood up and leaned over, grasping her arms and trying to hold her still. Suddenly the shaking stopped, and a long gasp of air exited her lips.

"Bess?" His grip tightened on her thin arms. "Bess? Damn you, answer me!" He shook her, but he already knew there was no life there. He moved back then, staring at her for several long seconds before screaming out her name and stumbling outside.

Lynda was the first one to see him heading for the main house, holding his arms around his head like a crazy man. She ran to him and grasped him.

"Tom, don't go in there!"

He looked at her with wild eyes, and Lynda felt sick herself at the horrible grief she saw there. "She's . . . dead," he groaned. "My Bess . . ."

She tightened her grip on his arms. "John is dying, too, Tom. Don't go to Father yet."

He shook his head and stumbled backward. "No. Why! Why, Lynda?"

She struggled to stay in control. Someone had to be strong for the moment. "I don't know, Tom. I asked myself the same thing when Lee was killed." She choked back tears. "I'm so sorry, Tom." She walked closer and he suddenly grabbed her and hugged her tightly, weeping on her shoulder.

Two fresh graves were dug on the little hill where Marie and her mother, David, and now John and Bess were buried. There was a headstone there for Lee, but no body, and there were the several graves of others who had died on Sax land. A sprawling, tree-size mesquite bush shaded most of the graves.

Tom stood staring at Bess's grave. He was still in shock. His eyes moved to the grave of his young stepbrother. He had two people to grieve for. How could he live without the woman who had become his life's blood? He'd promised Bess he would be strong, he would go on with life. But how could he keep that promise?

Six months. He'd had her only six months. So much joy and beauty had been packed into such a short time. An agonizing ache swept through him in painful spasms every time the reality of it hit him.

Bess was gone. She was dead. She was not coming back. There would be no sons and daughters. The cabin they had finally finished building for themselves would not be used. He had known grief, but never of this magnitude. Sometimes he wondered where his next breath would come from, for the heaviness in his chest was almost stifling. It was as though a huge boulder was crushing him. Nothing seemed real. Nothing mattered.

Tom looked over at his father, who knelt by John's grave. John had died in his father's arms, only three hours after Bess's death. He wondered how the man had borne all his own losses. Two wives . . . two sons and another unborn child who had been in Marie's belly when she was killed. And there had been others he had loved and lost in his lifetime. But Caleb Sax just kept going. Could he be that strong? At the moment it seemed impossible.

Caleb got to his feet slowly, as though he were ill. Sarah helped him up. Thank God their son James had been spared, as had Lynda and Cale. But the whole land smelled of death. Again the reality hit Tom, bringing the knot to his stomach, the awful ache to his throat as he fought the unmanly urge to weep like a child. Tom made the mistake of meeting his father's eyes. He knew. Caleb Sax knew the devastating grief; he understood it better than most. It took only that quick look to bring the floodwaters of grief to Tom Sax.

Caleb saw it coming, walked over and embraced his son, who could not hold it back now. He cried like a small child, withering in his father's arms and wanting to be held like that child. Caleb did the holding, tightly. How well he understood. And somehow having to help his son cope with his grief helped soothe Caleb's own torturous sorrow over losing John. Both his Cherokee sons were dead. The only remnant of the Cherokee family he had once loved was Cale, Lee's son. How thin was the line between life and death.

Lynda moved her own eyes to the headstone they had erected in Lee's memory. There was no body. God only knew what had ever happened to it. A year. It had been a whole year now since Lee left and never returned. She turned away. She could not bear the pitiful sight of her father and brother. Death! How it angered her. It was not fair. It was never fair. She walked away, heading down the hill and going to stand alone beside a small creek. There was a little water in it now because it was spring. But by midsummer it dried up. Died. Just like people. At least it came back to life every year. None of her loved ones would come back to life. How she ached for poor Tom. At least she had Cale, some remnant of Lee. Tom had nothing. All that suffering he had gone through for Bess. All for nothing.

"Lynda?"

She turned to see Jess Purnell standing behind her. She turned away again. "Go away."

He sighed, stepping closer. "We've gotten to be pretty good friends, you and me."

"What do you want, Jess?" she interrupted.

He swallowed. In spite of all his efforts, Lynda White-stone had remained as elusive as a butterfly, defensive, stubbornly independent. He didn't know how to approach her, how to get through her barriers.

"I want you to let me hold you."

She looked at him in surprise.

"Somebody has to," he added. "Don't you ever need holding?"

She moved her blue eyes toward the spot on the hill where Caleb still stood holding Tom. "Up there," she said quietly. "That's the reason I don't want anyone holding me. That's all it brings—terrible grief." She looked back at Jess. "Death is around us all the time. I don't intend to care that much again, Jess. I can raise Cale just fine by myself. I want and need no one in my life, certainly not another man." She turned away. "You give your heart and soul to someone, and then God decides to take him away. That leaves you with nothing but an empty shell for a body. That's what I am; an empty shell, with just enough emotion left to love my son. It's hard enough living with the constant fear of wondering if he will be next. Without little Cale I think I truly would end my life."

She walked past him and he grabbed her arm. "I love you, Lynda. You're a fine, strong, beautiful woman, and some day you'll belong to me. I've waited long enough to say it. Now it's done."

"Let me go."

"No." He yanked her close, grasping her wrists and forcing them behind her, pressing her against himself. "Not yet."

She met his eyes defiantly, but he kissed her anyway, a long, hard kiss to remind her of what she was missing in her life. He felt her stiffen, yet she did not truly try to get away from his lips, at least not at first. He sensed a tiny bit of surrender before she finally shook her head violently, leaning away from him.

"Bastard! You bastard," she wept.

He let go of her. "I'm not sorry. No, ma'am, I'm not sorry at all. I don't just love you, Lynda. I need you. I've got nobody. You have your parents and a son and brothers. I lost my folks a long time ago. You're the first woman who's come along who I want for my own more than anything in this world. You think about it, Lynda Whitestone. You think real hard about it."

She rubbed her lips with the back of her hand. "How dare you," she said in a shaking voice. "If you really loved me, you wouldn't . . . you wouldn't try so hard to make me care again! You would understand and let me be happy!"

"Happy? Are you happy, Lynda?"

Her chest heaved with heavy breathing as she struggled not to cry openly. "Yes," she almost hissed. "As long as I can keep from feeling anything, I'm very happy!" She turned and stomped away. He watched with an ache so fierce he wanted to bend over. One taste of her lips and he knew his nights would be miserable for a long time to come. But there had been that tiny hint of surrender. True, she was angry. But he had given her something to think about, and surely he had stirred old passions just a little. That was better than nothing.

He looked up at the little graveyard. Tom Sax had crumbled right to the ground. "Goddamned unfair," he muttered to himself. In a sense Lynda was right not to want to care again. But a man or a woman couldn't go through life alone and lonely just because of what might happen. Life couldn't go on that way. Lynda would realize that soon. He'd make sure of it.

Byron Clawson looked up from his desk as the man he'd sent to Texas came inside his office. He hadn't heard anything from Charles Hafer in a long time.

"Sit down," Byron told his informant.

"Thanks." The man moved into a red leather chair, fumbling with his hat nervously. He was a common drifter. Byron had picked him purposely because he looked like everyone else, didn't stand out in any particular way. He was unkempt and ragged, a man who would fit right in as a hired hand in a place like Texas. Byron wanted the truth, wanted this man to mix in on the Hafer ranch and find out if Hafer was doing his job.

"Well, Kent," Byron asked. "What did you find out?"

Stuart Kent seemed hesitant. "Charles Hafer is dead, sir," he finally answered.

Byron paled visibly. For a moment the messenger thought he might be sick right then and there. He could see Clawson struggling to keep his composure. Finally Byron took a deep breath and leaned back in his chair. "I've heard there has been a lot of cholera in Texas—"

"Not cholera, sir," the man interrupted. "A man by the name of Caleb Sax killed him outright."

He saw a look of utter defeat and near terror in Clawson's murky gray eyes.

"Tell me all of it," Byron told the man. The words came out in a near squeak.

"Well, sir, when I got there, there were only a few men left—living in Hafer's house like squatters, using it as a kind of hangout, living off his cattle and such. A big barn Hafer had built was burned down, and the place was pretty much deserted. I asked the men there what the hell happened to Hafer. They said there had been a big feud between him and this Caleb Sax—some neighbor to the south of him who's part Indian."

"I know who Caleb Sax is," Byron sneered impatiently.

Kent squirmed in his chair. He didn't like men like Byron Clawson. There was an element of evil to the man's power that made him uncomfortable, but he had been paid well to go to Texas and get the facts.

"Yes, sir," he replied. "At any rate, I guess at first the fight was over water. Hafer had diverted some from the Sax place to irrigate his own land for cotton. This Sax fella, he attacked Hafer's men and tore up the dam Hafer had built and got his water back. But I guess things got really heated up when this Sax man's son run off with Hafer's daughter."

Byron's eyes widened and he leaned forward. "His daughter!"

"Yes, sir. Seems the two took a shine to each other and the next thing you know, the young man snatches her right off a boat Hafer had put her on to bring her back to St. Louis and they get married. Hafer went after her but couldn't find her, so later he attacked Sax's place and stole the son and Sax's wife. He nearly killed the son—dragged him behind a horse. Said he'd return them when Sax brought him his daughter. Hafer was fumin' mad because the Sax boy was Indian. At any rate, his plan didn't work. Sax attacked in return. Somehow he knew just where his wife and son were being held. He got 'em back, and he killed a lot of Hafer men, burned the barn, too. And somehow Caleb Sax got in the house and killed Hafer. They found him stabbed to death."

Kent shifted in his chair again. "I mean to tell you, sir, those men are right scared of this Caleb Sax. They said they'd never go up against him again. Said now that Hafer is dead, they don't give a damn what happens. The Sax kid can have the girl for all they care. All most of them are concerned about is Mexico. They're kind of waitin' around to get in on the fightin' when it starts. They even—"

"That's enough!" Byron waved him off. "Go collect your money from my secretary. I want to be alone," he said in a shaking voice. He turned his chair around so that the back of it was to the man. Kent rose, glad to leave. He hurried out without another word.

Byron stared out a window. Sax! Caleb Sax was alive and well and still kicking! What if he knew? He bet that Sax knew the real owner of that land was Byron Clawson. His son had been nearly killed. The man already hated him enough to kill him. This would only make matters worse. He hit the arm of his chair with his fist.

"Fool," he grumbled, referring to Charles Hafer. "Goddamned fool! I never should have sent a goddamned farmer against someone like Caleb Sax!"

He whirled his chair and pulled open a drawer, taking out a bottle of whiskey and slugging some down. Caleb Sax! None of it had worked out as he had planned. Apparently Sax had more power in Texas than he thought, to get away with something that outrageous.

"He'll not keep that power or that land for long," Byron

sneered. "If I have to go down there myself to get things going against the Indians, I'll do it."

Surely by now, with so many Southerners going to Texas, there were rumblings against the Indians. A natural hatred was already harbored for the Comanche. That was understandable. But somehow Comanche hatred had to be directed at all the Indians. Someone had to accent the fact that a lot of Cherokee were going there, most of them probably squatting on land that wasn't even theirs.

That reminded him that there were men squatting on his own land. Squatters on Clawson land, living in the home Hafer had built with Clawson money! Now there was no one to watch over the property, no one to develop it. He took another swallow of whiskey. Hafer! He'd bungled everything!

He shoved the bottle back into the drawer. There was nothing he could do about it now. He was getting too involved in raising money and preparing to campaign for the primaries for governor. In another year they would be held. He couldn't become well known in Missouri by running off to Texas. The land was still his. What could happen to the land? It was always there. Besides, things were getting too dangerous down there, what with all the trouble with Mexico.

He leaned back, reassuring himself that he was safe by reminding himself that Caleb Sax surely wouldn't take the time to stop and come to St. Louis to kill him—not now—not with a whole family to support and the danger of war with Mexico. War! Yes. Perhaps the son of a bitch would be killed if there was a war. That was a pleasant thought.

Somehow Caleb Sax had to die, or Byron Clawson would never get a good night's sleep. Now the danger of Caleb wanting his skin was even greater. Why on earth hadn't Hafer just killed the man? Surely he could have had him assassinated somehow.

"Stupid goddamned fool," he muttered again. "I never should have told him it was worth more to him to destroy Sax financially and get him run out of Texas. I should have *ordered* him killed outright." The damned Indian always managed to win, to survive everything Byron threw at him, whether it was physical or mental torment. He stood up, going to look out the window.

"I'll get you yet, Caleb Sax," he growled in a low voice, speaking to nothing but the window. "I'll get you first." His eyes filled with tears of pure fear, and he shivered with the thought of Caleb alive and now aware that Byron had sent Charles Hafer to harrass and destroy him. As long as Caleb was alive, Byron could never be happy. He blamed Caleb for all his bad luck: for losing Sarah and her money; for his ugly, crooked nose.

"Perhaps I'll have to meet the enemy face to face after all and have it over with," he muttered aloud.

Yes. Surely there was a way to do that without dying. Not in combat. Lord knew he could never defeat Caleb Sax in combat. But maybe there was a way to look the man in the face and still defeat him. He would find a way. And Clawson set out to do just that.

Chapter Nineteen

It was 1835 when Santa Anna began an all-out campaign to "tame" the Americans. Surrounding provinces were secured by Mexican troops, their own militia disbanded. Military garrisons were established throughout Texas as a warning to the settlers. He hoped that the Mexican troops would in themselves be enough of a threat to settle the anger of the Americans, who were outraged that Santa Anna had declared their constitution invalid. Santa Anna did not like reform. He did not agree with trial by jury. He did not believe in religious tolerance, nor with the use of English in legal documents. The Americans were becoming too "American." They should obey Mexican law.

A group of merchants at Anahuac were arrested for creating opposition to heavy import taxes. Texans gathered in great numbers afterward in San Felipe to discuss what they should do about the merchants. More men joined the militia. William Barret Travis, a fiery young lawyer recently come to Texas, gathered together twenty-five men and a cannon and left San Felipe to attack the Mexican troops at Anahuac and demand the release of the merchants. Only one cannonball was fired, and the Mexican officer in charge fled with his forty-four men.

The merchants were released, but Texans were so torn over war or peace, and so worried about what the full Mexican army could do to them, that Travis returned to San Felipe to discover that most of the settlers were angry over his actions, declaring he had acted rashly. A letter of apology was immediately dispatched to the Mexican government.

But Santa Anna and the brother-in-law he had put in charge of Coahuila y Texas would have none of it. The Americans had dared to act against the Mexican government! Santa Anna demanded Travis be turned over for arrest. The Americans would not do it. They were upset with Travis, but they would not hand over one of their own to be shot by a firing squad.

Things were getting to the point of "fight or submit." Americans took hope in the leadership of Sam Houston, and in the return, in September of 1835, of Stephen Austin, more than two years since his arrest. Austin reinforced their courage and determination, describing Santa Anna as a "bloody monster," and declaring that war was their only recourse. The Mexican commander at San Antonio, Colonel Domingo de Ugartechea, sent a detachment to Gonzales to take back a small brass cannon given the settlers for defense against Indians. The Texans at Gonzales, angered that the Mexicans would dare to come and take away a needed weapon, sent out messengers to help them defend against Ugartechea's men. Their call for help was quickly answered, and the Mexican troops were met by one hundred sixty settlers and their long rifles. The Mexicans appeared and the Texans opened fire.

On October 9, 1835, a small troup of Americans attacked Mexican soldiers at Goliad, who were stationed there to guard some powder and shot. The Mexican soldiers, mostly criminals themselves, who were poorly fed and poorly paid, surrendered readily. They had no desire to fight the determined and independent Americans.

All these small victories of the proud and bold Texans fueled their craving to be rid of Santa Anna's cruel dictatorship. The Texas revolution had begun . . .

Tom Sax was among the men who fought to keep the cannon at Gonzales. He wanted a fight. He needed a fight.

He had left the ranch. Caleb understood. Tom had to get away from familiar things. But Caleb knew it wouldn't be long before he would also have to leave. War seemed inevitable.

Tom missed his father, miserably. Yet it was more miserable to stay around where he'd had those few months with Bess. Every day he had to look at the newly built but unused cabin. Every day he had to see the little graveyard on the hill. Every day was torture. Maybe he would die fighting Mexicans. It would be an honorable enough way to go. But somewhere deep inside he knew that some day his feelings would probably change. And he knew what it would do to his father if something happened to him.

Tom sat smoking, listening to Stephen Austin, their chosen leader. The poor man was ill. It was obvious his prison experience had nearly broken him. He looked terrible, and he coughed a lot. But the men had asked him to lead them, and he had agreed, for he loved Texas more than his own life. That was the strange part about it. They all loved Texas more than their personal comfort, their very lives. He realized how much he must love it. It had taken Bess from him, yet here he was, fighting for this cruel land.

What made a man do that? Mostly stubborn pride, he supposed. No man wanted to get "licked." He'd fight for Texas, then maybe he would leave it. But it would not be easy leaving his father. Maybe he was too dependent on the man. Except for his early years living with the Cheyenne, Caleb Sax and Texas were all Tom had ever known. He was twenty-two years old and had never been anywhere, except the one trip he made to St. Louis back in '32, where his name in the paper had attracted the attention of Sarah Sax and helped her find Caleb. He didn't even remember being with the Cheyenne as a baby.

But Tom hadn't cared much for the bigger cities in the East. If he left Texas, maybe he would go deeper into the wilds of the mountains to the north and west. Maybe he'd dig deeper into his Indian heritage, maybe even live among them. There had to be some way to get over Bess. The ache raged through his soul in cruel waves of sorrow that washed over him without warning, leaving the terrible crushing feeling on his chest again. He must not think about it. He must not think about all the hell he had gone through to have her, only to lose her to disease, something he could not fight. It made Tom feel so helpless. He guessed that was why he was here. Here he could physically fight something, vent his grief on the Mexicans.

There was not time to think about it now. Austin was telling the three hundred or so men present that he intended to attack San Antonio, a bold move indeed. There were fourteen hundred Mexicans at San Antonio; uniformed, trained men. Tom studied the American volunteers, mostly dressed in buckskins. Some wore boots, some only moccasins. Most were independent men who were difficult to lead, biting at the bit to "kill a Mexican"; rash men ready to do rash things.

Tom himself was among the ninety or so men led by Jim Bowie, a seemingly skilled, brave man who carried an unusually large, fancy knife and knew how to use it. Tom liked him and trusted him. The fiery young attorney, William Travis, who had won the victory at Anahuac, was also among them. They were all looking for a fight and Tom wanted one as much as any of them. Anything to keep from thinking about Bess. It was October 1835 when they all left for San Antonio, where they hoped to occupy a Spanish fortlike mission there called the Alamo.

* * *

Caleb lay sleepless. Tomorrow he would go to the convention in San Felipe and join with the others under Sam Houston's leadership, as they all discussed what to do. Already Stephen Austin and his men had been attacked outside San Antonio. In the ensuing battle, sixty Mexicans had been killed and only one Texan. Now the Texans were entrenched around the city but had not attacked, aware that their numbers were far too small. They were waiting for instructions and help from the rest of Texas, under Sam Houston. There would be a meeting first.

He lay beside Sarah in a bunkhouse on Handel property, a bunkhouse that was empty, deserted by men who had volunteered. Caleb's own ranch sat quiet, only a few Cherokee left to watch over things, including Jake Highwater. Most of Caleb's horses had been sold to be used by the militia, which was short in supply of everything. The few horses left could be watched by Jake and the four or five men left.

Caleb was now an active volunteer. There seemed to be no choice. He was a Texan, and Tom was also out there fighting. But he worried what this war would do to the ranch. He hadn't even got any money for the horses he'd sold to the militia; only promissory notes from a penniless new government. But he trusted they would make good on the notes. In the meantime, after this was over, he would simply start over. He could always start over. It seemed that was the story of his life.

James, now over two years old, slept in a cot nearby. Lynda and Cale slept in the main house with the Handels. Jess slept in a small shed nor far away. He would go with Caleb to San Felipe in the morning.

Caleb turned to Sarah then, and she to him, as though both sensed at just the right time what they must do.

He met her mouth and she returned the kiss with unusual savageness for his gentle woman. He was immediately on fire. They had made love already tonight but once was not enough. He would go to San Felipe tomorrow, perhaps march out that very day and not be back for a long, long time. His lips moved to her full breasts.

"Come back to me, Caleb," she wept. "Please, please come back to me!"

His only reply was to meet her mouth again, searching deeply as he moved on top of her. How long would it be before he did this again? What if he never came back? Who would care for her, love her?

It was the same for her, the worry, the wonder. It was all so wrong and unfair. Why did there have to be war? Everything seemed to be crumbling around them. Lee and John were dead, and poor Bess. Tom was off fighting somewhere, and the ranch sat making no money. Fate was again dealing its unpredictable hand to the Saxes.

Caleb told himself at least he still had the land. They would all go back some day. They would, after a while, all be happy again. There would be no more war in Texas.

He surged inside his woman with possessive determination. Sarah! God, how he hated leaving her. She arched up to him in return, wanting to remember this moment, every part of him, remember how it felt to be made love to by this man. No greater fear plagued her than losing him again after spending so many years apart.

At the main house Lynda also lay awake. Jess Purnell would leave tomorrow. Why had she been so mean to him? Why had it been so difficult for her to let herself care? Yes, it hurt to love and lose. But suddenly it seemed perhaps it would hurt more to lose a man without ever showing him she loved him. Over and over he had expressed his love to her. But she refused his advances, ignored her own needs, pretended they were not there. How terrifying it was to think of loving again! Especially now. Tomorrow he would leave.

Maybe he would never come back. And if he didn't, how would she feel then? He would die without ever knowing her love in return. She turned on her side. Her father liked and trusted Jess. Even little Cale liked him; loved riding on Jess's shoulders, ran to him as though he were his father every time he saw him.

She thought about his friendship, his beautiful, powerful body, the tender blue eyes and thick, sandy hair. She thought about the strong hands, the brilliant smile, the tanned face. He might die, never knowing that deep inside she really did feel love for him. But it was so terrifying to admit to that love.

She lay in torment. Which would be worse? Loving him, giving herself to him, and then having him die like Lee? Or letting him go off alone and lonely, his dying thoughts being of her, the woman he loved but never could have? What if he was wounded? Wouldn't he struggle to live if he knew she loved him and was waiting for him to come home? Or would he will himself to die because he was sure he never could have her? Surely this very moment her mother and father were making love, sharing those last wonderful, intimate moments together. Her father would leave knowing his woman loved him, leave with a determination to return to that woman, leave with much more courage in his heart because he had a real purpose.

She sighed and sat up. Maybe she was a fool. She pulled on her robe and went through a curtained doorway to the outer room, leaving a soundly sleeping Cale in her bed. The Handels slept in another room. Lynda walked on bare feet to the front door, her mind reeling with indecision.

She walked outside and over to an abandoned shack where she knew Jess slept. She reached the doorway and hesitated, turned. She wasn't even sure what she had expected. But just to wish him luck and tell him she loved him was risky. Just admitting it meant caring again, the risk of the awful loneliness again. It had been two years since Lee died. Two years. And it had taken her all this time to get over it, to feel like a whole person again. But she had never gotten over that loneliness. How could she take that chance again?

She started back for the house.

"Lynda?"

She gasped, turning to see a man come from the corner of the shed.

"Jess?"

He came closer. "What the hell are you doing out here?"

She swallowed. "Where did you come from? Why aren't you sleeping?"

"Couldn't. Too many things on my mind. And you didn't answer my question."

"I . . . I came to wish you luck . . . whatever happens to-morrow."

"In the middle of the night? In your robe?"

She looked down at herself, glad it was dark so he couldn't see her blushing.

"I couldn't sleep either," she replied.

He came closer and she couldn't make her legs move. "Thanks for coming to tell me." They just looked at each other, able to see well now by the light of the moon. Even though it was October, it was quite warm, yet a distinct shiver of desire moved through Lynda Sax Whitestone. "I'll worry about you," he told her.

"We will be all right. You'll be the ones in danger."

"God only knows where Santa Anna will strike, what his soldiers will do to women."

"They're supposed to be gentlemen in that respect."

"Men at war are never gentlemen. They can turn into savages."

"I can take care of myself."

"How well I know that."

She blinked back tears. "Jess, I—"

He waited, sure she had something important to say, afraid anything he said now might spoil it all.

"I love you, Jess."

There was a long moment of silence. He finally reached out hesitantly, reaching around her waist and pulling her close. She did not resist. She turned her face up to his and he met her mouth, her very willing, sensuous mouth. Fire ripped through his blood, and almost immediately she felt his hardness against her belly as his lips and tongue searched her mouth hungrily.

She had been too long without a man. Old, buried needs surged forward so that when his hands moved down to grasp at her hips she did not resist. She gripped him around the neck and let him push with his hand so that she came up and wrapped her legs around his waist, their mouths still tasting, searching. He turned and carried her inside that way, kicking shut the door behind him. Lynda White-stone was finally ready for a man again.

He lowered her to the bed, then moved on top of her. She hadn't even realized in the darkness that all he wore was his long underwear. They came off easily enough, while she sat up slightly, kissing wildly at his broad, muscular chest and arms. Somehow he'd been sure that when she finally submitted she would express almost more passion than he could handle. He'd seen it smolder at times in her haunting blue eyes, felt it emanate from her dark, slender body. He'd known there was one hell of a woman buried under all that hurt just waiting to break out again.

Now she had, and he would be the recipient. How he loved her! It all seemed so natural, so necessary. No questions were asked. He groaned with the taste of her mouth as he pushed up her gown. She wore nothing under it.

He hadn't even touched or tasted her breasts before he was moving inside of her with the eagerness of a younger man experiencing his first woman. She cried out with ecstasy, panting his name almost rhythmically as he buried himself inside of her, feeling half crazy with his need of her. He soon felt the pulsating contractions of her climax, exquisite muscle spasms that brought an ecstasy he had never experienced. She pulled him into herself with as much savageness as he was pushing.

He could control his pleasure no longer. His life poured into her in great, pulsating throbs that made him groan, then left him spent. He embraced her then, going limp on top of her.

"Lynda, God, Lynda," he murmured. "God, I love you. I love you."

She broke into tears. "Come back to me, Jess. You have to come back to me. I'm scared. I'm so...damned scared." She broke into heavy sobbing. He knew how hard this was for her, how terrified she was of losing again.

"I'll come back. You can damned well bet I'll come back," he told her.

He moved off her, pulling her gown the rest of the way up and over her head. Moonlight shafted through the window, and her brown breasts glowed softly in it. He bent down and kissed her throat, moving to her breasts, bringing more gasps of ecstasy from her lips as he gently sucked at the full nipples he had only dreamed about for months. Did a man ever stop needing this? It was as though he could draw strength and nourishment from these tender fruits, like a babe sucking its milk.

She kept whispering his name, squirming for more. He would give her more. He might be damned tired for a ride into San Felipe in the morning, but it would be worth it. And as soon as the war was over, he would come home and marry Lynda Sax Whitestone. She would be Lynda Purnell, and she would never be lonely again.

In December Texas militia, including Tom Sax, drove into San Antonio, startling the organized Mexican soldiers with their fierce, disorganized but determined effort to take the city in spite of the difference in numbers. The Mexicans, led by General Martín Perfecto de Cós, brother-in-law to Santa Anna, were in complete confusion as to how to fight these fierce Texans. They moved behind the protective walls of the Alamo mission, but Texans battered it with cannon until Cós could take no more. One hundred seventy-nine Mexican soldiers and six officers had already deserted. Many had been killed. Cós sent up a white flag, and the Texans marched into San Antonio. By then their leader was an old Indian fighter named Edward Burleson. Stephen Austin had gone to the United States to appeal for war funds and more volunteers.

Burleson's raw fighting skills had rallied the Texans, but he made one poor decision that was to affect Texas history forever, leading to one of its saddest events. He let Cós and some eleven hundred Mexican prisoners go free, with a promise from Cós that Mexican soldiers would never again fight Texans or deny them a right to their own constitution; in return for which the Texans agreed to remain a part of Mexico.

Burleson and his volunteers considered this courtesy a strong message to Santa Anna that they weren't after total independence. They never had been. They wanted only to be allowed to rule themselves, have their own courts, their own religion. Was it so much to ask? Surely, after this act of great humanitarianism, Santa Anna would back off and give them the same courtesy in return by leaving them alone now.

But Sam Houston saw it differently. He trained his volunteers at Washington-on-the-Brazos. Caleb and Jess were among those volunteers, both men eager to fight and tired of waiting to see what would happen after the Mexican defeat at San Antonio. Most thought that would be the end of it. Only Sam Houston was sure it was only the beginning. He sent out a letter to remaining Texans, urging all to rally to the standard in defense of Texas and not be fooled by the "temporary" victory at the Alamo.

Caleb struggled with worry over Sarah and his family, and Tom, who had been among those at San Antonio and who was now entrenched in the Alamo mission. Names of those killed had been posted. Tom was not among them. At least he knew Tom was all right.

San Antonio had been taken and he tried to tell himself there was nothing to worry about now. Every morning and night he prayed for his son, not just because of the danger he might be in, but because of the terrible burden Bess's death put on his heart. The boy had been long in recovering from her death.

He looked over at Jess, who sat leaning against a nearby tree smoking, his eyes closed. He'd noticed how Lynda looked at the man before they left, how suddenly they had embraced and kissed. It was certainly far more than the embrace of friends, and too lingering and intimate for a first kiss. He'd been fully aware of Jess's feelings for his daughter, but also aware of how Lynda had made it a point to stay away from him, to remain aloof, determined to ignore him. Caleb had said nothing about it all this time they had been here training, and Jess didn't bring it up, although for the first couple of days after leaving home, he had acted nervous about something, as though he had almost a guilty conscience.

Jess opened one eye to catch Caleb's intent look. His eyebrow arched and he came fully awake. "Something tells me I'm being judged and hung without even knowing it," he said to Caleb with a grin.

Caleb took a pipe from his pocket and began stuffing it, looking around to be sure no one else was close by. "You want to tell me about it?"

"About what?"

"About why my daughter suddenly kissed you like a long-lost lover the morning we left."

Jess colored slightly but held his eyes. "Sure. Why not? I intend to marry her soon as we get back. With your permission, Mr. Sax?"

Caleb finished stuffing the pipe, grinning a little. "You know you'd have my permission."

Jess leaned back again. "Yeah, well . . ."

Caleb knew what he was hinting at. He put the pipe to his lips and lit it, puffing it for a moment. "Her idea, or yours?"

"Both. Lynda came to me the night before we left to tell me she loved me. One thing just sort of led to another. She's a hell of a woman and I respect her, Caleb. I didn't want it to happen that way. It just did. I don't regret it and I don't think she does either."

Caleb puffed the pipe another few seconds. "Lynda's a full-grown woman and a mother. I have no say in what she does in the way of men. Lord knows I never did, anyway. She never knew me as a father until she was seventeen years old. That's a little late to be starting to tell a daughter what she should do with her life, not that I'd object to her marrying you," Caleb smiled. "You're a good man, Jess. You'd just by God better take damned good care of her and never hurt her."

Jess grinned. "No problem there."

"She has been hurt enough. Did she tell you about the gambler she lived with?"

Jess nodded. "I know all about it. I also know she was a damned scared child then, with no one to turn to. I don't care about that."

Caleb nodded. "Lynda is a fine woman. You're a lucky man."

Jess lit a cigar, feeling the pain of wanting her again.

"I'm well aware of that," he answered. Their eyes held. "Thanks for understanding, Caleb. I wasn't sure you would."

Caleb thought about Sarah, her savage eagerness that last night. "A man going off to war does something to a woman," Caleb answered. "To the man, too, I guess." He shook his head. "Probably the best lovemaking there is."

Jess grinned. "I don't doubt that."

God, how he wanted to be back home, in bed with Lynda. What a wild, beautiful, satisfying woman she was. There wasn't a woman alive who could make him feel like Lynda Whitestone made him feel, and Lynda was good and loyal and wonderful. What man could ask for more? It hurt to think about her. He ached for her, so much so that he considered deserting more than once just to go back and sleep with her again. But his manly pride kept him from doing it. Jess was not a deserter when he knew the cause was right. Hafer had been different. His cause was wrong. But to fight for Texas was to fight for Lynda Whitestone and Sax land, and he felt very much like a Sax now. He respected and admired Caleb.

"You think they're all right?" he asked Caleb then.

Caleb felt the old anxiety, but he had to think positively.

"They're at the Handels' and close to San Felipe. They will be all right."

Jess sighed. "I just worry about Santa Anna's soldiers, if they do retaliate. A lot of them are pretty worthless, not much better than bandits."

Caleb struggled against his own worry over possible attacks on San Felipe and surrounding settlements. "Handel will keep them safe. He'll take them on into town if necessary. We have to hope for the best. Santa Anna is still south of the border."

Jess stood up and stretched. "I just wish we'd get moving. This waiting is driving me crazy."

"I know. I hear we might go to Goliad." Caleb shivered. It was early February. Austin was currently in New Orleans negotiating loans and enlisting more American support. Pamphlets had been handed out to Southerners, calling Texas the "Garden of America" and urging volunteers to come help fight, in return for which they would receive free passage and eight hundred acres of land. More soldiers waited at Goliad, and it was rumored many had left the Alamo and returned home or joined troops elsewhere, sure the excitement at the Alamo was over now.

Caleb rose himself, staring to the south. Just how ferociously would Santa Anna retaliate for the humiliating defeat at San Antonio? And just how equipped were they to fight Santa Anna's full force? Texas was not organized. There were arguments over leadership, and although he considered Sam Houston one of the best—a true man of Texas and a man who understood what must be done—the man seemed to be languishing. It was time for action. Caleb hoped they would go to Goliad as it was rumored. This waiting and wondering was too strenuous. Maybe they would even go to the Alamo to bolster the declining garrison there. That would be good. He could be with Tom.

Emily Cox walked with her husband toward the meeting place where more volunteers awaited instructions. San Felipe was in chaos, with everyone arguing over what should be done next. None of their leaders was there: Houston was on his way to Goliad, Travis was at the Alamo, Austin was in the States. Texans were divided on the question of independence, as many still believed they could patch things up with Mexico.

The current leader at the Alamo, Colonel James Neill, complained that too many men had left for Goliad, men who planned to take the Mexican city of Matamoros at the mouth of the Rio Grande, where many liberal Mexicans lived who did not like Santa Anna's leadership. Sam Houston was totally against the idea, as was the new governor of the Province of Texas. But the general Council supported the plan and so they continued to argue in San Felipe, amid the influx of even more volunteers. Messages kept coming in from the Alamo, where men like Jim Bowie and Davy Crockett had gone with more volunteers. Those who had gone to Goliad from the Alamo had taken with them nearly all the medical supplies and more ammunition than the men there could spare should Santa Anna attack. But those who left argued that Santa Anna would not attack for weeks, and that the Texans' best move was to attack Matamoros.

And so the arguments raged, while the volunteers at the Alamo languished, caught in the middle, waiting for more men to come and help defend the huge mission-turned-fort that covered nearly two acres.

Howard Cox felt he had put off joining long enough. He didn't want to leave Emily, but neither did he want to be accused of not doing his part. Volunteers at the Alamo were dwindling to dangerous proportions and he was convinced, as were many others, that it would be the first target of Santa Anna. It was directly in Santa Anna's route north to invade Texas.

"I'm going to San Antonio," he told Emily as they walked to the meeting. "Those bucks that want to go to Matamoros are nuts. Stay in our own territory, that's what I say. Otherwise we look like the invaders, thirsty for war. We don't want war. We just want what's right. The ones at the Alamo, they're the ones who will need help. We'll find out more at the meeting."

"Oh, Howard, I'm afraid," Emily said.

He patted her hand. "I won't leave just yet, Emmy. But it will have to be soon. And don't you worry about ole' Howard. I've got my Emmy to come back to."

Several men rode by as they started across the street. One of them halted his horse, staring at Emily, who glanced at him and then quickly looked away, covering her scarred face with a lace scarf.

"Emily," the man shouted. "Hey, Emily!"

Howard stopped and looked at the man. "Don't pay any attention, Howard," Emily pleaded. "I never saw that man before in my life."

Cox frowned, confused. Why had he called her by name? The man turned his horse and rode up to them. "Emily Stoner! Since when did you get so high and mighty, turning away from an old customer?"

Emily kept walking, but the man rode his horse in front of her. "Hey, I'm talking to you!"

Howard yanked her out of the way, clenching his fists.

"What the hell do you think you're doing, insulting my wife, mister! Get down off that horse!"

The man frowned, leaning forward in his saddle and then grinning. "Your wife! Emily Stoner?"

"Her name was Emily Stephens, mister. Now it's Cox! You've got her mixed up with somebody else. Now leave her alone, or you'll be tasting your teeth!"

"Howard, please," Emily said in a shaking voice, keeping her head down.

The man on the horse started laughing. "Mister, somebody fooled you good. A man don't screw a woman as often as I screwed that one and then mix her up with somebody else. You married one of the biggest whores in New Orleans. Lucky man, you are. You've got all that good stuff all to yourself now—maybe." The man laughed again.

His horse reared and he laughed again as he rode off. Others stared, then moved on, while Howard just stood looking at Emily. She turned away from him, breaking into tears. Her grief was the proof of her guilt, and Howard stood in shock, feeling anger, disappointment, but most of all a great sorrow that moved through him with painful force.

"Emmy," he choked out. "Is it true?"

She started to walk away, devastated that her worst fear had been realized. He hurried up and grabbed her, spinning her around. "I asked you a question, Emily Cox. Is it true what that man said?"

"Yes," she hissed. "Yes! Yes! Yes!" She jerked away from him, suddenly hysterical. "I was afraid to tell you— afraid I'd lose you!" she screamed. "I love you, Howard. In you I saw a chance to live like a normal woman!"

The disappointment in his eyes tore at her heart. "Emmy," he groaned.

"You don't understand at all! I . . . I can explain, Howard. But I've never been untrue to you, and I never would be. You have to believe me, Howard. I love you. I love you!"

"Lies! All lies! You said you were a widow. You said—"

"I know what I said! How could I tell you the truth! I

wanted to be married—I wanted to get out of that life. These last few years with you have been the happiest of my life! Don't let it make you hate me, Howard!"

He blinked back tears. "I . . . I don't know what I feel. This is a damned poor time to find out—out here in the middle of the street—me thinkin' about goin' off to fight Mexicans. There's no time to feel anything, one way or the other."

"Tell me you love me, Howard," she sobbed.

He studied her eyes, then turned away coldly. A whore from New Orleans! How many times had that man bedded her? How many others had there been? "I have a meeting to go to. You go on back home."

They stood in the middle of the wide, dusty street as wagons and horses rode by them. "I'll be waiting, Howard. You come back . . . after the meeting. We'll . . . we'll talk."

He just shook his head and looked away. "I don't know. I just don't know what to think . . . what to do."

"You come back like I said," she said, hope in her voice. "I'll explain everything. No matter what you think, Howard, I didn't lie to hurt you. I just . . . I love you so, Howard. Truly I do. I'll always love you."

He looked at her, his eyes red with tears. "Go on home, Emmy," he said, a terrible sadness in the words. He turned and walked away, joining some other men who were headed for the meeting.

"Howard," she squeaked. She turned and walked slowly back. Ruined! All of it ruined in that one brief moment of recognition. She should have told him. She should have told him right in the beginning before she realized how much she really did love him.

The people moving around her, the talk of war, none of it was real to her now. She managed to keep walking on rubbery legs until she reached the little cabin, where she sank into a chair and wept . . . and waited. Night came. He did not return. The next morning she went to the meeting place, only to be told all the volunteers who had gathered there yesterday had left to help in the fighting.

"But he . . . he didn't come home to get his things," she said almost absently.

The man shrugged. "I wouldn't know about that, lady. He probably had everything with him he needed. Don't take much but a gun. What's your man's name. I can tell you where he went."

"Cox," she said quietly, staring at a map on the man's desk. "Howard Cox."

The man scanned a ledger. "Cox. Here he is." He read for a moment. "He joined them that went to help out at the Alamo. Maybe you'll hear from him when he gets back, or maybe you'll get a letter. They do try to get letters out. Don't worry. We'll end this thing right quick and send Santa Anna running back to Mexico where he belongs and your man will be back home. Sorry about the mix-up."

She just stared at him, then turned and left. Maybe he would write. It was all she could hope for. And maybe after he had time to think about it, after the fighting was over, he'd come back to San Felipe, back to his Emmy. Yes. When he was through at the Alamo, he'd come home to her.

Chapter Twenty

It was January 1836 when Jim Bowie rode to the Alamo with Houston's orders to blow up the mission and retreat. Tom joined the other volunteers in vehemently objecting to those orders.

"That's surrender, and we'll never surrender," men shouted.

"It's not surrender. It's the practical thing to do. Let

Santa Anna get deeper into Texas; then Houston will strike," Bowie told them.

"Santa Anna will never get deep into Texas. We'll stop him right here!"

"You don't have enough medical supplies, food and clothing, or even ammunition."

"We don't need much," another volunteer shouted. "It won't take us long to win this war. And Houston will see we get more when he realizes we're stayin' put. When Santa Anna comes, he'll meet our musket barrels, not our backsides."

The men laughed and cheered, raising their fists. They were here to fight, and that was what they would do.

That was fine with Tom. He just wished Santa Anna would hurry up and come. If he was lucky, he would be killed and this awful ache over Bess would be done with. He would be with her forever. Yet that would mean leaving this life and leaving his father, and losing another son would just about destroy Caleb Sax.

He noticed a man he'd seen come in with some new volunteers a few days earlier. The man looked familiar. Tom had kept mostly to himself since coming here, and he wondered if striking up a friendship would help this terrible new loneliness that had enveloped him since losing Bess and leaving home. He approached the big, bearded man just as the man was headed for the west wall to take his post there.

"Hey, mister," he called out.

The man turned. He frowned at first, then put out his hand. "You're a Sax. I've seen you in town."

Tom nodded, shaking his hand. "Yes, sir. Tom Sax. I've been trying to place you."

"Howard Cox. I was the blacksmith back at San Felipe."

"That's it." Tom smiled. "You're married to that woman my father knew years ago."

Howard let go of his hand, masking his anger and sorrow over Emily. What did any of it have to do with this young man? "Yes. Emily." Just saying the name brought back the remorse. He should have gone back first. He should have talked to her. She really did love him. Who was he to accuse her of anything without even talking it out first? After all, all that was before he'd ever known her. But it was too late now. He was here and he would stay until the fighting was over. "How have you been, Tom? How's your family?"

Tom sobered. "Things haven't gone so well. I lost my wife to cholera about a year and a half ago."

"Jesus, that's right. I remember hearing about that. I'm sorry, son. You lost a brother, too, didn't you?"

"Yes. John. He was a half-brother, my father's son by his Cherokee wife. John was only thirteen."

Howard frowned and shook his head, showing genuine concern. "My God, that's too bad, Tom. Your father has had his share of troubles, that's sure."

The pain moved through Tom again. "Yes. We all have."

Howard thought again of Emily. He didn't know anything about the troubles she'd had, why she'd been a prostitute. Why hadn't he talked to her before leaving? He'd make it up to her. Somehow he'd make it up to her. He'd just been so shocked and hurt. She'd understand that. They'd fine a way to start all over.

"Well, now, we'll have to kind of look out for each other, won't we?" Howard said aloud.

Tom smiled. "I suppose so. My father is with Houston, as far as I know. I wonder who will see some action first?"

"Hard to say. But I expect it will be us. We're closest to where Santa Anna has to come through."

"Well, I'm ready. I just wish he'd hurry up. I'm tired of all this waiting."

"Same here. You take care now, Tom. I've got to get to my post."

Tom nodded. "Good to see a familiar face, Howard."

Howard read the loneliness and sorrow in the young man's eyes. "I'm real sorry about your wife, son. But you're young. You'll be all right, Tom. I know it's hard to think that way now, but time takes care of a lot of things."

Tom nodded and turned away, and the two men parted, each lost in his own particular sorrow.

* * *

Jim Bowie became ill with a bad cough, so ill that he was bedridden. William Travis, who had been competing with Bowie for leadership at the Alamo, became the undisputed man in charge of the mission. The nights were bitterly cold, and since Santa Anna was known to be a man who liked total comfort, no one believed he would consider attacking the Alamo in such inclement weather.

"He'll wait till spring," Howard told Tom one night over a campfire. "He's got lots of men, which means lots of horses. He'll need the spring grass for grazing. By then we'll have lots of reinforcements."

"I hope you're right, but then I don't like the idea of sitting here until spring either," Tom replied. "It seems like no one is doing anything at all. We're all just waiting, and nobody knows how anyone else is doing. I am worried about my father and the ranch."

"I know what you mean, boy. Me and Emmy, we had kind of a problem when I left. I left angry, and it bothers me some. I've thought of writing to her, but I just don't know what to say."

"She will be all right. San Felipe is a big town now. She's safe there. That's where Mister Handel will take Sarah and the others if Mexican soldiers should get through that far and start attacking the ranchers."

"This must be hard on your pa, too. He'll be worrying about you and the rest of the family."

"Yes. I sent a letter not long ago telling them I'm still here. I hope they got it so they know I am all right."

"That's good. I guess I should think about writing my Emmy, maybe patch things up some before I go home. Maybe then she won't greet me with a fry pan and clobber me over the head with it for being such a fool."

Tom laughed. "I don't know what your problem was, but I don't think she would do that."

"Women can be mighty strange sometimes, son."

Tom's face saddened and he poked at the fire with a stick. "I guess I was never married long enough to find out."

"Hey, I'm sorry. I didn't mean to bring back bad memories."

Tom shook his head. "They aren't bad. They're beautiful." He picked up his musket. "I have to take my post. Good night."

Howard nodded in reply, watching Tom leave and feeling sorry for him. He sat back to think about a letter to Emily. But he never got to write it. The next day scouts reported Santa Anna was on the march, headed straight for the Alamo. Travis began sending out calls for more help. His messengers managed to get away from the mission by following brush-lined irrigation ditches that hid them from Mexican soldiers who by then were entrenching themselves around the handful of Americans who held the Alamo.

On March 3 the siege began. While delegates at Washington-on-the-Brazos were declaring Texas a free and independent republic, the Alamo was under full attack, and no one had been sent to help the brave defenders of the little mission. Some thought the Alamo had been abandoned, as Houston had ordered; the volunteers at Goliad refused to leave, thinking their own post more important to defend than the Alamo; and general chaos and an unorganized defense all combined to prevent help from arriving for William Travis and his men.

Howard thought he wanted to fight, but this was more than he had expected. It was as though the whole world was exploding. Everywhere Mexican cannon fire broke through the walls of the outer court, the Mexican soldiers poured over the walls, pushing the American defenders back into the mission itself. After three days of fighting and no sleep, with ammunition nearly spent, it was evident this battle was not going to be won. Howard thought of Emily. If only he'd written the letter. If only he'd gone back to see her in the first place. Would she realize he loved her?

He searched frantically then for Tom Sax as Mexican soldiers managed to overrun the mission itself. But there was too much mass confusion, and he was too busy trying to stay alive to search for Tom. He could only pray that somehow the young man would escape this hell. He fired his musket directly into the chest of a Mexican soldier, then felt the pain in his back as a bayonet found its mark.

"Emmy," the man groaned before collapsing over the bodies of comrades already fallen.

By the time the battle was over, 187 Texas volunteers had died, although the count would never be positively accurate, since so many volunteers came and went, and messengers had been sent out right up until the last heat of battle. The opportunity for Americans to take a truly accurate count would never come. Santa Anna ordered the bodies to be piled together and burned. The sickening smell of burning flesh filled the clear, cold air, the smoke wafting up into the bright blue Texas sky. Cannon and musket fire had stopped. The little mission sat silent and battered.

Santa Anna began his march northward, capturing militia volunteers at San Patricio, Agua Dulce and Refugio, promptly executing all prisoners. On March 20 Goliad was taken, and a week later 342 Texas volunteers, many of them already badly wounded, were led outside, blindfolded, made to lie facedown, and shot.

But already the news of the Alamo had reached those volunteers with Sam Houston, who had retreated from Gonzoles to the Colorado and then across the Brazos, where they had held up for two weeks, constantly drilling. It was Jess who brought the news to Caleb where he sat outside their tent cleaning his musket. For a moment Jess just stared at the man, wondering how he was going to find the words. But there was no way to get around it. It had to be said.

"I hope you're coming to tell me we're going to go fight someplace," Caleb told him kiddingly. But his smile faded when he saw the grim look on Jess's face. "What's wrong?"

"Scouts just came with the news, Caleb." He sighed deeply, looking away. "Santa Anna took the Alamo—killed every last man there and then . . . piled the bodies together and burned them."

There was a long silence, and Jess finally turned to meet

Caleb's eyes. "You all right? Do you understand what I'm telling you, Caleb?"

Caleb returned to cleaning his musket. "That's bad news. Gives us all the more reason to go after that bastard Santa Anna, doesn't it?"

"Caleb, Tom was at the Alamo," Jess said carefully.

Blue eyes lit into him angrily. "No! He got out somehow."

Jess frowned. The man wasn't going to let himself believe it. "Caleb, you know he was there. They were all killed. They say everybody at Goliad was killed, too. Even if he left and went there, he'd still be dead."

Caleb just kept rubbing the barrel of his gun. He shook his head. "I've lost too many sons, Jess. God wouldn't take that one from me—not my Tom—not my firstborn."

Jess wanted to be angry with him, because he didn't want to face the truth. His own heart ached with the thought of it. Tom! What a good friend he had become, and how sad the last months of his lonely life had been. What would this do to poor Lynda? If only he could be with her when she found out. He stared at Caleb. How was he going to handle this thing? He couldn't even share his grief with the man, because Caleb wouldn't believe it.

It was simply going to take some time. Caleb Sax couldn't face this one. This one was too much. Jess turned away, thinking of home and how easy it would be right now just to desert and run to Lynda. Others had run off. But how was Santa Anna going to be stopped if they all just gave up? They had to take a stand, and he wished Houston would do something. Now they had all the more reason to fight—the Alamo, and Goliad. There had been needless slaughter at both places.

He turned back to watch Caleb, who was lighting a pipe. "Sit down and relax, Jess," the man told him. "There's been some kind of mix-up. My Tom is out there somewhere, and when this thing is over with, we'll find him. Maybe he'll even be sitting home waiting for us when we get there."

Jess sighed deeply, turning away and blinking back tears. "Sure. You're probably right," he answered. He walked away. If the man wasn't going to face Tom's death, then Jess wasn't about to cry about it in front of him. Let Caleb face it in his own way, in his own time. He walked off to be alone. For the time being there was no one with whom to share this sorrow, and the sorrow was made greater by Caleb's refusal to face it.

He knelt by a gnarled old tree and wept. All those men —dead. It seemed incredible. And Tom Sax was surely one of them.

Lynda stood outside Emily's cabin. They had all come to San Felipe for safety—Lynda and Sarah and the babies, the Handels and what few men were left at the Handel ranch. By now it was possible both their ranches had been overrun by Santa Anna and his men, who were now camped outside the city. Everyone expected them to come through the next day, and now even San Felipe apparently was not safe. What few men there were in town would fight, but it would be useless.

Still, for the moment, there was no place else to go. At least with so many people in one place, Santa Anna's men would be less inclined to abuse the women. It was better than being caught alone on a remote ranch. Fleeing settlers who had suffered at the hands of Santa Anna's men had already filtered into town. More of his aids were marching through Texas at other points—men like Gaona, Urrea, Cós and Sesma. Rumor said that Houston was retreating from Santa Anna's push.

Lynda wondered if Jess and Caleb were still with Houston. Their last letters had said so, but there had been no letters now for weeks. Everyone said Houston was retreating closer and closer to the Gulf, and no one understood why. When would the man stand and fight?

Emily Cox was certain her husband had been at the Alamo. Their first few days in town the woman had carried on about how Howard had found out about her past just before he left. At first she was weeping and remorseful. Now she was quiet, hard, bitter. There were no smiles anymore, and she had aged. Sarah had tried to comfort her, but there was no comfort for such a woman. Lynda wondered where their own comfort would be if something happened to Caleb or Tom . . . or Jess.

The thought of losing Jess, too, was overwhelming, and she clung to the porch post and broke into tears. Where were they? Were they even alive? And what about Tom? Their last word was that he'd gone to the Alamo, and they knew now that everyone there had been killed. Even if he had been among the volunteers who left there and went to Goliad, he would still be dead. All those at Goliad had been executed by Santa Anna.

Tom. Jess. And her beloved father. Not knowing what was happening brought literal pain.

"Lynda."

She turned to see Sarah in the doorway. The woman knew all her thoughts, and shared them with equal concern. She'd thought once she'd lost Caleb Sax, lived without him for years. But this time . . . this time . . . if he didn't come back . . . how could she face it a second time? Lynda came to her and they embraced, breaking into tears.

"We've got to be strong, Lynda," Sarah finally said between tears. "All our men are alive. I just know it. Our job . . . is to keep ourselves alive and unharmed for them. We can't do anything for them right now but look out for ourselves and the babies. The Mexicans will come through here, probably tomorrow."

"Oh, Mother, it's all so horrible. I just . . . want to go home."

"We will, Lynda. We will go home again. I promise you that."

They awoke to screams and gunshots, and the acrid smell of smoke. Sarah looked out to see much of San Felipe burning. Wagons, carts, horses, and people on foot—all came running past the Cox cabin. Then old Wil Handel rode up with a wagon. "We must go," he shouted. "Hurry."

Emily Cox seemed unconcerned as Lynda and Sarah quickly packed carpetbags, preparing to flee.

"Come, Sarah," Wil shouted from the doorway. "Come

with us. They're burning it all down. I have your horse and travois."

Emily looked at them with bloodshot eyes. Her face was gaunt and hard. She was making coffee, still in her robe. "All burning but the saloons, I'll wager," she said calmly.

They had hoped the Mexicans would drive through, leave a few men to occupy the city, and go on from there. There were no Texas volunteers here to massacre. There were mostly women and children and men too old or injured to fight. Taking San Felipe was only a sign of "conquering" the Texans and putting them in their place. It was only one more strike along Santa Anna's march to the Gulf.

Sarah felt a desperate, sinking feeling. Was it wise to leave, or stay? If they fled, they would have to live out in the open. The nights were still cold, although it was now April. The rivers were swollen with spring rains and snow melts. It made her think of Blue Valley. That battle for water seemed a hundred years ago now. And what was it all for if they were all going to die and never go back home, leaving Texas in full control of Santa Anna's dictatorship? Blue Valley. She would like to be in that peaceful place right now, with Caleb, resting in his arms.

Closer gunfire brought her out of her thoughts. She closed her carpetbag. "Hurry, Emily," she told the woman. Lynda stood holding Cale and her own carpetbag. Outside their travois waited, pulled by the only horse they had left, carrying what few belongings they had salvaged before leaving home. They would tie the rest of their belongings to it and ride in the Handels' wagon.

Emily looked at Sarah with an odd smile. "I'm staying. I can handle the whole damned Mexican army if I have to, you know. Or have you forgotten what Emily Stoner really is?"

Sarah frowned. "You're Emily Cox, and you're a fine widow woman."

Emily laughed, almost like a crazy woman. She got up nonchalantly from her chair. "I'm Emily Stoner, destined to be a whore forever, and you damned well know it."

"Mother, we've got to go," Lynda said anxiously. She

looked at Handel. "Go ahead, Mister Handel. We're coming."

"We cannot leave you here."

"Come, Sarah," Mrs. Handel shouted from the wagon.

Lynda looked at her mother again, but Sarah was staring with pity at Emily. "Emily, please. You must come with us."

Emily tossed her blond hair. It was thinner now, showing some gray. "Did your husband ever tell you why he fled Fort Dearborn?" she asked Sarah with a sneer. "It was because of *me*! I was already a whore, way back then," she said, holding up her chin. "I'm the one who taught Caleb Sax all about women. They caught us together once and I screamed rape and almost got the poor boy hung. Did he ever tell you that?"

Sarah paled slightly. "Yes," she answered, lying.

Emily let out an odd hiss. "I'll bet," she grumbled. She held Sarah's eyes. "My wonderful preacher father caught us. I was scared to death of him. That's why I did it. Caleb had no choice but to get out of there. He never saw the Saxes again." She paused then, some of the crazy gleam leaving her eyes. "I always felt guilty about that."

"Emily, that was years ago. We were all children. None of it matters anymore. What matters is to get out of this city. Please come with us."

Emily shook her head, her chin stubbornly set. "No. You two get going. Stay with the others. You'll be safer."

Sarah's eyes filled with tears. "Emily, don't do this."

Emily blinked back her own tears then. "I'm a survivor, Sarah. And so are you and Lynda. We're all strong in our own way. I know what I have to do now, what I am. There is nothing those soldiers can do to me that a thousand other men haven't done."

"Stop it, Emily," Sarah said sharply. "You can't hurt me. You want us to hate you, but it won't work. You want it because you hate yourself. But you shouldn't. You were true to Howard. You were a good wife. And you had a *right* to try for happiness. He died for us. You can't just stand there and—"

"Go on!" Emily screamed. "Get going! They're coming!"

Sarah closed her eyes and turned away. This was the old, hard Emily—the one she had never really known. It hurt to think of Caleb being with her, but then he'd been just a boy, and Emily had been a mere child herself.

There were more gunshots, and she had no choice. She had to get out. She picked up James and hurried out the door, praying for the safety of her baby, grandson, and daughter. There was nothing more she could do about Emily Cox.

They were quickly drawn up in the swell of people who fled before the smoke. Mrs. Handel drove the wagon while Wil led Sarah's horse. James started to cry, and there was no way to soothe him. They had to keep going, run while they could.

San Felipe was soon mostly in flames, except for a few saloons . . . and one small cabin at the end of town.

"Welcome to San Felipe," Emily told the soldiers who were the first to arrive at the cabin. She stood outside facing them, wearing only a thin robe. "No sense going on after the women who have fled, gentlemen, when you can get all you need right here."

They just stared at her as she smiled seductively, hoping to divert their attention from the last women who had fled. Sarah Sax and Lynda Whitestone were not something soldiers would easily pass up a chance at raping.

"Spare my house, and I'll do what I can to relieve your needs before you move on. You had better hurry, though, if you want to catch Sam Houston. He's headed for the Gulf."

She turned and sauntered inside. Eight men sat on horses grinning at each other. One carrying a torch dropped it and they all dismounted, then moved to the door to have ther pleasure with the wild white woman.

Houston moved on to Harrisburg. When they heard San Felipe had been burned, Caleb and Jess both went almost wild with worry. The women! They should be with the women! Were they still at the Handels' or had they been in

San Felipe, where many refugees from outer areas had fled? Their only comfort was that the women were certainly not alone. And the best way to end this was to stay together with the militia and make a move against Santa Anna, something Houston surely intended to do eventually. Caleb wanted his turn at the Mexican soldiers. All any of them could think of was the Alamo and Goliad; so many men slaughtered; prisoners shot down like pigs; bodies burned. If Texas was going to be saved from the pompous, cruel Santa Anna, they must take a stand soon.

"Word is Santa Anna has ordered all his men to meet him here in the south," Jess came up and told Caleb then. "He'll get them all together full force before they come for us. At least that means they'll vacate San Felipe. The women should be safe. If we could defeat him now, we could go home."

Caleb looked at him with tired eyes. "Home?" He sighed deeply. "I wonder if there is a home to go to."

Jess nodded. "Sure there is. We have to believe there is, Caleb. You just remember Sarah and James—and your grandson—and Lynda. They're all waiting for us to come back."

Their eyes held. "And waiting for Tom, too."

Jess saw him tremble. Was he beginning to realize the truth? He nodded. "For Tom, too."

Their thoughts were interrupted when a messenger rode through camp and told them to make ready. They were marching to the Gulf. Santa Anna had arrived in New Washington. Warned by scouts, those citizens of New Washington who made up the central government of the new republic escaped by ship into Galveston Bay only hours before Santa Anna arrived. Now Houston was ordering his men to head in that very direction, toward the San Jacinto River, where Santa Anna was making camp.

Jess grinned, picking up his long gun. "This is it, friend. I knew Houston would come through. By God, we're going to fight, and we're going to win!"

Men were cheering, picking up their gear, making ready to break camp.

"Remember the Alamo," they were shouting back and forth to each other.

The words pierced Caleb's heart. The Alamo! Tom! He couldn't have been there. It couldn't be true. He would not believe it. He picked up his rifle. He was going to kill some Mexicans. Of all the men he'd killed, he knew he would enjoy this as he had never enjoyed killing before. He moved along with the rest of the men. Most were on foot. Horses and supplies had become scarce. It made him realize he'd have to round up some wild Texas mustangs all over again when he got home—start building his herd anew. He'd do it with the money the government owed him when all this was over. And Tom would help him. Tom was good at that. He doubted he could run the place without his son. Yes. He'd get this war over with and go home, and Tom would be there, waiting.

Caleb lay on his belly studying the camp through underbrush. The volunteers had chosen him to scout out the position of the Mexican troops because they knew his Indian skills at such things would be an asset.

He shivered from the cold. It was April 1836, but for several days it had been unusually cold and had rained constantly. They had marched through mud toward this place, sleeping little, exposed to the weather twenty-four hours a day so that Caleb felt weary and drenched to the bone.

But it was worth it. Before him, their backs against the San Jacinto River and Peggy Lake, were Mexican soldiers, perhaps fifteen hundred men. And there was no mistaking who occupied the fanciest tent, into which a giggling, pretty woman had gone. Only Santa Anna would live so high. He had completed his march through eastern Texas. Now he seemed ready to relax and enjoy the spoils of victory.

"Only you haven't won yet, you son of a bitch," Caleb hissed.

He headed back, moving through underbrush and swamp along Peggy Lake. When he made it back to Houston's camp, his story was confirmed by other scouts coming in from other directions and from San Felipe. The uncomfortable weather had caused delays and confusion among Santa Anna's three armies. They had become separated. Santa Anna himself was camped not far away, and they were in an open area, their backs to the water. It was an excellent advantage, even though the Texans were outnumbered two to one.

Houston had slept in that morning, his first full night's rest in nearly six weeks. The time had come. Santa Anna didn't even know Texas volunteers were near. If they could take the notorious Mexican leader, it would be the ultimate victory. To get Santa Anna's surrender would be to win the war.

The men milled around impatiently, wondering why Houston still did not move. It was difficult to keep some of them in camp. Finally Houston formed his troops, after the sun was already going down behind them.

"Siesta time," someone near Caleb said excitedly. "That's it! He's been waitin' till siesta time. All Mexicans take an afternoon nap. It's the perfect time to attack!"

Caleb smiled as the word was passed. Yes. They had every advantage. He thought again of Tom as the troops moved out then, marching through moss and oak behind Sam Houston, who rode a white horse, his sword raised. Drum and fife began to play, but the Mexicans slept so soundly they never suspected a thing.

Finally they were close enough for an all-out charge. Those on horses rode in at a gallop then, while the rest broke into a run.

"Remember the Alamo," they all were shouting.

The words cut into Caleb as though a Mexican soldier had sliced him with a sword. Tom! No, not Tom! Not Tom! He could not face it, yet the shouted words seemed to bring it all into reality. Dead. All dead. No survivors at the Alamo. No survivors. Tom had been there.

"Remember the Alamo! Alamo! Alamo!" The words pounded in his ears as he ran now, pulling his knife, his heart beating so hard with a building sorrow that his chest ached fiercely.

"Remember the Alamo," he shouted himself then. As

soon as he got the words out the tears came, tears of horror, anger, grief. Not Tom! Not Tom!

Suddenly he was in the heat of the short but fierce fight, as confused, shocked Mexican soldiers came out of tents to meet the wild, brave Texans. Caleb felt his knife sink into someone wearing a red coat. Then came another, and another. He slashed and slashed like a madman, wanting to kill all of them. The Texans yipped and called like wild Indians, shooting, slashing with swords and knives.

After several minutes of fighting, Caleb began slashing wildly at one soldier over and over, until Jess pulled him off.

"It's over, Caleb," the man told him desperately. "The man's dead and the battle is over."

Caleb threw him off with a power that seemed almost superhuman, sending Jess flying. He whirled then, still holding the knife.

"Caleb, it's me, Jess," the young man yelled. "Goddamn it, the fighting is over. We've won."

Caleb froze, staring at him strangely. All around them men began cheering, rounding up Mexican soldiers, their hands in the air in an act of surrender. Later the tally would show 630 Mexicans killed and 208 wounded, with 730 taken prisoner. The Texans, numbering nine hundred, had lost only nine men. Their victory had been quick and sure.

Sam Houston had been wounded in his right leg and his horse was killed. He was carried to rest under an oak tree. The prisoners were herded together, and as the Texans began frantically searching for Santa Anna, who had somehow slipped away, Caleb stood looking down at his bloody knife, not even aware of a wound in his own left side.

"Come on, Caleb. You're bleeding," Jess told him. He was battered himself but not badly hurt. His clothes carried the blood of those he had fought but not his own. He grabbed Caleb's arm and made him sit down, leaning against a tree. He pulled Caleb's buckskin shirt out of his leggings and examined a large gash in Caleb's side, then called for the doctor.

"In a minute," the busy man called back.

"Tom," Caleb mumbled.

Jess looked back at him. "What?"

"We have to find him."

Jess sighed, pulling off his own shirt in spite of the cold and holding it against Caleb's side. His long underwear would have to do for now. He pressed the shirt tightly against Caleb's wound

"We won't find him, Caleb. Tom is dead," he said gently. "They all died at the Alamo. We can't bring him back."

Caleb shook his head, another tear slipping out of one eye. "No. When we go home, we'll ask around."

"Damn it, Caleb, you've got to face facts. Sarah and Lynda will both need you to be a whole man when you get back. God only knows what they've been through. We'll all need each other. Before we go home you've got to face the reality that Tom is dead."

Caleb pressed his head back against the tree, his chest heaving. "No. We'll . . . we'll look for him. We'll go to the mission, ask at all the cities where volunteers congregated. And if we don't find him, I'll bet he'll be at home waiting for us when we get there."

"He won't, Caleb. He won't be there."

Their eyes met. "Remember the Alamo," someone nearby shouted again, as Mexican soldiers were shoved around, some kicked at. "You bastards didn't even leave us bodies to bury," another shouted. "Why'd you have to burn them, you lilly-livers!"

More tears slipped out of Caleb's eyes. Burned! They'd burned the bodies . . . all of them! That's what the scouts said. What if Tom wasn't even completely dead yet when they set fire to him? He looked down at the hard earth he sat on, grasping some of it in his fist. Texas. So many lives lost for Texas. And so many of them his own loved ones. Marie and her parents, their two sons David and John, Lee, and Bess. And now . . . no! Not Tom!

"Remember the Alamo," he said gruffly to Jess.

Jess's own eyes teared, and they reached out for each other and embraced. "Let's go home, Caleb," Jess said, his voice full of emotion. "Let's go home to Lynda and Sarah."

"Sarah," Caleb whispered. "Yes. I have to be with Sarah. Sarah, my Sarah. God, let her be all right!"

Chapter
Twenty-One

The Mexican prisoners were first moved to Galveston. Santa Anna had been found trying to sneak away disguised in peasant's clothing. It was not easy for Sam Houston to keep his Texans from hanging the man; but he finally convinced them that to let the man live and openly admit defeat was the best way to secure Texas independence. Santa Anna was forced to sign a formal surrender. When news of his defeat spread, Mexican soldiers elsewhere—up to four thousand men at Fort Bend alone—fled to the south, out of Texas territory.

Caleb and Jess had accompanied the prisoners' march to Galveston, which brought them to less than a hundred miles from home. Home. The word sounded good, but what would they find when they got there? They rode hard, heading first for San Felipe.

Sarah swept off the porch of Emily's cabin. They had spent weeks living in tent shelters, staying with large groups of refugees for safety until scouts finally reported Santa Anna's men had left San Felipe. For the time being there was no place else to go. Until Caleb returned, they could not go back to the ranch. Recently they had received word of Santa Anna's defeat at San Jacinto. Surely Caleb would be coming home soon. They would wait in town.

Wil Handel had returned to his ranch to try to get things in order again, and Mildred had insisted on going with him. Sarah and Lynda had no idea what was left of their own ranch, fearing the worst, since the Handel house had been burned. They could only hope things were still intact. Sarah refused to accept any possibility Caleb could be dead, and she kept telling herself there had to be a mistake about Tom. His last letter had been from the Alamo, but that was months ago. Maybe somehow he'd been gone when the mission was destroyed. It was impossible to imagine he could be dead; and worse, what his death would do to Caleb.

It was a warm day in May 1836. James, nearly three, ran up and down in front of the house chasing chickens, and Cale, just six months younger than his uncle, tried to keep up.

Sarah stopped and watched them with a worried heart. How much longer before fresh supplies came? And how much longer would the money Caleb gave her hold out? It seemed suddenly everyone was broke and food was scarce. The whole new Republic of Texas was in chaos, momentarily leaderless. Some said Sam Houston had been taken to New Orleans for special treatment for a badly infected leg.

"He'll be back," everyone said. "Sam Houston will be back and he'll be our next president. He'll get things going right. We'll be strong and prosperous in no time."

Sarah could not help doubting that. They would be a brand new country in their own right, with a brand new government. They would have to print their own money and to do that there had to be something behind that money to support it. The people of Texas had not been rich to begin with. They had donated arms and horses and supplies and what little they had in cash to build the Texas army. And who was going to trust a new, cash-poor republic enough to loan them anything? Not even the United States would be willing to do that. And some predicted Mexico would never truly recognize them as independent.

"There will still be trouble," some folks said. "Everybody thinks this war is over, but it isn't,"

"They should have hung Santa Anna," others shouted. "Kill the bastard! If he goes free, he'll make more trouble once he gets back home."

Sarah leaned against the porch post. She was tired. So tired. Living in the open, constantly on the move to avoid Mexican troops, had been taxing on her, for her health was not the best to begin with. When they finally returned to San Felipe she had looked for poor Emily, but the cabin had been vacated when they returned. Only several days later, when she saw the woman on the street dressed in red satin and laughing with a Texas volunteer, did she realize what had happened.

Emily Cox was Emily Stoner again, the old Emily Stoner of New Orleans. She had given up on the life she had so dearly wanted with Howard Cox and had returned to prostitution. She was hiding her grief now, putting on her shield of not caring, of liking the kind of life she was leading now, in a room above the Texas Belle Saloon.

A tent city had sprung up around San Felipe, the result of the thousands of people who had flowed into Texas for free land in return for fighting Mexicans. Now those thousands of newcomers languished near the towns, waiting for the new government to get organized, waiting for their promised land. Some of the original Texans were complaining that newcomers were squatting on their land. Everything seemed an utter mess.

What worried Sarah most was the kind of people coming now. Many were very poor, and most were Southerners. She knew instinctively that many of them were Indian haters, and now that the war with Mexico was over, the people of Texas would have more time to turn their attention to the new Republic and how it was to be run, which would mean new rules—their own rules. Sarah did not like the implications of a new Republic being claimed by land-hungry Southerners.

She closed her eyes. They had circles under them. She

was thin and so was Lynda. It seemed all there was to eat was beans and bread. She was sick of both. But none of it really mattered—not the poverty—not what had happened to poor Emily—not the hunger—not her worry over new laws and how the Indians would be treated.

All that really mattered was that Caleb, Tom, and Jess were still alive. All the tension and worry and sorrow for the loss of so many volunteers overwhelmed her then, heaving up through her insides and coming out in great sobs as she clung to the post.

Caleb! She could bear any of it, anything at all, if only Caleb would come home. She hung on to the post and cried, while James and Cale played in front of her, too young to understand the traumatic happenings around them, thinking it all just a wonderful adventure.

It was well after dark when Sarah awoke to someone knocking at the door. She rubbed her eyes and sat up. Lynda was awake then. She put a finger to her lips, turning the lamp up a little and grabbing up a musket. She cocked it and pointed it at the door and then signaled her mother to go to it. Sarah pulled on her robe and walked to the door. "Who is it?" she asked hesitantly.

"Sarah? That you?"

Her heart nearly stopped beating. "Caleb!" She threw open the door, and in the next moment strong arms were around her, blessed, strong, wonderful, warm arms, his arms, Caleb's arms. She buried her face in his neck, felt him kissing her hair. Were they both crying? Beside them Jess and Lynda were in a heated embrace, lost in each other, drinking in kisses, on fire with youthful passion. But youth did not hold the deed to passion, for when Caleb Sax's lips met his woman's, both were consumed with old, burning desires.

"I didn't know what I would find when I came here," Caleb groaned, after several minutes of just holding her. He kissed Sarah's neck. "I just thought I would try San Felipe first. I expected Emily to open the door."

They kissed again, and Sarah finally pulled away but he still held her. "Oh, Caleb, it's so sad. Howard Cox found out about her, just before he left with some volunteers. He was so hurt, and Emily couldn't forgive herself." She rested her head against his chest then. "She has gone back to prostitution, and has a room over the Texas Belle. Howard was killed at the Alamo."

She felt him stiffen. The Alamo! She pulled away again, and at her words Jess and Lynda also broke their embrace. Lynda looked past Jess at the doorway. The joy of the moment was dampened when she looked over at her father.

"Where is Tom? Isn't he with you?" Lynda asked.

Caleb's grip on Sarah's arms tightened. "I'm going to stay with Sarah a couple of days, then leave Jess with you and go look for him, before we go back home."

Jess's eyebrows arched. He thought Caleb had accepted the fact that Tom Sax was dead. He'd seemed to at San Jacinto. "Caleb—"

"He's alive," Caleb told the man quickly and firmly. "My son is alive and I'm going to find him."

Jess sighed, pushing Lynda away slightly. "Caleb, he was at the Alamo. There is no way he can be alive! Why are you doing this? The women need us now."

"He's my son," Caleb hissed.

"And he's dead," Jess answered firmly.

Lynda moved away and sank onto her bed. It was true then! Her beautiful, wonderful brother, Tom, so handsome and young and strong; so full of sorrow those last days, grieving over his beautiful Bess—he was dead. Now he and Bess were together.

Sarah watched Caleb with alarm. His face colored with anger as he glared at Jess. "You can believe what you want. You don't know yet how it feels to lose a son. I risked my life against the Comanche to save John, but I lost him anyway—and David. I've lost two sons. Two is enough for any man! They won't take Tom, too!"

"Caleb, stop it," Sarah spoke up, grasping his arm. "Here. Come here." She pulled him toward the bed, where James was stirring from all the voices. "Here is your son," she said gently. "We still have James."

The boy rubbed his eyes and blinked, then smiled a charming smile. "Poppy," he said in a sleepy voice. He reached up and Caleb Sax crumbled. He sat down on the bed, pulling the boy into his arms and rocking him, hugging him tightly and weeping, mumbling Tom's name over and over. Lynda lay down on the bed and sobbed. It seemed so unreal, yet she knew it had to be true if Tom had been at the Alamo. He had just walked away from home months ago to fight Mexicans, and he had never come back.

Jess came over to kneel in front of Caleb. "We'll go to every place where records are kept, Caleb. We'll make sure. But you've got to face it now. You knew at San Jacinto, didn't you? You knew when you kept stabbing at that Mexican soldier."

Caleb only wept, clinging to little James, who hugged his father in return, not sure what was the matter. Jess rose and faced Sarah, noticing how thin she was, the circles under her eyes. "I know you've been through hell yourself. But he's going to need you to be strong the next few months. Of all his losses, I think Tom will be the hardest."

"I know," she said weakly. Jess embraced her for a moment, then went back to Lynda, tortured at what this was doing to her also. Sarah stared at Caleb. Tom had been with him from the beginning. When he thought Sarah was dead, he still had his son Tom. Tom was there to sustain him when Marie was killed, and David. He'd been the only constant thing in Caleb Sax's life. Now it seemed he'd just blown away with the wind and had never existed.

Caleb moved back onto the bed, still holding James. He lay down with the boy and Sarah pulled off his moccasins and covered father and son. She crawled into bed, little James between them. She grasped Caleb's hand. There was absolutely nothing she could do but be there for him.

Jess bolted the door and turned down the lamp. He came back to the bed where Lynda lay, Cale on the other side of her. The deep-sleeping infant had never even awakened. Jess moved in beside Lynda to hold her. They weren't married yet, but he would sleep beside her and hold her anyway. Who gave a damn in times like these? He would marry her tomorrow if they could find a priest, and when her grief had mellowed they would make love again—and again and again. They had the rest of their lives to be together now. Tonight they would just cling together, taking what happiness they could from the fact that nothing had happened to himself or Caleb.

Outside lay a restless new Texas Republic, a big territory full of mass confusion and lawlessness, momentarily leaderless. But inside the little cabin Caleb and Sarah Sax had each other, and their son, and Lynda. The only children left were those who had been conceived by Caleb and Sarah themselves.

Lynda clung to Jess, so glad he had come back, that he still loved her. Thank God she still had her parents, and her baby brother, and her own little son—and Jess. She had to think of the positive side to this. She could not think about death. She must think only about life. Life . . . and love.

Tom struggled to stay on his feet. To fall meant a whipping. He had seen it happen to the other prisoners marching with him, and he was not about to add to the scars he already carried from the time he was dragged by Hafer men. Only at the moment, he would have rather been facing Hafer than to be at the gunpoint of Mexican soldiers.

If only he'd not been hit by that shrapnel; he wouldn't have gotten so dizzy and confused. He felt like a fool: an Indian scout sent out with a message, getting hit and running in exactly the wrong direction, right into the waiting arms of Mexican soldiers. What worried Tom most was that he had not been shot on sight. That meant only one thing. He would make a good slave, probably at some Mexican gold mine.

Tom had asked over and over what happened at the Alamo mission, but no one would tell him. All he remembered was the rumble of cannon and the screams of men before a message was slapped into his hand to be delivered, then something striking him in the head. When he came to he was carried on a stretcher by Mexican soldiers, and as soon as they realized he was awake they dumped him off and forced him to start walking on his own.

Everything was behind him—his father, Howard Cox, Jess, Lynda—home. Being forced south to an unknown

destination could mean never seeing any of his loved ones
or home again. He could rot away in some Mexican prison
or be worked to death in a mine, with no one ever knowing
what happened to him. The worst part of all this was
Caleb. What would this do to him?

He stumbled, and for the first time he felt the sting of a
whip. "Stay on your feet, Indian," a soldier commanded in
Spanish. Tom knew the language well, after having lived
so many years in Texas. "You will be nice and strong by
the time you get where you are going. Then you will be
worth much to us, no?"

The soldier laughed and Tom concentrated on staying on
his feet. He breathed deeply, remembering his father's way
of drawing on his inner spirit when extra courage and
strength were required.

Father. He would think about his father. He would not
die here to be buried in a common grave. He would live,
and he would find a way to escape and get back home. He
must concentrate on the ranch, on Blue Valley, on his beloved father. That would keep him alive. For the first time
since Bess's death Tom realized he did indeed want to live.
And even though she was dead, he would not think of her
that way. He would visualize her face, pretend she was
walking with him now, holding him up so he didn't catch
the whip. His beautiful, sweet Bess. He could almost see
her smiling face. He would stand straight and walk
proudly . . . for Bess . . . and because he was a Sax.

The main adobe house still stood, as did most of the
cabins, including Lynda's. Many of the Cherokee who had
been faithful to Caleb began to trickle back to Sax land.
Even the faithful Jake and Ada Highwater returned to help.
But there was no money to pay them. Everyone had to
work on a communal basis, planting gardens for food that
would be shared, and helping round up mustangs to rebuild
the ranch. Caleb, fortunately, had money saved, hidden
behind a stone in the root cellar in a place he knew no
squatters or Mexican soldier would find it. This money he
had refused to give up even for the new Republic. His

family came first. It was not a great amount though, and it would run out soon if he was not frugal.

Sam Houston did come back, to a new Republic that was penniless. The promissory notes given Caleb for his horses were no good. He would get no help from the government. But Texas was determined not to fail. Houston was elected their new president by a landslide, and a new constitution was ratified. Towns could elect their own mayors and councils. Counties were created, each with the power to elect its own administrators and a three-judge court. Duties were levied on imported items, but they did not come close to providing the cash the new Republic needed. The expensive Texas army was dissolved, and a militia system was instituted.

In order to settle their vast domain, Texans offered new settlers 1,280 acres absolutely free. Texas began to grow at an astounding rate. The city of Houston sprang up. Newspapers were printed. Nine out of ten newcomers were Americans, most from the South, including scheming speculators, Indian haters, slave owners and merchants looking to get rich. It was no surprise that a good share of outlaws also filtered in, seeking sanctuary and a new start in Texas. Many of the new settlers were cheated by speculators who sold them additional land cheap—but land that was not theirs to sell at all. And no one knew better than Caleb Sax the trouble that would come with such dealings.

Caleb poured his time into rebuilding, and Sarah worried about him. He worked from sunup to past sundown, hardly stopping to eat or rest. He was changed; harder, more quiet and remote. It was a long time before he had made love to her, even though Sarah knew the deep affection and passion was always there. But he did so almost mechanically, as if simply to satisfy her womanly needs.

Lynda began helping with the ranch work, against Jess's wishes. But there was no arguing with Lynda Sax Purnell. They had married before leaving San Felipe, and Jess discovered his new wife could be as stubborn as her father. She was intent on helping Caleb all she could, trying desperately to replace the son he had lost. Tom Sax had been her father's right-hand man. Lynda would ease Caleb's pain by doing what she could to take her brother's place. She could ride a horse, and she could shoot, and she knew how to chase down a mustang. And every time Lynda saw the gratefulness in Caleb's eyes for her help, she felt a certain joy and satisfaction. More and more she began leaving Cale with Sarah and spending long days riding with the men, devoting herself to rebuilding with almost as much enthusiasm as Caleb.

But for Caleb's part it was not total enthusiasm. Sarah knew it but said nothing. Caleb Sax was not eagerly rebuilding a ranch. He was trying to forget that Tom was dead. Sometimes he would bring up Tom's name as though he would be home any minute, then catch himself and stop short. It frightened Sarah that the man still had not seemed to face the reality that Tom really was not coming back.

Life went on that way for over a year. Sarah wept silently, for she was living with a stranger. She didn't even have the companionship of Lynda, who was always gone now, and Jess constantly argued that she should stay home and take care of Cale. He wanted a child of his own, too. But he worried that if Lynda didn't settle down, she'd never get pregnant. Every time they argued, Lynda soothed him with kisses and tears, begging to be allowed to help work the ranch. Her husband could never bring himself to truly put his foot down, for he had never loved or craved any woman the way he did Lynda. She always got her way in the end.

Slowly Texas began to flourish. Cotton quickly became the chief product of the new Republic, followed closely by the cattle industry. Many of the new settlers brought slaves to Texas with them, and tension began to mount over the slavery issue. Sam Houston was pro-Indian and antislavery, unpopular issues among a state made up mostly of Southerners. His popularity began to lessen because of it.

The Sax ranch began to grow again, along with the new Republic of Texas. But lawlessness prevailed everywhere, and hardly a week went by that Caleb and Jess did not have to chase squatters off Sax land. These were not refugee Cherokee. They were people with no concern for the property of others, ready to take whatever they could steal.

They had come to get rich the easiest way possible, and they had no morals and no conscience holding them back.

Caleb struggled inwardly, living in a lonely world of his own. Nothing was the way it used to be. Often he would ride alone, remembering the early days when he had come to Texas with Marie Whitestone's family, a man lost and lonely, thinking Sarah dead. He'd had Tom with him then, little Tom. There had always been Tom. When they came to Texas there was no one—only a few hundred original settlers scattered widely. The land was quiet. Even raiding Comanche were more welcome than these lawless, often filthy and disrespectful newcomers. How he wished it could be more like the old days, except that he hadn't had Sarah then.

That had been a different Texas, and he had been a different Caleb. Never in his life had he been happier than when Sarah and Lynda came to him. He'd had his whole family. Lee had been alive, and he and Lynda were so much in love. He'd had John too, so eager to please his father. How he missed John! And he'd had Tom, his life's blood, the son he all but worshipped.

The pain of losing both sons was at times almost unbearable. Caleb found himself turning to speak to them, but they were not there. Sometimes it seemed as if Tom was right beside him, whispering to him. He saw the boy in every hollow and on every hilltop. He was so Indian, smiling his handsome smile, sitting on a fine stallion, built like his father but with his mother's dark, dark eyes. They had been inseparable. Tom would have been twenty-four now ... twenty-four years since he had been born in the foothills of the Rockies, in those glorious days when Caleb Sax rode as Blue Hawk among the Cheyenne, married to Walking Grass. Now all of it was gone.

In Caleb's grief, his love for Tom was growing to such painful, unrealistic proportions while his love for the rest of his family who lived seemed to be getting lost in a world he could no longer face. He felt his feelings and his sense of reason running out of control, so that he hardly knew himself anymore, or knew what he wanted out of life.

* * *

Sarah watched in quiet agony as Caleb kept putting a screaming James on the pony. Caleb cajoled, soothed, urged, got up on the pony with the boy—all to no avail. Five-year-old James wanted nothing to do with the pony, and Caleb's patience was growing short. During the two years since he had returned from the war, Caleb had shown little patience for James, expecting much more from the child than he was able to give. Now he angrily pulled James from the pony, holding him out in front of him in a tight grip.

"What the hell is wrong with you?" he shouted at the boy. "Your brother rode a full-grown horse when he was only four!"

"Caleb!" Sarah charged up to them then, literally yanking the boy from Caleb's hands. "Give him time."

"Time?" Caleb threw his hands in the air. "My God, he's five years old."

"Yes. Only five."

"You're babying him!"

"And you are forcing him into things he isn't ready for yet. Every child develops differently."

"Cale already rides a pony. And Tom rode when he was only four."

"He isn't Cale. And he isn't Tom," she shouted back. "He's James. James. My God, what is happening to you!" She set James on the ground, and the crying child ran into the house.

Caleb watched him run and turned angry eyes to Sarah. Never in the years they had known each other had Caleb Sax even looked at his wife in anger, let alone had words with her.

"You're babying him to death," he accused. "You never had the chance with Lynda, so you're going overboard with James."

She stiffened at the words. "Maybe I am. But at least he knows I love him. At least he knows he's loved for James. I am not trying to make him replace someone!"

"And what is that supposed to mean?"

"You know damned well what it means, Caleb Sax. Tom

is dead. When are you going to face that and go on from there? James is alive! He's your son and he loves you. Stop trying to make him be Tom."

The back of Caleb's hand slammed across Sarah's face, making her stumble backward. Lynda and Jess were just riding in.

"Father!" Lynda leaped from her horse and went to her mother, who stood hunched over gasping for breath. Caleb looked at his hand as though it were some foreign object that had acted without his will. Sarah made a whimpering sound as Lynda put an arm around her, and Jess dismounted and stormed up to them. Caleb backed away, staring at Sarah, his hand shaking. His eyes widened at a white welt on the side of his wife's face.

"Sarah." He uttered the name as though in agony. He had hit Sarah. All the strain of their uncertain future in Texas and the horrible grief over Tom; all his losses had brought him to this. He glanced over at James, who stood crying in the doorway. His family had always been so important to him, and he was destroying it with his own grief. His eyes moved back to Sarah. "I . . . didn't mean to . . ." He swallowed. "My God, Sarah." He turned and stumbled to his horse, then mounted it and rode off at a hard gallop.

Sarah watched after him. Her face stung and her ears were ringing. This seemed incredible.

"Mother, what happened?" Lynda asked angrily.

Sarah looked at her. "It's all right." She blinked back tears. "I reminded him that Tom is dead. He got impatient with James, trying to make him do all the things Tom did at his age. He's got to realize that James is James and Tom is dead." She turned and walked wearily to the door, where she scooped James up in her arms.

"Mommy hurt," the boy wept.

"No. Mommy is fine."

"Daddy doesn't like me."

She cuddled him close. "Oh, yes he does, darling. Your daddy loves you so much. He's just very sad inside, James. We have to be patient with him. When he comes home, you tell him you're sorry you wouldn't ride the pony. I want you to try again tomorrow, James. I want you to ride that pony for your daddy. You'll find out it's fun, and your daddy will be very happy. You'll see. Will you try?"

"The pony will bite me."

"Oh, James, that pony would never bite a little boy. Wouldn't you like to ride around the corral with Cale? You can't let Cale beat you at things. You're his uncle." She set the boy down in a chair and he put a chubby hand to her red cheek. Lynda came inside, watching with tears in her eyes. "Did you know that in the Indian world, the uncles teach the young boys how to be riders and warriors and how to hunt?" Sarah asked James.

James shook his head.

Sarah kissed his cheek. "Well, they do. You ask your daddy about it when he comes back. He can tell you. And you're an uncle. That makes you very important, James. You should be teaching things to Cale, not letting him do everything first."

The boy frowned. "I want to be a good uncle. If daddy won't yell, I'll ride the pony again."

Sarah smiled, even though her heart was heavy with grief. She refused to show it i front of James. "I'm proud of you. You're very brave to try again, James Sax. Some day you'll be big and strong, just like your father."

"Will he like me better then?"

She took his hands. "He'll love you, just like he loves you now. You have to forgive Daddy. He still hurts inside because of your big brother who died."

"Did he love him more?"

She squeezed his hands. "No, James. He did not love Tom more. He just misses him."

The boy hugged her and Sarah looked up, her eyes meeting Lynda's. Her daughter's expression was full of love and concern. "Are you all right, Mother?"

"I am fine. And don't you hold this against your father. I don't think anyone understands better than I why he did what he did. If I can forgive him, no one else has any right not to."

Lynda put a hand to her stomach. "I love him so much. But when I saw him hit you . . ."

"Lynda, these things happen. Caleb is full of grief. The

worst of it is coming out of him now. It's like being sick and vomiting, then feeling better. You know what a good man he is. And you know ordinarily he would never lay a hand on me."

Lynda blinked back tears and nodded, moving to a chair to sit down. She looked pale.

"Lynda?" Sarah patted James's bottom and set him aside, going to her daughter. "What's wrong, Lynda? It isn't just what happened between me and Caleb, is it?"

The girl shook her head. "I . . . I'm pregnant, Mother. And I . . . feel so strange." She began to cry. "Oh, Mother, I think I'm going to lose it!"

"Dear God. Come on. Come in and lie down." She helped the girl into the bedroom and called out to James to go and get Jess.

Chapter Twenty-Two

It was after dark when Caleb rode up to the house to see Jess sitting on the veranda. Caleb dismounted and tied his horse, and Jess rose to greet him. By the light of a lantern that hung outside Caleb could see the man looked haggard, and his eyes were bloodshot and angry. Jess was too upset to notice the agony in Caleb's own deep blue eyes. He grasped Caleb's arm before he could go inside.

"Lynda lost a baby today," he said grimly.

Caleb frowned. "Lost a baby. Lynda is pregnant?"

"Was pregnant. I didn't know either. And the miscarriage is your fault!"

Caleb jerked his arm away. "What are you talking about?"

"Haven't you even noticed how hard she has been working to help you rebuild this ranch? Are you blind, man? We've been arguing over it for months! Don't you see what she's trying to do? She's trying to replace Tom!" Jess's blue eyes flashed with bitterness. "Goddamn it, Caleb, stop trying to find Tom in everyone else! Lynda is not going to work the ranch anymore, understand? I'll do my share, but my wife is staying off the goddamn horses. She's staying home and she's going to rest up good and she's going to get pregnant again and have a healthy baby!"

Caleb sighed, turning away and running a hand through his hair. "I'm sorry, Jess."

The man's agony was written so clearly on his face that some of the anger trickled out of Jess's heart. "Damn it, Caleb, I know what you've been going through," he said then in a calmer voice. "We all do. But we can't make up for it forever. That's what Lynda's been trying to do, you know. That girl loves you. She worships you. Other than finding Sarah, the happiest day of her life was when she discovered she had a father still alive. She treasures that blue quill necklace like it was made of diamonds and gold. And in your grief over Tom she feels that somehow you don't love her as much anymore. It's all that much worse for James, because he is too young to understand it. The living need you now, Caleb, not the dead."

Caleb felt a crushing ache in his chest. "I know. I have been . . . thinking. When I hit Sarah, I knew." His voice was quiet, defeated. He turned to Jess. "I really am sorry, Jess. I'll go talk to her. I'll make it my own order that she stays home. That will make it easier for you. I know how stubborn she can be." He glanced at the doorway and back at Jess. "How is she?"

"She'll be all right. She lost a lot of blood, and the cramps were pretty bad. But she's more depressed than anything else."

Caleb glanced at the door again. "Sarah?"

Jess sighed. "It has been a pretty hard day for her, to say the least. She's got a bruise on her face."

An agonizing sigh, close to a groan, came out of Caleb's throat, and he leaned both hands against the doorway, hanging his head between them. "There's no excuse. No excuse."

Jess reached outhere and talk to her. Talk to Lynda, too, if she's awake. I'll go for a walk and leave you alone for a while. Cale and James are asleep on the cot in the outer room. I'm going to come in later and sleep in a bedroll on the floor beside Lynda. I want her to have the bed to herself tonight. You and Sarah have been delegated to the loft, unless you want to go over and use our cabin. I just didn't want to move Lynda till tomorrow. I'm scared of the bleeding."

Caleb nodded, tapping on the door, and Jess walked quietly away. It opened, and Caleb met his wife's gentle green eyes. Sarah colored slightly, stepping aside and letting him in, closing and bolting the door again. She met his eyes boldly. He towered over her, feeling like an evil monster for having hit her. She looked so small and frail now. He knew he hadn't used anything near his strength earlier. If he had . . .

Pain seared through his chest. Caleb reached out, taking Sarah's chin in his hand and studying the bruise on the side of her face. His eyes filled with tears.

"If some other man did that to you, I'd kill him," he whispered gruffly. "I'd kill him without an ounce of regret!" Tears slipped down his cheeks, a rare sight on Caleb Sax. "As God is my witness, I'll never hurt you again, Sarah Sax. I don't know what happened to—"

She reached up and touched the tears, forcing back her own urge to cry. "It's over. This is me, remember? Sarah. Does anyone know better than I how much you love me?" She shook her head. "You are a lonely man, Caleb Sax. You always have been. All the love I can give you won't take away the loneliness you feel inside, not just from all your losses, but from what you are—a man torn between two worlds." Her voice broke slightly. "I understand the last two years have been pure hell, not just for you but for all of us. We just have to remember what's important, Caleb. We could lose this place tomorrow, but we still have each other. And the children we have left can't be made to feel guilty for those who have died."

He swallowed, and she saw his struggle to keep from breaking down completely. He reached out and pulled her close, crooking his arm around her neck, then moving his other arm around her, kissing her hair. "I want to make love to you, Sarah," he groaned, rubbing his hand over her back. "Let me make love to you. Let me make it all up to you. Forgive me and let me be the old Caleb for you."

She turned her face so that their lips met in a hot, fiery kiss that told her the real Caleb Sax had come home, not the stranger she had been living with for so long. Their kiss lingered as he pressed her tightly against him, and she could taste the salt of his tears. Finally he left her mouth, kissing her bruised cheek, her eyes, her hair. "Jess said we could use their cabin tonight," he whispered. "Come over there with me, Sarah. Jess will stay here."

She felt hot with the need of him. It had been so long, and this was a Caleb she had not known for a long time. "I've got to check on Lynda again first."

He sighed deeply, releasing her slightly. "I'm so sorry about Lynda. It's my fault. She has been working too hard. A woman can't go out tearing around on a horse every day and expect to carry a baby. I had no idea—"

"Caleb, you aren't to blame for everything. It's the war, our grief. It has taken a long time to heal, that's all. What Lynda did was a form of venting her own grief."

"But she did it for me. She has been trying to replace Tom."

Their eyes held. "At least you can talk about him now."

He studied her lovingly. "Is she awake?"

"I'll go see."

"If she is, I want to talk to her. Then we'll go over to their cabin."

She felt herself blushing like a schoolgirl. The old Caleb had come home. How she loved him! She grasped his wrists and nodded, then left him to go into the bedroom, and a shaggy little dog came trotting out from under the cot where the boys slept together in the main room. It trotted up to Caleb, wagging its tail wildly and biting at his moccasins.

"What the hell is this?" he asked. He felt lighter, happier, suddenly relieved.

Sarah stopped, smiled at the sight. "That is Pepper. He came straggling in earlier today from out of nowhere. James latched on to him and that was that. He was going to ask when you came back if he could keep him, but he's afraid you'll yell at him and won't let him."

Caleb looked over at his sleeping son. "What a fool I am," he murmured. He looked at Sarah. "I'll make it up to him, Sarah."

"I know you will. He loves you so, Caleb. He even said he would ride that pony for you tomorrow. I hope you recognize the courage that will take. For some reason he's afraid of the horses. Be patient with him, Caleb. He'll be a fine son."

She went into the bedroom and Caleb bent down to pick up the puppy, holding it out and studying it. "I guess you're a Sax now, pup," he told the dog. He set it back down when Sarah came out of the bedroom.

"She's awake," she told him.

Caleb walked past her in his familiar long stride, going through the curtained doorway to his daughter, who lay on her back, looking too pale even for her dusky complexion. Her eyes had dark circles under them, and it hit Caleb that he had hardly noticed her looks for a long time. He had paid no attention to all the danger signs. Nothing was worth losing this precious daughter.

Lynda opened her eyes and looked up at him. "Are you all right now, Father?" she asked weakly.

He shook his head in wonder. "Am *I* all right? My God, Lynda, what a question to ask." He came to the bed and leaned over her. "Lynda, I'm sorry. I'm so damned sorry. I never should have let you work so hard."

Her eyes teared. "I wanted to. I wanted to help. You didn't have Tom anymore, and—"

"You aren't Tom, Lynda. You're my daughter. And you are Jess Purnell's wife. Jess wants a child, and you're going to give him one. You're not helping with the ranching anymore—not for a good long time. You're going to take it very easy, and you're going to enjoy making love with your husband and you're going to get pregnant again. Those are my orders."

The words brought some color to her face and she smiled and looked away. "Now you're embarrassing me."

"I'm telling you the way it's going to be. You've been trying to make up for Tom, maybe somehow trying to *be* Tom. But you aren't my son, Lynda. You're my daughter, my very beautiful, strong, loyal daughter, maybe *too* loyal."

She met his eyes again. "Do you love me as much as you loved Tom?"

His eyes saddened. "That's a foolish question. If you ever doubted my love, you were very wrong. My grief over Tom has just distorted things, that's all. I love all my children equally, but each one in his or her own special way." He leaned down and kissed her forehead. "You are special because you are the product of the love I shared with your mother when we were young, the proof that no matter how hard someone tries to destroy that kind of love, it can't be done. Of course I love you, Lynda. You're very, very special." He touched her hair, smoothing it back from her face. "Somehow I'll make this up to all of you—Sarah, James, you. I've been a bastard to live with. I know that. It won't be that way anymore."

She smiled, reaching up and taking his hand. "I love you so much. I knew how you were hurting over Tom, and I couldn't figure out . . ." Her words broke as the tears came. ". . . how to make you feel better."

He squeezed her hand. "That wasn't your job, Lynda. Nothing you could have done, or Sarah or anyone else, could have changed how I was feeling inside. I just didn't realize until today how far it had gone. It won't happen again, I promise you. And no father could love a daughter more than I love you. Now you get some rest. Jess will be in in a minute to stay with you. Your mother and I are going to sleep over at your place."

She sniffed. "Poor Jess. He's been after m to stay home. He's so good to me, Father."

Caleb nodded. "I know. And he's the one you should devote yourself to first, Lynda. Not me. Jess is your husband. You listen to him and do what he tells you, understand? He's a good man. You've been hurting him by helping me. I don't want that." He kissed her again and rose. "Get some sleep now."

He gave her hand another squeeze, then left her, going into the outer room where Sarah was waiting. "Is she all right?" she asked.

"She's our daughter, isn't she? She's got your strength and my stubbornness. Of course she's all right," he answered, coming closer. He put a hand on her arm, looking at her sheepishly. "Will you come over to the other cabin with me?"

Sarah felt a sweet warmth move through her. The old Caleb was returning. She knew Caleb Sax well enough to realize he was sick inside over what he had done, and she knew it was only grief that had made him do it. Now he had finally faced that grief, was awakened to what it was doing to him and his family. She hugged him, burying her face against his chest.

"I'll come," she said softly.

He gave her a hug. "I love you," he whispered. "God, I love you so." He led her to the door and outside, where he left her a moment to go tell Jess they would sleep at his cabin.

Jess watched them walk into the darkness, relieved that Caleb Sax seemed to have overcome some of his grief over Tom. The great love between Caleb and Sarah was evident. No better proof could be had than the powers the woman had to heal Caleb of the worst loss of his life.

Caleb led Sarah into the cabin, closed the door and lit a lamp. He said nothing as he led her into the bedroom, where he made her sit on the bed while he picked up her foot and began unbuttoning her shoe. He pulled it off.

"You must be tired, Sarah. If you're too tired I'll just hold you and let you sleep." He picked up her other foot and began working that shoe off.

"No. I am tired, but we both need this," she said softly. "It's so nice to be with you again, Caleb," she added.

His blue eyes seemed glazed, for his desire for her was keen. The thought of hitting her . . . it made him ache inside. How could he have done that? He reached up under her dress, getting hold of her slips and bloomers and pulling them off. Her heart raced with anticipation as he pulled off her stockings and lightly kissed her feet, gently massaging her feet and legs, relaxing her more.

Their eyes held. Caleb sat beside her and began unbuttoning the back of her dress. It had its own supports, and because of the warm day she wore no other support under it. He slipped it down over her shoulders to her waist and she pulled out her arms, blushing, her heart pounding when he leaned down to lightly suck at her full nipples.

"Oh, Caleb, it's been so long," she whispered, grasping his long hair.

He kissed her breasts over and over, laying her back on the bed. He pulled the dress all the way off so that Sarah lay naked before him. He stood up, removing his clothes and moccasins. She studied his magnificent build, still so hard and strong; his powerful shoulders and narrow hips, flat stomach and strong thighs. He was so beautiful. She remembered that even as a little girl, when he was only a nine-year-old Indian boy, she had thought him beautiful.

He crawled onto the bed beside her, moving a hand gently over her stomach and down to explore that secret place that belonged only to Caleb Sax, making her shudder, feeling already on his fingers the sweet, satiny moisture that invited him inside. It tore at his heart to see the bruise on her face.

"From now on this is the only way I will touch you, Sarah Sax," he told her, his voice gruff with desire. "Gently . . . lovingly." He kissed the cheek. "I'm so sorry."

Their lips met then, and she was suddenly wild and bold, running her hands over his hard muscles, down over his back to his hips, feeling their strength, and moving a hand around to caress that part of him that made him so much a man. She pressed against him, opening her legs and wrapping them around him, guiding him into herself in great need and joy.

He groaned with the glory of it, the intense passions that

moved through him, a mixture of humble gratitude and almost agonizing love. Caleb surged into her as he kissed her savagely, wondering if he would ever get enough of her this night.

"Sarah, my Sarah," he groaned, burying himself in her as his lips moved to her neck. "Forgive me."

She arched up to him rhythmically. "Just be my Caleb," she whispered.

Texas abounded with talk of annexation to the United States. The new Republic struggled through terrible poverty, even going to England and France to secure financial aid and managing to negotiate trade agreements with both nations. Because of Texas's very shaky economy and the fact that Mexico still had not formally recognized it as a separate country, the United States hesitated at becoming involved at all. However, France's formal recognition of Texas as its own country brought about a new respect for the Republic, and the United States began to take another look. But Texas was filled with slaves by then, and the slavery issue began to loom as a major factor in whether or not Texas should be annexed by the United States.

It was that same year that a new president was elected for Texas—Mirabeau Lamar. He promised glory for Texas, recognition from other nations, especially Mexico; a national bank and a public school system; and harsh action against Indians on Texas soil . . . all Indians. Lamar won by a landslide. Sam Houston, a friend of the Indians and a foe of slavery, could not run for a second term, and even if he had, it was unlikely he would have won. His beliefs were not shared by the great majority of new Texans. Houston did, however, manage to be elected to the lower house of the Texas Congress, where he immediately formed a strong opposition to the policies of Mirabeau Lamar.

Mexico threatened renewed attack from the South. The Republic continued to be riddled with torn factions, poverty, and lawlessness. Lamar announced that Texas didn't need the United States, that rather than annexation they should be looking toward a powerful independent republic that would be recognized by all the great powers of Europe. They could take care of themselves.

The United States immediately dropped all renewed offers of annexation. Texas stood alone, ruled by a man of great dreams with no sure way of realizing those dreams and no money to support them.

But Caleb Sax had only one concern. Lamar was an Indian hater, and so were most of the new settlers of Texas. Caleb knew how white men thought. Their hatred of the Comanche, who continued to raid and bring great destruction and sorrow to Texas settlers, would be turned toward all Indians, even the peaceful ones. Jake Highwater also felt the pressure. Two of his sons had already left the ranch and headed for Indian Territory to settle there. But Jake and Ada stayed on with their remaining son. Jake knew all Cherokee were living on borrowed time, but Caleb Sax needed his help. Caleb had given him a home here and now he was in trouble himself. He would not desert his good friend.

At dusk one night in the spring of 1839, Emily Stoner's fancy carriage pulled up in front of the Sax house. The woman disembarked, wearing a dark blue dress of the latest fashion, a gown which, unlike her usual apparel, was deliberately modest. She wore a hat that tied with heavy lace around the sides of her face, hiding her scar. Caleb came out to greet her, embracing her, while Sarah hurried out behind him, followed by Pepper. Now over a year old, the dog was big and shaggy, and he stood watching Emily with a wagging tail, sensing she was friendly.

"Emily, where have you been? It's so good to see you," Sarah said while Caleb hugged the woman.

Emily pulled away from him and turned to Sarah, looking hesitant and apologetic. "Hello, Sarah."

Sarah reached out her hands, but Emily did not take them right away. Their eyes held. "Sarah, I . . . said some things to you the last time I saw you—"

"That was nearly three years ago. I know why you said them, Emily."

Emily nodded, taking her hands, then embracing Sarah.

The two women hugged tightly for a moment, and Sarah could smell strong perfume.

"Emily, come inside," Sarah told her then.

"No," the woman answered quickly. She pulled back and looked up at Caleb. "I just came to say a quick hello and to make sure you two were still all right. I . . . I can't come in. I shouldn't even be here."

Caleb frowned. "Why not? We're friends."

She fidgeted nervously with a handkerchief. "You don't want to go saying that in public, Caleb Sax. You're in enough trouble just being an Indian. You want to keep your family name respectable and not do anything to tarnish Sarah's reputation."

"I'll come and see my friends whenever I want," Caleb returned. "And where in hell have you been? We've both been worried about you. We've wondered about you often, Emily. You left San Felipe not long after the war was over. I know because I tried to find you."

She sighed and nodded. "I had to leave. I couldn't stand walking down the street and seeing that little cabin where Howard and I had lived." She blinked back tears. "I went back to New Orleans."

"And to prostitution," Caleb said. It was more a statement than a question.

Emily met his eyes. "Why not? It's what I'm made for."

"Don't talk stupid," Caleb answered. "You can come here and live with us if you want."

She laughed, a harsh ring to the laughter and a bitterness in her eyes. "You don't need that kind of gossip, my friend. I am where I was meant to be, and I don't have many years of that left. I'm not much for looks anymore, Lord knows. A hard life can make an old woman of you fast." She sighed and looked down again. "At any rate, I actually missed Texas. I came back with several pretty young things to set up my own . . . uh . . . boarding house, so to speak. It's a very pleasant place for a single man to stay—or a married man who isn't finding comfort in his own bed." She looked wryly at Sarah. "I don't suppose I'd be lucky enough to find out your husband has such a problem," she added with a crooked smile.

Sarah blushed and Emily laughed. "That's what I thought." She looked up at Caleb. "I'm back in San Felipe. Of course, I had to come here and see if you two were all right. God knows you can't come and see me. Don't you dare even try. If you're really my friends, don't cause me agony by coming to see me and creating problems for yourselves. If you see me in town, don't act like you even know me."

"Emily, that's ridiculous," Sarah told her.

"No it isn't. Please." She looked up at Caleb again. "Promise me. Once in a while I'll find a way to come here and visit, after dark like I'm doing now. I can trust my driver not to talk."

Caleb glanced at the man, who just sat staring ahead. He looked back at Emily. "I'm sorry about Howard, Emily. I wanted the chance to tell you that, but when I tried to come and see you, you had already left, and I had no idea where you went."

Her eyes teared, but she held her chin up as though undaunted. "I had him for a while. That's more than I ever thought I would get before I met him. I'm lucky to have had that much." She swallowed. "It's Howard I feel bad about, not myself. I'll survive like I always have." She held his eyes. "How about you? The war took its toll on everyone. How are you getting along?"

Caleb shrugged. "Money is tight. I'm feeling the squeeze from the Indian haters, having a little trouble selling my crops and horses."

She closed her eyes and sighed. "I was afraid of that." She studied the blue eyes. "But there's more, isn't there?" She looked past him. "Your family still intact?"

His lips tightened and his jaw flexed. He couldn't bring himself to say it. Sarah put an arm around his waist. "We lost Tom . . . at the Alamo."

Pain moved over Emily's face. She knew full well how important Tom was to Caleb, remembered how the paralyzed, bedridden Caleb she had once cared for talked constantly about his little Indian boy who lived with the Cheyenne and who he was going to go and get when he got well. Tom had been everything to Caleb then. She swallowed a lump in her throat, putting a hand on his arm. "My God, I'm so sorry, Caleb."

He nodded, visibly shaken. "We're all very sorry about a lot of things. It's over. Life goes on, I guess. We just keep doing the best we can."

"Lynda is married to Jess Purnell," Sarah spoke up, wanting to change the subject. "Do you remember we told you about him when we stayed at San Felipe?"

"Yes. I'm glad."

"They're down by the river with Cale. Lynda is pregnant again. James is six now. Please come inside and see him, Emily."

"No." She looked at Caleb. "I can't express enough how sorry I am about Tom. I'll try to keep you informed on what's happening in town, Caleb. There is an awful lot of talk about the Indians. Lamar is rebuilding the Texas army with the specific intention of rooting out all Comanche and Cherokee. I think he's more intent on getting rid of the peaceful Cherokee than he is the Comanche, just because a lot of the Cherokee own land. That same thinking could apply to you. Your only saving grace is that you're half white and your wife is white, and you were one of the original settlers under Austin. But Austin is dead now, and Houston has lost a lot of his power. The people don't seem to give a damn that he led Texas to freedom."

"Or that my husband himself fought at San Jacinto," Sarah added angrily. "How dare they even suggest—"

Caleb gave her a squeeze. "Never mind, Sarah. I've been expecting it." He looked out over the distant hills. "I've been expecting it."

Emily embraced them both together. "You have each other. That's all that's important. Remember that. If I can do anything to help, you know I will." She pulled away. "I've got to go."

"You'll be going back in the dark. Please stay the night, Emily. Who is going to know?"

"We can't take the chance. I love you both. I'm glad you're all right." She turned and hurried back to the carriage.

"Emily, don't do it. Stay with us," Caleb called out, leaving Sarah and walking toward the carriage.

She just laughed. "Don't ever worry about me, Caleb Sax. Emily Stoner does just fine. You have enough worries." She blew him a kiss and climbed in. The carriage clattered away. Caleb watched after it, remembering another time; a tall, young girl with haunting eyes, standing next to her preacher father who made her dress in long-sleeved and high-necked dresses, with gloves and hat, even in the hottest weather, so that no man would look upon her and lead her to sin.

Byron Clawson waited until his guest sipped more after-dinner wine. He had heard of Marston Biehl, a lawyer practicing in the new capital of the Republic of Texas. The man was in St. Louis on business. What better man to invite to dinner? Byron had far too much unsettled business in Texas.

"This is very fine wine," Biehl told the man. "It was kind of you, Mister Clawson, to invite me into your home."

Byron set down his own glass. The table at which they sat was long, but only the two men sat there. Byron's wife had retired to her sitting room. The Clawsons had little in common nowadays. His wife, Jayne, was the daughter of a local merchant, whose inheritance had been large enough to make up for the woman's plain looks and personality. He supposed they balanced each other, which was the only reason they were still together. She married Byron only because she was afraid if she didn't, she would never find a husband at all; he married her for money and social acceptance. Married men always fared better in politics. Married men with a family did even better, but Jayne had never given him children. It surely was her fault for being so cold in bed; things between them had gotten so that his only sexual enjoyment was with the local prostitutes. He had always preferred prostitutes. They were the only ones who understood his sexual needs. Jayne had long ago taken her own bedroom, but in the public eye they both put on a grand show of the happily married couple.

Still, it hadn't helped his political career the way he'd hoped. He had not won election to any state or local office, and in his own arrogant mind he simply could not imagine why. With all his money, he still did not have the ultimate power he would like to have. Maybe he could find that power somehow through his new connections to this place called Texas.

In the meantime he would keep his wife. She was relatively easy to live with. They simply didn't speak to each other; she never stopped him from visiting the prostitutes and she enjoyed spending his money. Besides, he did not want the embarrassment of another divorce. He'd spent too many years working at pushing his divorce from Sarah Sax under the rug and out of the public's mind. Some of his business associates didn't even know about that first marriage, including the prominent businessman he was now entertaining.

"Only the best for my guests," Byron said aloud. "And as I told you, my invitation is partially business, Mister Biehl. I just thought it good manners to wait until you were finished with your meal."

Biehl smiled. "Well, that was an excellent supper." He patted his stomach. "Now, what can I do for you in the way of business?"

Byron rose. "Come into my private office, Mister Biehl. I have some fine cigars. Bring your wine along."

Biehl rose and followed the man. There was something about Byron Clawson he didn't much like, yet he couldn't put his finger on what it was. There was an air of evil about the man, and he was quite homely. He was aware Byron Clawson had twice run for governor and lost, gaining few votes. But he was wealthy and respected as a businessman in St. Louis, if nothing more. And the fact remained the man owned a bank, and Texas needed money.

Byron sat down at his desk, then leaned over and offered Biehl, seated across from him, an open box of cigars. Biehl took one, thanking him, and Byron lit the cigar for him. He sat down then, leaning back in his own plush chair.

"I want to know about Texas, Mister Biehl. I have a

great interest in the new Republic, own a great deal of land there. I want to know if the war is realy over, and if it's safe to go there."

Biehl puffed the cigar for a moment. "I'd say so. Oh, we expect more problems with Mexico, but we're ready for it, much more ready than the first time, and more determined than ever. We've been a country of our own now long enough to want to keep it that way." He frowned. "Where is this land you own?"

Byron studied his glass of wine, thinking of Caleb. Where was he? Did he dare go within striking distance of Caleb Sax? "It's on the Brazos River, just north of some land owned by Caleb Sax. You ever heard of him? He's supposed to be one of the original settlers who came when Austin opened up that area."

"Sax." Biehl thought a moment. "It's somewhat familiar. But then I've only been in Texas a couple of years. I don't know the man personally."

Byron nodded. "Well, I'm thinking of going down there and checking things out myself. My wife has already agreed to let me go. I don't doubt by now that my land is covered with squatters. I had a man running it once, but he was killed—in some dispute with this Caleb Sax. But then I wouldn't go directly to my land. I'd hire someone to get things in shape, chase out the squatters and such. I would live in town—San Felipe, I'm thinking. I'd like to open up a bank there."

Biehl smiled. "That would be wonderful. And any money you might loan the government, to help shore up the army and such, would be most welcome, Mister Clawson. Texas is rather destitute right now. A man in your position could come there and get in on the ground floor and become quite wealthy. As an attorney, there might be ways I can help you. Of course I realize you're already a man of means, but Texas can make you even richer."

It was all Byron could do to hold back the eagerness in his eyes at the thought of gaining more wealth and new power in Texas. Yes, he had considered it carefully. He had failed twice at politics in Missouri. He was tired of losing. Perhaps in the new Republic he could finally be an important man, a man in control of the lives of others. Just think of all the poor Texans who needed loans. Maybe even Caleb Sax needed one! What better victory than to be personally responsible for ruining Caleb Sax financially. But there might be an even better victory.

"Tell me, Mister Biehl, what about the Indians? I've heard this new president—Lamar, I think his name is?"

"Yes."

"Lamar, yes. Well, I hear he's making an all-out campaign to rid Texas of its Indians. Is he just talking about the wilder Comanche?"

Biehl sipped more wine and then smiled. "No, sir. All Indians."

Byron nodded thoughtfully. "All Indians. Even the peaceful ones who might own land and are quite settled?"

Their eyes held. "All Indians." Biehl puffed his cigar again. "Lamar feels, as most Texans do, that the only way to be really strong is to get rid of the Indians. We can't have the trash some other state throws out move into Texas and create the same problems all over again. A lot of the Cherokee, Choctaw and the like who have been banished from the Southern states have trickled into Texas because they're not happy with the Indian Territory assigned to them; and, of course, that land is just north of Texas, so it's difficult to keep them out. But when Lamar is through, I don't think we'll have much trouble."

Byron smiled. "You have been a great help, Mister Biehl. A great help. I am going to give serious consideration to coming to Texas. I'm at a point in my life where I would like a change, and a challenge. And I have the money to do it, as well as money that could help Texas. I firmly believe that Texas will one day be another state, Mister Biehl, and when that happens, the land there will be worth a fortune, and Texas will be the biggest state in the Union."

Biehl smiled even wider in return. "You're a smart man, Mister Clawson. I share your hope that we will become a state. There has been a lot of bickering, especially over the issue of slavery, and Lamar continues to work with European countries to get loans and such. But that will all blow over, and in time Texas will definitely join the Union. I'm sure of it. But she will probably join as a slave state."

Byron shrugged. "A man has the right to own slaves. The North can't stop such a thing. Slaves are the basis of Southern economy. So what if it's a slave state? It's Texas." He sighed deeply. "I like the sound of it, Mister Biehl, I surely do."

Biehl finished his wine and set the glass on the desk. "Any man who goes there falls in love with her, Mister Clawson. Texas is like a woman, beckoning, beautiful, naked."

Byron laughed lightly, adding, "Now that *does* make me want to go there." How Byron would love seeing Caleb Sax ruined, preferably dead. He was tired of waiting, watching the shadows, wondering when Caleb would take his revenge for the botched up job Hafer did and knowing Byron was behind it.

Thank God for the war with Mexico. That had kept the man busy. Perhaps it had even killed him, and Sarah was down there alone. What a wonderful thought! He must go down there himself and find out. Surely if he stayed within the protection of a civilized town he would be safe. After all, Texas was full of Indian haters now. Caleb Sax wouldn't dare make a move that could cost him a hanging.

"Speaking of beautiful women," he said, "you're a single man, Biehl. I know where you can find some very pleasurable woman company while you're in St. Louis, if you're interested."

Biehl gave him a scolding look. "Oh, but you're a married man, Mister Clawson."

Byron leaned closer. "All the more reason to visit these ladies," he answered. "A man gets a little tired of the same one all the time. Proper women just don't seem to know how to enjoy a man, if you know what I mean."

Biehl shook his head, grinning. "You are a man of few morals, Mister Clawson."

Byron just laughed.

"I'll take you up on the women, Mister Clawson. My carriage, or yours?"

Byron rose, looking pompous and sure. "Mine, by all

means. You'll not be disappointed, Mister Biehl, I assure you. I'll just go tell my wife I'm taking you out to show you the town. And on the way we can talk more about Texas."

He left the room and Biehl watched after him. If Byron Clawson wanted to leave a wife at home and go romp with the whores, who was he to say otherwise? Lots of married men did that. But there was something more. He disliked the man without one concrete reason. Still, Clawson was planning on opening a bank in Texas. Texas came first. If it took men like Byron Clawson to help it along, then he was welcome.

Byron's own heart pounded wildly with the thought of it. Texas. Yes, he would get rid of all his fears. He would be a man and face Caleb Sax straight on, that's what he'd do. He'd go to Texas and finally win out over Caleb Sax, and he'd become a powerful leader of that baby republic. And when she became a state, he'd be right there, an important man, ready to step right into some office of importance, maybe even governor. Yes. Perhaps at last he could realize that dream in a new land where no one knew him and where he would make sure plenty of people depended on him.

He hoped, though, that there were some decent prostitutes there. Surely there were. Texas was full of burly, wild, unsettled men. Prostitutes followed that kind of man everywhere. Yes, there would be plenty of whores down there, too. Texas had everything. One thing, however, it would not have when he was through was Caleb Sax.

Chapter
Twenty-Three

It was February 1840 when John Thomas Purnell was born to Lynda and Jess. Named after his two dead uncles, Lynda was determined the boy would know all about them and love them, even though he would never know them.

Jess was beside himself with joy. It had been nearly three years since Lynda had lost their first baby. Cale was already seven years old when his little half-brother was born. Now Cale helped more with ranching chores, as did his uncle James, also seven.

The two boys were practically inseparable, in work and play, and both struggled to prove they could do their share in helping rebuild the Sax ranch. James felt closer to his father, and was proud to please him, no longer afraid of horses, and he and Cale were both learning how to herd mustangs.

The birth of a healthy son to Lynda and Jess helped ease the rising tension and sense of danger to the entire Sax family. President Lamar had spent hundreds of thousands of dollars, nearly depleting the Texas treasury, in his campaign against the Cherokee and the Comanche. Against the advice of Sam Houston himself, Lamar worked hard at ousting all Cherokee settled in eastern Texas, claiming they had no legal title to any of the land they occupied. The Texas army waged deliberate war against these peaceful Indians, forcing a series of bloody, needless battles that drove the Cherokee across the Red River into Indian Territory in the United States. Their leader, Chief Bowles, died in a fight to stay in Texas, and a sword given him by Sam Houston himself was pried from his hand. With this sad event came a hard division between the two leading factions of Texas—Lamar and Houston, who was furious over Lamar's treatment of the Indians.

The Sax ranch was left with very few men to help. Several Cherokee left of their own accord. The few hands who stayed, including Jake Highwater, remained out of loyalty, so far permitted by the government to stay because Caleb owned the land and gave them permission to live there. However, Caleb was plagued daily with the worry over when those in power would come along and tell him that he, too, could not legally own the land because he was part Indian. He was well aware that allowing Cherokee to stay on his land irritated the current government, but he refused to force them to leave.

Now when he rode the hills and valleys of his land, it was with a saddening heart. For years he had loved this place. He had nurtured it, developed it, watched Texas grow, even risked his own life and lost a son in the battle for Texas independence. Now all of it was threatened. His bitterness over his treatment by white men over the years, men like Sarah's father and Byron Clawson, and now the new government under President Lamar, simmered in Caleb's soul.

His finances worried him, for more than anything else he wanted to keep Sarah in a comfortable life-style. If not for the war, and now this new anti-Indian movement, he could have been a very rich man by now, with the finest horses in the West and a sprawling, prosperous ranch. He had always intended to build Sarah a bigger, finer home. But now all his energy and money went into just keeping the ranch going, as well as the little farming they did. The government had never come through on their promissory notes, and he knew they never would. It was getting more difficult to tend to the ranch and build it the way he should.

It was almost impossible to keep watch on horses that had to be ranged far from the main house, especially at Blue Valley. There were simply not enough men to help watch them, meaning he and Jess had to be away from the

women, who were less protected now that most of the
Cherokee had left. Keeping the horses close to the house
meant less grazing land, and left borders unprotected.

Squatters threatened incessantly. Time and again Jess
and Caleb were forced to route out freeloaders, but it was
an impossible task, for they could not constantly guard the
borders. Caleb seldom got to Blue Valley now, and it left a
distant ache in his heart. Blue Valley had once been a favorite place for him and Tom, in the early days, when he
and his eldest son built this land. It made him think of his
battle with Hafer over the water, and of Bess. Poor Bess.
Such sweet love so short-lived. It wasn't fair. But Tom and
Bess were together now. Perhaps they were better off. It
was those left behind who had to continue the struggle.

April came with heavy rains, so heavy that Lynda and
Sarah did not hear the horses approaching outside. It was
not until a knock came at the door that they realized someone was there. Caleb and Jess were far off in the north
pasture mending a fence, a necessary job in spite of the
weather. Sarah looked at Lynda, who immediately went for
a musket over the fireplace, while Sarah urged Cale and
James into the bedroom where little John lay sleeping in a
cradle. She ordered the boys to stay put.

Pepper growled as Sarah went to the door. "Who is it?"
she called.

Her only reply was another loud pounding.

"Who's there?"

"You Mrs. Sax?" came a voice in question.

Lynda leveled the rifle at the door. "Yes," Sarah answered.

"We're here to talk about buying some land off your
husband."

Sarah moved to peek out a window. She looked at
Lynda. "There are six of them . . . all men." She moved to
the door. "You'll have to wait outside until my husband
returns. He'll be back any minute," she called out louder to
them. She was not really certain when Caleb would come,
but she suddenly wished it would be quickly.

Both women jumped when something hit the door hard

then. They heard laughter, and suddenly someone was crashing his way through a window. Sarah screamed and stepped back and Lynda fired her rifle. The man in the window slumped, hanging over the sill, blood pouring from his head.

Lynda began reloading her rifle. There was no time to contemplate the fact that she had killed a man. The men outside began cursing, and someone began pulling the dead body back through the window.

"Jesus Christ, he's dead," someone shouted.

"But there's only a woman in there," someone else yelled.

"Woman or not, she killed Dressel."

"We'll get the Indian-loving whores," came another voice. Someone pointed a rifle into the broken window and fired. Then another man did the same, while the others began pounding on the door. Lynda and Sarah were forced to turn up the heavy kitchen table and duck behind it to avoid gunfire, and Sarah screamed at James and Cale to stay in the bedroom, to take the baby and get under the bed. She prayed Caleb had heard the shooting above the rain.

Pepper barked wildly and began leaping at the window. Lynda screamed for him to get away, but in the next moment there was another gunshot and the dog was hurled backward with a squeal, landing on his side and bleeding heavily from the stomach. He lay there panting.

"Pepper! Pepper!" James yelled from the bedroom.

"Stay there, James," Sarah ordered. "Don't you come out of that room!"

Another man appeared at the window. Lynda fired again but hit the sill. By then the wooden bar across the door began to crack. Lynda frantically began reloading, but could not do so before the door burst open and five men poured in, all with several-day-old beards and wearing clothes that bespoke men who had been riding for several days and cared little about bathing. Their wet, muddy boots began dripping on the floor as they all stood there grinning, some with guns in their hands. One suddenly charged toward Lynda, leaping right over the table and knocking the rifle from her hands. He threw it aside, holding her down to the floor then and staying on top of her.

"Well, looky here, Ben. You ever seen anything this pretty in all your born days?"

Sarah stood up, eyeing them all boldly. "Tell that man to let my daughter up," she said calmly.

The one called Ben only grinned, while the man on Lynda began trying to kiss her, grasping at her breasts through her dress. Lynda struggled wildly, scratching at his eyes, making him let go of her, but only for a moment. He yanked her up and backhanded her, sending her reeling toward the bedroom door.

"Mama," Cale cried out then, coming out from under the bed. The first man was on her again, pushing up her dress, but Cale jumped on his back, flailing at him with feet and fists. The man stood up, grabbing at the boy and throwing him back into the bedroom.

Little John began crying and Lynda, her head reeling from the blow to her face, scrambled up and ran into the bedroom, picking up John and holding him close, while Cale, refusing to cry in spite of hitting the bedpost hard, lit into the first man again, this time with James's help. The man managed to grasp them both around the throat, holding them at arm's length so they could not reach him with their little fists. He dragged them into the outer room, laughing at their struggles.

Sarah reached for James to get him away, but the one called Ben was beside her by then, pulling her back. He yanked her arms behind her and held them with one hand while he pulled her close, her back to him, fondling her breasts with his other hand.

Sarah struggled but he squeezed one breast painfully. "Give us what we want, or I'll let Henry there kill the boys." He looked over at a furious Lynda, who clung to little John, glaring at the men with the chilling hatred usually seen only in the fiercest Indian warriors. "Same goes for you, pretty thing. Put that baby down and strip them clothes off, else all three young ones are dead—right now."

James and Cale both began turning purple from lack of

air. Lynda looked at Sarah with tears in her eyes. The one called Ben suddenly ripped at Sarah's dress, exposing one breast. Sarah turned her face away from Lynda. "Let the boys go," she screamed. "You can take me in the bedroom. Just let the boys go!"

Ben grinned, rubbing at the exposed breast and pressing himself against her back. "That's better." He looked over at the first man. "Tie the young ones, Henry. You can be first at the younger woman there. I'm takin' this one in the bedroom."

Henry threw both boys to the floor. They coughed for air as another man brought over some rope to tie them. James looked over at Pepper, who now lay dead. "Pepper," he muttered.

"That's what happens when you got Indian in you, boy," one of the men laughed. "Life just ain't worth a shit."

Indian. Indian. It seemed to James that his father had had troubles ever since the boy could remember, and usually it had something to do with his father being Indian. It seemed strange to think of himself as part Indian. He didn't look Indian at all. But Cale did. And just because of that he got an extra kick while he was being tied.

Lynda quickly laid John back in his cradle in the bedroom, praying no harm would come to her baby. She wanted desperately to go to Cale, but dared not, and more than that she wanted to fight the one called Henry, who approached her when she came back into the main room. She had considered for a fleeting moment getting out through the bedroom window, but she would not desert the children or her mother. She eyed Henry with fear and hatred. If she fought, if either woman fought, the men would kill the boys. She knew instinctively it was not just a threat, and knew someone might also be killed if she had tried to escape.

Henry walked up to her and grasped her dress, ripping it open. He ran the backs of his hands over her nipples while the other men watched and laughed, anxiously awaiting their turn.

"We hear tell you're married to an Indian," Ben was telling Sarah. "You know what that makes you, honey?"

He kissed her neck and she felt nauseated. "That makes you a filthy whore, good for nothin' but spreadin' your legs for any man that comes along."

Henry began pulling Lynda's dress farther off, and the men delighted in the sight of her, tall and slim, slender thighs, dark skin.

"Now we come here to take this place over," Ben told Sarah, pulling the other shoulder of her own dress down. "They tell us it belongs to an Indian, so we figure it's up for grabs. We decided we want it. Shouldn't be any problem. We kill your husband, and that's that. 'Course you and the young woman there, you're welcome to stay on."

"My husband will kill you," Sarah told him, her voice calm but firm. She had decided she was not going to cry and beg for this animal.

"Well, he ain't around. You said so yourself. And you were lyin' about him comin' back any time, weren't you? Sure you were. By the time he comes, he'll have shared his white squaw with five other men, and we'll be waitin' for him."

James and Cale lay struggling on the floor, wishing they were bigger and stronger and could help. The words Indian, and white squaw, rang in James's ears. His precious dog Pepper had died because of Indian haters. How he'd loved Pepper, something that had been all his own. Now he lay dead, and these bad men were hurting and shaming his mother. He could not stop his tears, nor could Cale, whose own mother now stood completely naked before the men, who all gathered closer around her.

"One at a time now, boys," Ben warned them, shoving Sarah toward the bedroom.

"*White men*," Sarah thought. Here they'd been so afraid of a Comanche attack, and it was white men who had come. For years Cherokee had lived on their land, worked for them, yet never once had Sarah felt a fear of any of them.

So, this was the kind of scum that was coming into Texas. Squatters! Trash! Outlaws running from civilization and coming here to take what they could get for free!

"Get down on the floor, squaw," the one called Henry told Lynda.

She met his eyes steadily. "Not here. Not in front of my son. We'll go up in the loft."

The man's eyes moved over her appreciatively. "Fine with me." He grinned more, looking from the ladder back to Lynda. "You first."

They all laughed and stood at the foot of the ladder as she climbed it. She forced back her fear. Her father's keen ears had surely heard the gunfire. He and Jess would come, and these men would die. But would they come in time? She had no feelings of horror for herself at the moment. Her fear for her mother and her sons overshadowed that. There would be time later for letting this hideous event sink into her bones. In the bedroom Sarah was thinking the same thing as she obeyed the orders of the one called Ben and removed the rest of her clothing.

Ben laughed and set his gun aside, then, taking off everything but his underwear, as Sarah moved onto the bed, pale and shaking, wondering if she could get through this without vomiting. If only the children weren't here. How she would fight this slime then, to the death if necessary! Every muscle stiffened as he unbuttoned his underwear. She refused to look at anything but his scummy eyes as he approached the bed. One of the other men came to stand in the curtained doorway, leering at them. Ben straddled Sarah, then looked over at the man.

"Get out of here! I can't do it when somebody's watchin'. You'll get your own turn."

The second man moved his eyes over Sarah hungrily before he left. Ben looked down at Sarah.

It was then Sarah sensed another presence. Her eyes moved to the bedroom window. A week ago James had accidentally torn the screen, and Caleb had removed it. It still wasn't fixed. She saw someone look in, then dart back. It was raining so hard she couldn't see the face clearly, but she did not doubt it was Caleb. The rain had helped to hide the sound of his approach.

She had to help him get inside somehow. The window was locked. If the men knew he was out there, they'd kill everyone inside, or perhaps use the boys as hostages to get out. Ben leaned down to put his mouth over her breast and she pushed him.

"Wait!"

His eyes hardened. "Don't make me do this the hard way, woman," he sneered, grasping her hair and making ready to hit her.

"It's so warm in here," Sarah objected. "I just want you to open the window."

Her heart pounded. She prayed it would work. Ben looked over at the window, then back at her slyly. "It's raining out there."

"I know. But it's so stuffy. Please. I . . . feel like I can't breathe."

"All right. But you make one move to get off this bed, and I'll beat you so bad you won't be able to walk straight, let alone what I'll do to your kid."

He moved off the bed and Sarah lay still. Ben raised the window and a light breeze moved through the room. "That *is* better," he declared. "Gonna get your floor a little wet, but we don't care about that, do we?" He turned around to come back to Sarah, and with the quiet stealthiness only an Indian could possess, Caleb leaned through the window and flung his big knife. It sank into Ben's spine, making a sickening scraping sound. Sarah shuddered and looked away as Ben, wide-eyed in impending death, stumbled to the bed and fell over her. Caleb was quickly through the window, and he quietly pulled the body off his wife and lowered it to the floor, yanking out the knife and wiping it off on a piece of Ben's clothing.

Sarah immediately pulled a blanket over herself, fighting a need to scream. She saw the horror and fierce revenge in Caleb's eyes as he leaned close, grasping her hair and pressing his cheek against hers quickly and reassuringly. "How many?" he whispered.

"Three more in the outer room," she whispered in reply. "One up in the loft with Lynda."

Caleb left her. Oh, how he wanted to hold her! What had they done to her? What were they doing to Lynda? Water dripped from his clothing as he moved to the curtained doorway and pulled out his pistol. He looked through a tiny opening where the curtains came together and saw Cale and James lying facedown on the floor, their hands tied behind them, both boys crying and mumbling "Mother" and "Mama." John lay in a cradle in the bedroom, and three men stood at the foot of the ladder telling someone in the loft to hurry up.

Caleb darted into the room then, firing his pistol at one man point-blank. The man stumbled backward.

"Father!" James shouted.

"Son of a bitch," one of the men yelled, pointing a gun at Caleb. But Caleb's knife was out and thrown before the man could fire. Jess burst in then from the front, shooting down the third man.

Lynda screamed in the loft then. Jess started up the ladder, but the fourth man appeared at the top, holding a naked Lynda in front of him. "You men make another move and she's dead," the man growled. "Back off!"

Jess's eyes widened with heated hatred as he backed away, as did Caleb.

"Drop your weapons," the man ordered.

Caleb's knife was still imbedded in the chest of one of the others. His pistol had been fired and there had not been time to reload. He threw it down but inched his way toward the dead man whose body held his knife. Jess stood there with his pistol still in his hand.

"I said to drop it," the man in the loft growled.

"Get your stinking hands off my wife," Jess hissed.

Henry only grinned, grasping a breast. "She's a right good squaw, mister," he leered.

Lynda took advantage of the moment. She lurched sideways away from the man and shoved, sending him over the edge. Caleb dived for his knife, yanking it out of the dead man, then turning and landing it with a whir and a thud into Henry as soon as the man hit the floor. The man gasped, staring wide-eyed at Caleb in terror.

Caleb walked up to the man, who began jerking violently. "He's still alive," he muttered. He looked up at his beautiful daughter, who stood holding a blanket clumsily in front of herself. The side of her face was bruised. Sarah appeared at the doorway of the bedroom, wearing a robe she had quickly pulled on, her green eyes wide and horrified. Rage consumed Caleb. He yanked his knife from Henry's still living body and dragged the man toward the door.

"Caleb," Jess called to him, shaking with his own rage. "That one is mine."

Their eyes held, and Caleb understood. He kicked the body out the door, then held his knife out to Jess. "He's all yours. Here's your chance to be an Indian."

Jess walked toward him, a determined look on his face. He took the knife from Caleb and went outside, dragging Henry's still-live body farther away from the house.

Jess held a trembling Lynda in his arms. They were in their own cabin, and the trauma of the day had not left her. The one called Henry had humiliated her with prying hands and explorations, but Caleb and Jess had arrived before she was actually raped.

Jess held her tightly, his own rage still burning in his soul. He knew the humiliation of the day would be with both Lynda and Sarah for a long time. Jess had finally managed to calm Cale, and little John slept soundly, too small to understand any of the day's events.

Lynda huddled close to Jess and he kissed her tears. "It's all over," he told her. "And until we can get more help, Caleb and I aren't leaving you again, not even for a little while."

"They saw me," she whispered. "The boys. My father."

"Hush. Do you really think they care about anything but the fact that you're all right? My God, Lynda, loved ones don't remember things that shouldn't be remembered. To Cale you're as sacred as Holy Mary. And to Caleb you're just his little girl, whom he loves very much." He kissed her hair. "And to me you're still my woman, and I damned well love you more than any of them."

"Thank God you weren't hurt. I was so afraid for you. I don't know what I'd do, Jess, if anything happened to you—"

He put his fingers to her lips. "It's all over. And it won't happen again."

"Make love to me, Jess," she whimpered.

He frowned, smoothing back her hair. "Surely that's the last thing you want, honey."

"It is . . . and yet . . . I don't know." Her chest heaved in a sob. "They made it all so ugly. Make love to me. I want to know it's all right—that it's still beautiful for us."

Desire cut through him. He'd wanted to make love to her, out of his own sheer need to prove she was still his. By God, she *was* his! How dare those bastards even think of touching his wife! Henry's cries of pain still hung in his ears like music when he remembered having the pleasure of finishing the man's life with Caleb's big knife.

He met Lynda's trembling mouth, kissing it gently. He would make this good—nice—gentle. Of course it could be beautiful. He would work at helping her forget. She returned his kisses almost frantically, crying, pushing against him.

"Calm down, Lynda," he told her, pulling away slightly. "Nothing can change what we have between us, or change my love for you. I'm just so damned sorry you had to go through that. It will never happen again." He moved a hand over her naked body. "I'd die for you."

He met her mouth then, demanding by his touch and kiss that she relax and let him make the moves. Gently and slowly he kissed every part of her, reminding her that every inch of her belonged to Jess Purnell. How she loved him —so strong and sure and brave.

He moved on top of her and gently entered her, being careful not to do anything to make her remember the bad things, trying desperately to soothe her memory of the day's horror. It seemed unusual she would want to do this, yet he understood her need to act quickly so that today's experience did not come between them and make her afraid to share her body again.

He took her rhythmically, always enjoying being inside this brave, exquisite woman he had fallen in love with in one glance. Could that really have been over seven years ago? Cale had not even been born yet! It seemed only yesterday, and then again it seemed he'd loved her all his thirty years. She was eighteen and he was twenty-three that first day he saw her. So many things had happened since then: the fight with Hafer, the war, that beautiful night she'd come to him before he left for San Felipe. Never once since then had he made love to her without experiencing the same glorious ecstasy of being wrapped within the body of Lynda Sax. It never got old, and her wild joy in taking a man never ceased to bring out the animal in him. But he was careful this night not to be careless or too aggressive.

Lynda took him gladly. She never wanted any other man but Jess to touch her now. She never dreamed she could love this much again, but it had happened. Her whole world was Jess Purnell, and Jess was determined that the scum who had attacked her would not spoil this beautiful part of their love.

In the main house Caleb lay holding Sarah, treasuring her just as fiercely as Jess treasured Lynda. It had taken him a long time to calm her after the reality of all that had happened sunk in, the humiliation torturing her mind. That was when the shaking began.

She had been brave when necessary, to protect James and Cale. But once it was over, Caleb could not hold her long enough or hard enough. Jess had ridden to find help from the few Cherokee left on the north section of their land. There were five men to be buried, and Caleb could not leave Sarah.

Now, finally, she had fallen asleep. He needed to make love to her, haunted by the memory of seeing the filthy squatter bent over her.

He hugged her tightly, kissing her hair. Poor Sarah. All her suffering was for being married to him, for living with an Indian. He knew she didn't care. But it broke his heart to think of his Sarah suffering for any cause.

He kissed her hair. How long could he stay on here? He wanted desperately to stay. What else could he offer her? How could he just leave Texas and wander with a woman like Sarah, so beautiful and delicate? Sarah Sax needed a solid home, a hearth, stability. He couldn't make her wander like an Indian. It didn't matter for himself. He had lived that way before and he could do it again. But not her.

Crying in the loft interrupted his thoughts. It was James. Caleb moved cautiously away from Sarah. He'd convinced her to drink some whiskey, and it was doing its job. He and Jess had scrubbed away the blood as best they could and now all was quiet. But how long would it be before people like the men who'd come today would return? And how could he run a ranch if he couldn't leave the house?

He moved out of the bed and went through the outer room and to the ladder that led to the loft. The blankets over the feather mattress, where the one called Henry had beaten Lynda and almost raped her, had been changed. Now James lay there crying. Caleb climbed the ladder.

"James?"

The boy sniffed and sat up. Caleb could see him by the dim light of a lantern that had been kept lit in the main room.

"They killed Pepper," the boy sniffled. "They killed my dog and hurt my mother just because we're Indian. Why'd they do that, Pa?"

Caleb climbed into the loft and lay down beside him, pulling the boy into his arms. "Because they're bad people, James. Because they don't understand what's really important, what makes a real man. They judge people by the color of their skin, lump people together instead of treating each man as an individual."

The boy rubbed his nose and eyes. "What's wrong with being Indian?" he sobbed. "Why do they hate Indians?"

Caleb hugged him tightly. "I don't even know that, James. I'm forty-five years old and I still don't know the answer. But things like this have been happening to me all my life, James. I just remind myself I'm my own person, and I'm a man, good as the next. And so will you be."

The boy pressed his face against his father's strong chest. "But I don't look like an Indian. Maybe I should never tell anybody I'm Indian when I grow up."

Caleb frowned, petting his hair. "Don't ever deny what you are, James. It's wrong. And it will leave an empty place in your heart, a guilty feeling that will stay with you and keep you from being happy."

The boy's lips puckered. "I won't ever be happy if everybody always hates me."

"They won't all hate you, James. There are a lot of good ones, like Tom Sax, the man who raised me. And like the Handels, and Jess. There are some good ones. You'll find your own way when you're a man, and you won't have to deny your Indian blood to do it."

The boy shook in another sob. "I want Pepper. He was just trying to protect us. Pepper was my friend."

"We'll find you another dog."

"I don't want another dog. I want Pepper. He's all alone now. He needs me."

"He's sleeping peacefully now, running around someplace where dogs have nothing but fresh meat and green grass and all the chickens to chase that they want."

He held the boy tightly as he kept mumbling about Pepper, finally growing more sleepy. Caleb wondered how much more his heart could take. He had never quite gotten over being short with this son when he was going through that final mourning over Tom. He often wondered if he'd truly made it up to him yet. James rode a horse just fine now, but sometimes Caleb saw a strange look in his son's eyes, a mixture of fear and rejection. Could they ever be as close as Caleb and Tom had been? How he loved James. But every child was different, and even though James was only seven, he felt this son slipping away from him and had no idea how to stop it. What had happened today had only made matters worse. Already he spoke of denying his Indian blood.

His own eyes teared. How could he make life better for this son? Everyone he touched and loved seemed to suffer. If only Pepper hadn't died. If only he could present James with his dog. He wondered if deep inside, the boy blamed his father for the death of his dog and the humiliation of his mother. If Caleb Sax were not an Indian, perhaps none of it would have happened. Was that what James was thinking?

Still, the boy clung to him now, turned to his father for

comfort. Yes, the boy loved him. But he was also still very young and dependent.

There would be no sleep for Caleb Sax that night. He had too much to think about. How much longer could he hold out? How much longer could he subject his family to the growing dangers here? He had worked so hard for this land, lost so much for it, risked his own life for it. Now he might have to leave it.

Caleb thought of the words of an old Mexican he had known when he first settled in Texas. The land was filling with Americans, and Caleb asked him why he didn't leave and go farther south into Mexico.

"*Mis raices estan aqui*," the old man had told him. "My roots are buried here."

Yes. That was the way it was for Caleb. The words came back to him so clearly. "*Mis raices estan aqui*." The land. Blue Valley. All the memories. Marie. Young David and John, two sons gone. And Tom. Three sons. Three sons! He clung tightly to James. Not this one. He might lose this one in a way worse than death; he might be denied by his own son. That would be the worst loss of all. If only James knew how much Caleb loved him. But they were worlds apart. He could only love this son from a distance.

A wolf howled outside, and a chill swept through Caleb. Tom. It still haunted him that he had never even had a body to bury. It still seemed as if the young man's spirit walked beside him, and sometimes it was a comforting feeling, as though Tom was right there telling him everything would be all right. He felt the presence now and hugged James closer, remembering when Tom was this young. Why was it still so hard to think of his eldest son as dead? He had told everyone else he'd finally faced that reality, forced himself to go on with life and to stop taking the loss out on all of them. But deep inside his heart Tom Sax still lived.

Caleb sat up wearily, picking a groggy James up with him and carrying him to the ladder, holding him over one shoulder as he descended. He didn't want Sarah or the boy to wake up alone tonight. He carried James into their bedroom and lay the boy down beside his mother, then crawled into bed with them, putting his arm around them both. No one was going to take these two from him, nor would anyone take Lynda or his grandchildren. No one! Whatever he had to do to keep what was left of the Sax family alive and together, he would do it.

Chapter
Twenty-Four

Caleb couldn't shake the feeling. Something was beckoning him. He had worked hard that morning helping Jess finish branding the few colts that had been born that spring. Caleb longed to take the whole herd to Blue Valley but didn't dare expose these new, carefully bred steeds to the thieving hands of squatters. The old Hafer place was covered with them now, and Caleb could not help wondering if Byron Clawson knew, or if the man even still owned the land. The last he'd checked, it was still in Byron's name. Maybe now that the war was over . . .

He grinned. No. Byron Clawson wouldn't be so stupid as to leave his sanctuary of an office in St. Louis to come to a place like Texas, especially when he knew Caleb Sax would be his next-door neighbor and was aware of what had happened to Charles Hafer. Still, Byron was pompous and unpredictable.

None of that mattered now. What mattered was this urgent feeling to go to Blue Valley. Were the spirits telling him he would find a fine bunch of mustangs there? Was something wrong? He hung up his branding iron on special hooks in the barn.

"We've got some fine horses to sell at the docks this

spring, Caleb," Jess said, coming in behind him. "Maybe now that the squatters know they can't mess with us, we can start building things up again."

Caleb turned to look at him. "Maybe. But this isn't over yet, Jess. What happened a couple of weeks ago might be just the beginning." He leaned against a support beam. "I'm not so sure we can stay here much longer."

Jess hung up his own branding iron and walked closer, resting his hands on his hips. "You're not going to give up now, are you, after all you've been through on this place?" He studied Caleb's tired eyes. The man was still hard and handsome, but age was beginning to show around the eyes and there was a touch of gray in the otherwise shining black hair.

Caleb held his eyes. "I might." He sighed deeply. "It would be like cutting out a piece of my heart, but every time I picture that son of a bitch on top of my wife—" His eyes flashed angrily and he walked over to pick up a horse blanket.

Jess watched him, his own memories of that day still bitter. "I know what you mean, Caleb. It was hard on both of them, and the boys, too. I've been wondering myself about staying, but it's your place and I didn't want to say anything. I know how much you love it."

Caleb went to a stall and took out his favorite horse, a white and gray speckled Appaloosa gelding. "I love my family more." He threw the blanket over the horse's back, then went to the wall to take down a bridle. "I just don't like the idea of turning Lynda and Sarah into wandering nomads. I don't have the faintest idea where in hell I'd go if I had to leave Texas." He turned to meet the man's eyes again. "It's tearing me apart inside, Jess, trying to decide what's right to do."

Jess walked closer, petting the Appaloosa's nose. "Whatever you decide, Caleb, I'm with you. And so will the rest of the family be with you. You know that."

Caleb turned and slipped the bridle bit into the horse's mouth. "I know. I appreciate your support." He pulled the bridle over the horse's ears. "When we take the herd into San Felipe, we'll have to take the women and kids along.

We have no choice. We can't leave them here. Besides, we need some supplies, and it might be good for them to go into town." He eased up onto the horse's back. "Tell Sarah not to wait lunch. I won't be back for a while."

"Where are you going?"

"Blue Valley." Caleb started to turn the horse.

"Blue Valley!" Jess grabbed the bridle. "Alone?"

"No. I'll take my musket and pistol."

"You know what I mean. You can't go up there alone. The north section is crawling with squatters from Hafer land."

"I can take care of myself. Besides, a lot of them got out of there after we killed off those that came to the house."

"What the hell are you going there for?"

Caleb sighed, looking down at him with weary eyes. "I don't even know, Jess. All I know is that all morning I've had this urge to go there, like someone came and told me I had to go. Maybe the spirits are telling me something. I don't know. I can't explain it. Besides, it's been a while since I was there. It's my favorite place. I feel closer to Tom there."

"Caleb, let me go with you."

"You can't. You've got to stay here with the women. I'll tell Jake to help keep a watch when I go by his place. Tell Sarah I'll be back sometime after dark but not to worry if I'm not back till tomorrow morning. It's a long ride."

He turned the horse then and trotted to the barn entrance, where his musket stood on end. He picked it up and rested it across his lap.

"Caleb, you're crazy to go there. Sarah will have a fit when she finds out."

"I know. That's why I'm going without telling her." He rode out.

Jess started to go after him, but Caleb was already heading north at full gallop. "Damned, stubborn Indian," Jess muttered. "Spirits!" He stalked toward the house.

Caleb made his way down the stony escarpment, the surefooted Appaloosa picking its way carefully so as not to spill its rider, yet sensing that would be difficult to do.

Caleb Sax sat a horse as well as he walked on his own two feet, maybe better, and the Appaloosa could feel the power of its rider.

It had rained that morning in Blue Valley, and with the rising heat of the day mixed with the moisture still in the ground and the grass, the land seemed to steam. Everything was hazy, and the colors of the hills on the other side of the Valley melted together as the day settled into dusk.

Caleb stopped partway down, studying the Valley below him, seeing no sign of squatters. His keen eyes moved along the distant hills. The Appaloosa tossed its head and snorted, waiting for another command. Caleb made ready to continue the descent, but suddenly he saw a lone figure on the distant ridge.

He stared, an odd tingle moving through his blood so that he shivered. He had no idea who it was, but a sixth sense told him it was not some kind of enemy. He could barely make out a man on a horse through the mist. Why Caleb was so struck by the figure, he couldn't understand, but he sat there motionless for a long time, watching it move along the ridge, stop a few times, move again, then come down toard the Valley.

Caleb finally found his faculties and urged his Appaloosa downward again. He had ridden hard, and made good time reaching the Valley. Why in the world had he been in such a hurry? He had felt moved by superior forces, led along by some invisible hand.

The day hung still and humid, a shadow slowly moving across the Valley as the sun began to sink behind the hills that protected it. The lone figure Caleb had seen was still descending and had nearly reached the Valley itself. Caleb reached bottom then, too, pausing for a moment as the figure started across, then stopped.

Whoever it was, he had seen Caleb. Caleb gripped his rifle, his eyes quickly moving to either side of the figure to see if there were others nearby, but the man seemed to be alone. He started ahead slowly, the chill sweeping through him again with sudden fury, for in that instant Caleb thought of Tom. The figure resembled his son.

He cursed himself then for being such a fool. Why did

he let everything lead to thoughts of Tom? Why did he allow the memory to haunt him so? It was still having its effects on others, especially James. Poor little James. James was a beautiful child, inside and out. He was the product of Caleb and Sarah's newfound love after years of being apart. A son was a son.

And there was Lynda. Even she had wondered if she was loved as much. Oh, but he did love her dearly. Why did children doubt such love? Perhaps because it was so very important to them. He remembered when he was a small boy, and the Sioux man who had adopted him took a new wife and they had a baby boy. How jealous Caleb had been of that baby! He was sure that new son was loved more than he. Now, as a grown man, he knew better. Apparently children needed that constant security and reassurance.

He brushed away thoughts of Tom, or at least tried to, as he trotted the Appaloosa ever closer to the approaching figure. The figure stopped again, and so did Caleb. How could he forget about Tom when the man he was watching looked more and more like him the closer he got? His heart pounded furiously and his breathing quickened when the figure raised a rifle into the air and let out a familiar Indian war whoop.

"*Tsehe-heto,*" the man shouted then.

Father! The word meant "my father" in Cheyenne. Caleb felt suddenly weak. Was he going mad? Was this some kind of vision? He clung to the reins of his Appaloosa, and the animal whinnied and pranced sideways as the figure came close then. He wore black, from shiny black boots to black pants to a handsome black shirt and hat. His hair was long, tied into a tail at his back. A fine silver and turquoise necklace graced the dark skin of his neck and a matching bracelet was wrapped around his broad wrist. A silver and turquoise belt circled his slender waist, and he rode a fine black stallion. At the moment his handsome brown eyes brimmed with tears. He flashed a brilliant smile.

"Father," he said then, reining his horse next to Caleb's. "Are you not glad to see me?"

Caleb stared, trembling. "Tom?"

The young man nodded. His smile quickly faded when he saw that his father looked ready to fall right off his horse. He quickly dismounted and reached up for the man. When his hand touched Caleb's arm, Caleb actually jerked back, tears welling in his eyes and his throat constricting. He held the young man's eyes. "You . . . we thought you were dead . . . the Alamo . . . everyone was killed . . . the bodies burned."

"I was sent out, Father, with a message. I was knocked senseless by shrapnel, and in my confusion I tried to crawl back to the mission, but I crawled right into a Mexican camp. They took me prisoner and sent me back into Mexico with some soldiers who were returning to Mexico City. I was in a Mexican prison for three and a half years. They kept me alive because I was young and strong. They used me to work in a gold mine."

Caleb continued to stare. Did he dare let himself believe this was real? He slowly slung his leg around and slid off the Appaloosa, standing before the young man, who stood as tall as his father. He kept looking at him with total shock in his eyes, then reached out, carefully touching Tom's chest as though to convince himself this was not a ghost. He began trembling visibly then, touching Tom's face.

"All these years . . . I've been struggling to face the reality of your death," Caleb choked out. "Yet somehow deep inside I . . . I knew. I could never quite accept it."

A tear slipped down Tom's cheek. "I have been dreaming of this day," he said, his voice gruff with emotion. "All the time I was in that prison, I thought of you . . . Lynda . . . the ranch. And I knew through all the pain, I had to live . . . for my father. Sometimes that's all that kept me going."

Caleb's eyes moved over him and he began shaking. Tom reached out and embraced him. "It is all right, Father. I am here."

Caleb's arm came around him and he wept. Tom. How could this be? The spirits had most certainly smiled upon him this day. No matter what happened now he would make it. Tom had been spared! Tom had come back to him. Tom was not dead. All his inability to accept his death made sense now. His inner spirit had somehow known his son was still alive.

The shock of it moved through him in waves of near faintness so that he half hung on to Tom just to stay on his feet. The young man held his father tightly. Oh, how he loved the man. What had happened since the war? Was everyone still all right? Why weren't there any horses in Blue Valley? He had passed through several squatter camps on Hafer land. Where had all the people come from?

How long they stood there clinging to each other, neither could know. Now Caleb understood why he'd had such an urge to come here. Perhaps the spirits thought it would be better for father and son to meet first, before any of the others knew.

"When we fought at San Jacinto, all I could think of was you," Caleb groaned. "We all shouted 'remember the Alamo.' We won the war, but I lost my son . . . and I wondered if it was worth it. Why didn't they let you go? Why didn't they let you go after we won?"

Tom pulled away suddenly. "I don't know. I think they just forgot about me. I was thrown in a dungeon for a long time, then sent to the gold mines." He wiped his eyes. "Come and sit down, Father. Are you all right?"

Caleb nodded and Tom kept an arm around the man, leading him to a large, flat rock where they both sat down. His father had aged, and Tom knew it was because the man thought he had lost his son. What else had he lost? Tom was almost afraid to ask. But at least in spite of the added lines around the man's eyes and the gray in his hair, Tom could still sense a hard strength. Caleb Sax didn't go down or give up easily, not even at the loss of his most treasured son. Tom suspected Sarah Sax had a lot to do with that.

"I was treated pretty bad, in the prison and at the gold mines," he told his father. "I didn't think I'd live at all. When they finally let me go, I had no horse, no money, no gun, and just the tattered clothes I wore. One old Mexican who befriended me at the gold mines told me of a man he had once worked for who was very wealthy, fair and kind. He said if I needed anything when I was ever freed, I should go to him. I went there and asked for work. He gave me a job and paid me well. I worked until I was healthier and had enough money to buy clothes and this horse I am riding. I wanted to come back right away, but I was hundreds of miles from home, sick, and without a horse. I never would have survived. I could find no one willing to carry a message all the way to Texas for me."

Caleb had been hunched over, struggling to regain control of himself. He wiped his nose and eyes, turning to look at Tom. "Is it really you?"

The young man smiled through his tears and nodded. "It's really me."

Caleb grasped one of his arms. "I'm afraid you'll disappear."

Tom sniffed. "I won't disappear, Father." He looked the man over. "Are you all right? Were you injured or anything? What about Sarah, and Lynda?"

Caleb just kept looking him up and down. "I was wounded at San Jacinto, but not badly. Lynda is fine. She's married to Jess Purnell, and they have a son. Sarah is well. So are James and Cale."

Their eyes held again . . . so much time past, so much loss. Caleb knew the young man was thinking of Bess.

"Time heals a lot of things, Tom. But somehow it hadn't healed my pain over losing you." He ran a shaking hand over Tom's arm and shoulder. "Now I know why." He sniffed, unable to control more tears that ran down his cheeks. Tom was alive. No man's face could display more joy than did the face of Caleb Sax at that moment, as the reality of it hit him all over again. He was not dreaming. He was not mad. Tom Sax was alive. He was touching him this very moment. For four years he'd lived with the agony of thinking a son was dead. He was twenty-eight now. Twenty-eight already! Four years had been lost, but he had his son back. That was all that mattered.

He looked around at the deepening shadows. "We'll camp right here tonight, in the Valley," he said in a husky voice. "This was always our favorite place. It's too late to head back tonight. We'll go back in the morning."

Tom nodded and smiled again. "God, it's good to see my father's face."

They embraced then, laughing and crying at the same time.

"*Ne-mehotatse, na-eha*," Caleb groaned, hugging the young man so tightly Tom could barely breathe.

"I love you, too, Father. It was so terrible—missing you—thinking about Bess." They hugged several more seconds, and for that short while Tom felt like a little boy again. This man had always been here for him, in his best and worst moments. What would he have done without these strong arms when Bess died?

And yet perhaps Caleb Sax had always made things too easy for him. In his years away he'd realized that loving Bess had been part of the process of becoming his own man. He'd realized that to truly find Tom Sax he could not always be with his father.

He'd had time to think about a lot of things, and one of them was that he had to strike out alone some day soon. He had heard a lot about California from other Spaniards at the ranchero where he had worked. It was a place, he was told, of sunshine and lush vegetation. He had given serious thought to going there.

But he would not bring it up now. It was too good to be home again, and his poor father had thought him dead. Caleb Sax would not want to hear anything about his son leaving for other places. And it was possible the man needed him right now. What had happened since the war? Caleb Sax had always been there for his son. Now Tom Sax would be here for his father if his father needed the extra help. Besides, for the moment it was too wonderful just being near the man again. Tom felt stronger already.

He pulled away then, but his father wouldn't fully let go of him. "At first they only told me about the Alamo," Tom told him. "It was a long time before they told me the truth —that Santa Anna had surrendered at San Jacinto."

Caleb noticed the young man had picked up a slight Spanish accent from being imprisoned so long with other Mexicans, and probably from working among them. Considering his injuries and imprisonment, Tom looked good, a little thin, perhaps, but good, healthy. Caleb finally let go of him, getting up and going to his Appaloosa to retrieve a pipe and tobacco from his parfleche. "We'll smoke," he told Tom.

Tom smiled and nodded, and Caleb still could not quite believe it, sure the boy would evaporate at any moment. "You look good, Tom. And that's a fine horse. You look like the man you worked for paid you well."

"He did. He liked me, and he knew I was anxious to come home. They aren't all like Santa Anna, Father."

"Of course they aren't. It isn't men like us who make these wars, Tom. It's dictators like Santa Anna, and it's politics. I remember how the Indians suffered when the British and the Americans fought back in 1812, each power bribing and tricking the various tribes into helping them, pitting Indian against Indian. People bigger than us plan the wars, and we end up fighting them. Old Tom Sax tried explaining that to me once. I was just a kid then, but the same things have been going on ever since."

Tom gazed around the Valley. "Where are the horses, Father? It's so quiet here. This is a time when the horses should be thick in this grass, and the branding irons should be lying hot in the fires." He turned and saw the distant fear and the sad longing in Caleb's eyes.

"There aren't many horses now, Tom," Caleb answered. "It's been hard rebuilding, and I was never paid for the horses I sold for those promissory notes. Jess and I have been running the place almost all alone since the new president of Texas ran out most of the Cherokee." He sat back down on the rock beside Tom and began stuffing the pipe.

"The Cherokee! They're more peaceful than any other people here."

"They were. They're gone now," Caleb answered bitterly, lighting the pipe and sucking on it for a moment. "Texas wanted to get rid of its Indians. They're concentrating now on the Comanche."

He puffed the pipe once more and handed it to Tom. Their eyes held. "And what about you?" Tom asked. "You're Indian."

He saw a hardness come into his father's deep blue eyes. He took the pipe from the man and puffed it quietly, already realizing it was a good thing he'd gotten here when he did.

"Things are bad, Tom. No one has flat-out told me to leave, but I feel it all around me."

Tom felt a lump in his throat, turning and looking out over the Valley again. "You can't leave this place, Father. Our blood is here. Marie and David, John and Bess, Marie's parents, Lee—"

"I know, Tom. Every time I think about it I feel like someone is pulling my heart out with their bare hands. But I have to think about Sarah and James and the rest of the family. I'm not losing any more of my family over Texas, Tom."

He moved farther back on the rock and sat cross-legged, facing his son. "When I thought I'd lost you, too, I knew—" His voice broke and he looked down. "No more, Tom. I need my family—what's left of it." He looked at Tom again, new tears in his eyes. "I can't believe you're really alive! Just seeing you . . . sitting there—" He sniffed and wiped his eyes, looking down again. "Damn," he whispered.

Tom reached out and touched his shoulder, handing back the pipe. "Have another smoke. It's going to be all right, Father. I'm here to help, however you need it. If you think we have to leave Texas, we'll leave. Hell, we can make it wherever we go, as long as we all have each other. You still have a daughter and two sons—and now two grandsons. And you still have Sarah."

Caleb nodded, his shoulders shaking. Tom knew full well his father's old fear of losing everyone he loved. He understood what it must have been like for the man to think he was dead. He had already watched his father lose one entire family. This second family and Tom himself, who was a remnant of Caleb's old love for a Cheyenne woman, were all-important to the man. How strange that Caleb Sax had once been as wild as the wildest savage, still could be when necessary, yet he could love with such passion. Sarah was the rock in his life, the wind that carried him.

It was several minutes before Caleb could speak again. Tom sat quietly beside him, smoking the pipe to keep the embers going. He studied the Valley. There was a little light left, but the moon was beginning to make an appearance above the far hills. He thought how big Texas was. Yet apparently soon there would be no more room here for men like Caleb Sax. Tears of fury welled up in Tom's eyes to think of all his father had given up for this land.

Caleb stood up and walked away for a moment. He threw back his head and breathed deeply before finally turning to face his son. "You've really thrown me, Tom. What can a man say or do when his son walks back from the dead?" He smiled through remaining tears and shook his head. "Wait till I come riding back with you. It will be impossible for Sarah to be angry with me then."

Tom frowned. "Why would she be angry?"

"Because I came here alone." He looked out over the Valley. "This place is dangerous now, son. Squatters crawl around like maggots. I can't leave the horses anymore or they will all be stolen. Some squatters even attacked the house a couple of weeks ago. If Jess and I hadn't got there when we did—" His eyes flashed with renewed anger. "They had James and Cale tied, Sarah and your sister stripped and manhandled. Five more minutes and they both would have been raped."

Tom's face darkened with his own anger and he rose, setting aside the pipe. "My God! You killed them all?"

"With great pleasure, and with Jess's help. None of us was badly hurt, but Jess and I don't dare leave them alone now. Most of the Cherokee are gone except for a couple of families that are settled just north of the Valley. That makes it impossible for me to ranch the way I should. I'm just about out of money."

Pride and determination glowed in Tom's eyes. "I have some money. Juan paid me a lot more than I should have been making." He turned to his saddle bags. "He was a good man, a kind man. He hates the current Mexican government and was angry when I told him what had happened to me. He said I should get back to my father quickly." He reached into the saddle bag and pulled out a smaller leather bag that was tied at the top with rawhide drawstrings. He brought it to his father. "Gold. Juan gave me some of it. The rest I stole, from Mexican soldiers."

Caleb's eyes widened. "Stole! Are they after you?"

"They'll never know who did it. There was only a small encampment—five of them. You would be proud of how Indian I was that night. I stole this pouch right off the waistbelt of one of them while they slept. They never even woke up! That man is probably still hunting all over for his money pouch." They both laughed and Tom shoved the gold into his father's hands. "Here."

Caleb sobered. "I don't want your gold, Tom."

"*Our* gold. I did it for Texas—but mostly for revenge, and for you. I want you to have it. If we have to leave Texas, it will help. And I have something even better, Father, much better than gold."

The young man went back to his black stallion, pulling a rifle from its boot and bringing it over to his father. "This will help, too, especially if we can get more. We can handle any squatters who come along—or Indian haters. And if we have to leave, they will protect us from outlaws and Comanche."

He held out the long rifle and Caleb stared at it, lowering the bag of gold. "What the hell kind of a gun is that?"

"It's a repeating rifle."

"Repeating?"

"It's made by a man named Samuel Colt. He makes repeating pistols, too." Tom pulled a long pistol from a holder at his side. Caleb had been so engrossed in the fact that his son was alive at all, he hadn't noticed the young man's weapons. Tom held the revolver in one hand, and the rifle in the other. The pistol was silver, and long, perhaps fifteen inches or so. It had a fine woodgrain handle. The rifle was very long, a handsome piece with Spanish designs carved into the woodgrain butt. "One of these rifles can do what it would take ten or twenty men to do. If you are inside the house and enemies come, you can fire over and over, instead of firing once and then handing your rifle to someone to reload while you fire another. It's like having ten men shooting back instead of just one!"

Tom put the pistol away in its holster for a moment.

"Look." He turned and pointed to a mesquite bush, aiming the rifle and cocking the hammer. He fired, shaving off the tip of a branch. The horses jumped. Caleb stared in wonder as Tom fired again and again, eight times, and all he did each time was pull back the hammer of the rifle. He turned to his father then, his face gleaming. "And you can carry extra cylinders, already loaded. You just pop out the old one and shove in the new one. One man becomes ten men."

He handed the rifle to his father, who looked at it in awe. Tom whipped out the pistol. "This is just as handy but does not shoot as far. See?" He cocked it and fired, then cocked and fired again. He turned grinning to his father. "Get one of these or a rifle for yourself and Jess, and we can defend ourselves against anyone. I bet if Sarah and Lynda had had one in their hands when those squatters came, they never would have got close to them."

Caleb studied the rifle, then handed it to Tom. "Give me the pistol."

Tom gave it to him gladly. Caleb got a feel of it in his hand, then pointed it and fired, cocked it again and fired. "I'll be goddamned," he murmured, studying the instrument. "Where did you get these?"

"Juan got several of them in Santa Fe. Not him exactly. He sends men there to buy supplies that come in from the States. There is a great road of trade between St. Louis and Santa Fe now, through Colorado Territory and a place called Bent's Fort. It would be a good place to sell your horses, Father, if you have trouble here. Men make good money at both Santa Fe and Bent's Fort. These guns are made in the States. The rifle is about a hundred and fifty dollars. But I got mine and the pistol for nothing. I saved a prized stallion from dying. Juan gave me the guns as a gift. And I'll bet you will find they are starting to show up in San Felipe. I have enough gold to buy two or three rifles, and pistols. If they don't have any, you can have someone order them for you out of St. Louis."

Caleb studied the pistol more, then took back the rifle, handing the pistol to Tom. He studied the instrument, lifting it and aiming. There were two shots left. He fired them, then studied the rifle again, shaking his head.

"You can even shoot them after they've been under water," Tom explained. "And they are much safer. They won't explode on you like old muskets can do."

"To think of how many times I could have used guns like this," Caleb said quietly. "Marie might still be alive, and David, maybe even Lee." He faced his son. "You are a Godsend, Tom, a miracle. The spirits are truly with me this day. Before today my heart was so heavy. There have been times when, if it were not for James and Sarah, I would have ended my life. Now, Texas or no Texas, I have so much to live for." He breathed deeply, holding up the rifle. "This has been the best day of my entire life!"

Caleb's eyes sparkled. With the rifle upraised, his tall, muscular body silhouetted now in the faint light of dusk, Tom suddenly saw the Indian again—the victorious, wild Blue Hawk who had waged his own personal war against the Crow.

Yes, Caleb Sax was still strong, and inside he was still young. The return of his son had brought back a strength and determination he had been lacking for months, as well as a confidence that whatever happened, everything would be all right. He hugged Tom again, just to make sure this was all real. They stood there together, father and son, in the lingering twilight, in Blue Valley, but a place they both knew might have to become only another memory. It didn't matter. Tom Sax was alive, and for the moment nothing else in the whole world mattered to Caleb Sax.

A wolf howled in the distant hills, its wail seeming to exemplify the mourning of those who had lost so much in this land, the distant longing for things that used to be but are no more. Texas was changing.

Chapter
Twenty-Five

They rode into San Felipe, proudly, for they were the Saxes, and they had been among the first to come to Texas. Caleb and Tom rode in the lead, herding ahead of them twelve of Caleb's finest horses. Each man sat tall on his horse, Caleb wearing traditional buckskins, Tom dressed in his fine black clothes and riding the black stallion, sporting his new rifle and pistol.

Behind them rode James and Cale, each on his own horse. James kept an eye on the Appaloosa colt he had taken a liking to. It would be sold with the others. He had hoped that now that he could ride, his father would present him with a horse that would be all his own, a sign he had truly been accepted as an honorable son. The colt had somehow eased his sorrow over losing Pepper, for the little horse had taken a liking to James and was like a pet to him. But Caleb Sax made no sign that the animal was any more special than the other horses.

Cale proudly displayed the blue quill necklace around his neck. It was a little big for him, but it was his grandfather's and then his mother's. Now it was his. He knew the story of how his mother had kept it as an orphan, hoping to some day find her parents. The necklace was very special, made by his Cheyenne great-grandmother. He would keep it and treasure it forever, and he would never be ashamed of his Indian blood.

Sarah and Lynda rode on either side of the boys, little John riding papoose-style on Lynda's back. A wagon clattered behind the women, driven by Jake Highwater, brought to town to carry back supplies. Jess rode behind the entire entourage, a rear guard, to watch for Comanche or any other culprits who might have an eye for the horses and the women.

Lynda watched Tom proudly. He had been home ten days. And still all of them wondered if they were only dreaming this miracle. Her brother lived, and her father had never looked happier or healthier. For the rest of Lynda's life, she would not forget the sight of Caleb and Tom returning from Blue Valley. What incredible turns her life had taken—from growing up a frightened orphan to finding a whole family. No matter what happened now, she could not complain. God had blessed her greatly.

James took his eyes from the colt and looked ahead at his big half-brother, a mixture of near worship and jealousy. Surely Tom was the favored one. If only his father would do something to make James feel just as important. It was only natural that for now the man would act as though Tom Sax was the only son who existed. After all, Tom had literally returned from the dead. James admired Tom. He was everything James would like to be, and he hoped to be as big and strong some day. But since his return, it had been difficult for James to get his father's attention. Perhaps Caleb hadn't seen how close he was to the Appaloosa, how faithful the boy had been at feeding and caring for the horse. Or maybe he was still inwardly angry for the time James had refused to ride. But the excitement of the day seemed to help ease the boy's worries. The whole family had come to town, bringing the finest horses in all of Texas as far as James was concerned.

People stared. Some whispered. The entire atmosphere had changed from when Caleb used to come to town. He felt it. This was a new crowd. Stephen Austin was dead, and Sam Houston at the moment had lost control. Travis was gone, too, gone down at the Alamo, along with Bowie and Crockett, all men who had been a friend to Indians. But things could still change. President Lamar had done some foolish things that had cost an already-poor Texas badly needed money, and Sam Houston was instigating a vigorous campaign against the man. They were holding their own on the ranch, and now they had Tom to help.

They rode through the streets toward the docks. From an upper window over the "boarding house" that belonged to Emily Stoner, an aging, painted, blond woman watched them.

"Caleb Sax," she muttered with a half grin. "Still hanging on." She frowned, noticing the young man with him. "My God, it's Tom," she uttered in astonishment. She almost called out to them but checked herself. People were watching the Saxes. The last thing Caleb needed was to have a known whore yell out to him like he was an old friend. But then he *was* an old friend. How sad she could not acknowledge that. If only she were still married to Howard and could present herself as a respectable lady. But that was over. She watched sadly as Caleb and Tom rode by.

Someone else also watched, standing at the window of his new office. He had been in San Felipe six weeks, long enough to establish his importance, long enough to jump in on the anti-Indian fever and help feed its fires. Caleb had not been to town in months, due to the trouble he feared he would find there. He had no idea that San Felipe had a new citizen, and another new bank.

Byron Clawson watched him now, fear slinking down his spine with a sudden chill. So, there he was! He smiled at how people were watching Caleb as he rode by, hatred on their faces. If there was ever a good time to confront Caleb Sax and watch him crawl, this was it! He could almost smell trouble.

He threw down his cigar and ran outside. He would stay out of Caleb's sight until the time was right. He was safe here. Caleb couldn't touch him! Byron's whole body was damp with nervous anticipation. He'd never dare face Caleb Sax alone, but here in town . . . He almost laughed out loud at the situation. Sarah was with him. That made it all even better.

He hurried down the street as Caleb herded his horses toward the docks.

Below, Caleb moved through the main street, nodding to the few people he still knew, looking down his nose proudly at those who gave him dark, disapproving looks. Yes, this was a different breed of people.

Caleb and Tom yipped and called, moving the herd to the stockyards near the docks and into an empty pen. Tom closed a gate and waited with the others while Caleb dismounted. He would walk to the building where the men worked who handled shipments in and out of San Felipe, most going to or from New Orleans. He'd dealt with them many times, usually getting a written receipt for the horses and collecting the money for them right there at the docks. The animals were then sold to the earliest arriving buyer from New Orleans. The horses were easy to sell. Everyone knew that animals bred by Caleb Sax were good stock.

Tom watched as Caleb headed for the small building. Pain stabbed at his heart. This was where he had seen Bess getting ready to leave Texas. This was where they'd made their plans to run away together. Sometimes his memory of Bess was so vivid, and he ached for her. Would he ever find another woman like her? The only women he wanted now were the ones he didn't have to care about. There had been a few accommodating Mexican girls on Juan's ranch. But there had not been that fulfilling ecstasy he had found with Bess. Perhaps he would never feel that way again.

Tom stiffened defensively when several men stepped into Caleb's pathway before he could reach the building where he was headed. As ordered, the women and children stayed on their horses, but Sarah's heart pounded as she, too, saw what was happening. They had all been aware that several men had continued to follow them through the street and to the docks, their looks menacing. But they had not expected a true confrontation. Ten or twelve men stood in front of Caleb, arms folded as though to set up a wall that would not let him by.

"Goin' somewhere, Indian?" one of them asked.

Caleb had seen them coming, and had known instinctively what they would do. He rested his hand on his knife.

"I'm going to see whoever is in charge of the docks. I have horses to sell. Now get out of my way."

They moved closer and Tom turned to the women. "Stay put," he said softly. He edged his horse closer, as did Jess.

"Nobody around here buys anything from Indians," one of the men told Caleb.

"I've been selling horses here for years, mister. I've been in Texas since before you learned not to wet your pants. Now get out of my way!"

"What you gonna do about it, Indian?" another spoke up. "Kill somebody? Go ahead, just try it. That way we could string you up right quick and get rid of one more Indian."

"How'd you manage to stay in Texas, anyway?" another asked. "I thought we got rid of all the scum around here."

"Let him through," Tom growled, pointing his rifle at the men. "Unless you want ten holes in your fat gut!"

"Put it away, Tom," Caleb told his son, his own eye still on the men who threatened him. "They want you to use it. That's what they're waiting for."

One of the men grinned. "That's a pretty fancy gun you got there, boy. You steal that off some innocent Texan?"

Tom rode up close to the man, cocking the rifle and pushing it against the man's neck. "I earned this gun, after sitting in a Mexican prison for years. Unbelievable, that I fought for Texas independence so the likes of you could come here and live free," he growled. He gave the gun barrel a shove, knocking the man backward to the ground. The man grunted, grasping at his throat then and rolling to his knees.

Tom backed up, waving the rifle. "We are here to sell horses," he told them all. "Now get out of the way, all of you!"

"You won't use that gun, mister," another shouted. "It don't take much to get an Indian hung around here. You'd be pretty stupid to shoot one of us."

"Put the gun away, Tom," Caleb warned again, never once taking his eyes from the men who threatened him.

Jess rode up behind them. "Get out of the way and let us through," he told the crowd.

One of the men snickered. "Must be an Indian lover."
His eyes moved to Lynda, who sat proudly in the distance.
"'Course that's easy to do when the Indian looks like that
pretty thing over there. I hear tell Indian women just love
white men—*all* white men. They ain't too particular. And
they'll give a man a wild ride."

The man had barely finished the sentence before Jess
rode his horse closer, nudging it against the man, who
jumped away. "You stinking white trash," he growled.
"Get out of our way!"

"You're white same as us, mister," the man yelled, his
accusing eyes moving then to Sarah. "And so's that slut
squaw woman who lays with Caleb Sax."

Jess's foot kicked out then, landing hard under the man's
chin and sending him sprawling. Two men jumped on
Caleb and Sarah screamed his name, watching in horror as
all hell broke loose. Tom shoved his rifle into its boot and
was off his horse, charging into the two men on Caleb,
pulling one away, but another man grabbed him from behind. Tom whirled, backhanding the man and knocking
him down, while Caleb kicked and punched in well-aimed
blows that sent both his attackers sprawling. By then Jess
was involved in a fist fight with three friends of the man he
had kicked.

Caleb ran over to Jess, yanking one man away and turning him, landing a big fist into his nose. He heard a snap-
ping sound, and blood poured from the man's nose when
he went down. He stayed down. Caleb grabbed another
one who was preparing to hit Jess from behind while Jess
fought the third man. Two more men jumped on Tom, who
elbowed one hard in the gut and kicked the other.

As men went down, more came to take their place.
Lynda felt sick at the sound of the punches, watching the
mêlée in terror, as did Sarah, both women feeling helpless.

"I'm going to help," Cale declared, starting his horse
forward. Lynda grabbed the reins.

"No! One blow from a grown man could kill you!"

"But they're hurting Jess and Grandpa."

Her eyes teared. "Stay back, Cale."

"Pa," James whimpered. Sarah reached over and squeezed his arm. "You can't do anything, James."

Jake started to get down, but someone from behind yelled out for him to stay put or he'd be in big trouble. The voice sounded familiar. Sarah turned, her eyes widening in horror at the sight of Byron Clawson. He stood before her in an expensive suit and eyed her with an evil grin.

Sarah felt as though all the blood was draining out of her as Byron came closer. He had aged, and with age he had become even uglier, thinner, his gray eyes duller. Years of heavy drinking had not helped his already plain looks, and his nose was still twisted and crooked from the powerful blow Caleb Sax once dealt him.

"Hello, Sarah dear," he told her, bowing slightly. He looked over at the battle that still raged. Caleb, Tom, and Jess all sported their share of blood by then but were still putting men down. The crowd seemed hesitant. After all, two of them were Indians. Would they pull knives? One never knew what an Indian would do.

"I see your husband is still as untamed and vulgar as he was when I knew him," Byron said with a grin. "You can never quite get the uncivilized wildness out of an Indian, can you?" His eyes ran over her greedily. "But then that's what you always liked about him, right?"

Sarah's face was pale and she struggled against the old shaking. "What are you doing in San Felipe?" she asked, finally finding her voice.

"Just taking care of business. I happen to own a bit of land, you know, next to your husband's."

Lynda rode closer. "Get away from my mother, you bastard," she shouted. She'd met this man only once, in St. Louis. He was responsible for her being put in an orphanage and never knowing her parents. She hated him worse than any enemy she had ever had.

Byron just smiled at her, seeming very calm. He turned and walked toward the fighting. Several men lay sprawled out half unconscious. Caleb, Tom and Jess were tiring, taking their share of blows by then. A sheriff followed Byron, and Sarah could hardly breathe, her heart pounded so hard. Byron Clawson! What was he going to do? Why was the sheriff with him?

The sheriff pulled his gun and fired it into the air twice. Men backed away, some pulling off the remaining fighters so that Caleb, Tom, and Jess were left standing alone near the sheriff and Byron.

"Back off and get back to your own business," the sheriff called to the crowd.

"Arrest those men, Sheriff," someone from the crowd shouted. "They're troublemakers. The white one started the whole thing, and the other two are worthless Indians."

"Yeah! That Caleb Sax even killed a bunch of squatters a while back," someone else yelled.

Caleb whirled to defend himself to the sheriff, but words would not come when he saw Byron Clawson standing next to the man. Byron grinned at Caleb's shocked face. Caleb looked quickly at Sarah, who looked fearful. The noise of the surrounding crowd diminished for Caleb as his eyes moved back to Byron, filling with bitter hatred. He gathered his composure. A chill swept through Byron. He paled visibly, struggling to keep a smile on his face. With blood streaming down his face and over his clothes, and the wild, hate-filled look in his eyes, Caleb was every bit the fierce warrior.

This had all seemed like such a good idea to Byron, until he saw Caleb Sax again face to face. It had been years, long enough for Clawson to forget just how big and fierce the man truly was. Was he really safe just being in the middle of town? Of course he was, and he had the entire control of this situation. Yet he could barely control the sudden urge to run fast and hard. He forced himself to stay put and look confident, letting his eyes move over Caleb scathingly, while the crowd raised fists and yelled for the sheriff to do something about the "troublemakers."

"Hello, Caleb," Byron finally said.

"I was wondering when you'd show your face, Clawson," Caleb growled, blood pouring from a deep gash on his forehead and a bruise forming under one eye, a small cut in the center of it. "Somehow I knew you'd come here yourself some day! You've got to be the dumbest son of a bitch who ever walked!"

Byron's eyebrows arched, and Sarah watched in trembling horror. The sheriff continued to try to quiet the crowd, while Caleb and Byron just stared at each other.

"Come now, Caleb. You touch me, and this very angry crowd will have you swinging in no time at all."

"Who the hell is this, Caleb?" Jess spoke up.

"This is Byron Clawson," Caleb sneered. He didn't have to say more. Byron felt himself weakening as Jess looked him over, as did the younger man dressed in black, who looked very Indian. Surely he must be the son, Tom Sax.

"You're the one who put Lynda in an orphanage," Jess hissed, stepping closer.

"And who are you?" Byron asked haughtily.

"I'm her husband," Jess growled.

Byron's eyes moved over the man as though he were scum. "She was the bastard child of my wife," he hissed, his eyes moving back to Caleb. "I did Sarah a great favor by marrying her and giving her some respect. But the child looked too Indian. I had to get rid of it." He looked back at Jess. "If you were low enough to marry her, that's your problem."

"You bastard," Jess sneered, clenching his fists.

The sheriff was so involved quieting the crowd that he didn't even notice the conversation between Byron and the Saxes.

"Not here, Jess," Caleb said in a quiet but determined voice. "There will be a right time." His eyes never left Byron's.

Byron just grinned again. "Caleb, Caleb. Why can't you ever forgive? I can. I'll show you." He turned to the crowd, raising his hands into the air. "Quiet! Quiet," he shouted.

Everyone lowered their voices. Byron might be new in town, but everyone knew he was very rich, a man who could save a lot of them from poverty. He was already known as the big banker from St. Louis who was handing out low-interest loans.

"I came to San Felipe thinking the town had grown and

progressed," Byron told them in a loud voice. "And all I find is a lawless land. Do you want Texas to grow? Do you want cities like St. Louis to take shape in Texas?"

"Yes," they all answered in various ways.

"We'll be a state some day," someone yelled out.

"Lamar wants us to stay to ourselves," someone else shouted.

An argument broke out then over statehood, some men mentioning slavery, and voices raised again until the sheriff again fired his pistol and Byron yelled for quiet.

"Mister Sax was an original settler," Byron told them. "His blood has been spilled for Texas. He is a big landowner. As far as his killing those squatters, fighting squatters is something all landowners have to do. Today he and his family have been insulted. He reacted as any of you would react to such a thing. Now since he was an original settler, I say you should all get out of here and give the man another chance. He deserves that much. If not for men like Caleb Sax none of you could be here."

The crowd mumbled. "But he's Indian," someone called out.

"That issue is still an open one in Texas. I am told Mister Sax runs a fine ranch and has lived here for years without causing trouble. Now show me you're fine, civilized citizens by backing off and letting the man go. It's time for law and order in Texas, not brawling and hangings."

"Tell him to stay on his ranch and out of town if he knows what's good for him," another man yelled. "His women, too."

Caleb's fists clenched in rage. Byron smiled, looking up at the man. "It might be in your best interest to stay out of San Felipe, Mister Sax," he said, loud enough for others to hear, pretending to have just met Caleb.

Caleb's jaw flexed in anger. "You know I have to come here to sell my horses and get supplies."

Byron looked over at the horses. "Well, I suggest that today you go back home, with the horses. Maybe there will be a better time."

It was all Caleb could do to control himself. He needed the money, and he needed the supplies, and Byron Clawson damned well knew it. Caleb didn't want to use his son's gold. That was Tom's money. But there might be no other choice. Byron actually put out his hand then so that others could see his valiant effort at keeping the peace in San Felipe. "My name is Byron Clawson," he told Caleb.

Caleb wanted to tear him from limb to limb. What was this man up to?

"You'd better shake my hand, or the crowd might get out of hand," Byron said then in a quieter voice.

Caleb reached out and took the hand, squeezing hard.

"I've opened a bank in San Felipe," Byron told him, "to help people like yourself who are hurting for cash. And I hear the land I own borders yours, Mister Sax. I'll have to pay you a visit sometime."

The crowd began to disburse, but Caleb kept a grip on Byron's hand, squeezing even harder, until he saw beads of perspiration on Clawson's forehead. "What the hell are you really doing here, Clawson?" he sneered, his voice lowered. Tom and Jess stood nearby threateningly, both wiping at blood on their faces and knuckles.

Byron's eyes narrowed. "I just saved your life, Sax. Do you intend to break my hand for that?"

Caleb lightened his grip. "I'll break more than that when I get the chance," he glowered. "And if you just saved my life, it was for a *reason*. God knows you tried your best to take that life once, and don't think I've ever forgotten the hell you put me through, let alone what you did to Sarah and Lynda!" He towered over Byron, his very size and wild look draining all of Byron's confidence. "You come near my place, or any member of my family, Clawson, and your guts will greet the sun! The only thing that has kept me from killing you before now was distance. Now you're in *my* territory, and you're a goddamned fool!"

He gave Byron's arm a shove when he let go of his hand, and the man stepped back slightly, flexing the hand to get the blood back into it. "I'm no fool, Sax. You can't touch me as long as I'm in San Felipe. An Indian doesn't dare make a wrong move in this place and you know it. You're already walking on thin ice, being allowed to stay in Texas at all!"

"You ugly, back-shooting coward," Caleb growled, step-ping closer.

Byron backed away more, putting up a finger. "Ah! Watch yourself now, Caleb. People are still watching." He put on a smile.

"Come on, Caleb. Let's get the horses and get out of here," Jess told him.

"I need to sell them," Caleb answered angrily, his eyes still on Clawson.

"Maybe another time. We can make do."

"Forget it today, Father. I've got money," Tom told the man, struggling with his own temptation to light into Byron Clawson.

"I don't need my son's money." Caleb stormed past Byron then toward the corral. Tom and Jess grabbed the three horses and followed, and Byron strolled behind them.

"If you're going broke, Caleb, I'd be glad to float you a loan," he called out deliberately, a broad grin on his face. He looked up at Sarah. "You should have stayed with me, Sarah. I could have done so much more for you."

Lynda rode between her mother and Byron. "Don't you even talk to my mother!"

"What's wrong here?" the sheriff asked Byron, coming up behind them. "These people being ungrateful?"

Byron just laughed lightly. "That's the way some people are, Sheriff. Comes from living with Indians—so uncivilized, you know. Everything is fine. You go ahead and clean up the mess these people made. Maybe after this they'll know how to conduct themselves when they come to town."

The sheriff walked away, and in the distance a few people still stood mumbling about the "damned Indians." Caleb opened the gate to the corral, then turned and eased up onto his big Appaloosa, riding over to where Byron stood near Sarah.

"Get away from my wife and daughter, or by God I'll kill you here and now, hanging or no hanging!"

Byron backed off, struggling to appear unruffled. But inside he seethed at the thought of Caleb winning Sarah first all those years ago. How he hated her, and Caleb.

Lovers! Wild young lovers, enjoying each other—Caleb Sax stealing her virginity before Byron could do it! It made him feel so much less a man. He struggled to stay in control.

"I'm certainly glad I didn't bring my dear wife to this place," he answered evenly. "I wasn't sure Texas was a place yet fit for ladies." His chilling eyes moved to Sarah and Lynda. "Now I can see it isn't, for I've yet to meet a proper lady since coming here."

Caleb edged his horse closer to the man. "What are you after, Clawson? It must be pretty important, for you to show your face in front of me."

Byron's eyes narrowed to slits of hatred. "Just your land, Sax. And your ultimate destruction. I'll have both. I've got the money—*and* the power."

"Then try destroying me. You already tried it through Charles Hafer. You know what happened to him. Now I truly hope you try again. You won't die as quickly as Hafer did. I can promise you that!" Caleb's hand rested on the handle of his knife. "Now get out of my sight. Right now I'm thinking a rope around my neck would be worth the feel of sinking my blade into your guts."

Clawson breathed deeply. Caleb Sax seemed to have grown more fierce, and even bigger physically, than when Byron had known him. But then that was nearly twenty-four years ago. Could so much hatred really live that long and spring forth so readily in a man? Yes. Apparently it could, and apparently his wealth and power had little effect on Caleb Sax.

"We'll see which one of us stays in Texas, and which one goes," Byron sneered. He turned and stalked off. Tom rode up next to his father.

"There goes a dead man," Caleb said. "His days are numbered."

"You'll have to be awful careful, Father."

Caleb wiped some of the blood from his face. "I'll know when the time is right."

"Caleb, stay away from him," Sarah spoke up in a trembling voice. "Don't let him take you from me by getting you hung."

Caleb rode up to her, reaching out and pulling her onto his horse in front of him. Feeling her tremble, he knew another spell of shaking was trying to possess her. Caleb held her tightly.

"Don't you ever let that man get to you again, Sarah. Don't let him do this to you. I'll kill him as sure as I'm sitting here on this horse, and I promise you I won't hang for it. You just remember I'm here, and he'll never hurt you again. And he by God won't be the cause of our being apart again."

She broke into tears and he squeezed her harder. "Stop it, Sarah. Do you trust me?"

She sniffed and wiped at tears and he jerked her again. "Do you?"

She nodded then and he bent forward and kissed her cheek. "Then you leave it all up to me, understand? You put Byron Clawson right out of your mind. He'll not trouble you or insult you again. I told you that a long time ago and I meant it. He's scared—so scared he's come here to check on me himself. He's made the dumbest move of his life."

He looked at Jess and Tom. "You two all right?"

They both grinned through battered lips and bruised faces. "We'll live," Tom spoke up.

"So will I," Caleb answered.

"You sure can fight, Pa," James spoke up. "Tom and Jess, too. I never saw a fight like that!"

Cale held up his small fist. "We were gonna help."

Caleb gave the boy a grin. "Some day you and James will fight better than any of us," he told the boy.

"What do we do now, Caleb?" Jess asked.

"We take the horses and go back. We'll stop at the Handels. Wil is still a good friend. I'll pay him to come into town with the horses and sell them for me. We can give him a list of supplies and have him pick them up." He looked at Tom. "Including a couple of those Colt rifles and pistols. It looks like we might need them."

"Are we leaving Texas?" Tom asked.

Sarah turned to look up at him, shocked at the suggestion. Lynda and the others looked at Caleb and Tom both in surprise. It was the first time such a thing had been mentioned seriously in front of them, and Sarah's heart ached at the terrible sadness that came into her husband's eyes. Caleb turned to watch the crowd breaking up, noticing a few men stood and still watched to make sure they all left with the horses.

"I don't know yet, Tom. I only know I don't like what happened here today." He looked back at Tom. "And I especially don't like the presence of Byron Clawson. But whether we stay or go, I think we'll need the best guns we can get." He looked at Sarah then.

"Caleb," she whispered. "Leave our home?"

His chest hurt at the thought of dragging her out into the wilderness again. He would never forget the first time he had done that, when they ran away together and she had gotten so sick.

"I'll do whatever I have to do to protect my family, Sarah. You're all I have left. Land is land, and there's more in other places. It never goes away. But people can't be replaced. I'm just sorry for the insults you've suffered being married to me."

Their eyes held. "You don't really think it matters, do you?"

He kissed her lightly, pressing her close with his arm still around her. No, it didn't matter, and that was why he loved her so much.

He rode forward then, and Lynda took up the reins of Sarah's horse and led it along beside her. Jess and Tom routed the horses out of the corral and herded them along the street. The Sax men watched the onlookers carefully, all three of them with a grip on their pistols.

It sickened Sarah to think of what just happened. She held up her chin proudly as she rode down the street in front of her husband, sure there wasn't a man there who could hold a candle to Caleb Sax.

Chapter Twenty-Six

It took five days for the Saxes to get home from San Felipe. They stopped first at the Handels and had to wait for Wil to take the horses back to town and pick up needed supplies. The old German couple's steadfast friendship bolstered Sarah's faith.

James was excited when old Wil returned with the Appaloosa colt, but his joy faded quickly. He learned it was only because Handel wanted to buy the animal himself, in addition to two fine horses Caleb had already given him for his help and friendship.

"You don't have to pay me for the colt," Caleb told the man. "I'll throw him in for all your trouble."

"No! No," Handel insisted. "This one I pay for. It is fair. And you should not turn away money, Caleb, especially if you might be leaving Texas."

James's heart tightened. Leave Texas? This was the only home he'd ever known. Pepper was buried here. And how could he leave behind the colt? If he could have kept the animal, it would have been like taking a part of home with him.

James wanted so much to be proud of his Indian blood, but it seemed that everything bad that happened to them was because they were Indian. If admitting to having Indian blood meant living in constant misery and harassment, how could he think of owning up to his heritage? He didn't look a bit Indian with his light skin and sandy hair that lay in thick, curly waves. Every day he was more glad he looked white. His eyes were blue like Caleb's, the one thing his son was glad he had inherited.

James fought tears as Wil Handel handed his father the badly needed money for the colt. How could he argue against it? His father needed every penny he could get right now.

Caleb turned away from the corral gate, catching the look in James's eyes. The boy stood staring at the colt, his lips puckered, his face blotchy red from wanting to cry. "What's wrong, James?"

James looked up at him. His emotions were so mixed about this man. He was in awe of his own father. He loved him, but sometimes he wished someone else were his father—a white man. "Nothing," he answered.

Caleb looked from the boy to the colt and back. "Is it the colt? I've seen you with him a lot."

The boy just nodded, then shrugged. "It's okay."

Caleb walked up and tousled his hair. "I'm sorry, James. But I can't turn down any sales. There will be other colts. And the time is coming when one will be all your own. You're a good rider now. I'm very proud of that."

The boy's heart lightened and he looked up then. "You are?"

Caleb grinned. "Of course I am. Come on. Let's get home."

The boy touched his arm. "Pa, are we going to stay?"

Caleb lost his smile. "I don't know."

"I don't want to leave."

"I know that. None of us wants to leave. But we might have no choice. You're going to have to be a man about a few things, James. I'm just sorry there's been no time for you to be a little boy. That's the way it was for me when I was growing up. Sometimes I wonder if I was ever a boy." He bent down and hoisted the boy to his shoulders with strong hands. "Let's go get your mother and head out."

Sarah felt her husband's tenseness. She knew his rage toward Byron Clawson was greater than ever, and it worried her. Seeing Byron Clawson had brought back all the bitter memories: his loss of Sarah, the thought of Clawson beating her and forcing her to submit to him, the agony over knowing her baby had been taken from her and that she'd been drugged so badly that it had had a lifetime effect on her.

As soon as Sarah moved under the covers, Caleb drew her close. Sarah belonged to Caleb Sax and no one else. She needed that reassurance just as much as Caleb did, and their lips met in heated passion. She wondered why she had even bothered to put on a gown. In no time it was off, and Caleb himself had come to bed naked. He raked his hand through Sarah's long, tumbling hair, still so beautiful and thick, glinting a red-gold color. His hand left her hair and moved down her bare back, massaging her hips, moving around and dipping between her legs to find that secret place that he had been first to claim.

In her own need to assure herself this was Caleb, and that it would always be Caleb, Sarah gripped his muscular arms tightly, returning his kiss with equal hunger and passion. She wanted him to touch, to taste, to claim her. She raised up to him, pressing her breasts against his chest. Neither of them needed to explain the urgency they both felt to give and take and share and be one.

Sarah began to think of their uncertain future, and felt tears coming.

Caleb kissed them gently. *"Ho-shuh,"* he whispered, soothing her with the Cheyenne word for "be still." "No one will hurt you ever, ever again," he added, meeting her mouth then as he moved on top of her. Sarah opened her legs, welcoming him readily. She gasped when he entered her with a hard, strong thrust that left her almost breathless. He moved then with wild rhythm, a deliberate, determined act this time, proving to himself and to Sarah that he was her man and there would never again be another—not filthy squatters and not Byron Clawson!

Caleb's virility and demanding claim whetted her womanly needs and she moved with him, her excitement building until he felt the pulsating explosion that drew him even deeper into his woman and told him he had pleased her greatly. The joy of this glorious union would never change, he was sure; and from it he drew new strength. He held himself back, wanting to keep the pleasure going for as long as possible. But, finally, there was no stopping the release of his life, and he groaned her name and clung to her tightly.

He relaxed beside Sarah, holding her close. Yes. He was already contemplating how he would stop Byron Clawson. It would take some planning, but he would do it.

It was later that same night that they came. Caleb heard horses outside. He leaped out of bed, pulling on his buckskin leggings. "Get a robe on and get in the loft with James," he ordered Sarah, grabbing up his new Colt rifle and revolver. Comanche would not come in the night. These were either outlaws, or squatters up to no good—or maybe Rangers.

Sarah hurriedly pulled on a robe, her heart pounding as she ascended the ladder to the loft, where James was already awake from the shouting outside.

"Stay there, James," she told him, moving into the loft and around a corner out of sight. Caleb went to a window and threw open a shutter. Several armed men sat outside on horses, some of them holding torches. Two wagons full of Cherokee who had been living on Caleb's land were with them, some of the Cherokee men bound.

"Caleb Sax!" someone shouted.

Caleb hoped Jess was shoving Lynda and Cale and the baby into the hidden wall at their own cabin. He cocked his rifle.

"Who the hell are you and what do you want?" he called back.

"We're Texas Rangers, sent by President Lamar to get rid of all remaining Indians, you included. You have five days, Caleb Sax. Five days to gather what you can carry and get out of Texas."

Sarah held James close, feeling him trembling. "It will be all right, James," she whispered.

"This is my land. I settled it before any of you ever came to Texas," Caleb growled back. "I have a former wife and two sons buried on this land, and a daughter-in-law. I lost a son-in-law to Comanche and I fought at San Jacinto and was wounded!"

"We can't make allowances, Sax. We've rounded up the Cherokee living on this land illegally. They're leaving with us tonight and at daylight they head north to Indian Territory. The only reason we're giving you five days is because you did fight at San Jacinto. You're lucky you have that much time."

"What gives you the right to come onto my father's land like this?" Tom shouted from behind the men, pointing his rifle at them. Jess moved up beside him. The leader of the Rangers whirled, and Caleb unbolted his door, moving outside, steadying his own rifle.

"This is no longer Sax land," the apparent leader answered Tom. "It belongs to the local county and will be auctioned off as soon as you're gone."

"And there isn't a hell hot enough for the likes of you," Tom answered angrily. "The ground under a snake couldn't be any lower."

"You had better watch it, boy. We're Texas Rangers, with full authority to do whatever is necessary to make sure orders are carried out. If you want to get out of Texas alive, you'd better put down that gun. There are a lot more of us than there are of you, and we're all carrying the same repeating rifle you're holding."

Tom moved around them, still cradling the rifle and coming closer to his father.

"Who arranged to have you men suddenly come here like this in the middle of the night?" Caleb asked. "Byron Clawson? I'll bet he's ready to do some heavy bidding at the auction, too!"

"We can't name names, mister. We just carry out orders."

"You don't have to name names. Clawson never was good at fighting his own fights or meeting a man straight on." He was counting. There were twenty of them. There was not a chance in the world against them. He could get away with killing squatters. But he didn't dare pull a trigger on these men.

He glanced at the wagons, his heart aching at the forlorn

looks on the faces of the banished Cherokee. It appeared they'd been allowed to take only what they could grab in a matter of minutes. A deeper sorrow engulfed him when he saw Jake and Ada. Caleb looked back at the leader of the Rangers. "I want to talk to these people before you go."

The man cocked his own rifle. "Only if you lay down your arms first—you and that young man there and the one standing behind us. Have him come around where we can see him better."

"Jess! Come on around," Caleb called out. He looked at Tom. "Put the rifle down. There are too many of them. We can't shoot it out with Rangers."

Tom's face was black with rage as he stared at his father.

Caleb jerked the rifle from his hand. "I'm not going to lose one person in this family over land," he said firmly. "Where is your pistol?"

Tom's jaw flexed with repressed anger and sorrow. "Still in the bunkhouse."

Caleb carried the two rifles to the doorway and stood them against it. He turned to Jess. "Put yours up there, too."

Jess hesitated, then nodded, setting the rifle against the door and standing by it while Caleb walked to the wagons. He reached out and touched Jake's arm. "I'm damned sorry, Jake. If I could stop them, I would."

The man nodded, looking suddenly very old. "I understand. When you leave, Caleb, if you have no place else to go, come to Indian Territory and look for us. We will help you settle."

"Thanks, Jake." Caleb fought tears, looking around at the tortured faces. Some of the women were quietly crying and a couple of children were whimpering. These people were so dear to him! It was Cherokee who had helped him in his first terrible years of struggling alone after losing Sarah. These people had been chased out of the south. They had hoped to find a home and some peace in Texas, but that was not to be. "Some day people will know the truth, Jake," Caleb told the man. His voice choked.

"They'll know the truth, and it will be to the shame of this country."

Jake nodded, as one of the Rangers moved his horse up behind him. "That's long enough, Sax. We've got to get these people moving."

Caleb clung to Jake's arm. "They're my friends, you son of a bitch! They helped me settle this place. If I want to—" He was not allowed to finish. The Ranger swung a club, landing it hard in the middle of Caleb's back with a crushing blow that sent Caleb reeling sideways, landing face-down.

"Father!" Tom started to go to the man, but three Rangers moved in front of him, all holding rifles on him.

"Stay put," one of them told him.

Tom stood there with clenched fists, and inside Sarah pulled away from James, looking down from the loft. What had happened! Why had Tom called out "Father"?

Caleb groaned, trying to get to his knees, but nothing would move. "Get these wagons rolling," the Ranger who had hit Caleb told the others. He turned the horse, looking at Tom and Jess. "Remember. Five days, whether Caleb Sax can get up on two feet or not. We'll be back, and if you're still here, there will be hell to pay."

The wagons rolled away, old Jake staring at Caleb, tears running down his cheeks. Tom was so furious he wondered if his head would burst from the pain that charged through it now. As soon as men and torches were out of sight he ran to Caleb.

"Father! How bad are you hurt?"

Sarah hurried down from the loft and ran outside. "Caleb!"

Tom rolled him onto his back. "Can't . . . move my legs," Caleb groaned. "Old injury. God, it's . . . back. It's back."

Sarah felt faint. He'd not been troubled for years from the gunshot wound Byron Clawson had given him in the back, the wound that had paralyzed him. He'd had occasional numbness in the legs, but that was all. She looked at Tom.

"What happened?"

"One of the Rangers hit him in the back with a club."

"Dear God!" Her eyes teared. "You and Jess carry him inside."

Caleb cried out with pain when they picked him up.

"Go get Lynda out of the hiding place," Jess called to Sarah. She ran over to their cabin, taking down the tapestry.

"Lynda, come out. They're gone."

Lynda pushed out the hidden door, wincing with pain from being so cramped as she got out.

"Come to the house," Sarah ordered. "You father's been hurt."

Lynda quickly followed, leading Cale by the hand and holding John in the other arm. She followed her mother inside, where Caleb lay facedown on the bed. A huge bruise was already swelling on his back. Tom looked at Sarah. "What can we do!"

Her eyes teared. "Nothing. We can't do anything but wait and hope it passes. He said this happened once before, years ago, when he first met Marie and her family and helped lift a wagon that was stuck in the mud. After a few hours the feeling came back." She leaned over Caleb, smoothing the hair back from his face. "I love you, Caleb. I love you so," she said, bending close to his ear.

His only reply was a groan. Sarah looked up at Tom and Jess. "Get two wagons ready and start packing—everything practical and necessary first, then anything else that fits. We'll get everything ready and hope Caleb recovers quickly enough to help us know what to do next. We have to be ready to leave."

Jess nodded, turning and going out. Tom just stood there staring at his father. "How can all those years of work and sacrifice be for nothing?" he choked out. "It isn't right!"

Sarah leaned over again, stroking Caleb's hair. "It wasn't for nothing. Your father helped settle this country in a lot of ways, Tom. Some day men like him will be recognized for the heroes they were." She straightened, looking at Tom. "When a man does what is right, it's never for nothing, Tom. Your father can be proud of everything he's done, and so can you. If we have to start over, then that's what we will do. The last thing I want is for Caleb to lose one more loved one. Now go and help Jess."

Tom gripped the bed rail and kept watching his father. He moved his eyes to meet Sarah's green ones then. "And what about all my years in that stinking prison? I was at the Alamo! I tried to get out with a message while Santa Anna's men poured against the walls! Now they tell me I have to leave the only home I've ever known! What good has it done me or my father to do what's right?"

Sarah frowned. "What are you saying, Tom?"

"I'm saying a man who will never be accepted anyplace he goes might as well take what he can get where he can get it and not worry about what's right. A lot of good it did my father to do what's right. It comes down to the law of survival—and who has the most guns. And what few laws there are are made by *white* men! I fought Mexicans, yet a Mexican man was kinder to me when I got out of prison than any white man has ever been. And if there is any way to fight men like those who came here tonight, I'm going to do it, even if it means joining the Comanche or the Apache or Mexican outlaws. They tried to take my Bess from me, and now they're taking my home from me and almost killed my father. I have no room left in my heart for patience, Sarah; no desire left to do what's right. I don't *care* any more!"

Tom stormed out, brushing past Lynda, who stood in the doorway. She grasped his arm as he went by. He whirled to face her. "I heard you in there," Lynda said, her blue eyes burning into him. "Don't you do something stupid, Tom Sax. Father needs you. He needs all of us."

He jerked his arm away. "You think I don't know that? I'm not going to do anything stupid, not now anyway. I'm just going to get my revenge some day, that's all."

"And how would you do that?"

"I don't know yet."

"Don't you break our father's heart."

His eyes softened slightly. "It has been slowly broken to pieces already over the years. And when he was my age he was riding against the Crow, taking his own form of revenge. I am our father's son, and I have *my* revenge to find. I sat rotting in prison for almost four years, dreaming of coming home to my father and this ranch. Now I find it was all for nothing."

"You lived! That was worth everything else Father might lose. That's all that matters to him—family. And right now we're going to do everything we can to save what's left of this one!"

He walked toward the door and hesitated. "Don't worry, little sister. I will be a part of this family for a long time to come. But now that I know what to expect from life, it helps me know what to do with mine. I'm sorry, Lynda, but all feelings of goodness and doing right have left me for now." He turned to face her. "The only feelings I have left are for this family. They go no farther."

She closed her eyes and looked down. "What you need, Tom Sax, is a good woman to settle you down."

He let out a disgusted sigh. "I *had* a good woman. White men kept us apart during precious months when we could have been together. Because of that I had only six months with her, and then white man's disease took her away from me. I will never love again the way I loved Bess."

She met his eyes. "Yes, you will. I thought the same thing when Lee died. But then I found Jess. You'll marry again, Tom."

He shook his head, smiling bitterly. He turned and walked out. Lynda looked toward the bedroom, where she could hear her father groaning. She couldn't blame Tom for the way he felt.

Caleb deliberately defied the pain. By morning he insisted on trying to get up. There were things to be done. He had no doubt the Rangers would come back. With the help of Jess and Tom, who each took an arm, he managed to sit up. Jess moved his legs off the bed for him, alarmed at the way Caleb's feet fell to the floor. Jess glanced at Tom, who scowled with anger, both for the man who had first wounded Caleb so many years ago, and the Rangers who had come the night before.

"Help me up," Caleb groaned, perspiration coating his face.

"Caleb, you might do yourself more harm," Sarah tried to argue.

"It's the only way," Caleb answered. "The longer I lay there the weaker I'll get. The first time . . . Emily made me move around . . . had men help carry me to the river so I could exercise. The water helps . . . your body is lighter. But there's not enough water in the Brazos . . . right now." He reached up and Jess and Tom each grasped him under a shoulder and helped him to his feet. Caleb cried out, his legs almost useless.

"Father, maybe you shouldn't—"

"Walk with me," Caleb interrupted Tom. "Come on! Walk with me!"

Sarah turned away, forcing back tears.

"I've got to keep moving . . . not let it set in," Caleb was saying. "Got to get the family . . . out of here . . . go kill Clawson."

Sarah's heart tightened. Kill Clawson! What was he saying? She turned to see Jess and Tom half dragging Caleb out into the main room. Just the night before, Caleb Sax had made love to her with great passion, his virile body moving over her as only Caleb could do, before the Rangers came. Now he could barely make one foot move in front of the other in his awkward attempt to walk. Without Jess and Tom holding him, it would be impossible.

"Take me to Marie's grave," he was telling Tom and Jess.

"You sure, Father?"

"Yes, damn it! Quit . . . arguing with me." There came another groan. "I want to see the graves once more— Marie, Lee, David and John, Bess. We'll visit them once more . . . before we go. Later I want to have a family meeting. Are you . . . packing the wagons?"

"We've got a lot done already, Caleb," Jess answered.

"Good. I'll be walking . . . in a couple of days. I've got to figure out how to get Clawson. I can't . . . fight them all. I'll leave Texas . . . but not without taking care of the man responsible . . . for all of this. He might think he's won. But he's lost."

The words rang in Sarah's ears as she watched Caleb struggle out the door. Byron Clawson. Everything that had happened to them when they were young was because of Byron. Now the man had come back to haunt them again. Even without his physical presence he was there. The old gunshot wound to Caleb's back had reared its ugly head, crippling her virile, strong husband a second time. All due to Byron Clawson.

She walked to the window. Caleb was taking small, weak steps now. Her heart tightened with dread at his words of killing Byron. She wanted the man dead as much as anyone, and Caleb Sax deserved to do the killing, but how could he in this condition? And how could he hope to get away with it?

She hung her head, feeling guilty for wanting a man dead. But she did. She wanted Byron Clawson dead more than the squatters or Comanche or any other enemy who had ever threatened them. Dead, for what he had done to Caleb, what he had done to her and to Lynda. But even Byron Clawson's death was not worth losing her Caleb. It all seemed so hopeless. Caleb was determined now, more than ever. She feared there would be no talking him out of it this time.

It was late the next afternoon when Emily Stoner arrived in her fancy carriage. Sarah hurried out to greet the woman, who stiffened when Sarah hugged her, always feeling awkward when Sarah treated her kindly.

"Emily! It's so good to see you."

Emily drew away, studying the tired lines about Sarah's eyes. She glanced at the wagons that sat in front of the house, heavily packed. "They've already been here, haven't they?"

Sarah's eyes teared. "Yes. They dragged off the Chero-kee and told us we had five days to get out. That was the night before last." Her words began to break. "They hurt Caleb—hit him hard in the back with a club. The paralysis came back. He's forcing himself to walk. He's so damned determined, Emily, but he's in so much pain, and all he talks about is killing Byron Clawson before he leaves."

Emily sighed, closing her eyes. "You are leaving then."

"Yes. We have no choice, Emily. We can't survive here any more. Caleb can't even go to town to sell his horses."

"I know. I saw what happened last week in town. You didn't see me, but I was watching. I decided then and there to get on the good side of your Mister Byron Clawson and find out what I could. The man has no idea I know you and Caleb. I made it a point to get some business from him. It took me about five minutes to figure out the man has a weakness for prostitutes and a sickening sexual appetite that only whores could—"

Sarah reddened deeply and turned away.

"I'm sorry, Sarah. My God, how did a woman like you stand being married to that bastard?"

Sarah wiped at her eyes. "It was a matter of submitting willingly or risk losing my baby from his beatings. Even so, Lynda came early because of a beating. After that he kept me so drugged I didn't know what was happening most of the time."

Emily put a hand on her shoulder. "Byron told me he was stirring up resentment against Caleb still owning land here. He's responsible for sending the Rangers out here."

"We already guessed that."

"Sarah, I have to talk to Caleb. Last night Byron Clawson told one of my girls he's not giving Caleb the full five days. He's going to send the Rangers back in just a couple of days, only they won't be real Texas Rangers. He's paying local trash—Indian haters—to pose as Rangers and come out here to kill Caleb and the other men."

Sarah covered her eyes. "My God," she whispered.

Caleb suddenly appeared at the doorway, supporting himself with two canes. "Emily," he called out. "You picked a poor time to visit."

Emily left Sarah, walking closer to Caleb and looking him over with tear-filled eyes. "How bad is it?"

Caleb smiled bitterly. "About as bad as when you got me on my feet after I was first paralyzed. Only then there wasn't much feeling. This time there's a lot of pain. But

I'll survive, long enough to kill the bastard who's responsible for this!"

She stepped closer. "In your condition? Forget it, Caleb. I came here to warn you to get out by tomorrow if possible. Byron Clawson is sending men here in a couple of days, only they won't be Texas Rangers. He has plans for all of you, including the women. You've got to leave as soon as possible."

He studied her closely. "How do you know?"

A sly grin moved across her mouth. "Byron Clawson has no idea I know the two of you, and he has a keen appetite for prostitutes." She made a face. "It's no wonder. No decent woman would do the things that man thinks up. But the girls and I put up with it because once we can get a little booze into him, he loosens up and brags about his money and power—and laughs about taking over your land."

Caleb's eyes were lighting up as she spoke. "He comes to your place?"

She frowned, folding her arms. "What are you thinking, Caleb Sax?"

Caleb looked over at Sarah. "Sarah, go inside."

She came closer, putting a hand on his arm. "Caleb, we need you. You can hardly walk. Please let's just leave."

His eyes were stern. "I told you once to trust me in this. Neither of us will be happy and free until that man is dead. Now go inside like I asked."

She turned away and Caleb moved to the steps, putting canes down first, then his feet. "Come away from the house, Emily."

She watched him, shaking her head. He was going to be more stubborn than ever this time. She walked slowly with him away from the carriage and the house. He turned to her then, his blue eyes pleading. "Help me, Emily. Help me kill him."

Her eyes widened. "Don'tbe a fool, Caleb."

"Goddamn it, Emily, I have to kill him," he almost growled through gritted teeth. "I *have* to!"

She closed her eyes and reached out to grasp a fence rail. "My God, Caleb, do you know what you're saying?

What about Sarah—your family? Just get the hell out, Caleb."

"Not that way! Not with my tail between my legs! I'll leave Texas, but by God, I'll not leave without watching that man die a slow death!"

Emily turned away. "I shouldn't have come at all. I just wanted to warn you—"

"When, Emily? When does he come to see you?"

"No, Caleb."

"Damn it, woman, when does he come! All these years you've said you think you owe me, even after all those months of helping me walk again. Well, you could never help me any more than now. The man almost destroyed Sarah and Lynda, and he tried to kill me and left me a cripple. All from his goddamned jealousy and greed and arrogance! I'm losing everything I've worked for, Emily. I can't let it all be for nothing. I can bear it as long as I know Byron Clawson can never threaten Sarah again! He has never won yet, and he won't win this one. Now are you going to help me, or do I have to just march into his office and kill him outright and *hang* for it?"

She sighed deeply, looking up at him then. "He comes almost every night, usually after ten o'clock."

"And where is your room?"

She shook her head. "Caleb—"

"Where is it?" he shouted.

She folded her arms and sighed in resignation. "Second story, first window on the right as you face the boarding house."

He nodded. "All right." He looked out over the landscape he had learned to love, thinking quietly. "Today is Tuesday." He bit his lip. "Tuesday." He thought a moment longer, then looked down at her. "Saturday. Saturday night. You have him in that room Saturday night, about eleven o'clock. Can I get in through that window or a side window?"

She swallowed. "Just around the corner is a side window. There is a stairway leading to the second floor and a balcony off all the windows."

"Good. Leave the side window unlocked. Just make sure

that around eleven the man is so involved in sexual pleasure he won't notice me come inside."

She frowned. "Even I would be embarrassed to have someone walk in on me, and you of all people."

He grinned, the taste of victory giving his eyes a wild look. "It will be worth it, believe me. And by God, I won't be giving a damn that night about what I see nor blame you for anything you do to keep his attention. That's the important thing. Keep him occupied. Emily, you can do that, can't you?"

She had to grin. "There were many times when I wished I could keep you occupied that way, damn you."

He smiled in return, suddenly as excited as a little boy. "You won't get in trouble. If people come around the next day asking about him, all you have to do is tell them he was there to see you and then left. You wouldn't have any idea what happened to him after that. You can suggest maybe he got attacked in some alley. There are all kinds of no-goods coming to San Felipe now. No one would suspect. I'll come in through the window, and I'll use my own technique of getting him out without a sound. I won't leave you suspect, Emily, I promise."

Her eyes teared. "I'm not worried about that." Her lip quivered. "But I'll miss all of you so much. You don't dare come back, you know."

"I plan to have alibis. I was well on my way out of Texas when Mister Byron Clawson was killed. I'll make sure it takes them a while to even find the body, or what's left of it."

A chill moved through her. "I sure am glad I'm not the one you're after."

He leaned down and kissed her forehead. "Thank you, Emily. I might never see you again after that; never be able to thank you or make it up to you. I'm sorry. We'll all think about you often, and pray for you."

She shrugged. "Don't bother with the praying part. But I know you'll think of me, just like I'll be thinking about you."

Their eyes held, and all the years swept before them. Wasn't it only yesterday she was a young, confused girl, virtually imprisoned in her own house by a fanatic preacher father? Wasn't it only yesterday Caleb began meeting her in her barn, learning all about women for the first time? She reached up and grasped his face, then stood on her tiptoes and kissed his lips. "I'll do it," she told him. "Saturday night." She let go of him, her hands lingering on his chest. "What about you? How are you going to do it in this condition?"

"I'll be strong enough by then. That gives me four more days. I'll draw strength from my hatred of Byron Clawson. That should be all I need."

She hung her head. "Caleb, if anything goes wrong—"

"It won't. Believe me, it won't. It's *my* turn now, Emily. *Maheo* brought me Lynda and Sarah, gave me James, brought my son Tom back from the dead. The spirits will be with me on Saturday night."

She studied the determined blue eyes. "I hope so, Caleb Sax. I surely hope so. God forgive me for helping you if something goes wrong."

Chapter
Twenty-Seven

The supper table was quiet. Sarah knew Caleb was planning something, and she had no doubt it involved killing Byron Clawson. She could only nibble at her food. Would these be their last remaining days together? Perhaps it was not even a matter of days. Perhaps it was a matter of this one night.

Caleb had insisted they all eat together this evening.

Emily had left after saying good-bye to each one of them and wishing them good luck. The woman made no mention of what she and Caled had talked about.

When they finished Caled leaned back, looking around the table at all of them—Sarah, Lynda, James, Tom, Jess, Cale. Little John lay in a cradle nearby. Lynda picked up a plate and started to rise.

"Sit down, Lynda," Caleb told her.

She looked at him with a frown and slowly sat back down, waiting for him to speak then. Caleb stopped to light a pipe, while Sarah stared at her plate and Tom watched his father anxiously, ready for action.

"I know this is home to most of you," Caleb spoke up then. "It's been the only real home I ever had." He puffed the pipe for a moment. "In a sense this ranch will always belong to us. Our loved ones are buried here. It's like the old Spanish saying I told you once. *Mis raices estan aqui.* My roots are buried here. At least it seems that way, even though my own real roots are with the Cheyenne. It's harder for Tom, and James and Cale. This is all they've ever known. But now we all know it's time to move on. Emily tells me Byron Clawson plans to send men out here who are not Texas Rangers. I don't think that needs any explaining."

"Bastard," Tom muttered under his breath. James blinked back tears and Jess picked up Cale's hand and squeezed it reassuringly.

"We don't have help any more, and even if we three men use those new repeating rifles we might hold them off for a while. But they'd win in the end, and what they would do to us, and to you women, wouldn't be worth the fight. I told all of you before that I will not risk the lives of any more of my family for this land. And according to Emily, we've got to get out fast. Clawson isn't giving us the full five days. He couldn't face me like a man in San Felipe. He has done everything behind my back . . ." He puffed the pipe again. ". . . including shooting me," he added bitterly. He shifted in his chair, his pain obvious.

"You can all be proud of what we did here. But we've got to move on. In a sense this whole country belongs to us, you know. I guess I always knew I couldn't own a piece of it for myself. The white man in me wanted to, but the Indian side of me told me this land was only borrowed. The land belongs to itself. It isn't right to divide it up and try to own pieces of it. The only reason I did what I did was to settle with my family—to stay in one place and build something for their future. And when Sarah came, that became even more important. She's not a woman to go wandering like an Indian. But now I'm going to have to ask her to do just that."

His eyes moved to Sarah, his heart aching at her obvious struggle not to break down. "But Sarah Sax is a strong woman. God knows she had to be to survive living with Clawson." He looked at the rest of them. "And Sarah understands, as I think all of you do, that staying together and surviving is all that's important. And that's what we are going to do."

His eyes moved to Tom. "Tom, we leave tomorrow morning. You'll be in charge. You're to take the family first to Wil Handel's place. Have one of Wil's men go into San Felipe and buy whatever supplies we might still need. At least then if we get raided, no one will be here. You have Wil hide our wagons and all of you until the supplies come."

He puffed the pipe again, and they all waited quietly for him to continue. "Then you will all leave for Unorganized Territory. Head for Bent's Fort. You'll have the remaining horses to herd with you. Stay as far east as possible, away from Comanche country. I had Wil get me a map when he took the horses into San Felipe. This Bent's Fort is on the Arkansas River in southeast Colorado Territory. Head up into Indian Territory to the Arkansas. We'll follow it up to the Sante Fe Trail and follow that to Bent's Fort. It's the long way around but safer. To go directly northwest into Colorado would be suicide. The land there is crawling with renegade Comanche and Apache.

"Once we reach Bent's Fort we can get organized and decide what to do. The country there is still wild and free and belongs to no one in particular, except the Cheyenne. In a sense I'll be going back to my own true roots—your ancestors. Maybe that's good. Maybe we'll even settle right there and do a good horse trading business with travelers to Santa Fe. We'll be starting over, but we've done it before. Either way, you'll head out of here by Friday morning and make as many miles as you and the horses can stand the first day."

Jess frowned. "You talk like you won't be with us."

"I won't."

They all looked at him as he puffed the pipe again. "Don't do it, Caleb," Sarah pleaded. "We'll never see you again."

Caleb's eyes glittered with determination. "Oh, yes you will. It's all planned. It will work."

"You can hardly walk, Father," Lynda protested.

"I'll be strong enough by Saturday. Years ago when I took part in the Cheyenne Sun Dance ritual, I learned how to ignore pain, Lynda. You move into another world in your mind and you draw on a strength that in normal situations you don't even realize you have. That's what I'll do when I kill Byron Clawson. And I will not leave Texas until that's done."

Sarah closed her eyes and looked away.

"If raiders happen to come to the Handels, Wil will tell them we've already been there to say our good-byes and have gone on our way—all of us, including me," Caleb continued. "By the time Byron Clawson dies, as far as the rest of them know we'll have been gone two or three days. They can't connect us to his death. Besides, I don't expect he'll be found for quite some time."

"They'll suspect. They'll come after us," Sarah said quietly.

"They won't. All they want is the land, Sarah. It's that simple. Byron wants my hide, but he won't be around to collect or to instigate others to come after me. Once we're gone, this place will be swarming with bidders. Out of sight, out of mind. No one will come after us if Byron is out of the way."

"Let me go with you, Father," Tom said. "I'll gladly help you kill him."

"No. Extra people means extra risk. I don't want you

involved. Besides, Jess can't handle the women and children and horses all by himself. You're good with those guns, and the six of you will need all the protection you can get. I'll ride hard to catch up."

"How will you find us?" Lynda asked.

Caleb grinned. "I'm an Indian, aren't I?"

Lynda sighed, smiling sadly. "Yes. You certainly are that."

"And so are you." His eyes moved to James. "All of you, except Sarah and Jess. But they're Indians at heart." He leaned forward, reaching out and taking Sarah's hand. "You'll leave Handel's by Friday morning. I'll catch up by the next Friday." He squeezed her hand tightly, but his eyes moved around the table. "If something should go wrong, which I don't expect—but if it does, I'm counting on all of you to stay together. Go on to Bent's Fort and decide from there what you will do. The horses will belong to all of you collectively. Sell them and divide up the money, or keep them and raise more."

James and Cale both began to sniffle, and Tom's own chest hurt so badly he kept taking deep breaths to try to ease the pain. This was home. Texas was all he could remember. Vengeance swelled in his soul like something alive. They were really leaving this place. He had planned on going to California, but he'd always thought he could come back here. Now he could not consider California, at least not for a while, not until Caleb Sax was resettled with his family. And there would be no more Texas. Texas was gone. Bess was gone. His feelings of fury were overwhelming, and he wondered if he would ever feel calm and happy again.

Everyone moved mechanically after that. The table was cleared and remaining dishes were packed. It was not an easy job. They were not prepared for this, and there were not enough crates and boxes. They didn't even own a covered wagon. They would have to sleep on the prairie in makeshift tents. Sarah didn't mind any of it, as long as Caleb showed up to make the journey with them. She felt numb, struggling not to think the worst. But Caleb was so badly injured, and Clawson probably kept himself right in the middle of town where it was almost impossible to get to the man.

"He keeps people around like flies hang around a dead animal," Emily had said.

So how was Caleb to get to the man? What had he planned with Emily? Sarah moved in a near daze. Everyone was quiet and pensive. Tom took his quietly crying little brother and his nephew Cale outside to talk to them and encourage them, reminding them that they would have to be men now, and help their father and grandfather, as well as help protect the women and horses on their journey. By the time he finished with them the excitement of what was to come helped still the boys' sadness over leaving the only home they had ever known.

Inside Sarah walked into the bedroom. The mattress was bare. They would sleep on it that way, folding the two light blankets they would use for covers in the morning and packing them, too. The night's leftovers would be lunch tomorrow, on the way to the Handels.

Sarah removed her clothes and pulled on her gown. She just stood there then, looking around the room. Here in this house she had found life again, in the arms of Caleb Sax. Here, after eighteen years of being apart, they had come together again in love. Nothing could compare to making love with the man a woman loved beyond all things; a man she had thought dead, a man who had been her friend in childhood, her love in their early years. To find him again had been a moment of joy never to be forgotten. They were nervous strangers at first, but in a few days all the old passion was back and he'd made her his legal wife and had taken her back to his bed. She'd taken his life again and had given him another child.

Sarah heard his footsteps behind her, the light tap of the canes, then the slow steps. A chill moved through her. Under normal conditions, Caleb Sax could handle ten Byron Clawsons. But how could he expect to handle even one now? She felt Caleb come close behind her but she did not turn around.

"I'm sorry to put you through this, Sarah; sorry to uproot

you. I had big plans for you. A big, sprawling hacienda and—"

"Don't torture yourself, Caleb. None of those things matter to me and you know it." She twisted her fingers nervously. "Just come back to me."

He moved one cane over to the other hand and used his free hand to reach up and touch her shoulder.

"I will. But you remember that we have never really been apart, Sarah, even when we were physically apart. Even before I loved you as a man loves a woman, when I lived among the Cheyenne and knew you were growing up in St. Louis, I thought about you, missed you, wondered if I'd ever see you again. The moment I did, I knew who would be the most important woman in my life. And then when I thought you were dead, I could still picture you, feel you with me so many times. That's how it will always be for us, Sarah. Not even death can separate us."

"Don't say that," she whispered.

"It's the truth."

She turned and hugged him around the middle, crying against his chest.

"Be strong for me, Sarah. You're such a strong woman and you don't even realize it. We're going to make it through this, I promise. And the place we're going to will be new and beautiful, closer to the mountains. You'll like it there. It's cooler—greener. And the Cheyenne are there." He hugged her close. "It's so strange. My life seems to be making a great circle. I'm going back to my beginnings in a sense. That's the way the Cheyenne look at life; as one big circle, never ending. And you and I will never end. We'll go on and on, through James and Lynda and their children."

"Oh, God, Caleb, I can't live without you now," she wept, clinging to him. "I can't go through that a second time."

"You won't. You just head north and keep watching the southern horizon. In a few days you'll see me coming. But you remember what I said, about how we will always be together. We've made our own circle, and it can't be broken by man, Sarah, and especially not by Byron Clawson.

You just put him forever out of your mind. He will never bother you again. You'll never see his face again or hear his voice again. And he'll never threaten you again. That I will make sure of, no matter what the consequences. And if something happens you'll go right on, because you've got our son to raise."

He let go of her and urged her to the bed. "Come on now. Lie down and get some rest. We leave by sunup for Wil's place. James and Cale are going to sleep at the bunkhouse with Tom. He's telling them enough tall tales to keep their minds spinning all night. They'll be all right. Children adjust."

She lay back on the bed. Caleb set his canes aside and held the head rail of the bed for support, letting himself down slowly.

"Yes, children adjust," he told himself. He had been raised by a Sioux man, then lost that family and had been adopted by a white man. Caleb had adjusted to a whole new world then, but had been thrown back into the Indian world as a teen. Again he had survived, only to find himself led back to the white man's world. Now he would wander again like an Indian, perhaps never to own and settle land again the way he had in Texas.

Sarah pulled the covers over them. It irritated Caleb that he couldn't even make love to her tonight. It seemed important. Yet she was so upset it probably didn't matter. Tonight their feelings went beyond making love. They went even deeper. He winced with pain as he lay on his back, putting out his arm and taking her close. This was enough for tonight, to hold each other this way.

Byron rode in a carriage. He was not accustomed to riding a horse for hours at a time, and it was a long ride to the Sax ranch. Scouts had reported all of Caleb's help was gone. Only the Sax family was left. The fifteen armed men he rode with were certainly enough to subdue three men, two women and a couple of children. And the thought of watching the men rape Sarah Sax in front of Caleb was much more inviting to Byron than waiting in town for these men to return. He wanted to be there himself for this one.

His heart quickened when the house came into sight. Scouts were already returning to give them an idea of the best way to approach Caleb, who would surely put up a fight. He waited impatiently for the good news, squinting when the scouts rode up so hard they stirred up too much dust.

"There's nobody there, Mister Clawson," they reported.

Byron's eyes widened in annoyance. "What?"

"They're gone."

"They can't be gone! They had five days to get out, and Sax was hurt bad."

"Go look for yourself, sir. The place is empty, except for some furniture. The barn's empty, horses gones, everything."

Byron climbed out of the carriage, staring at the house. "Someone warned them," he sneered. He looked around at them. "One of you is a spy!"

"Like hell," one of the men answered. "Excuse me, Mister Clawson, but there isn't a man here who would have warned that Indian."

Byron gritted his teeth and kicked at the carriage wheel. "Damn! We've got to find them. They can't have gone far."

"Who cares now? They're gone. Ain't that what you wanted?"

"I want Caleb Sax dead. *Dead*! Do you hear? As long as he's alive I can't get a good night's sleep. After this he'll be after my hide more than ever. I don't just want him out of Texas. I want his skin stretched out in the sun to dry."

The man paced a moment, his heart racing. Caleb Sax had gotten away. The man could be anywhere! There was no doubting Caleb's sincerity that day in San Felipe. Now that Byron Clawson was in Sax territory, he had left himself open for disaster. If he couldn't find Caleb Sax, he might as well find some excuse to go back to St. Louis. Sunday. If they didn't find him by Sunday, he'd leave. He liked his new power and importance here in Texas, but he valued his life more, and he'd be safer in St. Louis. Sunday was when the next boat was headed out of San Felipe for the Bay and New Orleans. Byron would be on it if Caleb wasn't found by Sunday.

He looked toward the houses. "Burn every building."

"But Mister Clawson, they're good buildings. They make the place more valuable."

"Burn them," Byron shouted angrily. "Everything. And when we're through with this mess you can ride onto my property and get rid of all the squatters. I'll pay you men well to guard both this place and my own. I'm laying claim to all of it." He puffed out his chest, calming himself. "Some day this land will be worth a fortune, especially if Texas becomes a state." He looked at the two scouts. "Did Sax have any friends who might have helped him?"

"Not that we know of. The closest place is Wil Handel's, but it's toward town. Sax wouldn't go that way."

"You can never tell what Caleb Sax will do, just to try to trick you. Go burn the buildings and we'll check out the Handel ranch."

"Yes, sir."

Byron waited in the distance. He didn't like actually getting his hands involved in the real dirty work, other than the day he had helped Sarah's father chase Caleb Sax out of St. Louis and took the liberty of shooting the man in the back.

The barn went first, for it was still full of hay. Byron watched smoke billow from each end, then break through the roof. Next went some bunkhouses and two cabins, then the main house. Smoke wafted upward, and it was not long before the buildings began falling in. The only Saxes there to watch were those buried on the hillside not far from the main house. Byron noticed a cloud far to the north. A storm was coming.

In Blue Valley it was already raining, and an eerie, moaning wind moved through that place, as though several people were weeping in a great chorus.

"Where is he, Handel?" Byron questioned the old German. "You've seen him, haven't you?"

It was raining hard now, and Wil Handel stood at his doorway, out of the downpour, gun in hand. "I told you,

Tom Sax was here a couple of days ago to tell us they was leaving. He told me about what your men did. That was bad. The Saxes, they are gone, and we have lost our best friends."

"You'll lose more than that if you don't tell me where they went," Clawson threatened.

"I told you and told you. That Tom, he came to tell us good-bye because his father was badly hurt. He could not even move. Tom say they will head north, into Indian country. That was three days ago, sir. Now get off my land."

"Not until we search this place!"

Handel wanted very much to pull the trigger. But there were too many of them. "Then go ahead. You will find nothing."

Byron nodded his head and several men stormed into the house, muddying the floor with their boots while Mildred Handel scolded and shouted. A few men went to the barn. Straw covered a doorway in the floor that led to a cellar dug farther under the ground. It was a place to hide from Comanche, but these days such spaces became useful against squatters and people like those who investigated the Handel place now. Deep in the dirt cellar sat the entire Sax family; all but Caleb, who had left alone on a horse during the night. He had gone off alone to pray for the strength he would need to do what he must do. Sarah worried that he would not even be able to stay on his horse. Perhaps he was lying somewhere out on the plains needing help, cold and wet. The torture of not knowing was physically painful to her.

The Saxes heard booted feet pound over their heads, but due to the rain, the men above did not notice the hollow sound their steps made. Sarah could hear them talking. "Maybe we should beat Handel into telling us if he knows more," one of them said.

"Maybe we should just burn his place down, too," said another.

Sarah stared at the door above. "I've got to give myself up," she whispered. "All Byron really wants is me. They'll hurt Mister Handel!" She started to rise, but Tom grabbed her from behind, forcing her down and holding her tight, putting a hand over her mouth against her weeping.

"You stay put," he whispered hoarsely. "If you give yourself up, they'll kill us all. And you will ruin Father's plans for Clawson. They won't really do anything to Handel. He's *white*."

She squeezed her eyes shut. Caleb! All those men! He was going to get himself killed!

Tom lightened his grip and she covered her face and huddled close to him, shuddering as she heard Byron Clawson's voice. It was all Tom could do to keep from charging up himself and killing the man, saving his father the trouble. But he knew there were too many others with Clawson. He would only risk all their lives.

"Is there anything here?" Clawson was asking the men.

"Nothing, sir."

They prayed the men would not find the two loaded wagons, which were hidden under stacked bales of hay.

"We'll get some answers out of Handel," Byron said.

"I wouldn't do that, sir. Handel is a respected Texas citizen, one of the first settlers. The government wouldn't like that. You don't want to jeopardize your own standing in the community."

There was a moment of silence. "Yes, of course."

"I would give it up, sir."

"I told you I can't trust Caleb Sax. The man has to die."

Sarah cringed, and Jess held James closer when he started to whimper.

"They could be anywhere. If they've been gone as long as Handel says, it would take too many men to spread out across the plains to look for them. I don't know about you, but I'm not going to risk my neck against Comanche no matter what you pay me. I'm sorry, sir."

There were a few more footsteps. "Bastard," Byron shouted then. "Bastard! How did he do it? Who warned him? I should have known better than to come to this stinking, uncivilized cow country!"

"Sir, you're talkin' about Texas," someone answered. "I'll kill Indians for you and rape any white squaw that lays with one, but I won't tolerate you insultin' Texas."

"I'll insult anything and anyone I want for what I pay you, you fool!" The footsteps thundered out of the barn then. After waiting a few minutes to be sure the men were gone, Tom let go of Sarah and climbed the ladder slowly to open the door. He saw men heading back to the Handel house. He signaled Jess to come up. They would watch from the barn. If it looked like Handel might be in real trouble, they would help in spite of the danger.

Jess followed him up and the women and children waited with pounding hearts. Handel's men had returned just that morning with supplies from town. They would leave today if Byron and his men would just get going.

"It's a good thing Caleb Sax isn't here, Handel," Byron told the man grudgingly.

"You're a bad man, Mister Clawson," Handel answered. "You got no right coming to my place and making a mess and saying I am hiding someone. I will tell the county about what you did. Texas was a good place till the likes of you came along."

"I've come here to help Texas," Byron answered impatiently, climbing into his buggy. "You people ought to be more grateful to ones like us who come here to loan you our hard earned money to help you get back on your feet."

"You should have been here when we were fighting Comanches and outlaws—when we were fighting Santa Anna. You should have been here in the beginning, Mister Clawson, when we struggled against drought and flood and disease. We will survive, Mister Clawson. We got along all right before you came. You are not what Texas is made of. Nor are these scoundrels who ride with you! They are scum, and you are scum! It is men like myself and Caleb Sax who built Texas. Men like you will come and go again. The real Texas is in the hearts of we who built it."

Byron waved the man off and turned his carriage, whipping his horse into a trot. He and his men rode off, splattering through mud. Tom and Jess waited for several minutes before running over to the trapdoor and opening it.

"Come on out," Jess told the women. He reached down, and Lynda handed up John. Jess took him and Tom helped both women climb out then. Cale and James climbed up with the agility of children. Wil and Mildred Handel were walking to the barn then.

"They are gone," Wil shouted. "You'd better get the wagons ready to go, Tom."

Tom and Jess began removing bales of hay from around the wagons. Sarah walked up and embraced Mildred Handel. "I'll miss you so, Mildred."

"And we will miss you, Sarah. You have been good neighbors. It will be so lonely without you. These new people, they are not like the rest of us. I feel so ashamed that you must go."

"It's not your fault, Mildred. You've been such good neighbors to us. What would we have done without you? God bless you, Mildred."

The women pulled apart, both of them crying. "Ah, now you must leave. It is not right. Not right." She shook her head. "This country is so good in many ways, but it has much to learn. They let us foreigners stay, and they chase away the true Americans. We do not understand this."

"Caleb better be careful," Wil spoke up then. "We will pray for him. I hope that he lets us know before he leaves so we will know he is all right."

"I'm sure he'll try," Sarah told them.

There was a round of good-byes. There was no time to waste. It was all happening so fast. Wil Handel decided not to mention that Byron Clawson had told him he had burned down every building on the Sax ranch. Why add to their sorrows? They should remember it the way it was. Memories were all such people had.

Jess and Tom quickly hitched the wagons to teams led by their own horses. Luckily Byron and the men who had accompanied him were not familiar with Caleb's horses, or they would have recognized the few that grazed in the nearby pastures, as well as those in the stalls in Wil's barn which belonged to Caleb Sax. So far things had worked the way Caleb had hoped. The alibi had been set up. Caleb was supposedly well on his way north, and just as he had predicted, no one was willing to chase him down. He was gone, and that was all they cared about.

Sarah climbed into the seat of one wagon, holding baby John in her arms and pulling a poncho over both of them to protect them from the rain. Jess sat beside her and picked up the reins. James and Cale rode in the back, covering themselves and their belongings with a large piece of canvas. Lynda drove the second wagon and Tom saddled his horse, riding out to round up the few horses that would go along.

Rain mixed with their own tears as they headed north.

Sarah felt as though her heart was being torn from her chest. It was all over, and the only thing that would make this all bearable was when Caleb rejoined them.

The Handels waved until they were small dots on the horizon. James watched with silent tears. He would never see his colt again. It had run behind them for a ways until Tom chased it back. For the rest of his life James would not forget what it meant to be Indian.

Chapter
Twenty-Eight

Emily lit a thin cigar, relieved that it was nearing eleven o'clock. Byron Clawson had come earlier than she had anticipated. Even a whore could take only so much, and the man's fantasies seemed to have no end. She thought she knew all the ways there were to please a man, but Byron Clawson thought of things even Emily had never tried.

"So, you say this Sax fellow was gone," she said, hoping to take a little break by striking up a conversation.

Besides, she had to be sure everything was going as planned.

"The son of a bitch got away from me. I wish to hell I knew who informed him. I'd have his hide," Byron fumed.

Emily smiled to herself, then turned to face Byron. He was such a pitiful sight, so thin and white—the most important part of him lying pink and limp between his legs. She puffed the cigar. "Well, maybe it was just a sixth sense. They say Indians have such things, you know."

He grinned, motioning for her to come back to bed. He didn't seem to mind her aging body or the scar on her face. She would do all the wild things he liked to do. That was all that mattered to him. She walked over and sat down beside him. He moved a hand up to toy with her breast.

"You ever lay with an Indian, Emily?" His eyes lit up with hideous curiosity.

She struggled to hide her revulsion of this pitiful specimen of man. She preferred turning her thoughts to Caleb. "Sure. A few times."

"Who? When?"

She tossed back her hair. "Don't tell me you haven't heard where I got this scar."

"It's true then? You were a captive of the Potawatomies?"

Her eyes narrowed. "It's true."

He only grinned. "Is that why you're a whore?"

She struggled to keep from slapping him, taking another puff of the cigar. "Partly. It's really none of your business, Byron. The point is I know how to show you a good time."

He laughed, sitting up slightly and kissing her thighs. "Are Indians really bigger than white men?"

She got up from the bed. "All men are about the same."

He flopped down on the bed. "That Sarah Sax—she was a bitch. I gave her baby a name and saved her reputation by marrying her, but she never knew how to please me. Damn! I wouldn't have minded getting my hands on her one more time. I would tie her down and make her do every damned thing there is to do! She'd be sorry she laid with that big buck! She's never known a day of luxury with that half-breed. I could have given her the world. All she had to do was to be a normal woman in bed. But she was cold as ice."

Emily looked at the time. It was five minutes before eleven. She put out her cigar. "I can't imagine how she could be that way with someone like you—a man with money, power, and so good in bed," she answered, wanting to laugh. She turned to face him again, then sauntered closer. "What will you do now? Are you going after this Sax?"

"I'd like to, but no one will try to find him. These worthless ruffians around here are satisfied that he's left. None of them is brave enough to go out looking for him." He sighed. "I will be going back to St. Louis soon to hire someone to take care of my new bank here, and the land. I'm a little nervous with this Sax fellow loose."

He sat up and reached over, picking up a bottle of whiskey and taking a long swallow. His eyes were becoming glazed with alcohol and desire. "I'm safer in St. Louis. At any rate, that's why I came early tonight. I won't see you again for a while, unless you'd like to come back to St. Louis with me. I could set you up very well, Emily."

"That's a generous offer, Byron, but I like my setup here too much to move." She tried to keep the harshness from her voice. What a detestable man! She forced a smile, coming back to the bed. It was almost eleven. The last thing she wanted was for Caleb Sax to see her this way, but she reminded herself that she was helping him kill this depraved man.

She moved her hands over Clawson, toying expertly with that part of him that repulsed her the most. In moments he was laughing and panting. It seemed his ability to go on and on with these things was endless. She lay back, pretending to enjoy it when his own fingers explored her with crude probes, and maniacal grunts came from his throat.

Emily kept watching the window. Finally a buckskin-clad leg appeared. She began laughing, sprawling out on the bed wickedly to keep Byron's attention away from the window. Then she suddenly rolled off the bed. "Catch me, Byron," she teased.

He grinned hideously, licking his lips. He raised up to go after her, but suddenly he felt a strong arm come around him from behind, pulling tight against his throat, and the tip of a big knife pressed to his cheek just under his eye.

"One sound, and this eye gets popped right out of its socket," Caleb warned.

Emily quickly grabbed up a robe and pulled it on, while Byron gaped at her. "You," he squeaked. "You're the one!"

Caleb bent his arm even harder, choking the man. "I told you not to make a sound," he growled. He looked at Emily. "My pockets—some straw. Take it out and stuff it in his mouth."

Emily nodded, wide-eyed with the tenseness of the moment. Byron began struggling wildly, but he was no match for Caleb. He pulled and tugged at Caleb's arm, but his struggles only caused Caleb's knife to cut into his skin and the sharp pain made him begin crying like a little boy.

Caleb's hold on his throat was so tight he couldn't get enough air, and Byron began to get weary. Emily walked over beside Caleb and grabbed straw from the pockets of his buckskin jacket. Caleb stood at the edge of the bed while Byron was still on it, his thin, naked body squirming while he cried. He kept his lips tightly shut.

"Open your mouth, you son of a bitch, or I'll by God cut your balls off right here and now," Caleb hissed.

The man shook violently. He opened his mouth and Emily stuffed straw into it. Caleb yanked the man from the bed then, shoving him to the floor and planting a knee against his chest so hard that he could breathe barely enough to stay alive. Caleb shoved his knife into its sheath for a moment, taking out a bandanna and quickly tying it around Byron Clawson's mouth tightly so he couldn't make a sound. He jerked the man to his feet. Emily was astounded at Caleb's strength. If Caleb Sax was in pain, no one would know it, nor would a person believe the man had been a near cripple just a few days earlier.

"Get dressed," he ordered Byron. "I want nothing of yours left in this room. For all intents and purposes, you left of your own free will." He shoved the man over the bed and Byron rolled off it to the floor on the other side, grasping at his throat, choking on the dusty straw and trying to get his breath back from having Caleb's knee against his chest. He was sure a rib had cracked.

He crawled to his clothes, hardly able to get them on straight, he shook so badly from fear. Byron could only hope Caleb Sax intended only to frighten him. Surely the man wouldn't dare kill him. Everyone would suspect. But then maybe not. Everyone, including himself, thought Caleb Sax was on his way out of Texas.

He hastily pulled on and buttoned his pants, failing to get the right buttons into the right holes out of nervousness. He pulled on his shirt but left the tail hanging out. He stuffed his tie into a pocket of his suit jacket and pulled the jacket on. Tears ran down his face as he eyed Caleb, who seemed to fill the room with his size and power. Where had his strength come from? He was supposed to have been badly wounded by the Rangers.

The stinking whore Emily Stoner was helping Caleb Sax. He should have known! He should have known. Why had he come to Texas? And why had he come here tonight? If only he hadn't drunk so much. He'd have been more alert. It was that damned whore's fault! She got him drunk on purpose.

Caleb watched his every move, sensed the man would make a dash for it, which he did. Caleb was ready. He lunged before Byron could get to the door, grabbing the man back and whipping one arm behind him, bending until he heard a snap. A muffled groan came from Byron's gagged mouth and Emily put a hand to her stomach. She was beginning to see just how ruthless Caleb Sax could be. Byron's shoulder moved oddly as Caleb pulled both arms behind the man's back and tied his wrists, then his ankles. He left the man lying on the floor and rose, facing Emily.

"Look around good. Make sure there's nothing of his here."

She turned away, scouring the room with her eyes. She walked to the bed and straightened the sheets, then looked under the bed. "Just his shoes and socks." She picked them up and held them out. Caleb took them and tied the shoes to his belt, then stuffed the socks into another of Byron's jacket pockets. He turned to Emily, stepping closer.

"Thank you, Emily. I'll get as far away as possible. I came into town after dark and my horse is tied at the side in the alley. No one saw me. You stay in the room until everyone else has gone. If people ask, Byron decided to stay most of the night with you. He left early in the morning. That's all you know."

She nodded. "Good luck, Caleb. Be careful!"

Their eyes held. "I'm so goddamned sorry about everything, Emily—Howard and all. I'm sorry we couldn't have stayed here. I'll always think about you, wonder about you."

She blinked back tears. "I'll be doing the same. Try to write me sometime. Wait a while, until things settle around here."

"I'll do that." He put a hand to her face. "I'll never forget this."

"And I'll never forget you, Caleb. Take good care of that beautiful family."

He smiled, tears in his eyes. She thought it odd that he could be so loving and gentle, yet could turn around and be as ruthless as he was with Byron Clawson. Caleb bent down and met her lips. How could he not give her one more kiss for old times' sake? He would probably never see her again. The kiss lingered in a moment of old curiosity over what could have been. She had been Caleb Sax's first awakening to woman. Where did time go? Why was youth such a fleeting thing?

He left her lips. "You know I love you, Caleb. I always have."

He smiled sadly. "We love each other, in a special way." He kissed her forehead then. "Good-bye, Emily." His voice was choked. He turned then, reaching down and picking up Byron, slinging the man over his shoulder like a sack of potatoes. "Turn down your lamp," he said quietly to her.

Emily obeyed, watching his shadow disappear through the window then. She hurried over to it, but could see nothing in the darkness below. That was good. If she couldn't see him, then neither could anyone else. She heard a horse trot quietly away toward the back of the building.

Her eyes teared as she clutched at a pain in her stomach. How could she tell him what the doctor had told her? She was dying. The symptoms had become manifest in the past few months, and it wouldn't be too long before they intensified. What was the sense of adding that burden to all those he already carried? He might try to do something foolish if he knew, like try to come back for her. It was better this way.

Emily put her head down on the windowsill and wept. She would never see Caleb Sax again. She would die in this wild land called Texas and that would be that. Caleb Sax was off to new land, even more unsettled land. That was what he was made for. Texas had become too civilized for the likes of men like Caleb.

They made camp for the night. Sarah did as Caleb had ordered and kept her eyes on the southern horizon, waiting. They had been traveling for nine days, two days longer than Caleb had said it would take. Perhaps he wouldn't be able to find them. She couldn't let herself think anything worse than that. He had just been somehow delayed, or he'd lost their trail. He would come. Yes, he would come. He'd promised.

She turned and helped pitch a tent, while Tom staked out a rope to tie all the horses up for the night. He would be glad when they reached hillier country. There was no place to hide on these open plains, but so far they had not been bothered.

He, too, was worried. But he refused to voice his feelings. Sarah was already a nervous wreck, and Lynda kept looking at him with those big, blue eyes full of sorrow. Jess did all he could to comfort and reassure her.

Both men were weary. They needed another man. If Caleb didn't show, this journey would not only be difficult, but full of crushing sorrow. They all felt like lost sheep without a shepherd.

Jess tried to liven up the group after a meager supper of

beans and biscuits by starting up some singing of humorous songs he had learned when he worked on docks along Lake Erie. When that didn't work he began telling all of them about the Great Lakes, and they all tried to picture how big they must be, convinced that Jess exaggerated. But Sarah assured them it was true, telling them about Lake Michigan, which bordered Fort Dearborn, where she and Caleb had grown up. It all seemed so long ago, and it made her think of Caleb, the young Indian boy who had come to live with them when they were children. She remembered how fascinated he'd been over that big lake. *"Maxe-ne hanenestse,"* he called it.

The boys began asking questions about the lake, but suddenly Sarah stopped talking. Her eyes were glued to the horizon behind them and they all turned. Far off they could see a man on a horse. But there was another smaller horse with him. How could it be Caleb? He would be coming alone.

Sarah rose, her heart pounding. The figure had apparently spotted them and turned his horse into a gallop. Tom and Jess both reached for their rifles. "It's him," Sarah said boldly. "It's Caleb!"

She began to run.

"Sarah, wait," Jess called out.

But she didn't have to wait. She knew her husband, even from such a distance. She knew those shoulders, the way he sat a horse. She could see the dance of the fringes of his buckskins. "Caleb," she called out.

Tom and Jess lowered their rifles.

"Oh, God, Jess, I think it's him," Lynda said in a shaking voice. She started to run out behind her mother, but Jess caught her arm.

"Wait. Let them be."

James stared, hardly able to believe his eyes but sure that the smaller horse with his father was the Appaloosa colt. Was it possible?

Caleb saw her coming. Sarah! It was over. He was leaving his beloved Texas, but not his memories. They could go with him. And so would Sarah and his family. He thought of some of the things Tom Sax and his good trapper friend Bo had said to Caleb so many years ago, when Caleb was just a youth.

"Half of you is their kind, Caleb. All manner of things will happen to you before you're an old man. For all you know some day you'll settle in the white man's world."

He had tried that. But he knew now he could never quite live completely as a white man.

"Life keeps turning around, Tom," he had told his own son once. *"I guess everything is a matter of perspective. There's good and bad, no matter which side of the fence you're on."*

Caleb rode hard until he was close to Sarah, then slowed his horse, reaching down and sweeping her up with one arm, perching her in front of him. She sat sideways, reaching around his neck and weeping uncontrollably.

"It's all over," he told her. "Byron Clawson will never cross your path again, and they'll be a long time finding him."

She clung to him, unable to speak. He kissed her hair, her cheek, her neck. She felt good, and he felt stronger than ever. Killing Clawson had given him a new energy and purpose, releasing long pent-up hatreds and vengeance. Open prairie or not, he would find a way to make love to this woman tonight, even if he had to send the others on ahead.

"Come on, Sarah. Stop your crying. I told you I would come. You have got to have more faith in me, woman."

"Oh, Caleb," she finally managed to speak between sobs. "I can go anywhere. Anywhere! It doesn't matter. Just don't ever let us be apart like that again!"

"That's a promise, Sarah Sax." He urged his horse into motion, heading at a slower pace toward the camp. He grinned when he saw the look on James's face as he came closer, leading the Appaloosa colt.

"Father!" Lynda came running up to him, hugging his leg. Caleb's eyes moved to Tom, who just stood staring, tears on his cheeks.

"It's goddamned good to see you, Caleb," Jess said, coming up and squeezing his arm.

"How about getting your wife off me so I can get down," Caleb teased.

Jess smiled, gently pulling Lynda away. Caleb gave a still-weeping Sarah a squeeze, easing off his horse and lifting her down. He urged his horse back out of the way and reached for the colt, keeping one arm around Sarah as he led the colt over to James. Cale stared at his grandfather as though he were some kind of spirit returned from the dead as Caleb handed out the colt's reins to James.

"He's all yours, James," he told the boy.

James looked from the horse up into his father's blue eyes. "Mine? I thought . . . I thought Mister Handel bought him."

"He did. I bought him back. You have been brave about all of this, and it's not been easy on you. I want you to have the colt."

The boy's eyes teared and he hugged his father, a lump so big in his throat he couldn't talk. Caleb looked at Cale. "You take your pick from the younger horses of what we have with us, Cale. Take whatever horse you want and its your own."

The boy's lips puckered. "I'm glad you're back, Grandpa," he sniffed. "Will you help me pick out a good one?"

"If you want. Why don't you take James and his colt and go look at the other horses?" He gently pulled James away. "Go on, son. Brush down your horse."

James wiped at his eyes. "Thank you, Pa," he muttered. He grabbed the colt's reins and ran off with Cale.

Caleb kept hold of Sarah, eyeing Tom. "Everything all right?"

Tom just nodded. He quickly wiped his eyes. "We could use some meat," he told the man then, his voice strained. "Jess and I didn't want to go off hunting and leave the women alone. Now that you're here, we can all take turns."

Caleb nodded. "Tomorrow we'll cover as much country as possible. We've got to get to some hills. We're too open here."

Tom swallowed. "Something tells me we're going to make it just fine."

Caleb grinned then. "I've been thinking the same thing." He walked with Sarah over to the campfire. "I'm kind of excited about going someplace new. I guess I'm a wandering man at heart anyway. Lord knows I've lived about everyplace there is to live in this land. So has Sarah."

"So have all of us," Lynda added.

Tom shrugged. "All I've known is Texas—and Mexico, but not exactly in a pleasurable way."

Caleb met his son's eyes. "And you're yearning to know what else is out there, now that we've been displaced," Caleb told Tom.

The young man sighed. "How did you know?"

"I was your age once, that's how. All I ask is that you help us get settled first, Tom. Then if you want to do a little wandering, I won't stop you."

Their eyes held. It would be hard to leave Caleb Sax. And it would be hard on Caleb. But Tom Sax had to be his own man. "We won't worry about it now," he told Caleb. "Right now you look so damned good to me I can't even begin to think of leaving."

Caleb smiled. "You will, in time. And somewhere out there another woman is waiting for you. You had just better hope she's as good a wife as Sarah."

Tom smiled sadly. "If she's as good as Bess was, I'll be satisfied."

Caleb looked over at James, who was hugging the colt around the neck. He looked back at Tom. "No sad thoughts tonight. We've left a lot behind, but we have each other and we're going someplace new. Maybe it's for the best."

Tom nodded. "Maybe."

Cale came running over, the blue quill necklace in his hand. "Hold this for me, Mother," he told Lynda, handing it to her. "It gets kind of heavy on my neck." He ran off again and Lynda clasped the necklace, looking down at it.

"This necklace . . . it's kind of like a good luck charm," she said, looking over at her father.

Caleb hugged Sarah close. The necklace had brought his family together, and every time he held it himself he felt a certain strength. Perhaps it possessed some powerful Indian spirit. All he knew was he had his family, and Byron Clawson was dead. There was no looking back now, no going back. It was done. They would go to Colorado—to the mountains—to Cheyenne country. But a good share of their hearts and spirits would forever belong to Texas, and memories of loved ones now buried there would forever live in their memories.

* * *

"There is a right time for everything:
  A time to be born, a time to die . . .
  A time to kill, a time to heal . . .
  A time to destroy, a time to rebuild . . .
  A time to cry, a time to laugh . . .
  A time to grieve, a time to dance . . .
  A time for loving, a time for hating . . .
  A time for war, a time for peace."

  Ecclesiastes 3: Various verses from 1 through 8.
  (The Way, The Living Bible)

You'll also want to read these thrilling bestsellers by *Jennifer Wilde* . . .